Little ROBOT

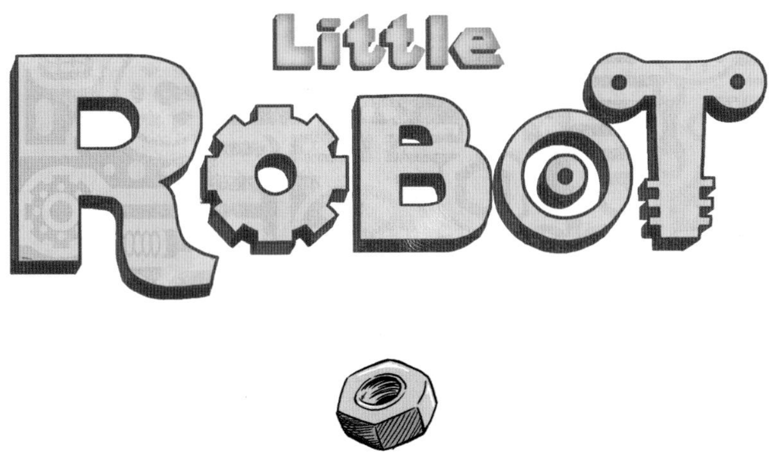

Little RoBoT

Ben Hatke

:01

First Second
New York

First Second

Published by First Second
First Second is an imprint of Roaring Brook Press, a division of Holtzbrinck Publishing Holdings Limited Partnership
175 Fifth Avenue, New York, New York 10010

Cataloging-in-Publication Data is on file at the Library of Congress

ISBN 978-1-62672-080-0

First Second books may be purchased for business or promotional use. For information on bulk
purchases please contact Macmillan Corporate and Premium Sales Department at
(800) 221-7945 x5442 or by email atspecialmarkets@macmillan.com.

First edition 2015
Book design by Danielle Ceccolini
Printed in China by Toppan Leefung Printing Ltd., Dongguan City, Guangdong Province

10 9 8 7 6 5 4 3 2 1

For my DAD,
who showed me
how COOL *it is to*
MAKE THINGS

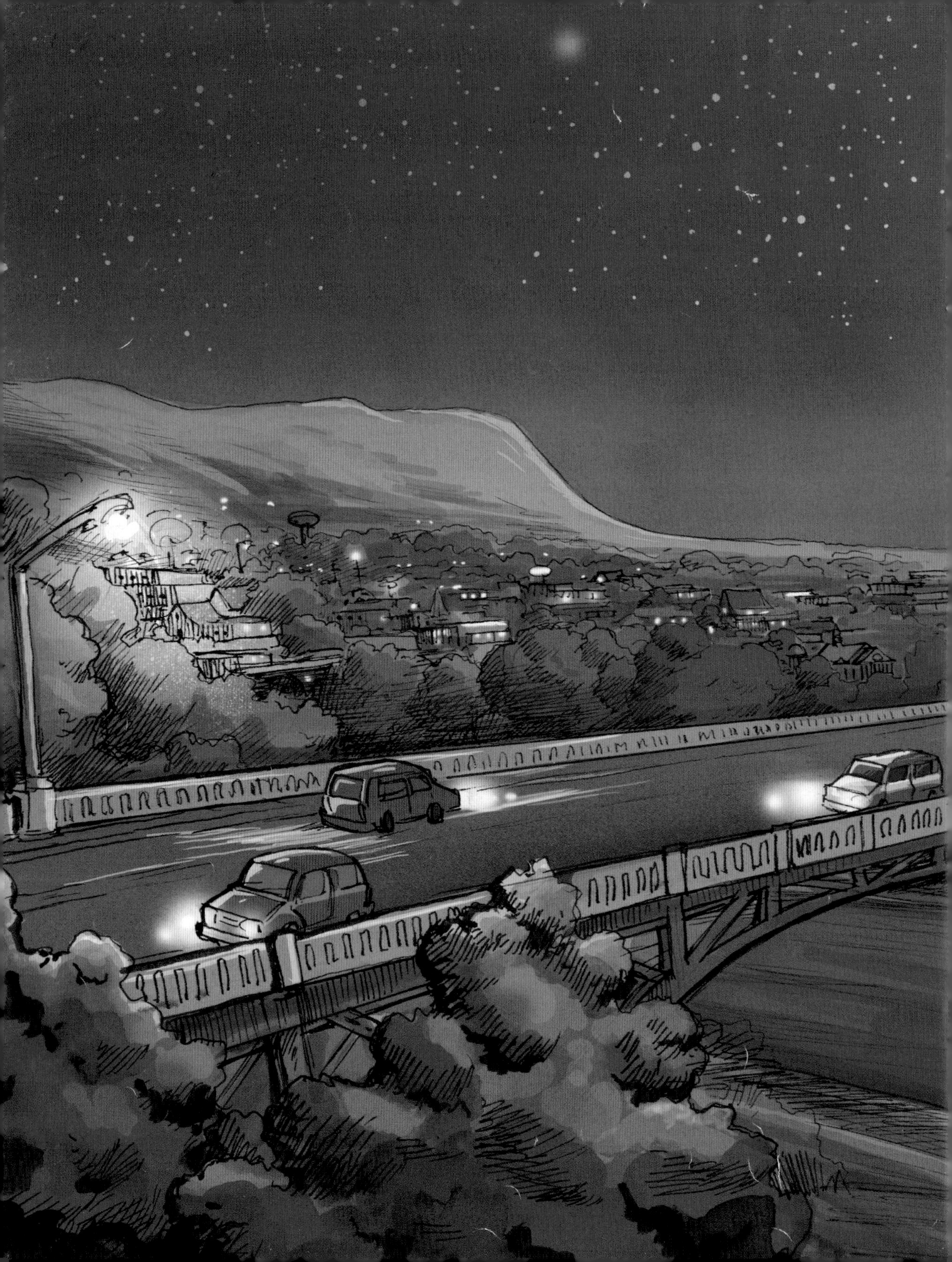

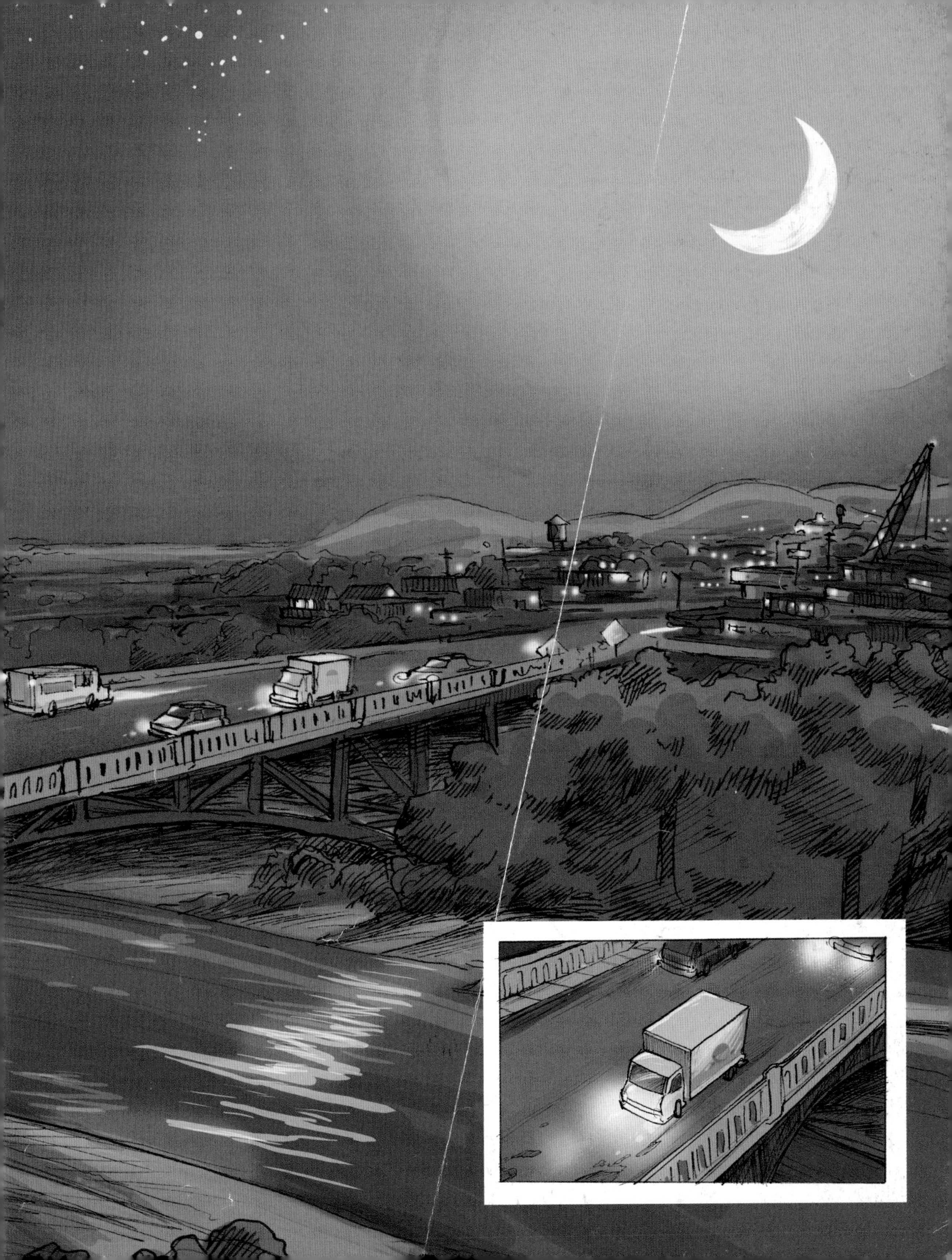

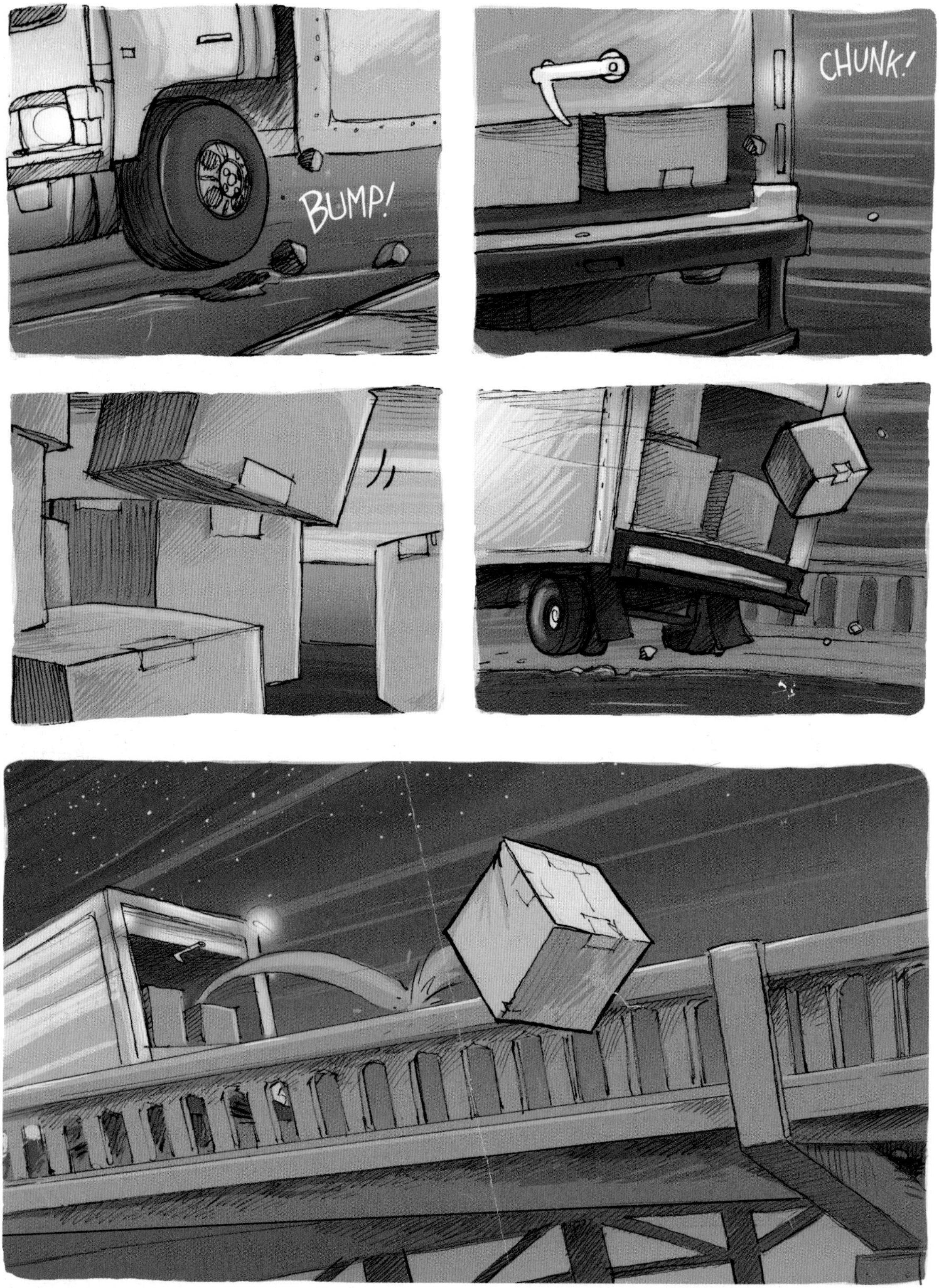
BUMP!
CHUNK!

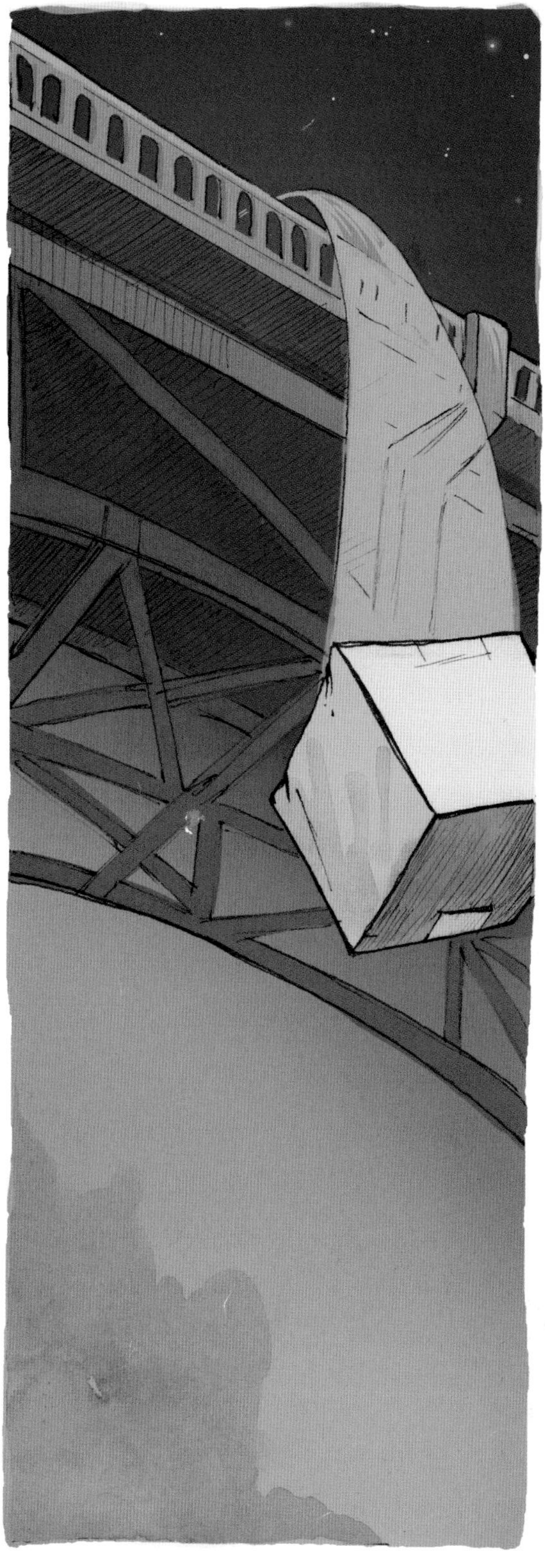

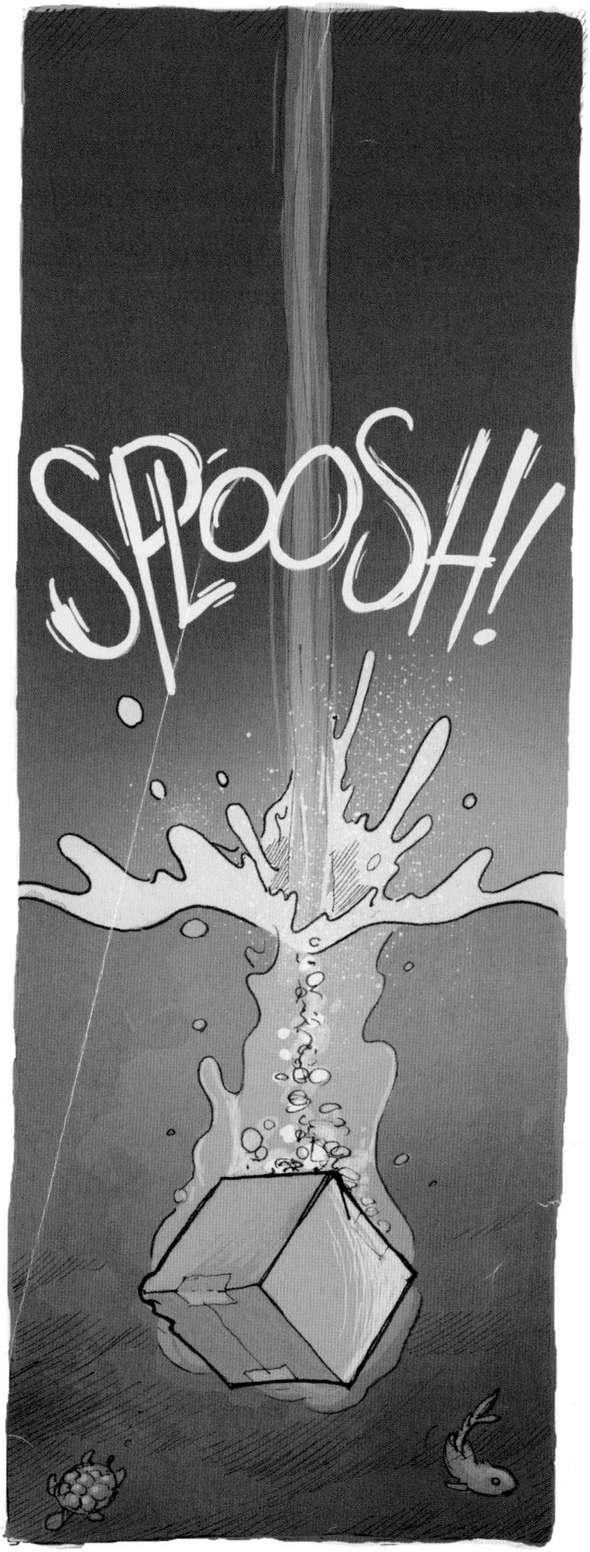
SPLOOSH!

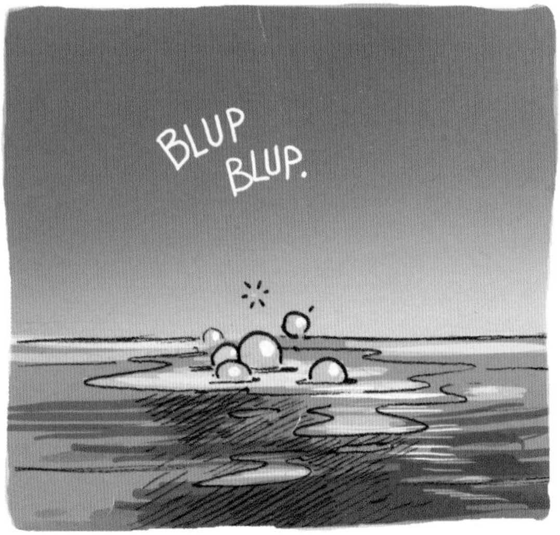
BLUP
BLUP.
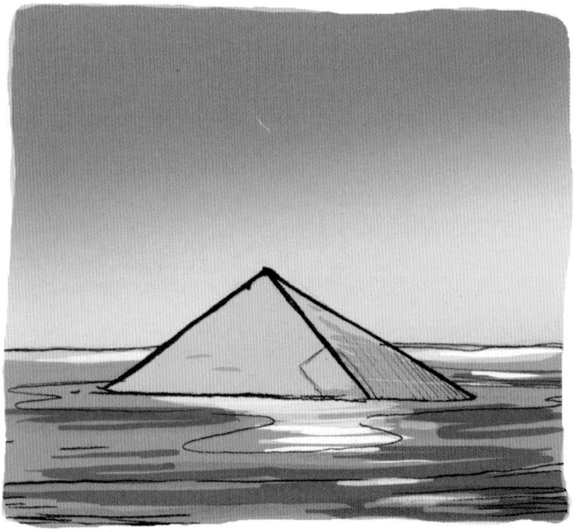
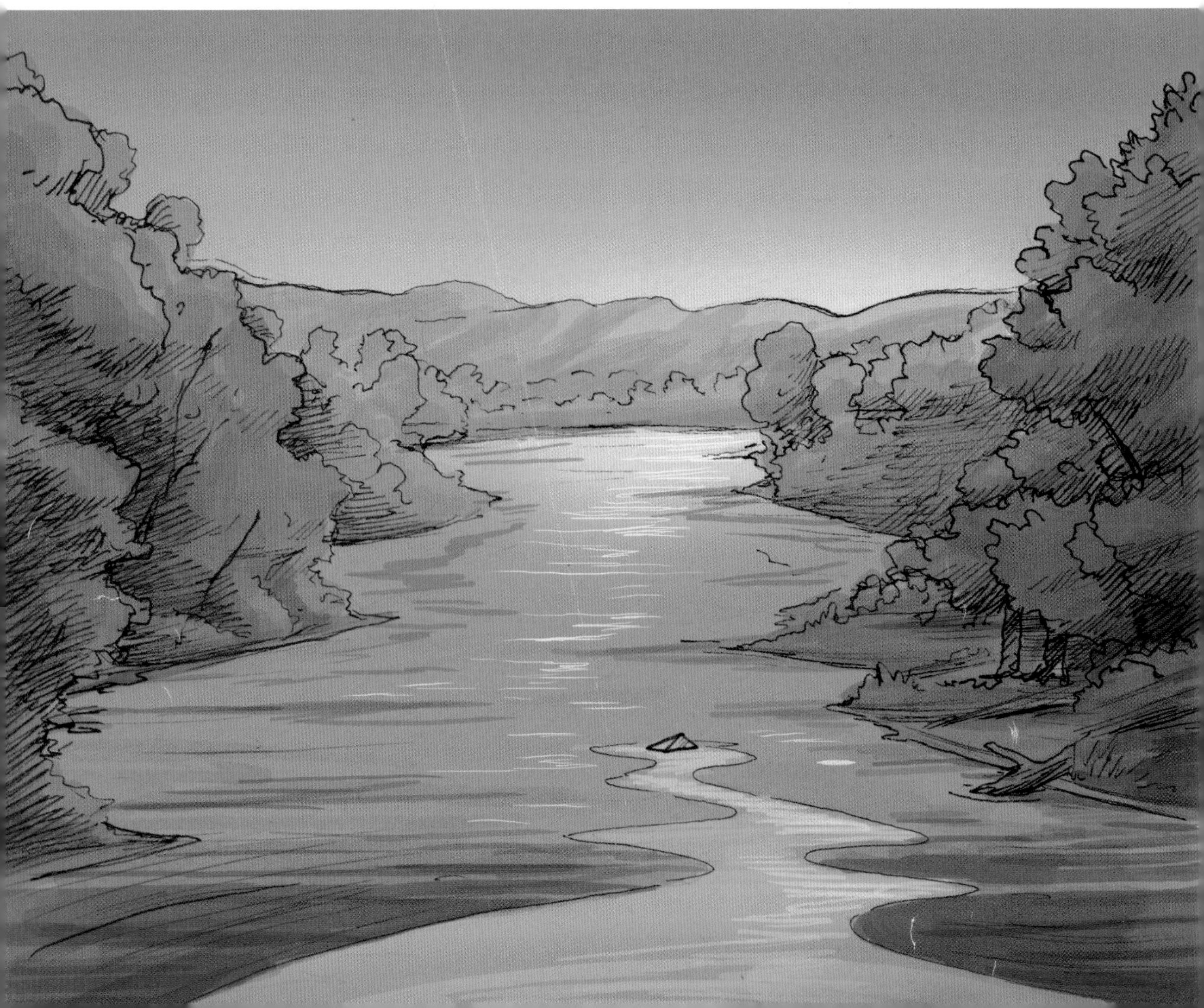

CHAPTER ONE

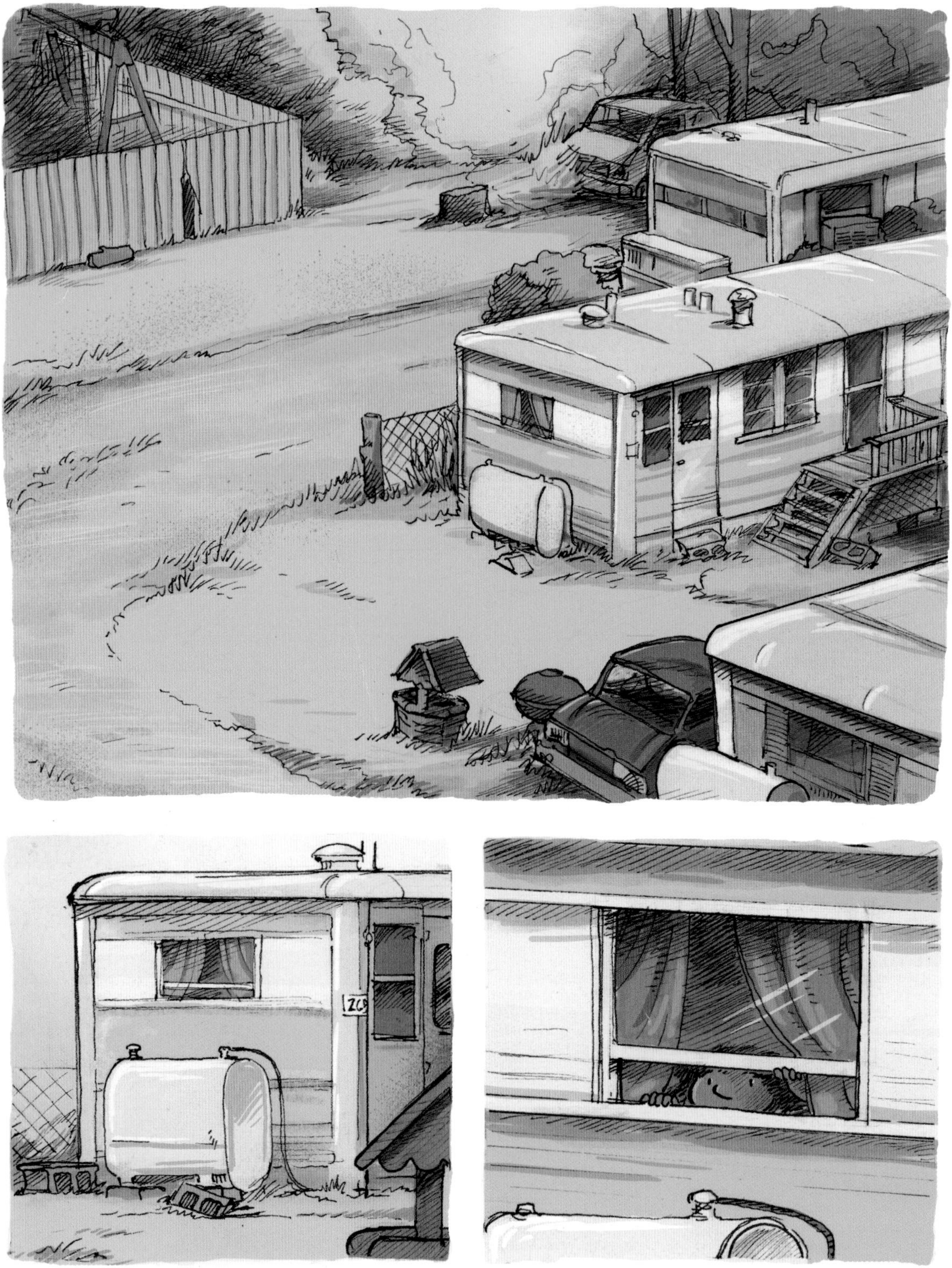

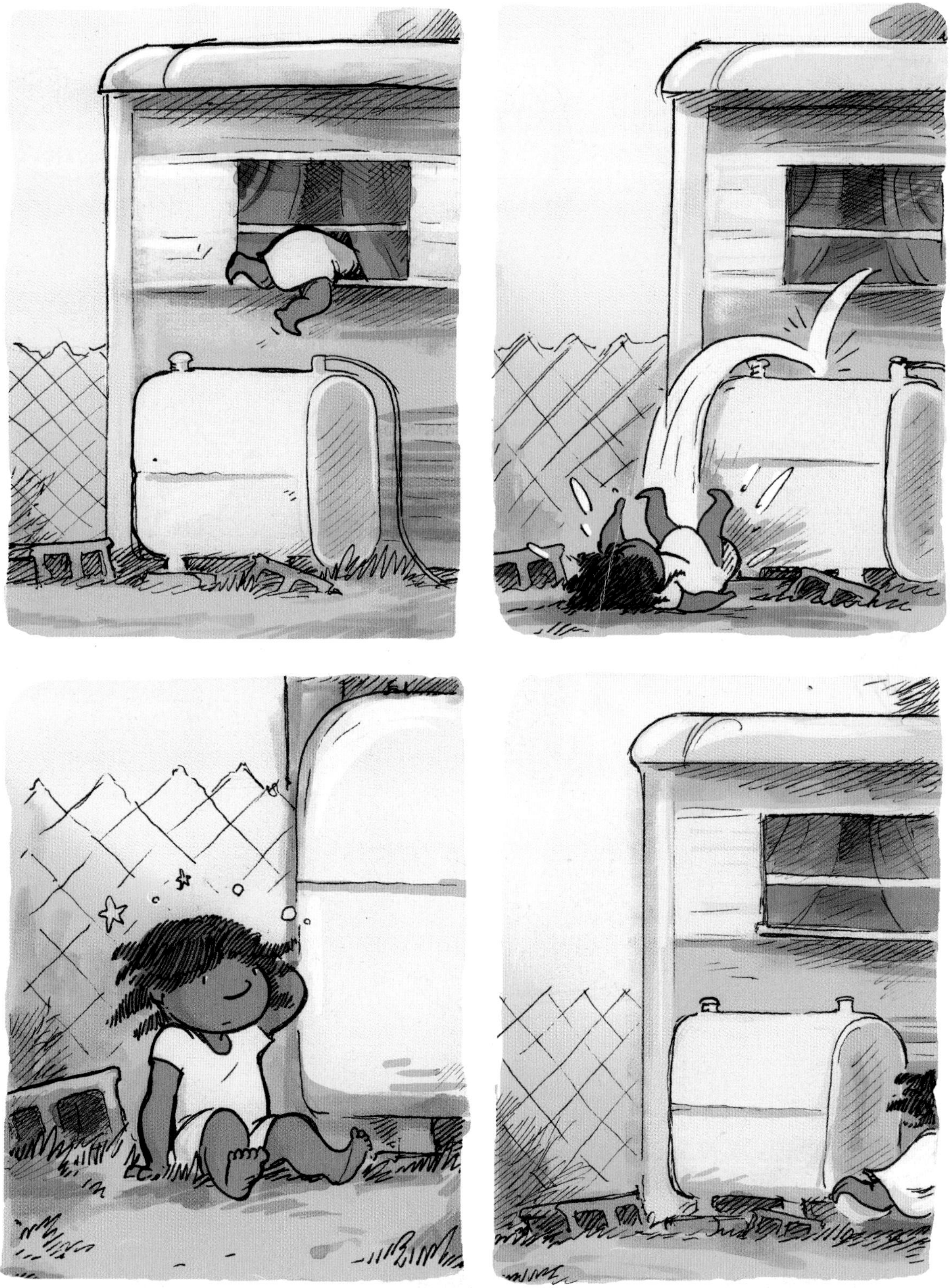

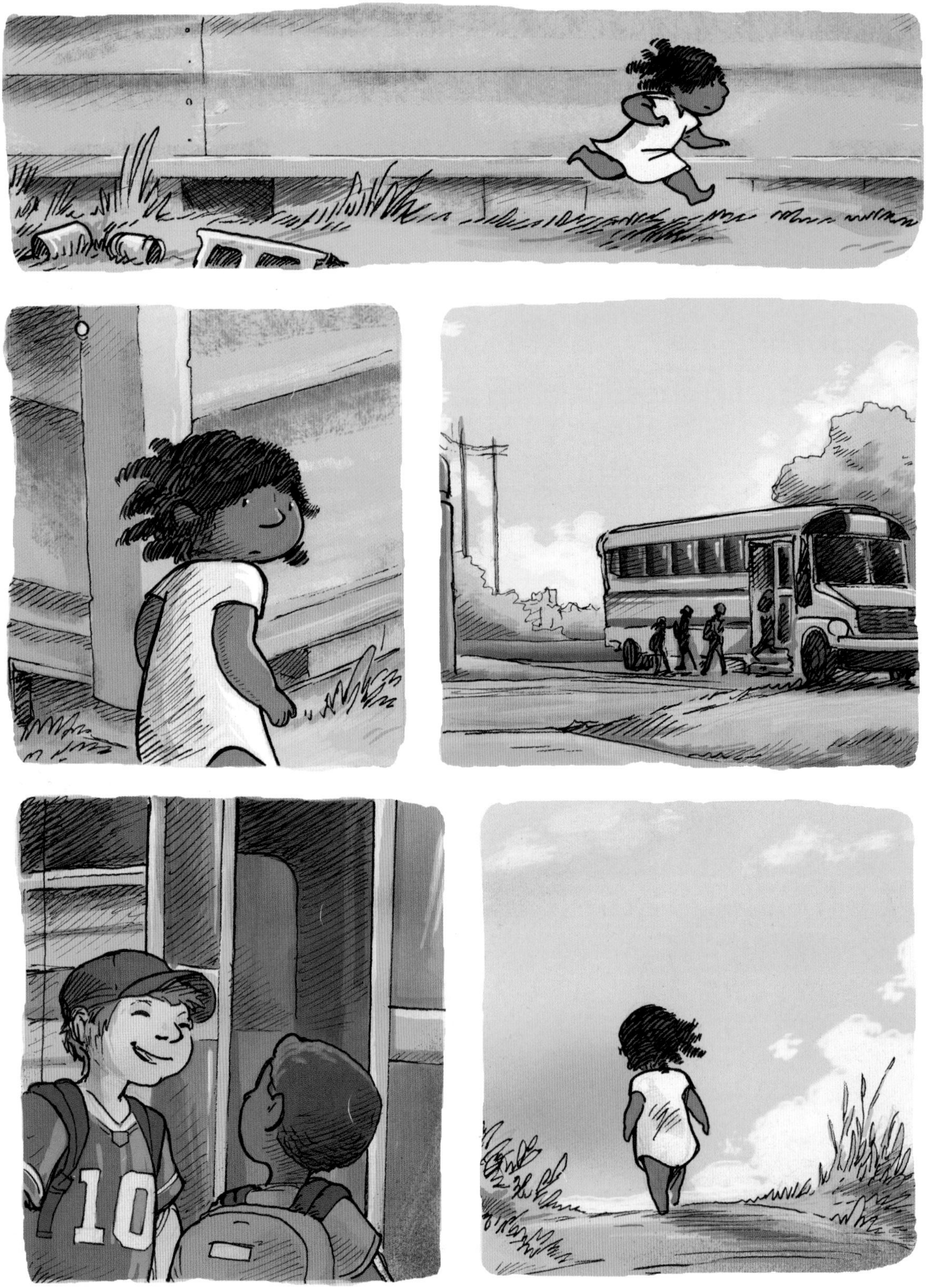
10

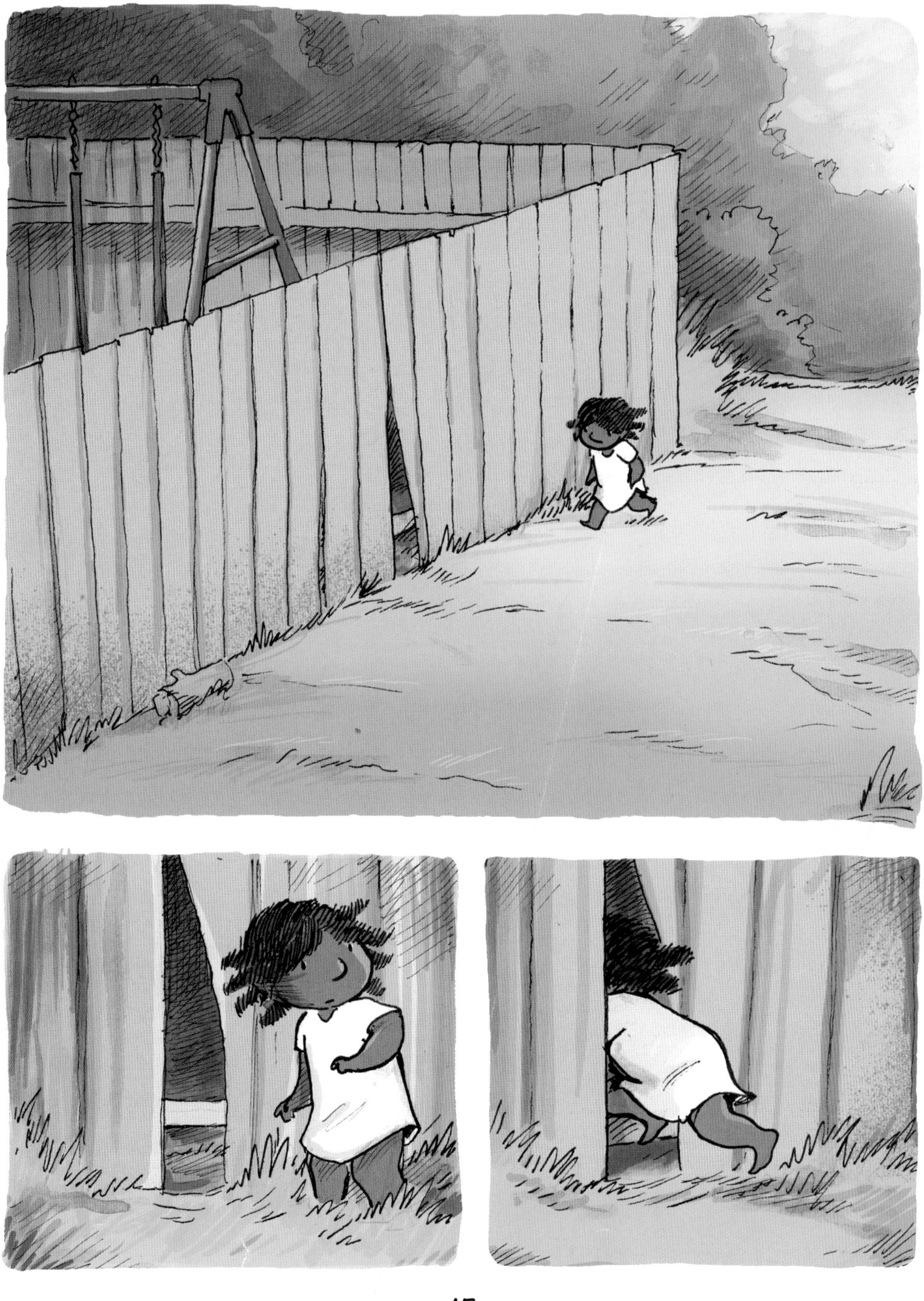

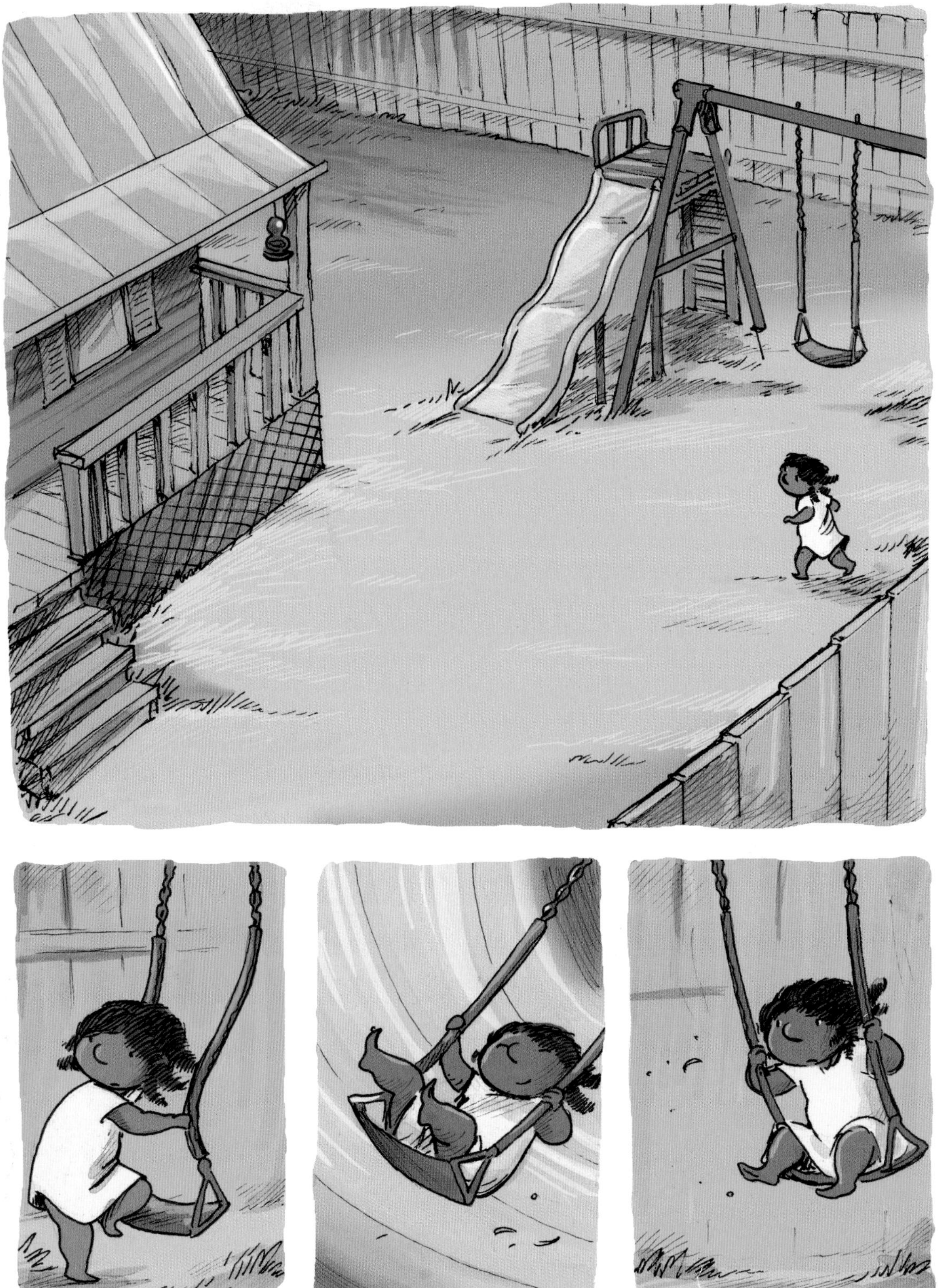

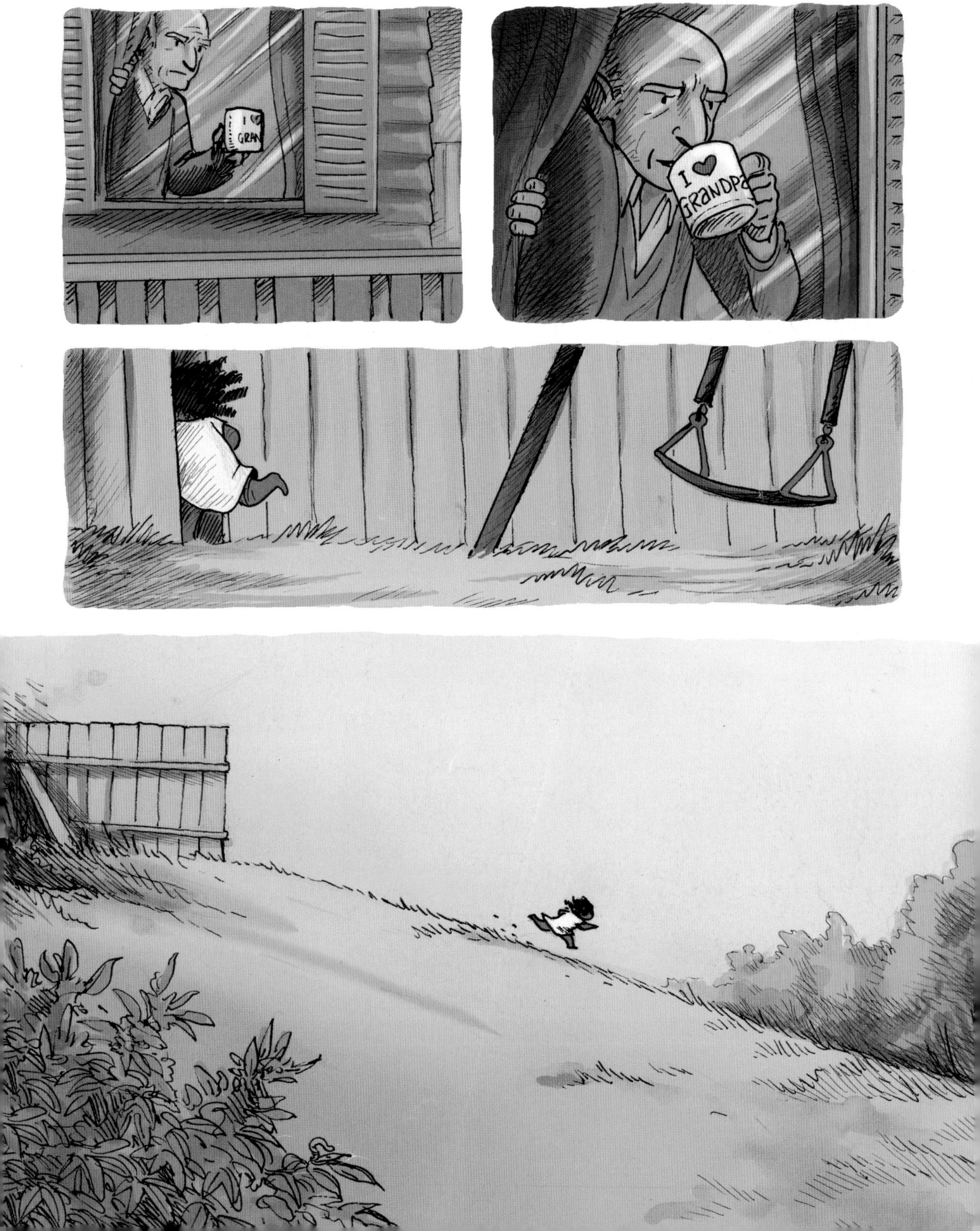
I ♥ GRAN
I ♥ GRANDPA

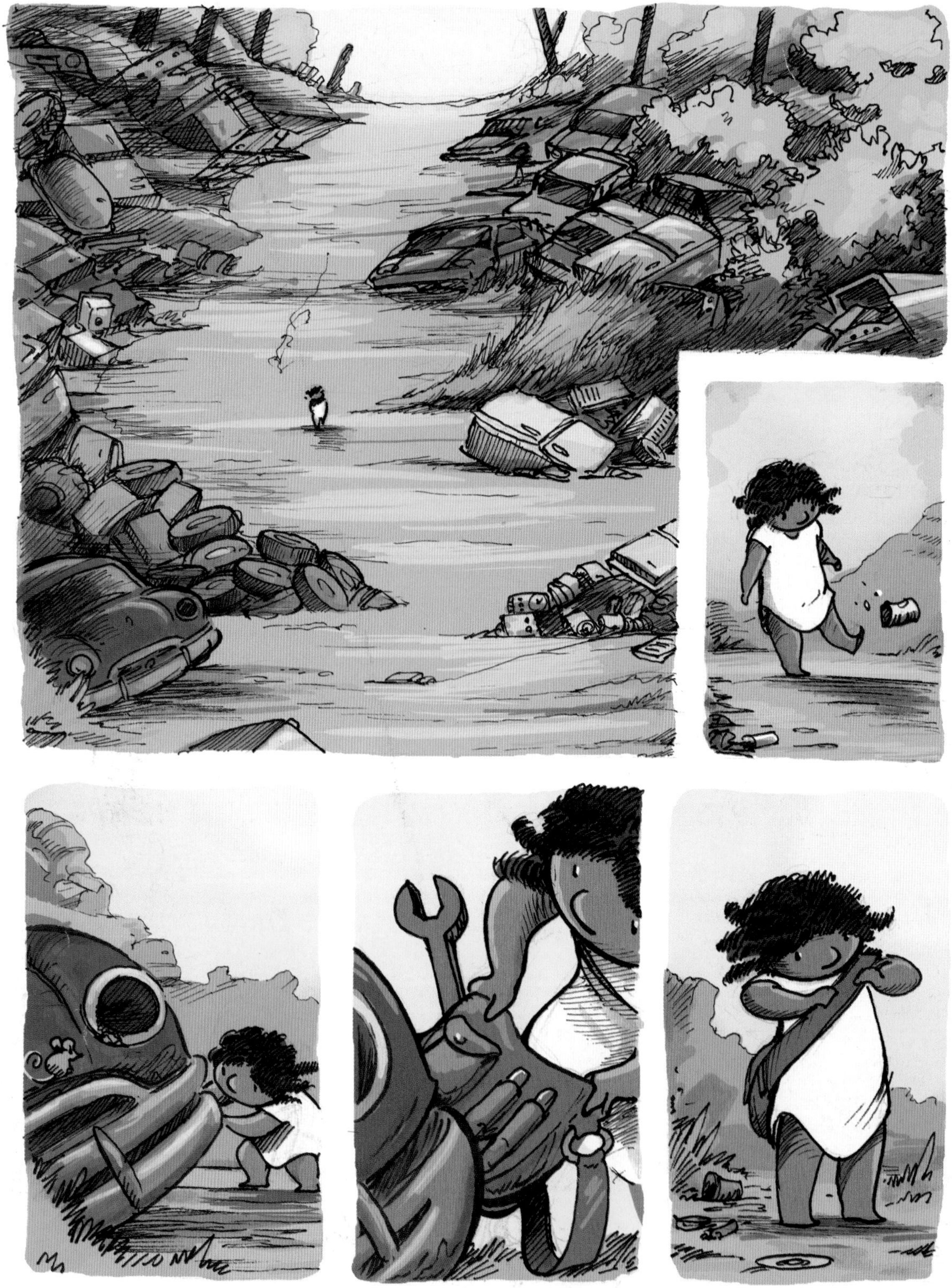

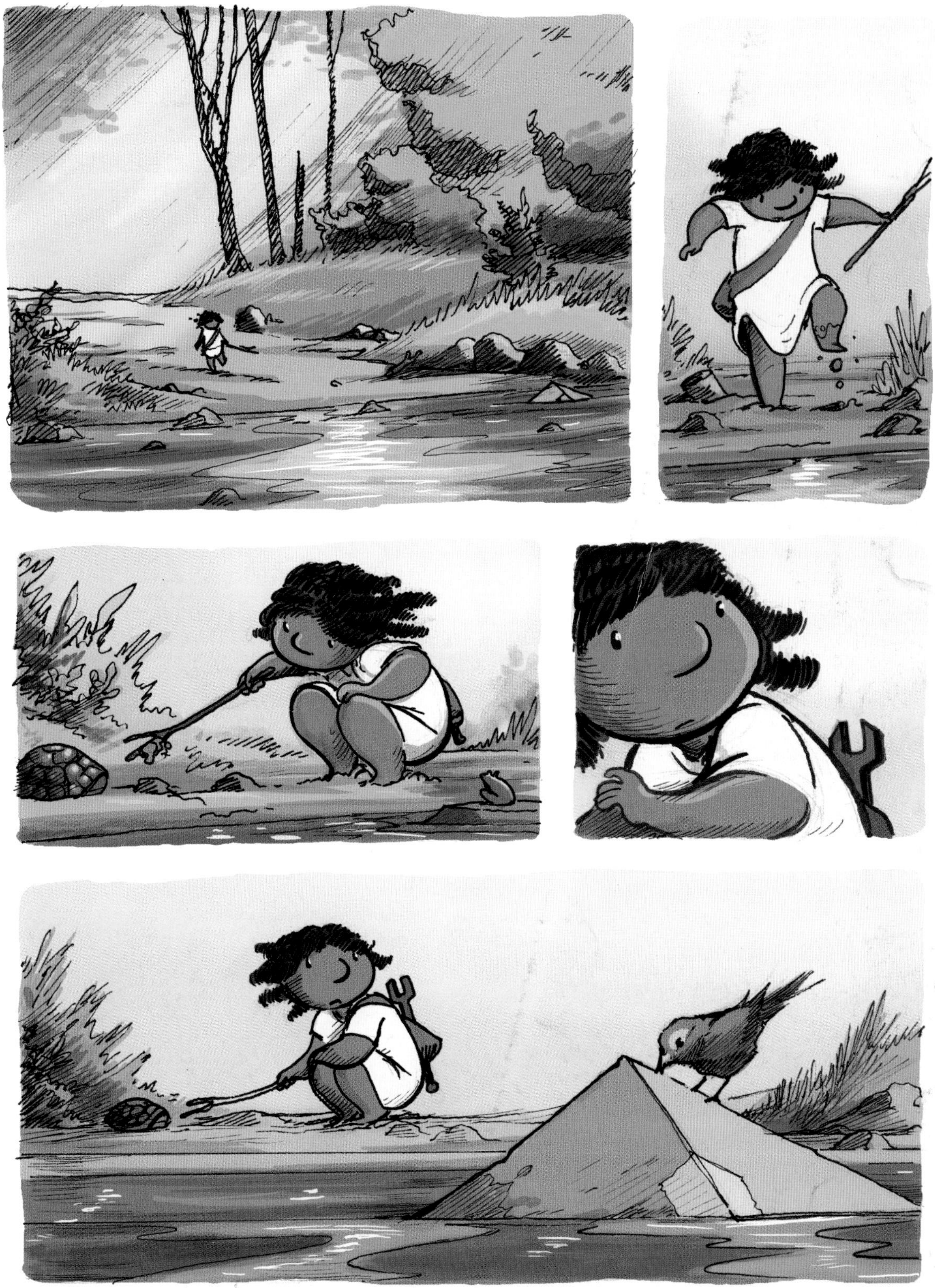

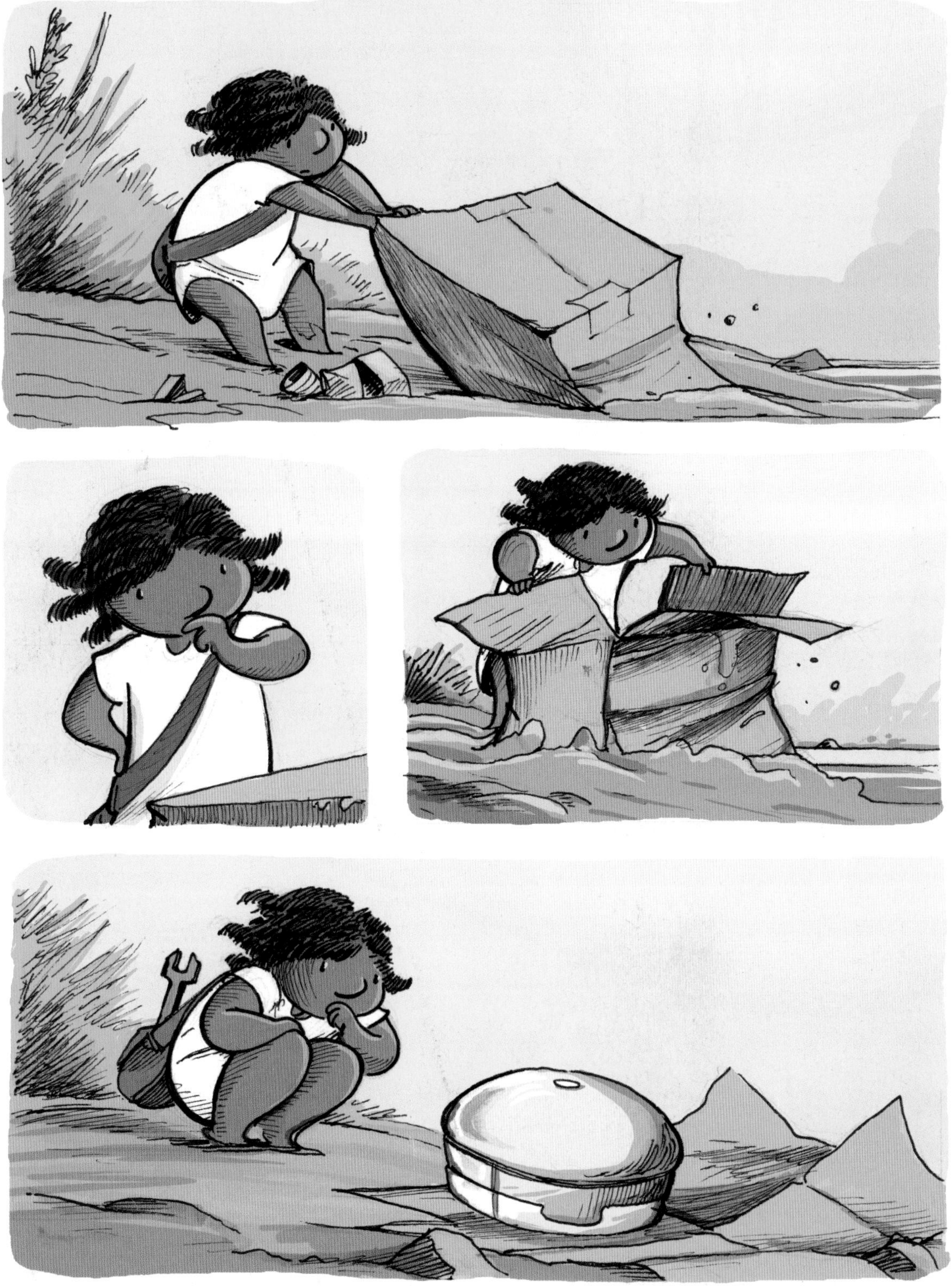

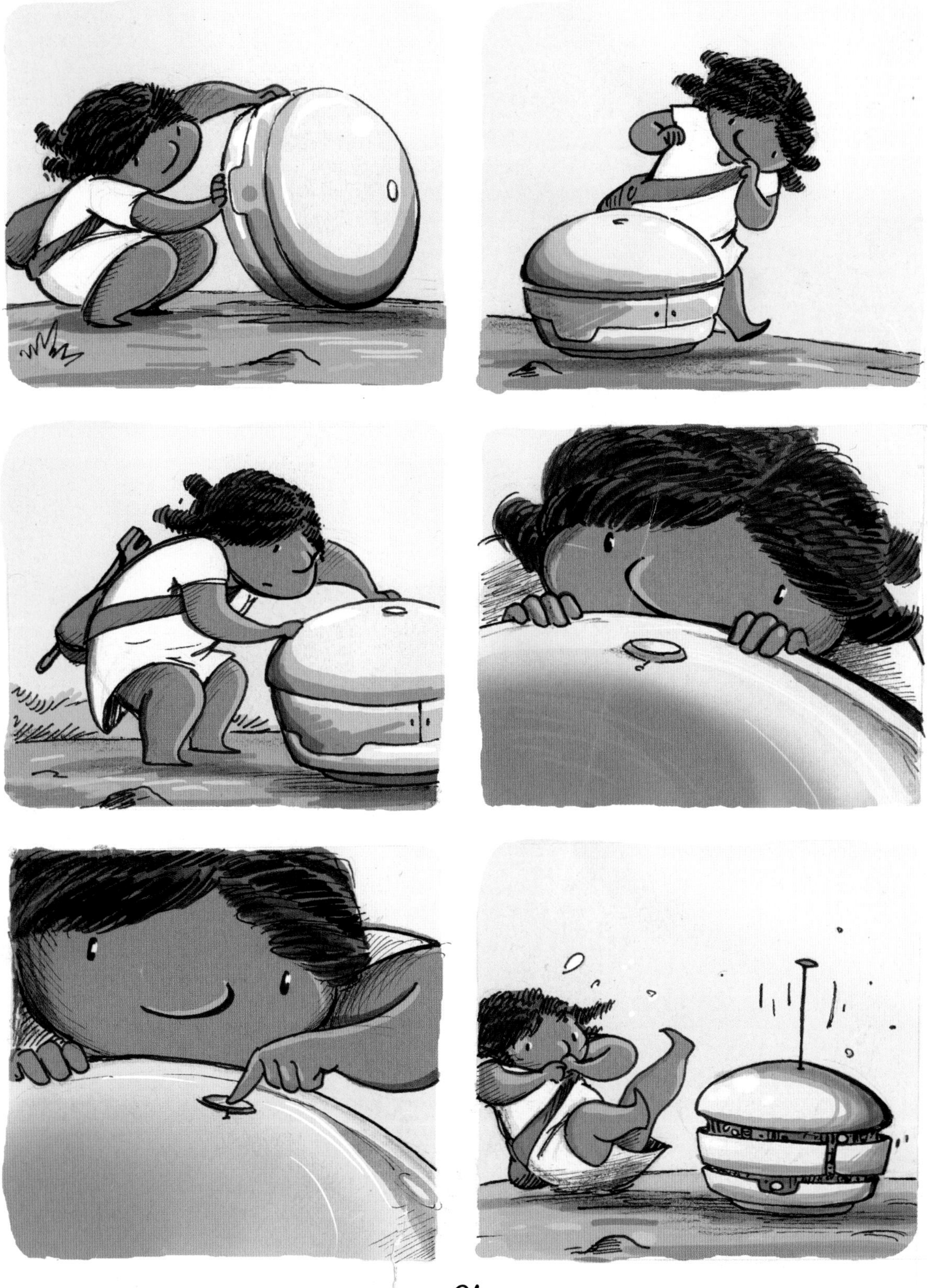

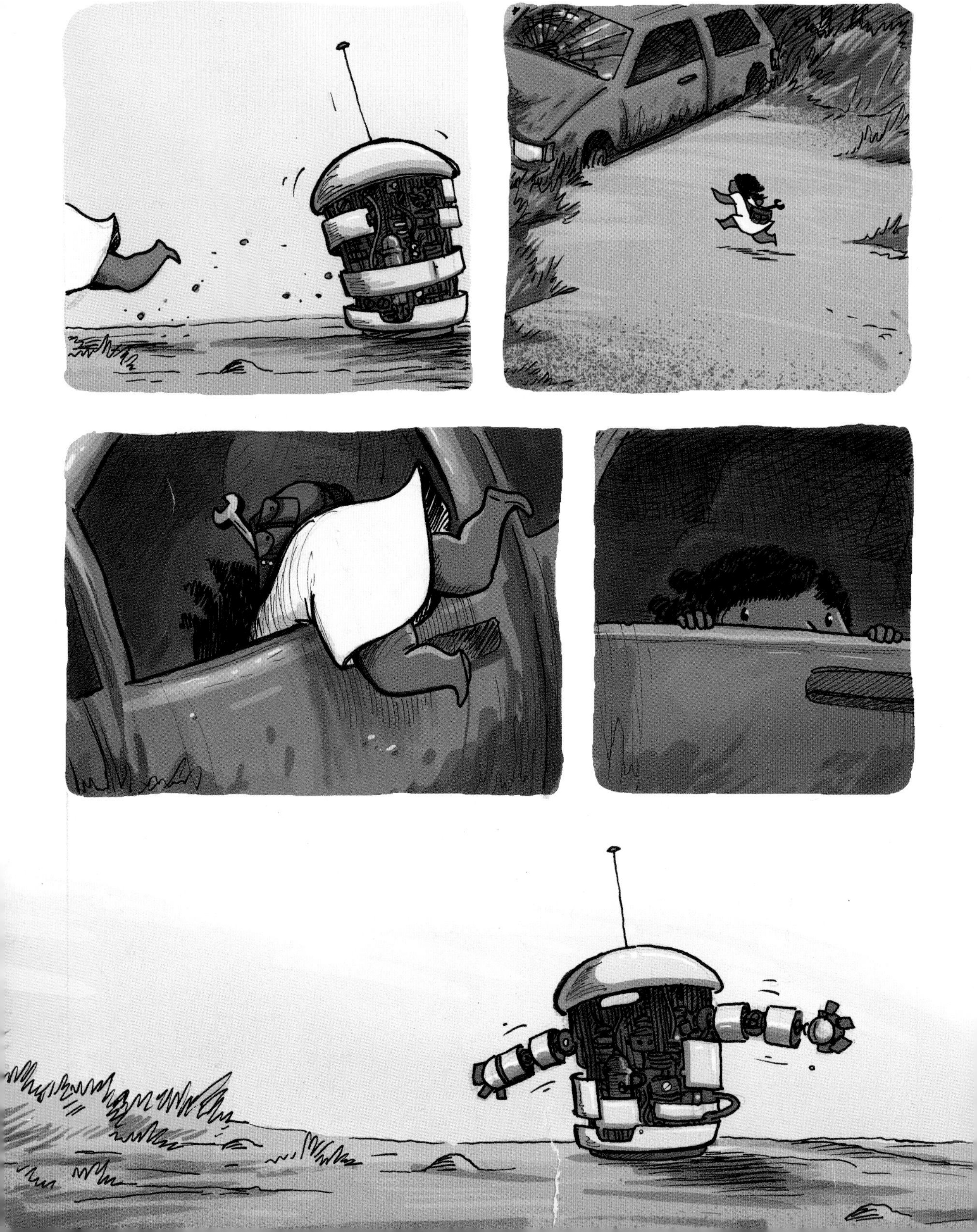

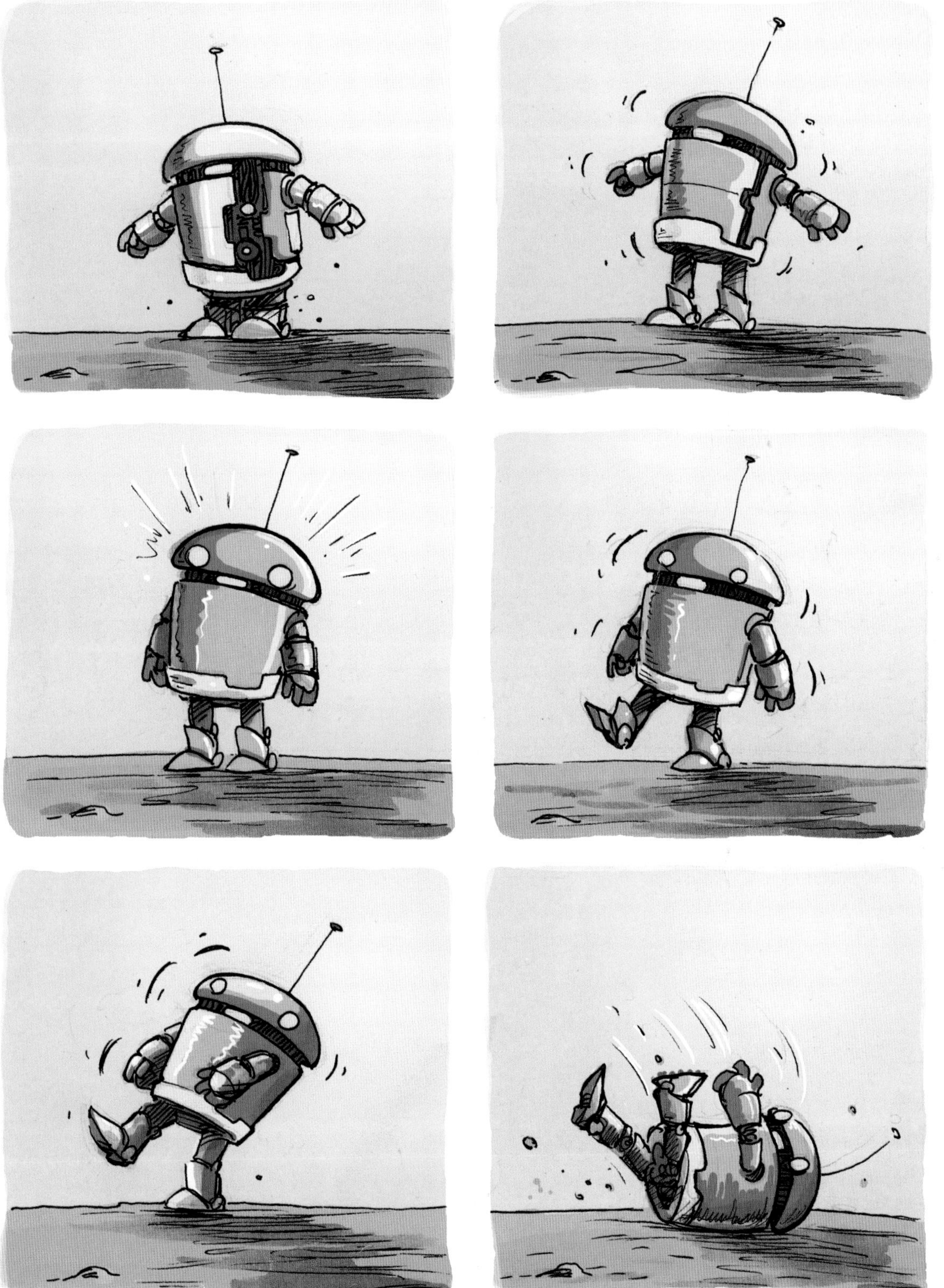

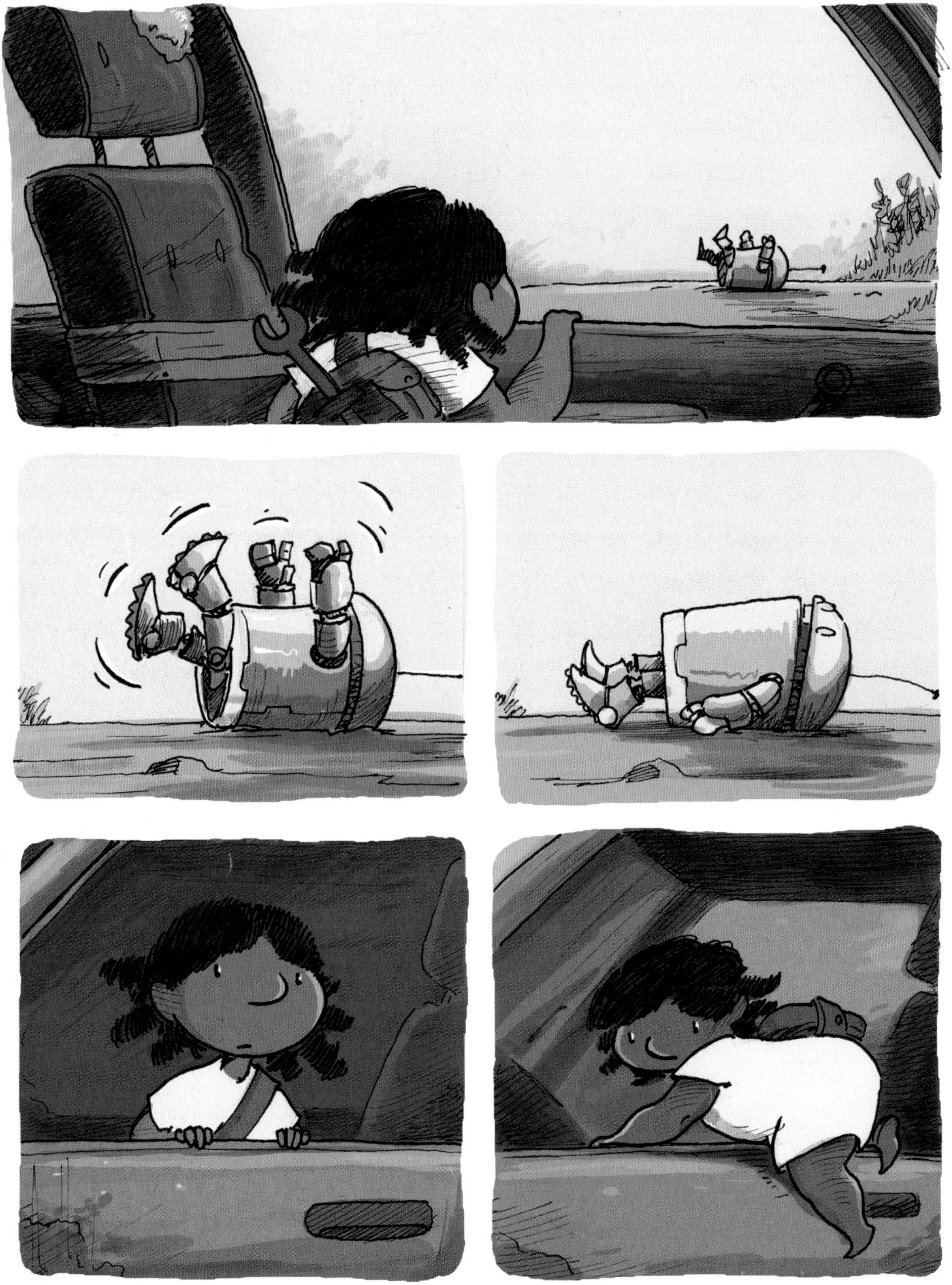

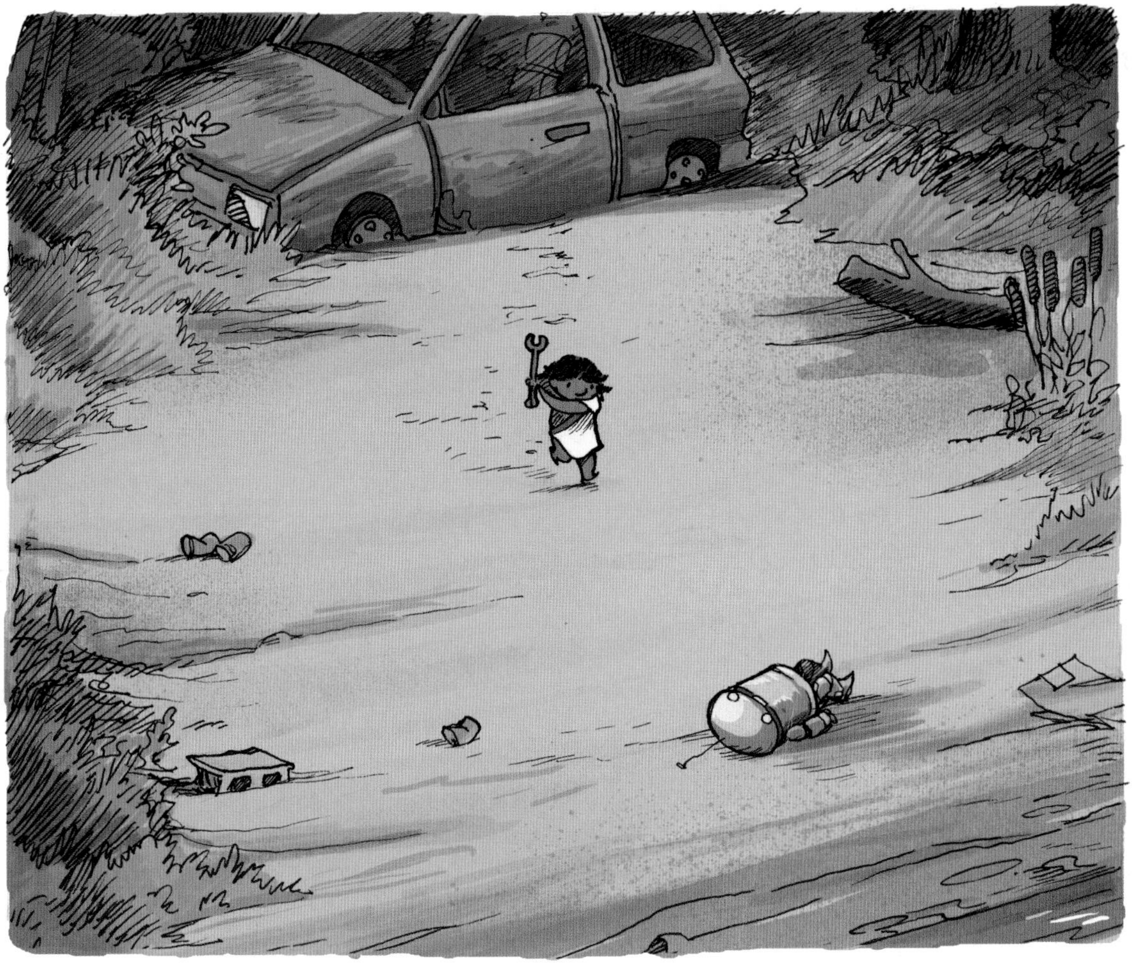

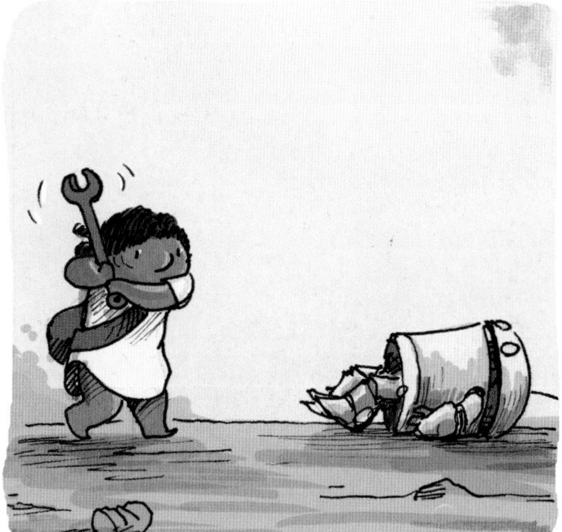

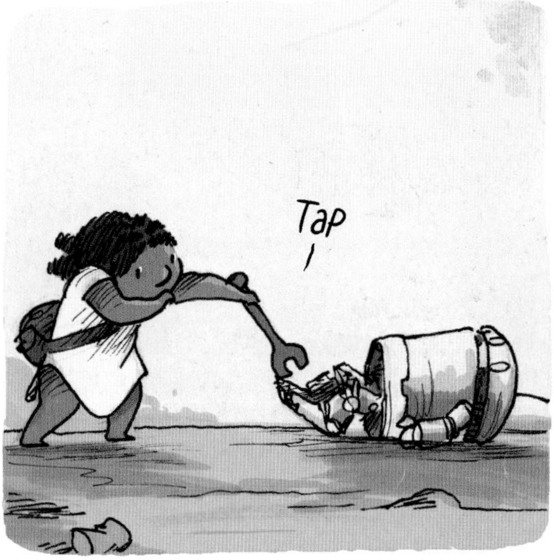
Tap

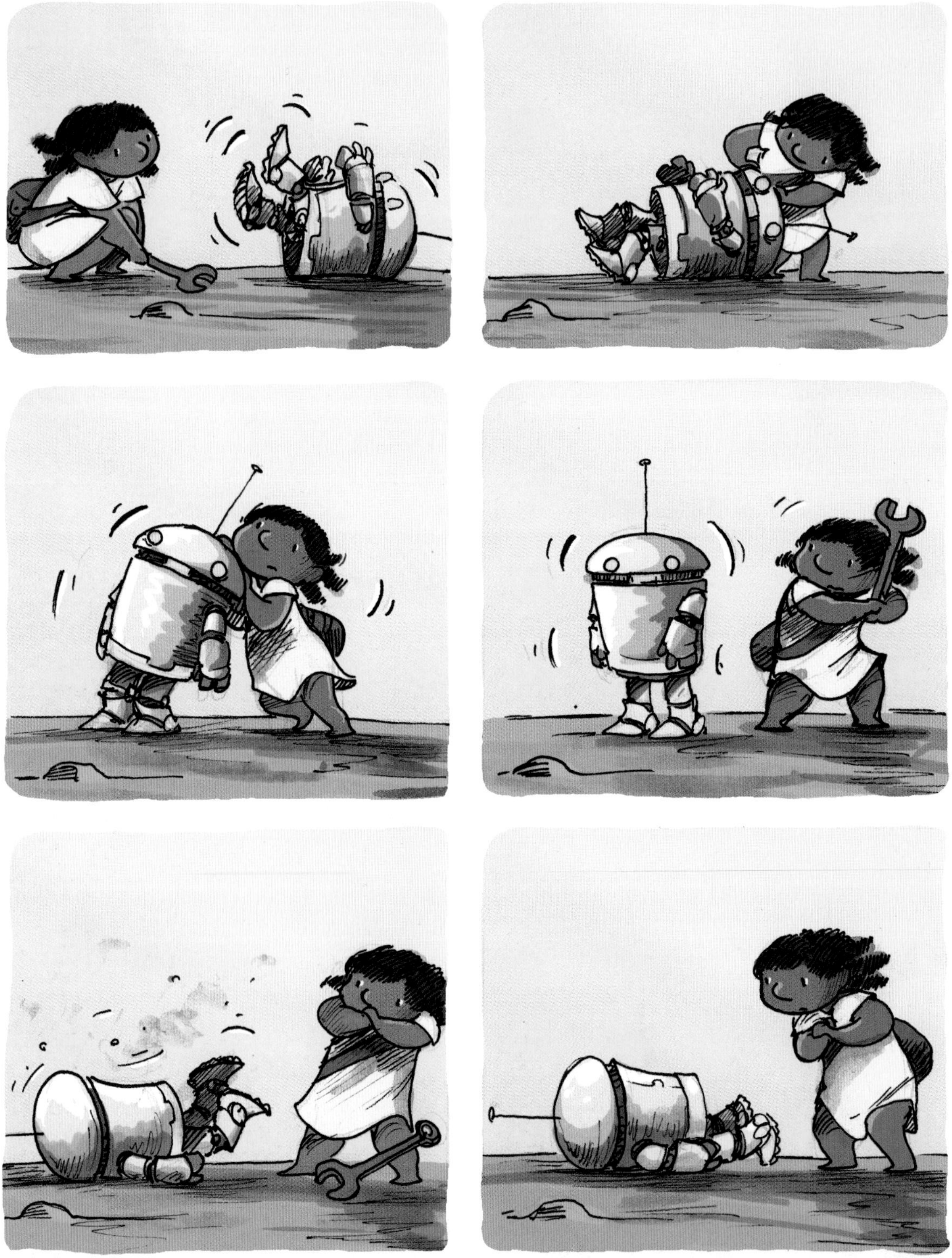

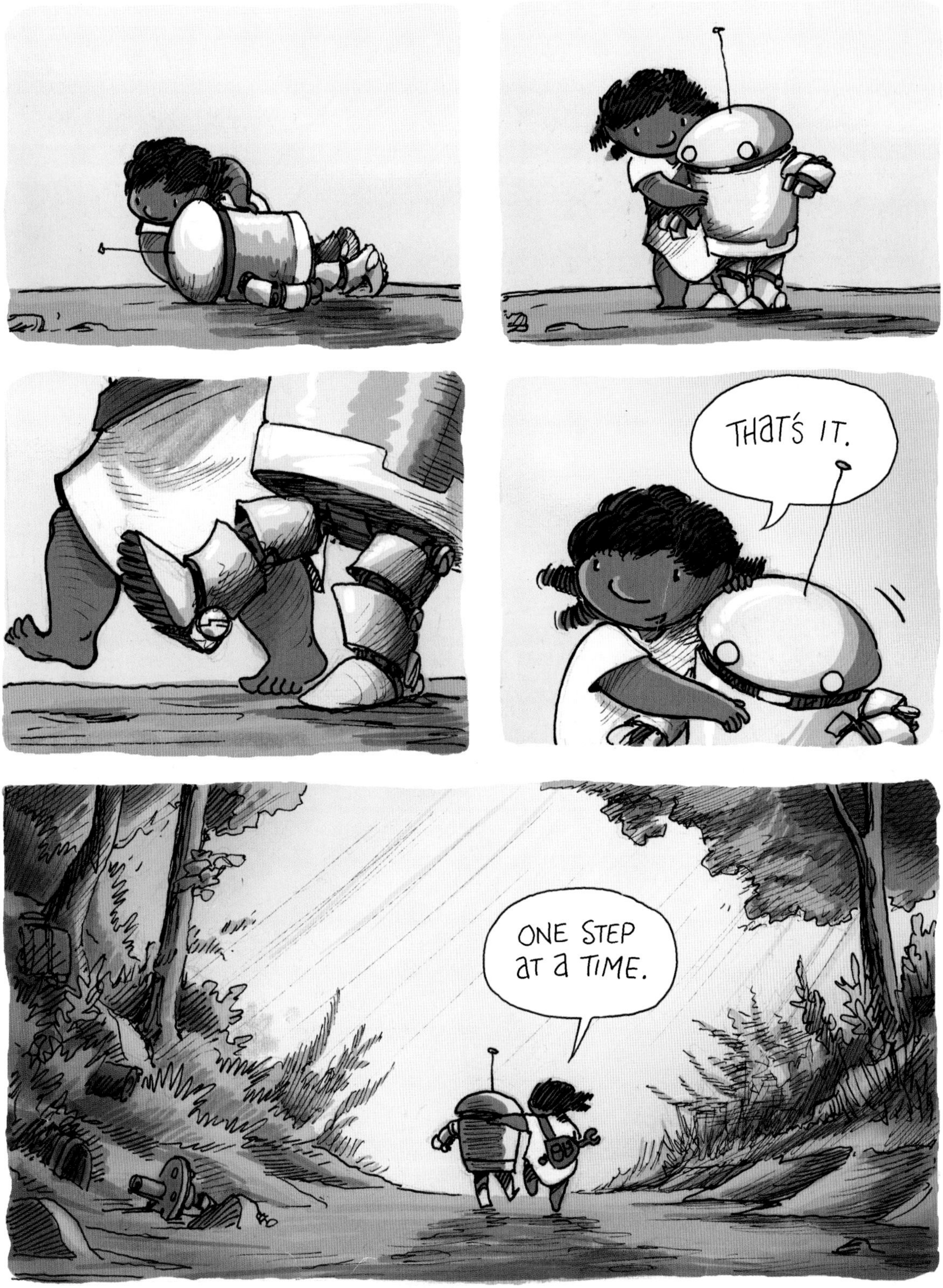
THAT'S IT.
ONE STEP AT A TIME.

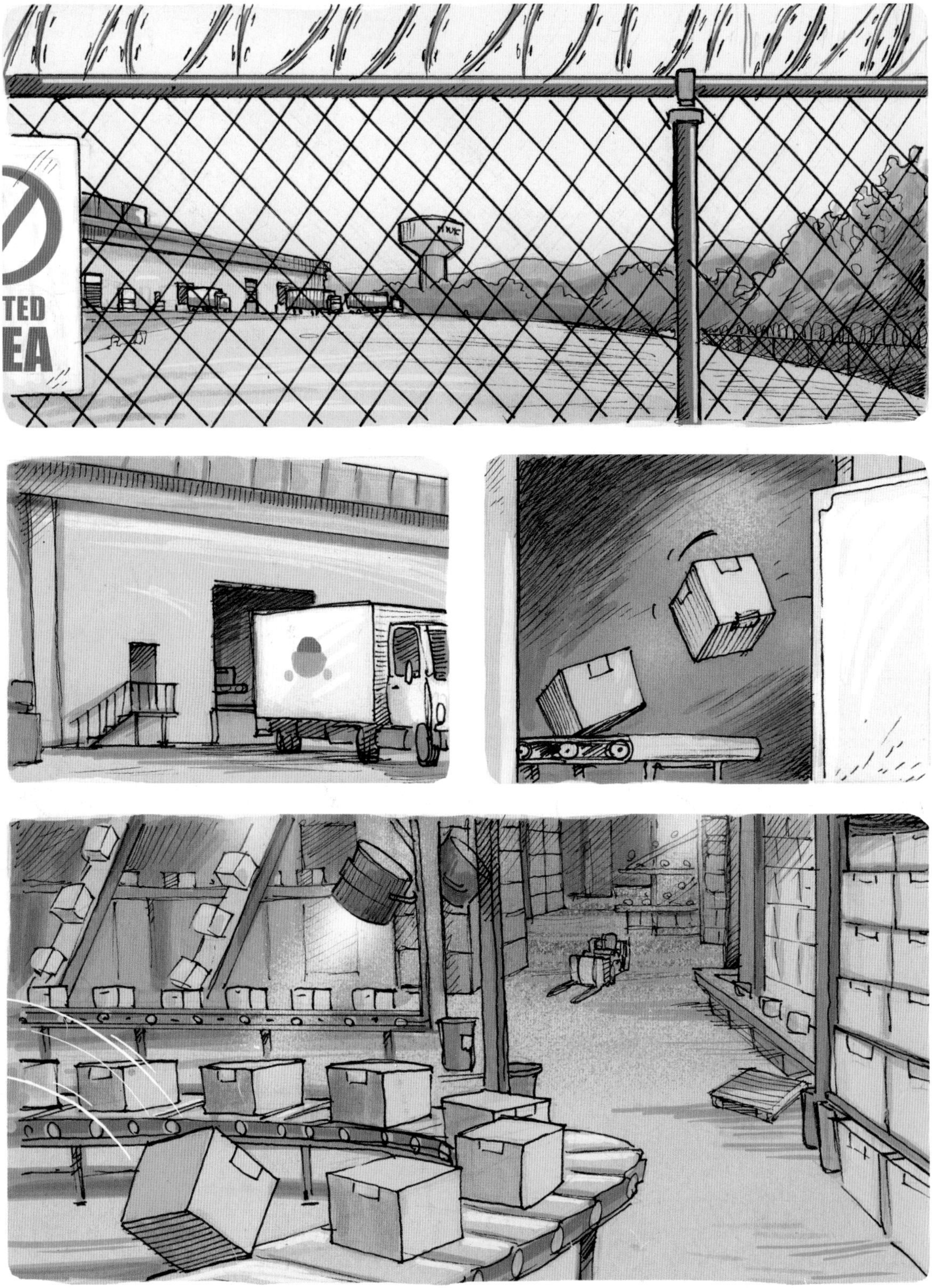
TED
EA

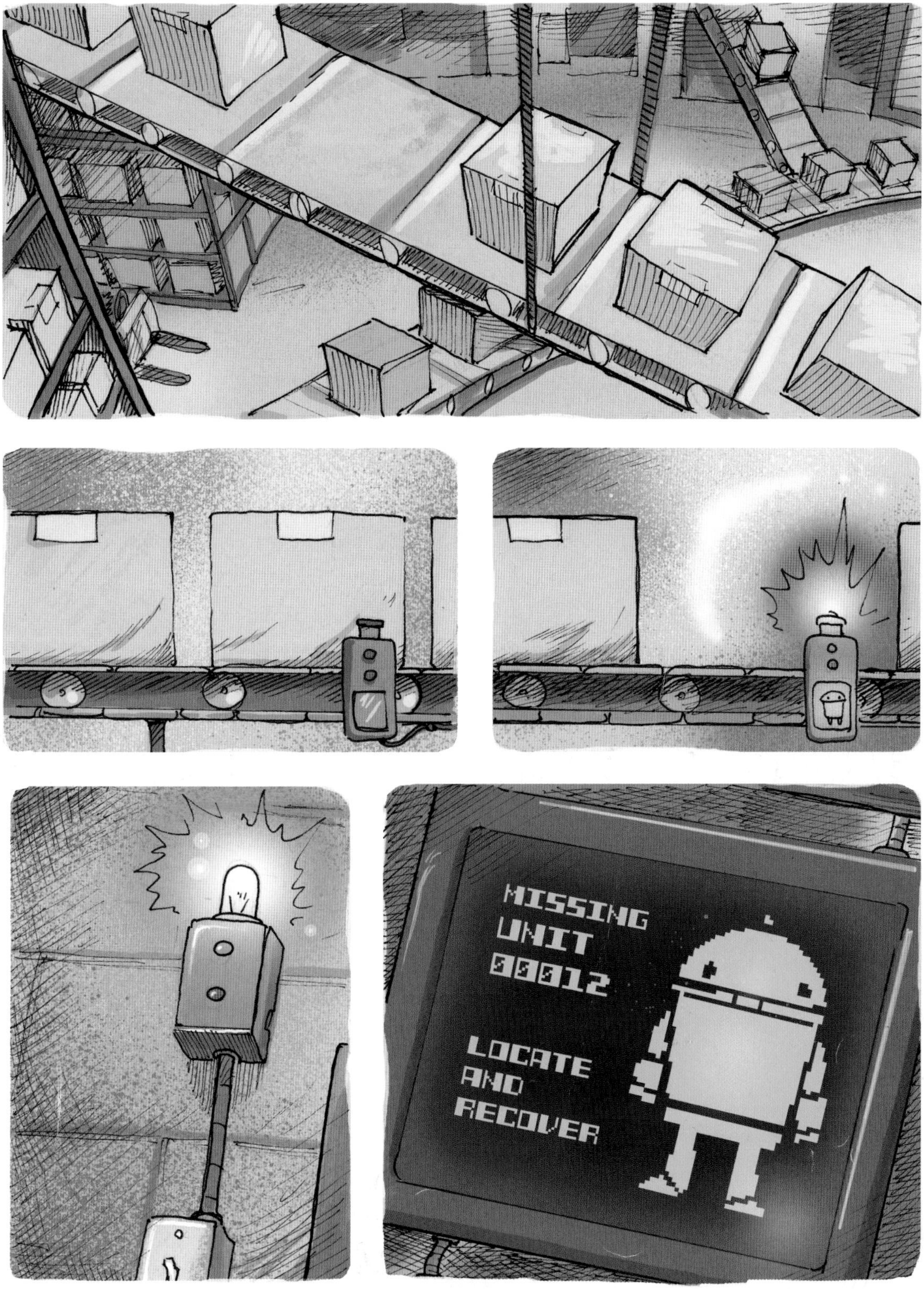
MISSING
UNIT
00012
LOCATE
AND
RECOVER

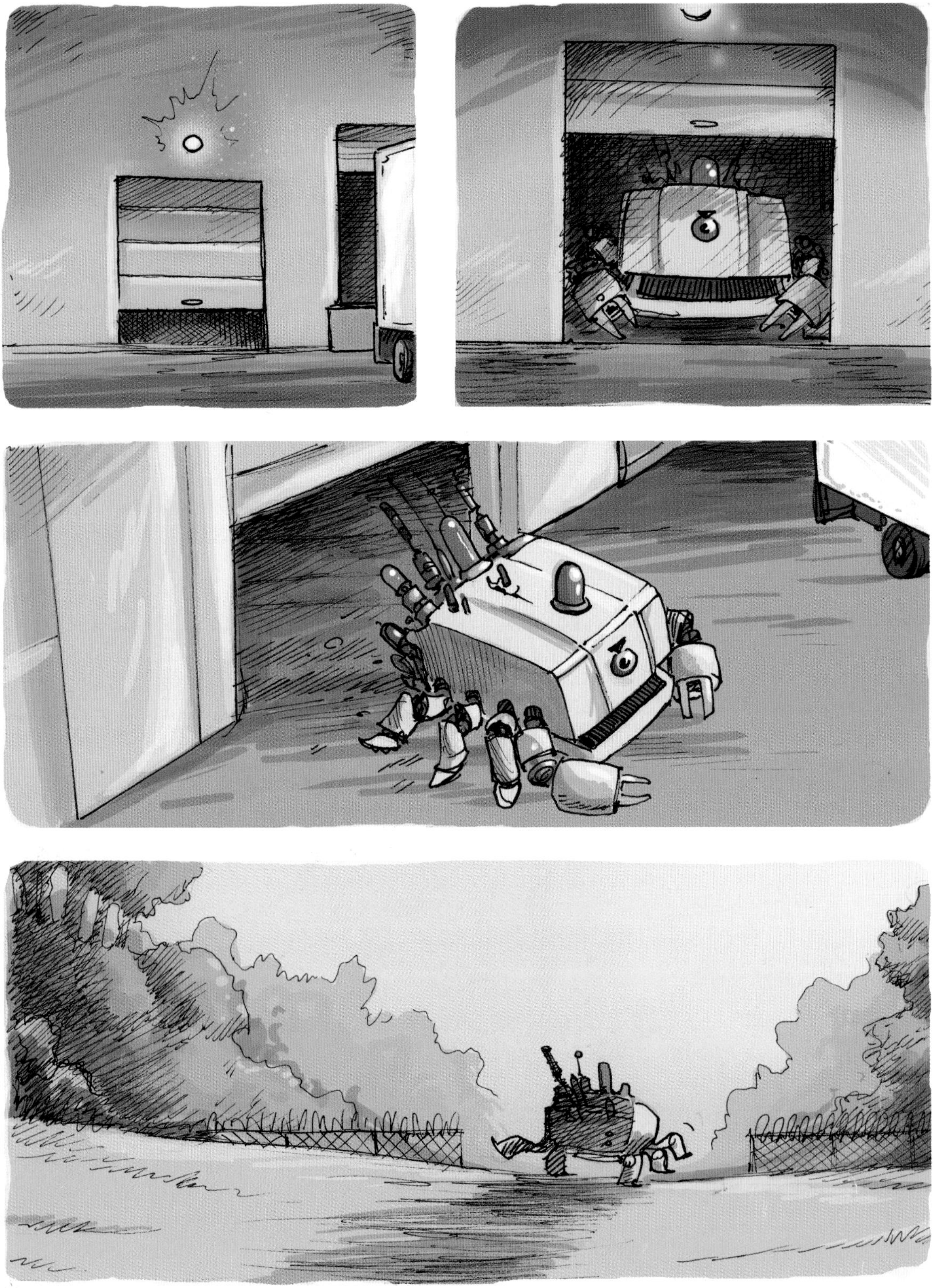

CHAPTER TWO

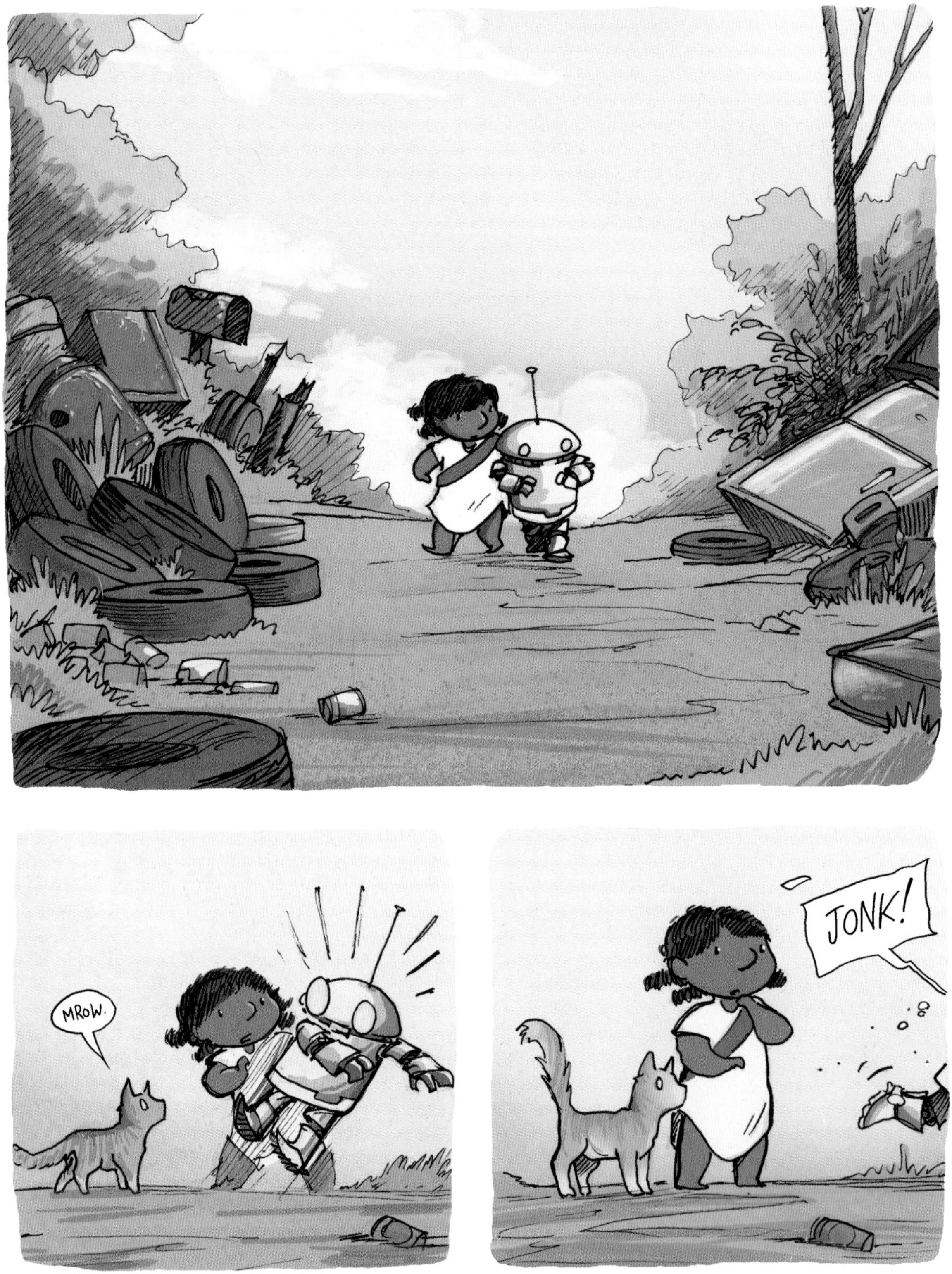
MROW.
JONK!

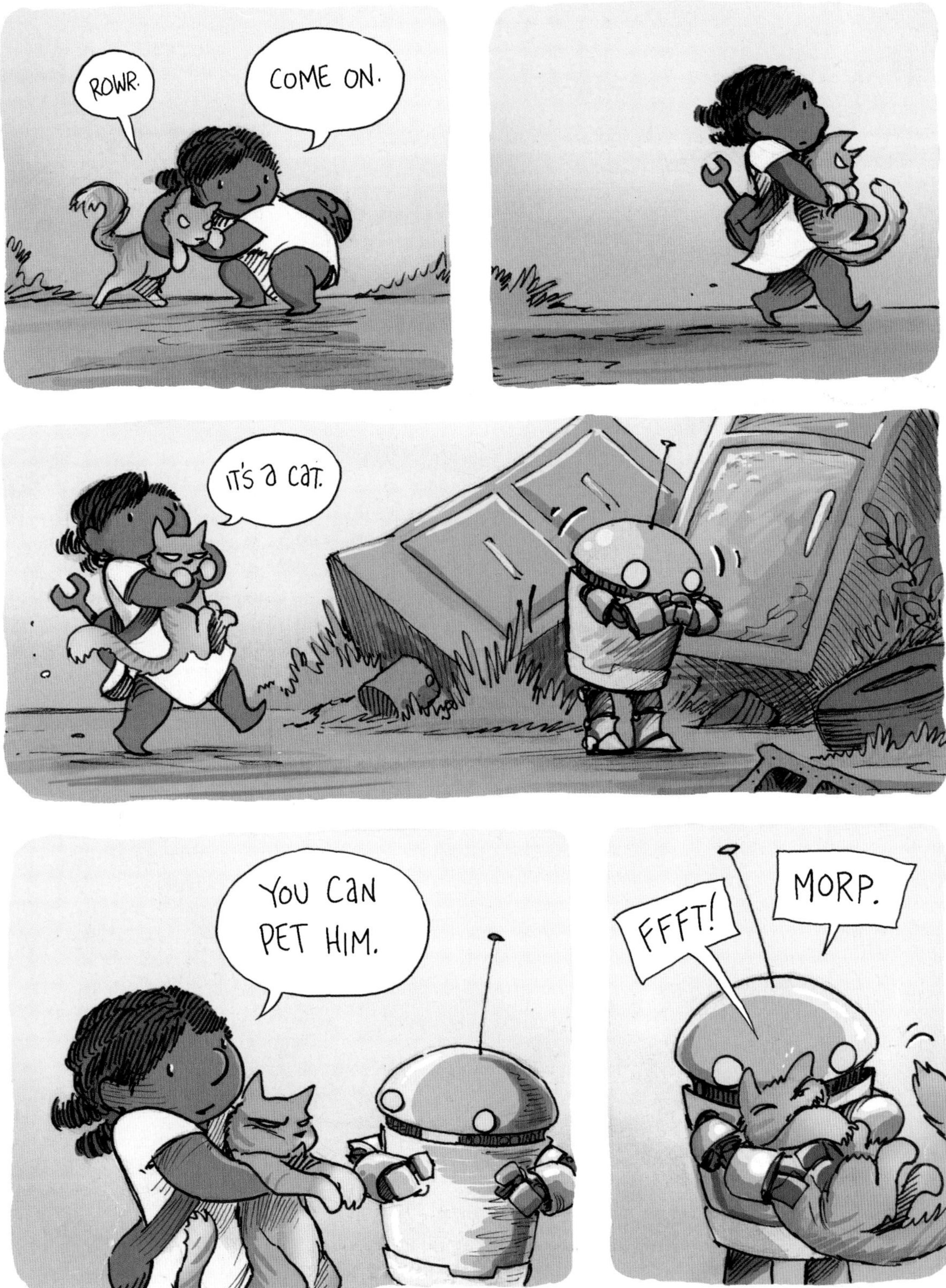
ROWR.
COME ON.
IT'S A CAT.
YOU CAN PET HIM.
FFFT!
MORP.

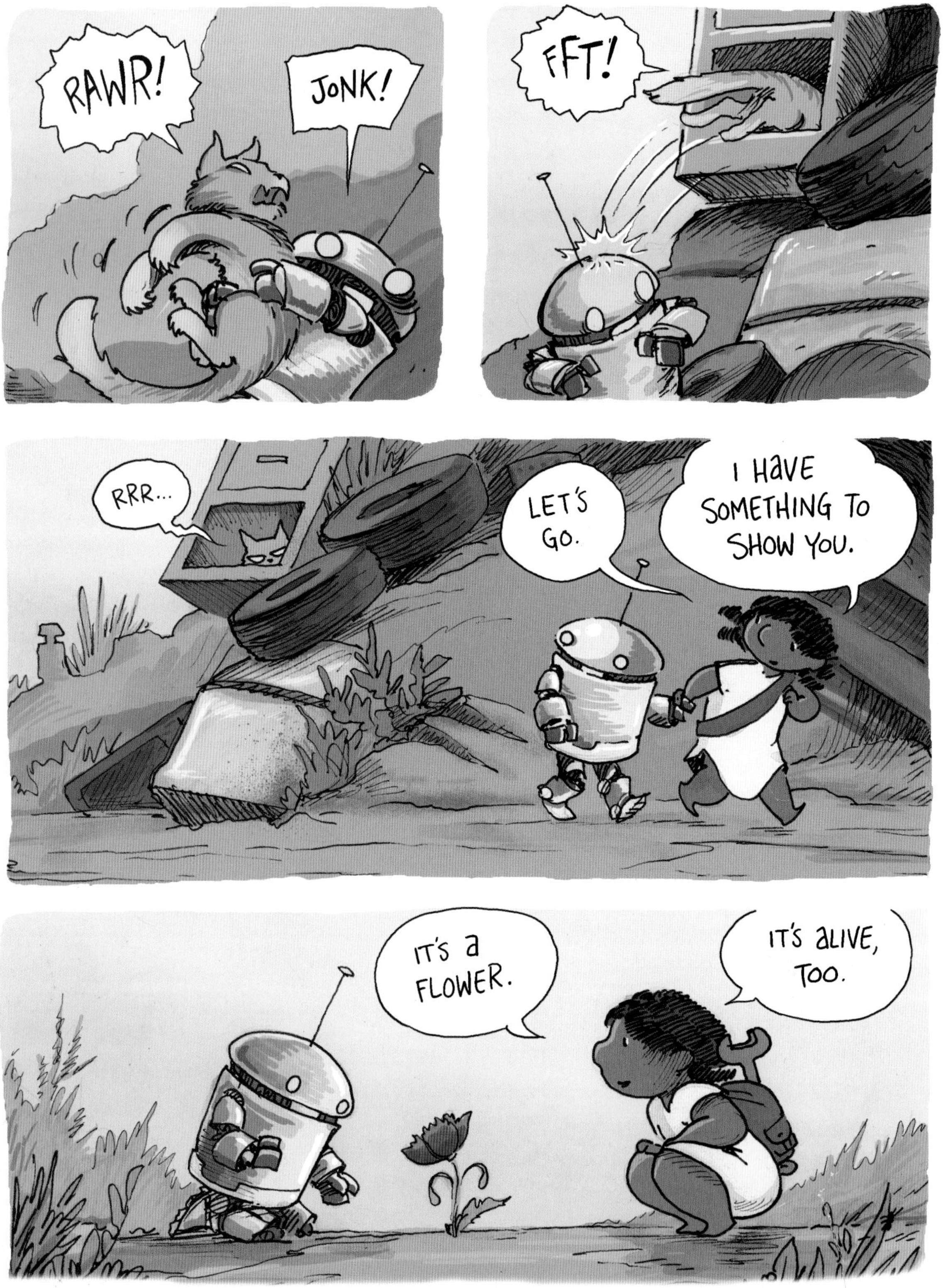
RAWR!
JONK!
FFT!
RRR...
LET'S GO.
I HAVE SOMETHING TO SHOW YOU.
IT'S A FLOWER.
IT'S ALIVE, TOO.

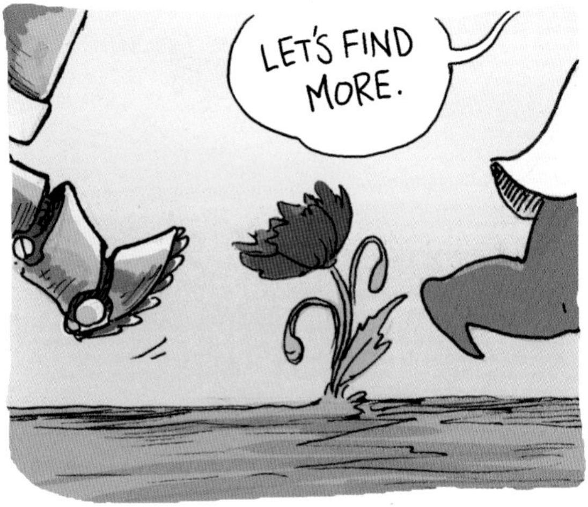
LET'S FIND MORE.

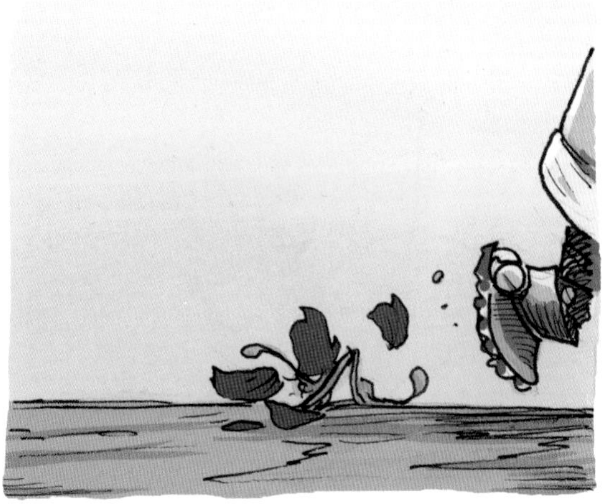

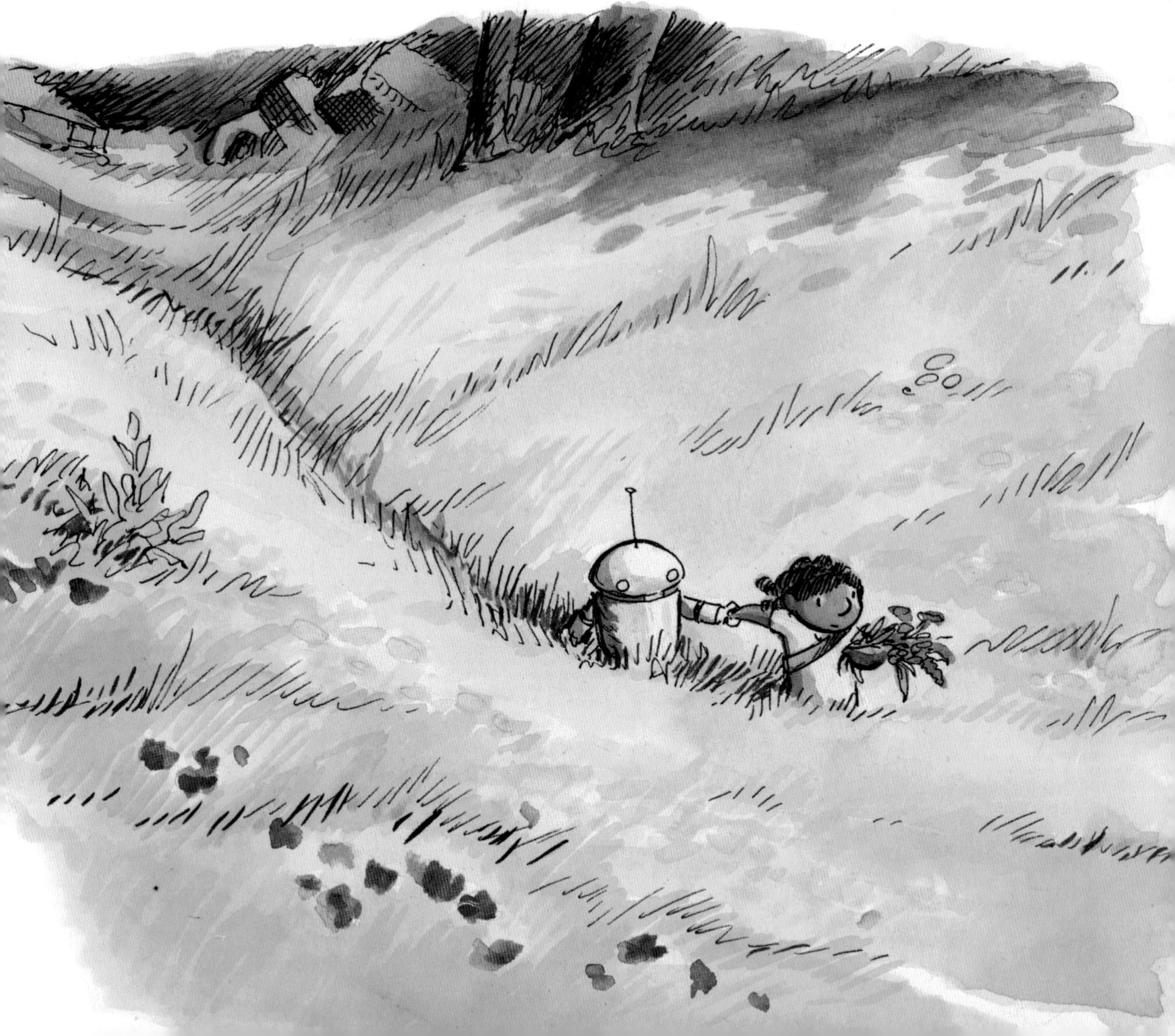

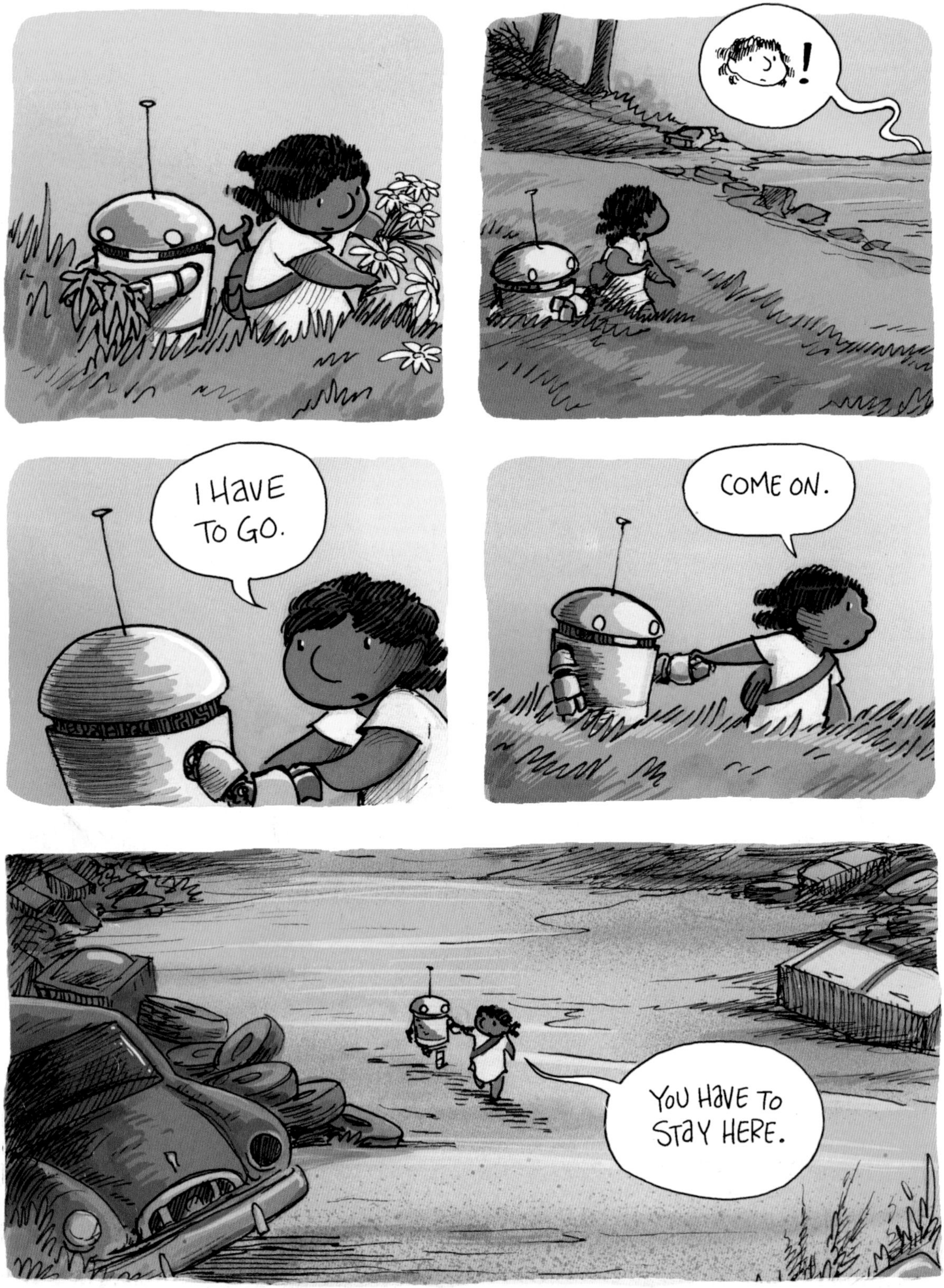
!
I HAVE TO GO.
COME ON.
YOU HAVE TO STAY HERE.

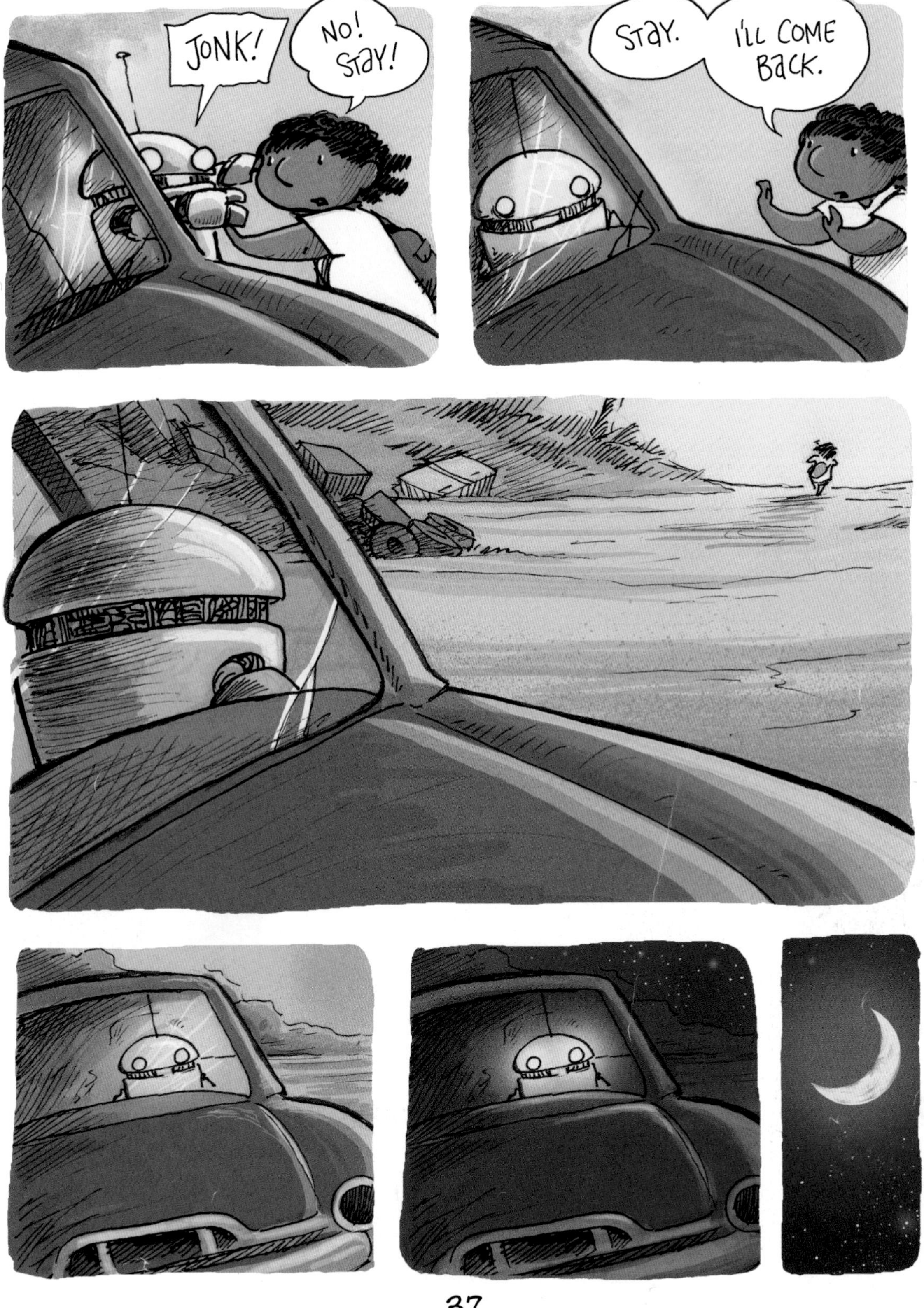
JONK!
NO! STAY!
STAY.
I'LL COME BACK.

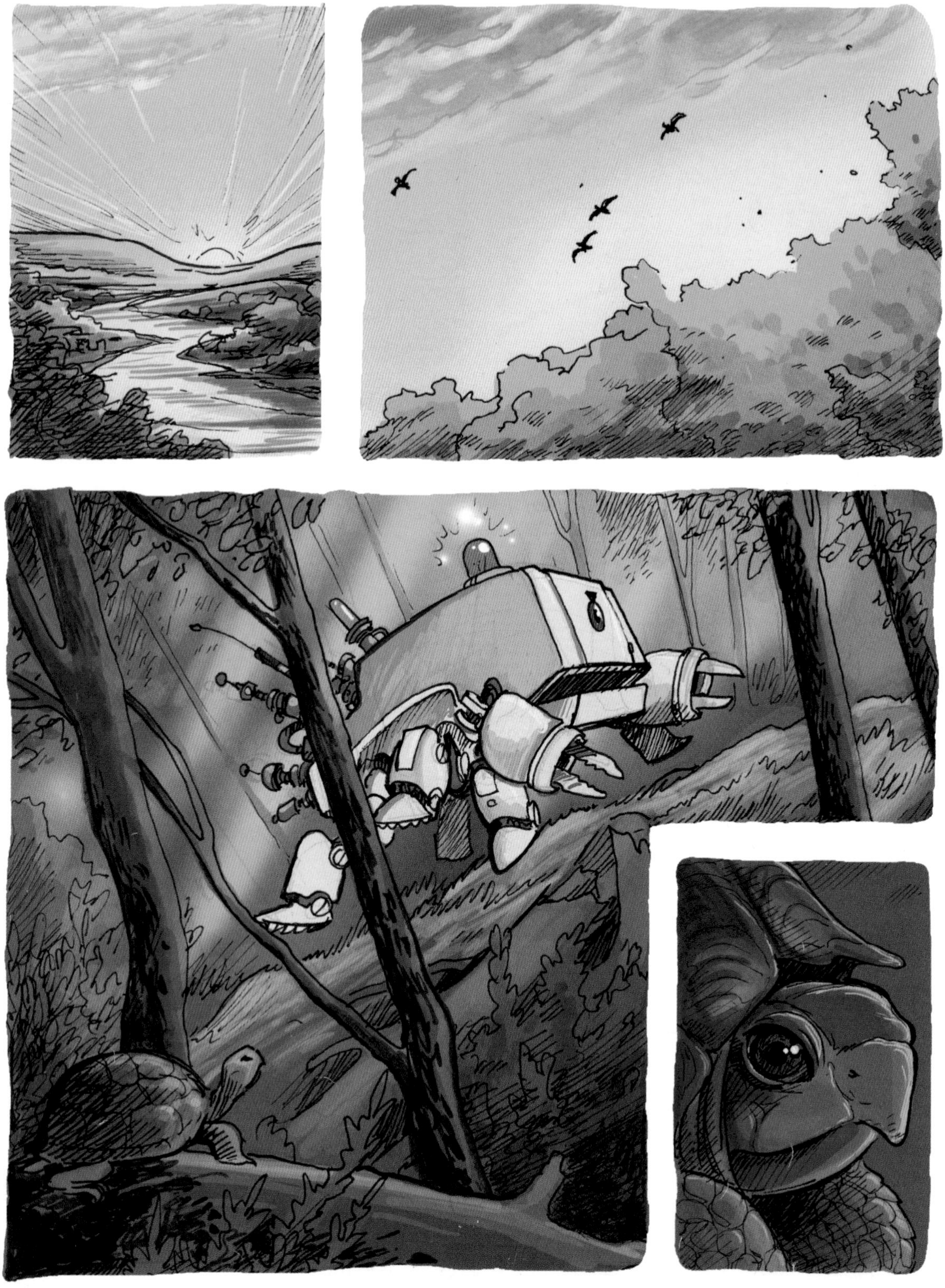

CHAPTER THREE

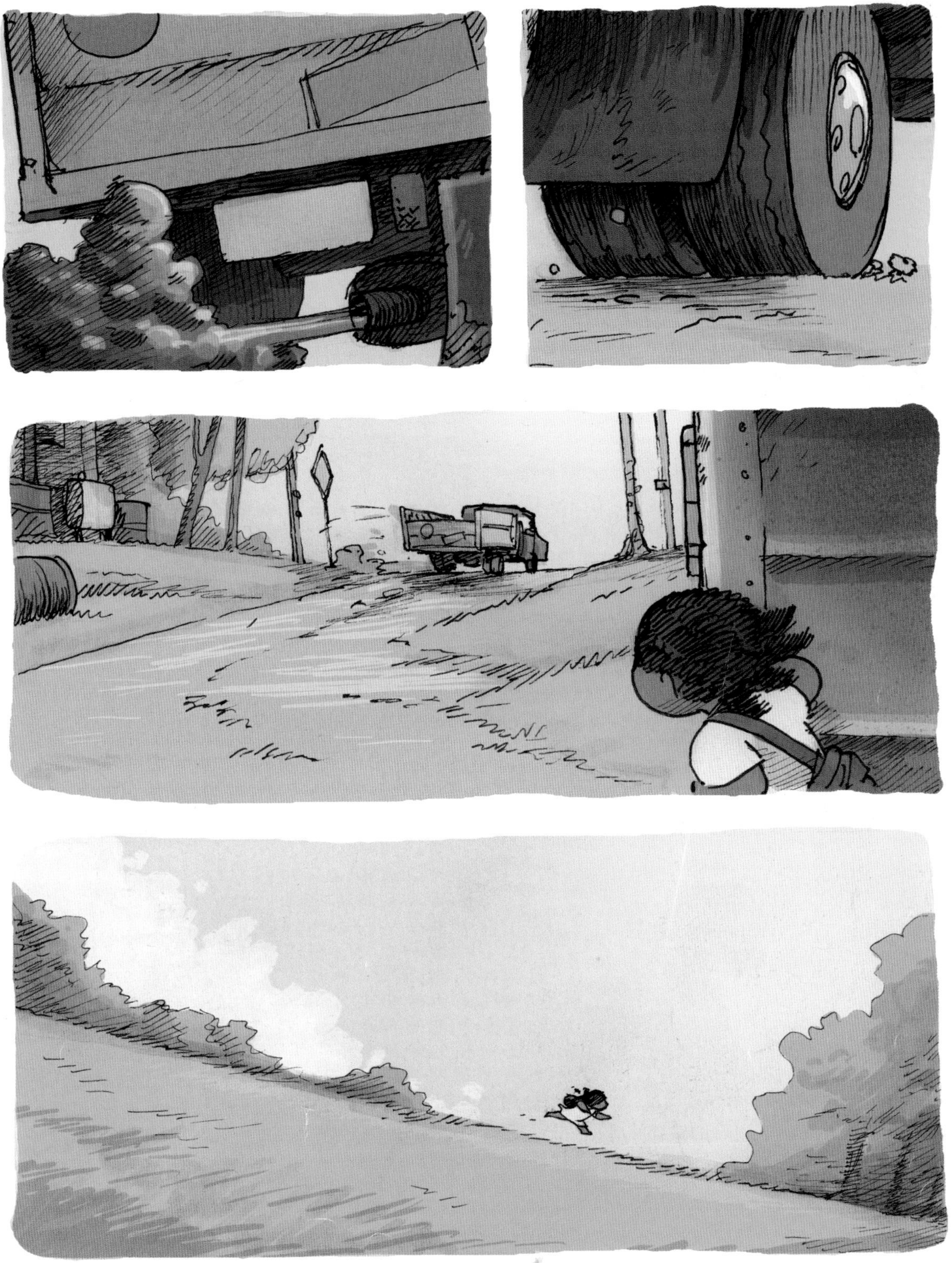

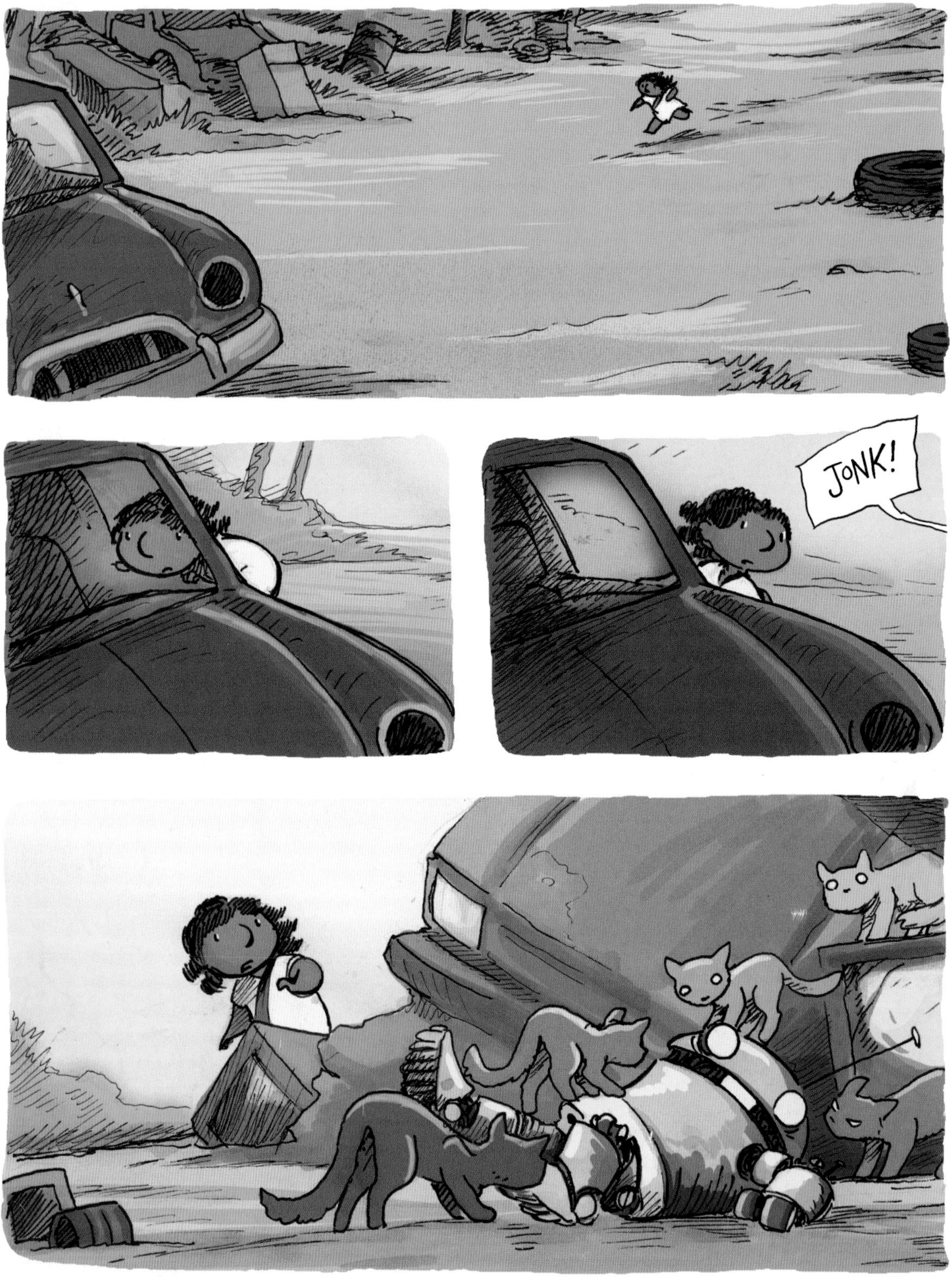
JONK!

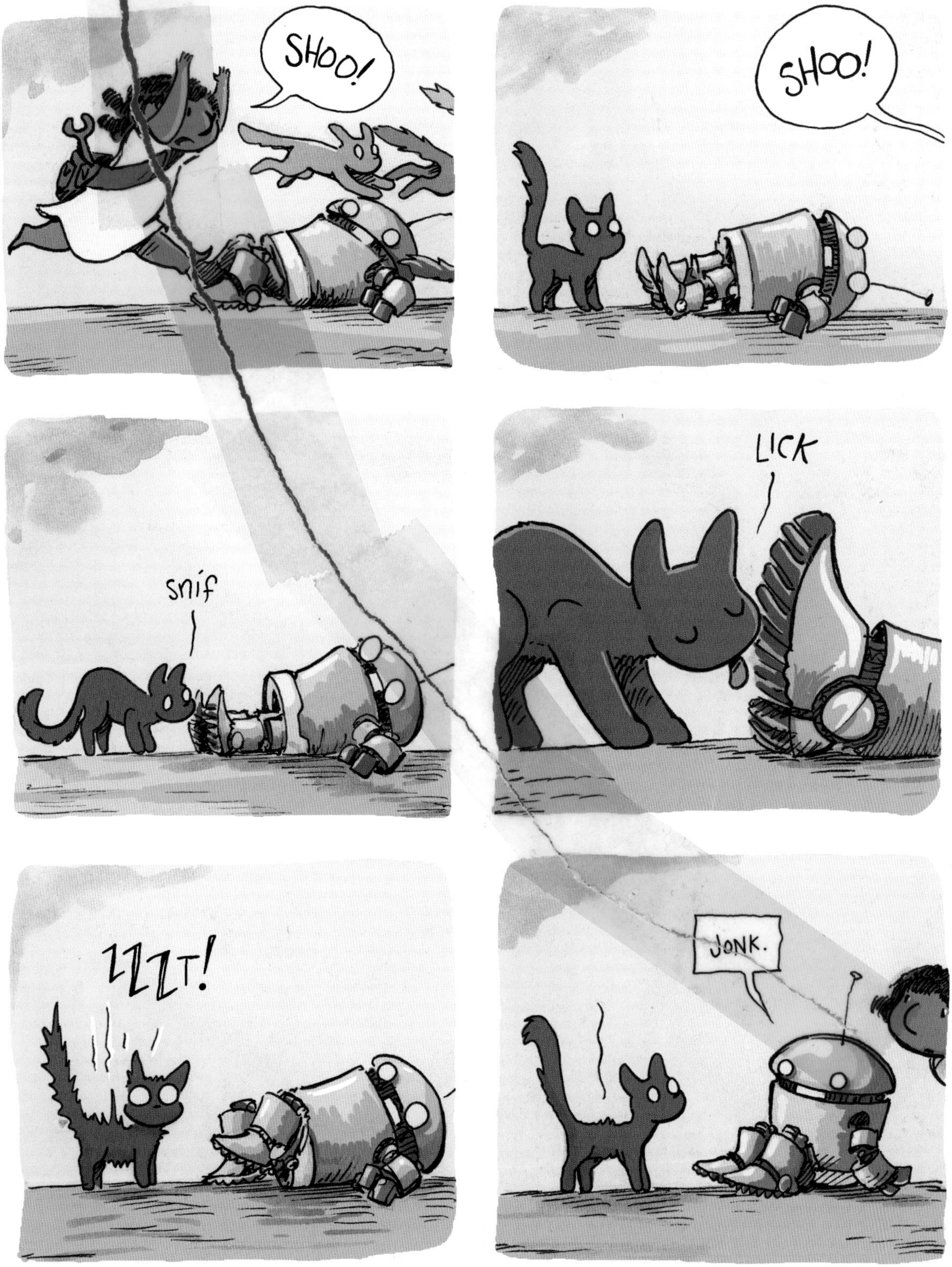
SHOO!
SHOO!
snif
LICK
ZZZT!
JONK.

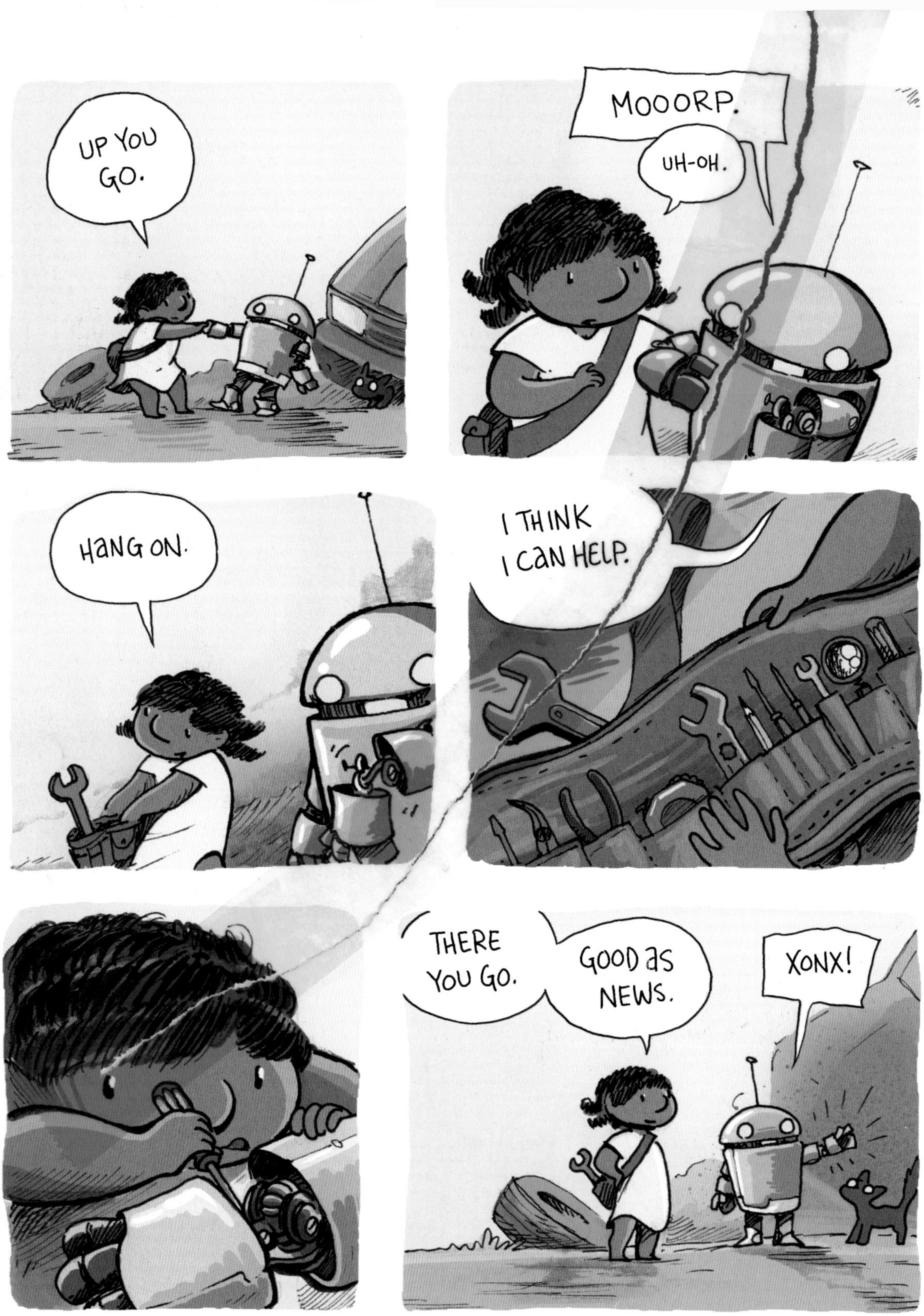
UP YOU GO.
MOOORP.
UH-OH.
HANG ON.
I THINK I CAN HELP.
THERE YOU GO.
GOOD AS NEWS.
XONX!

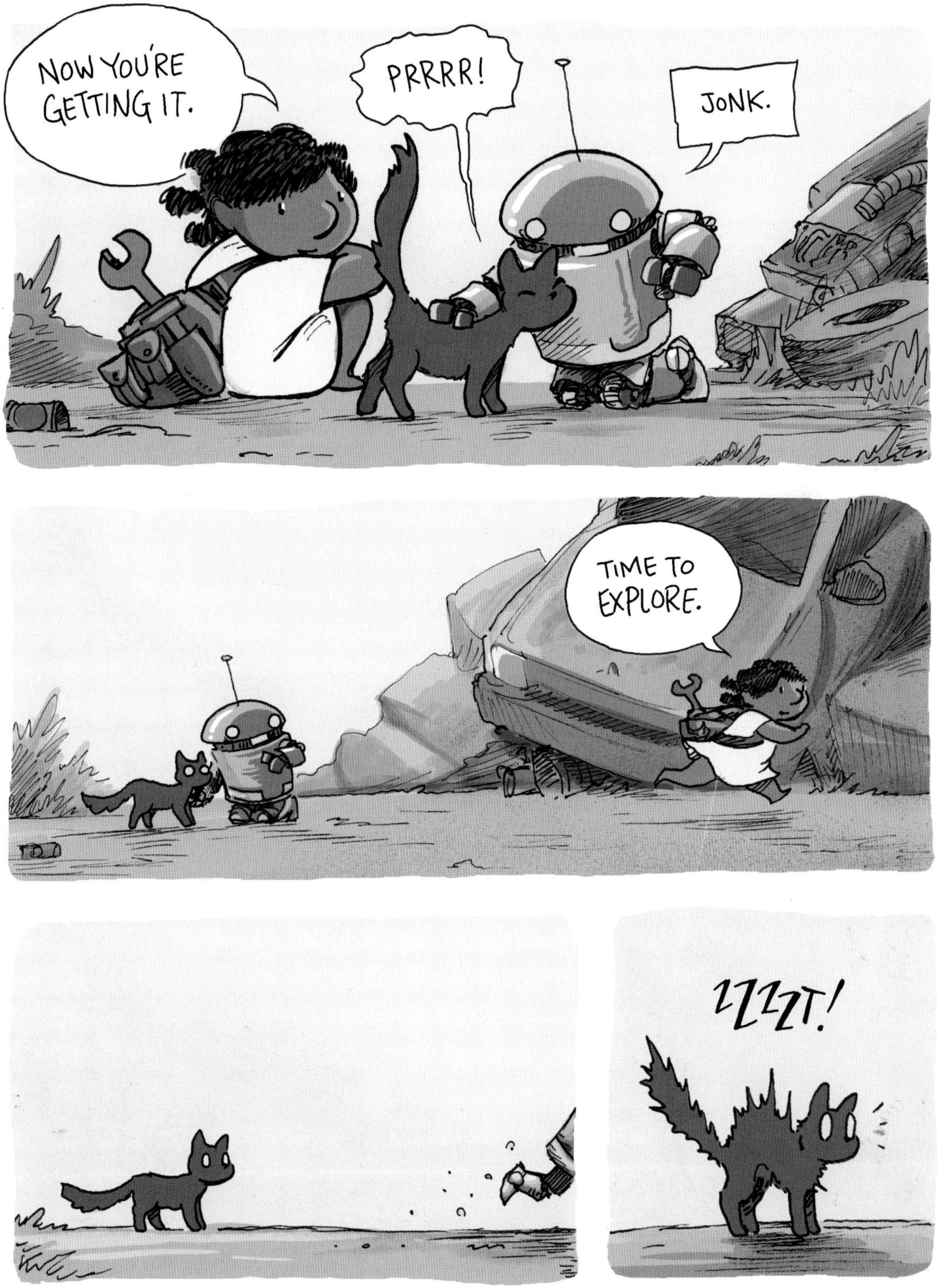
NOW YOU'RE GETTING IT.
PRRRR!
JONK.
TIME TO EXPLORE.
ZZZZT!

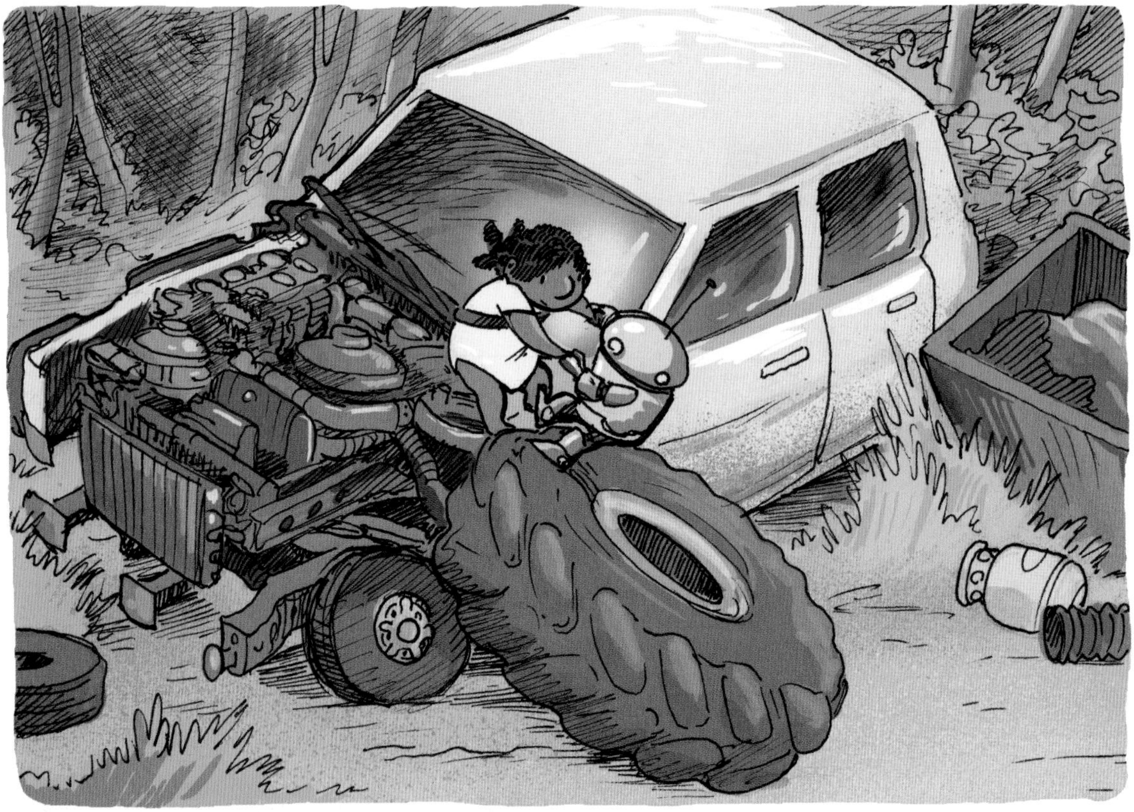

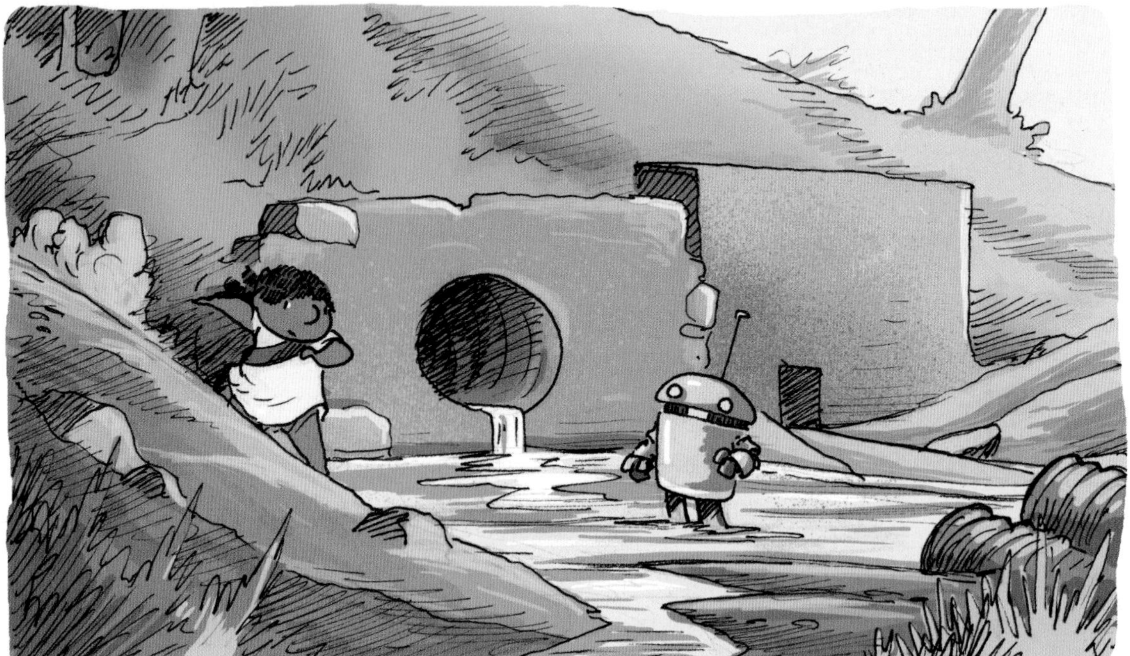

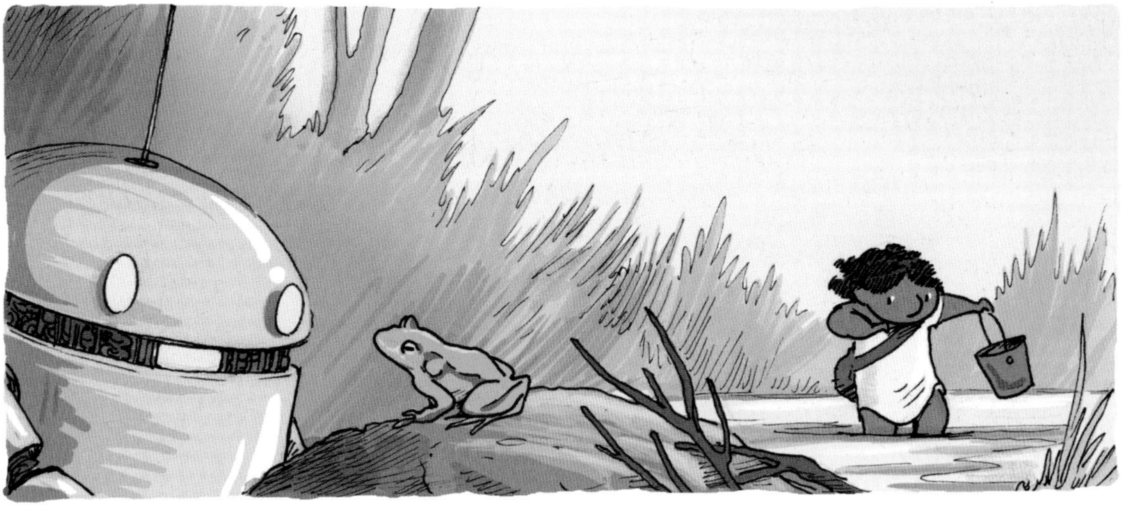

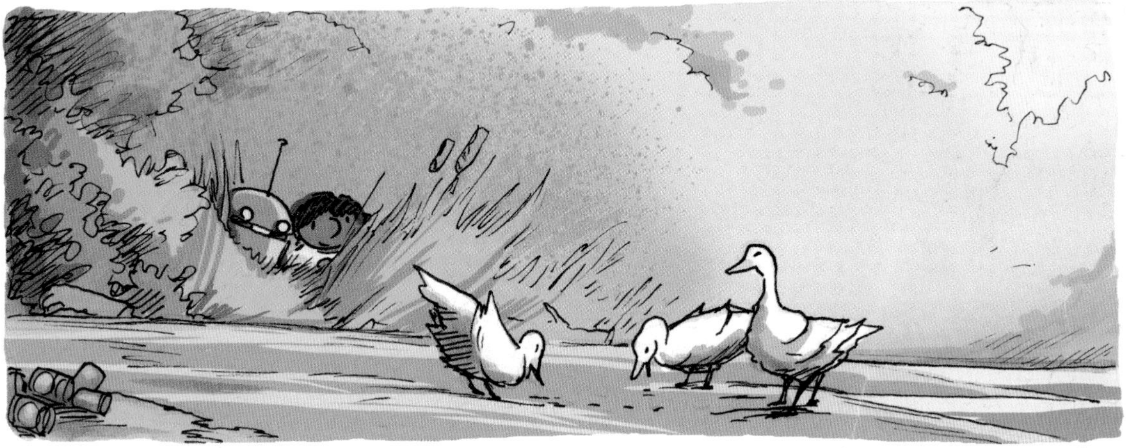

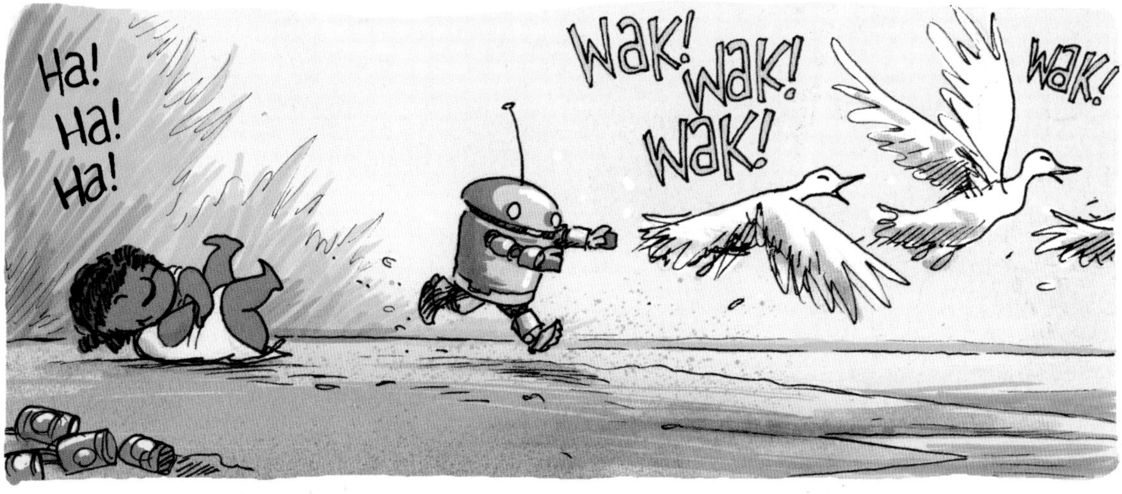
Ha!
Ha!
Ha!
WAK!
WAK!
WAK!
WAK!

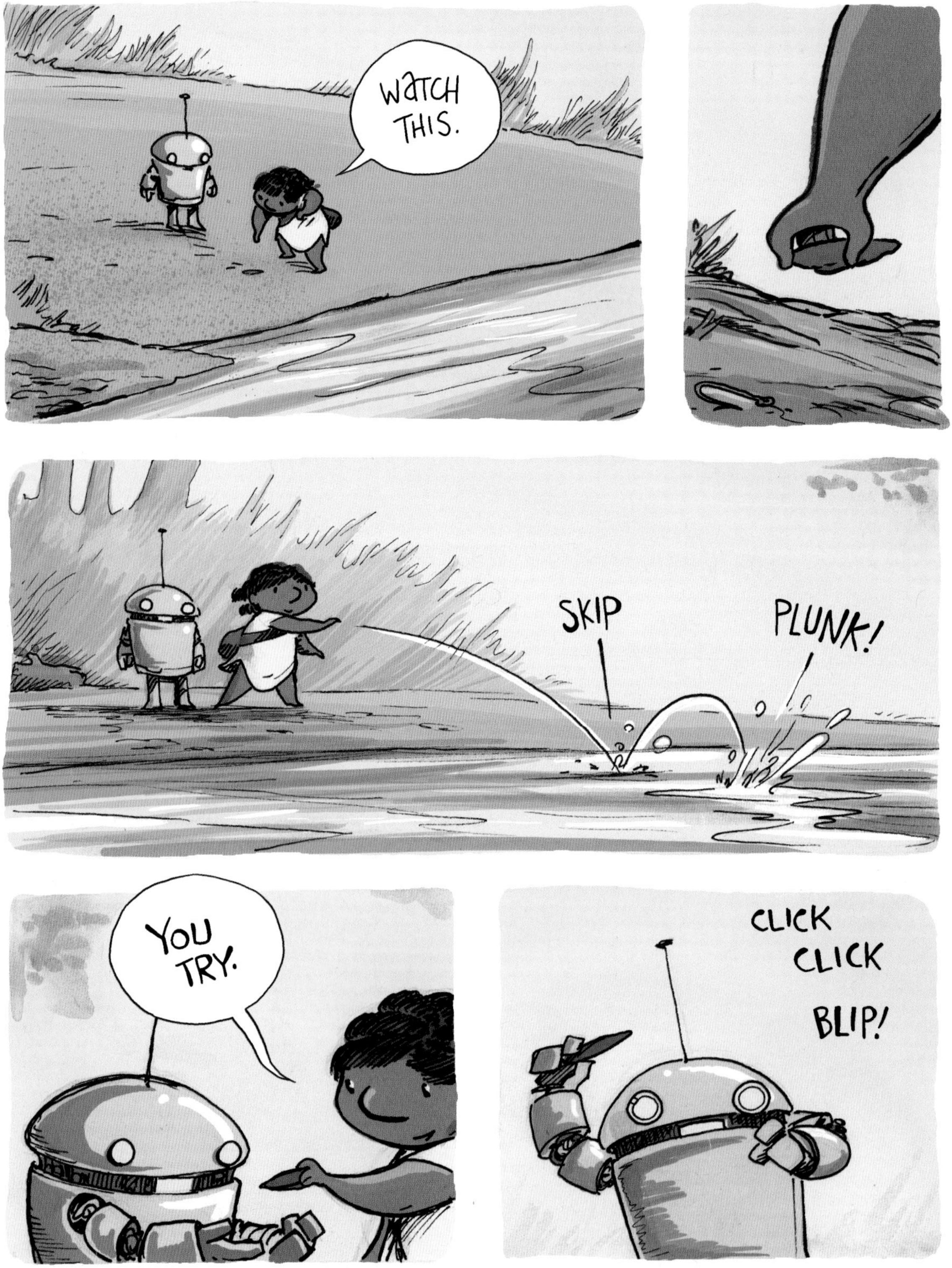
WATCH THIS.
SKIP
PLUNK!
YOU TRY.
CLICK
CLICK
BLIP!

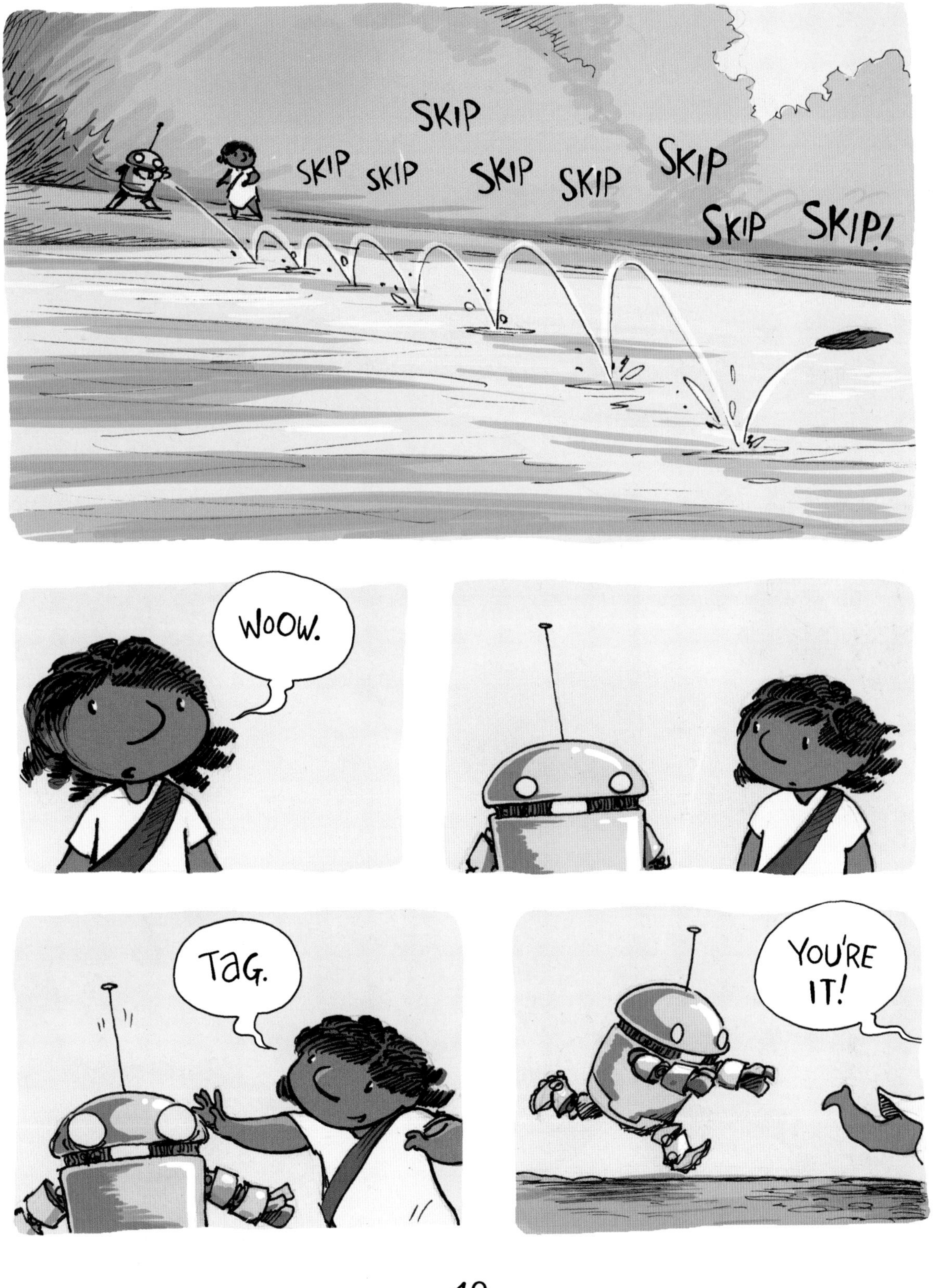
SKIP
SKIP
SKIP
SKIP
SKIP
SKIP
SKIP
SKIP!
WOOW.
TAG.
YOU'RE IT!

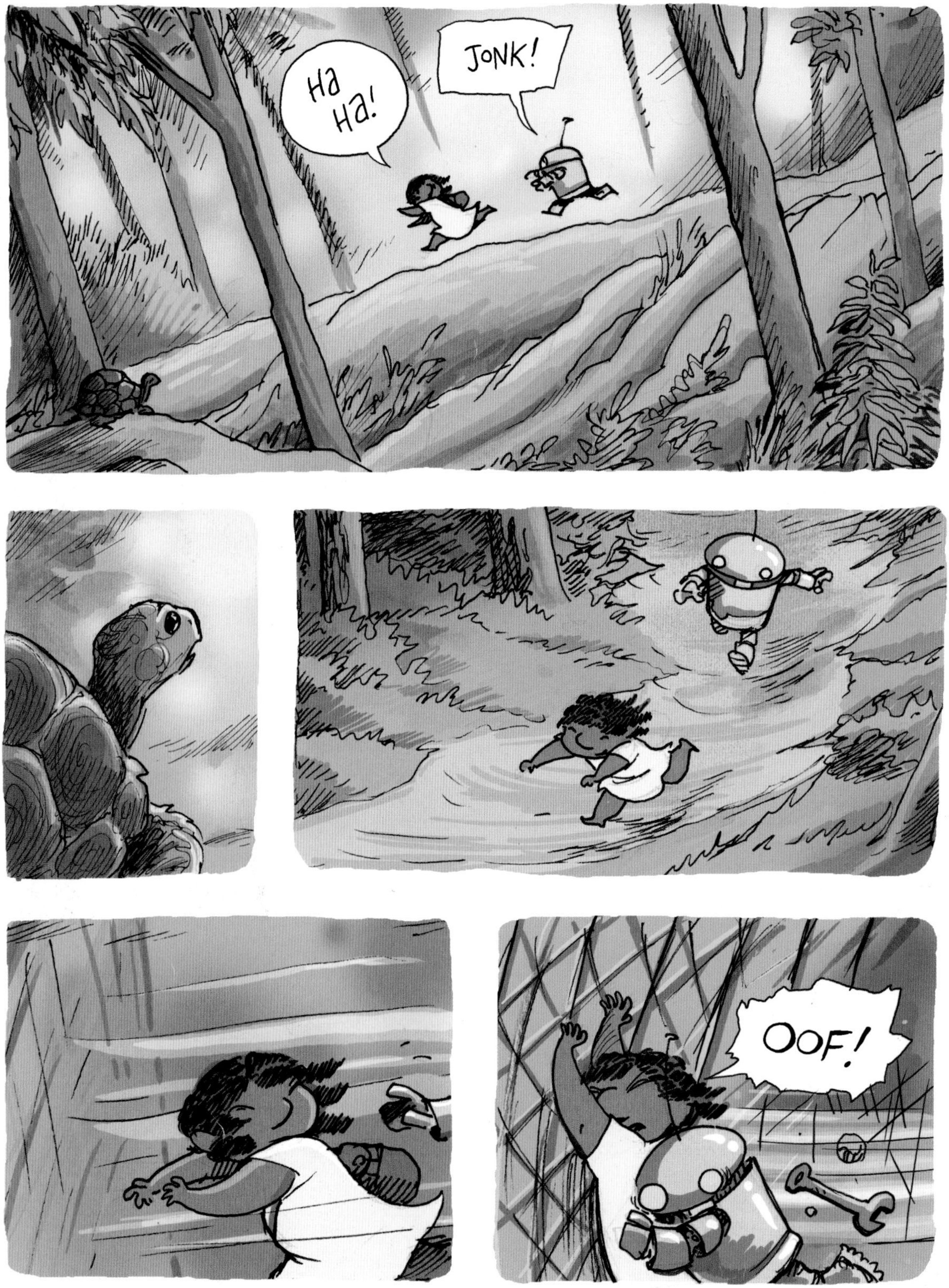
Ha Ha!
JONK!
OOF!

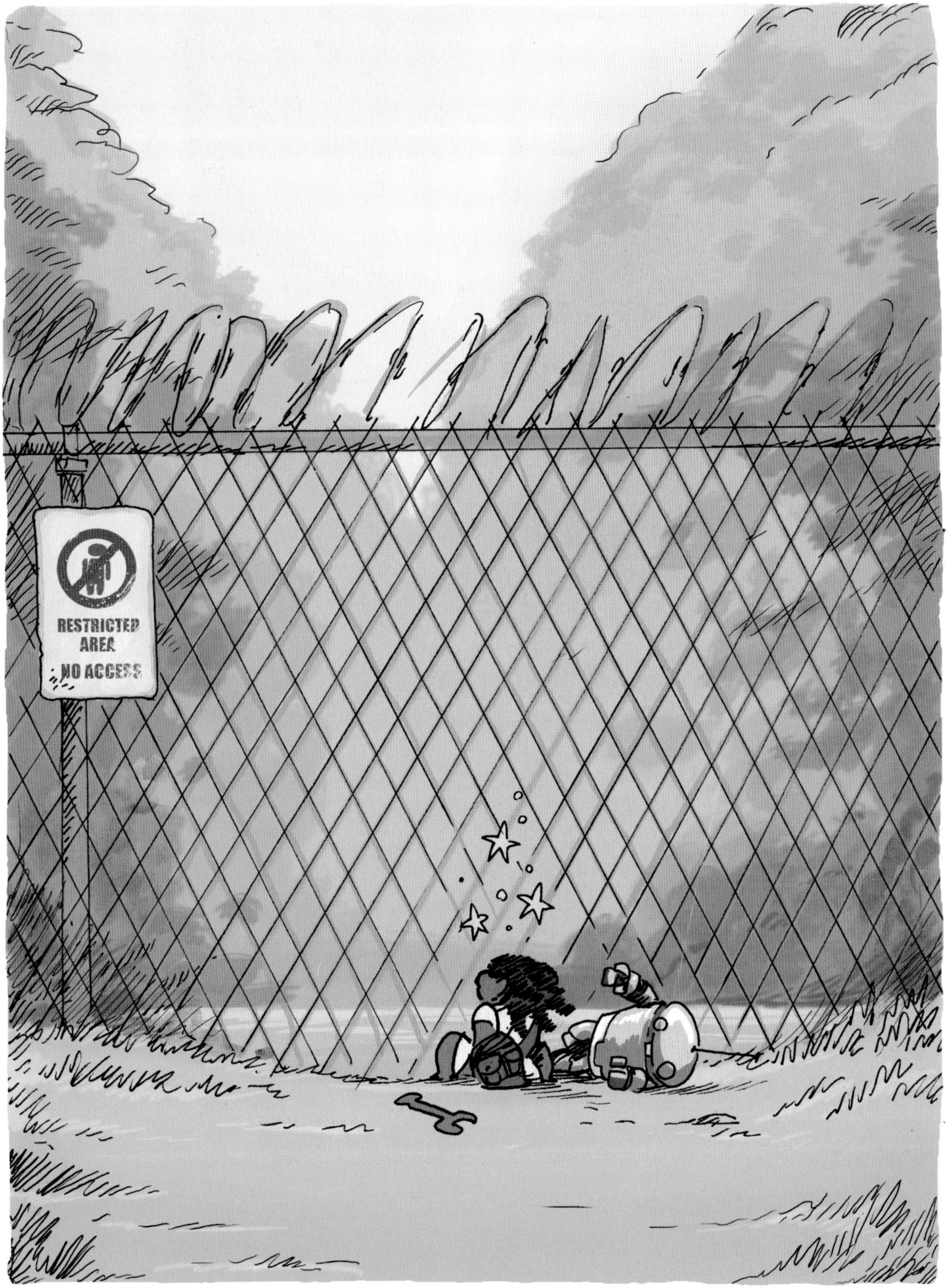
RESTRICTED
AREA
NO ACCESS

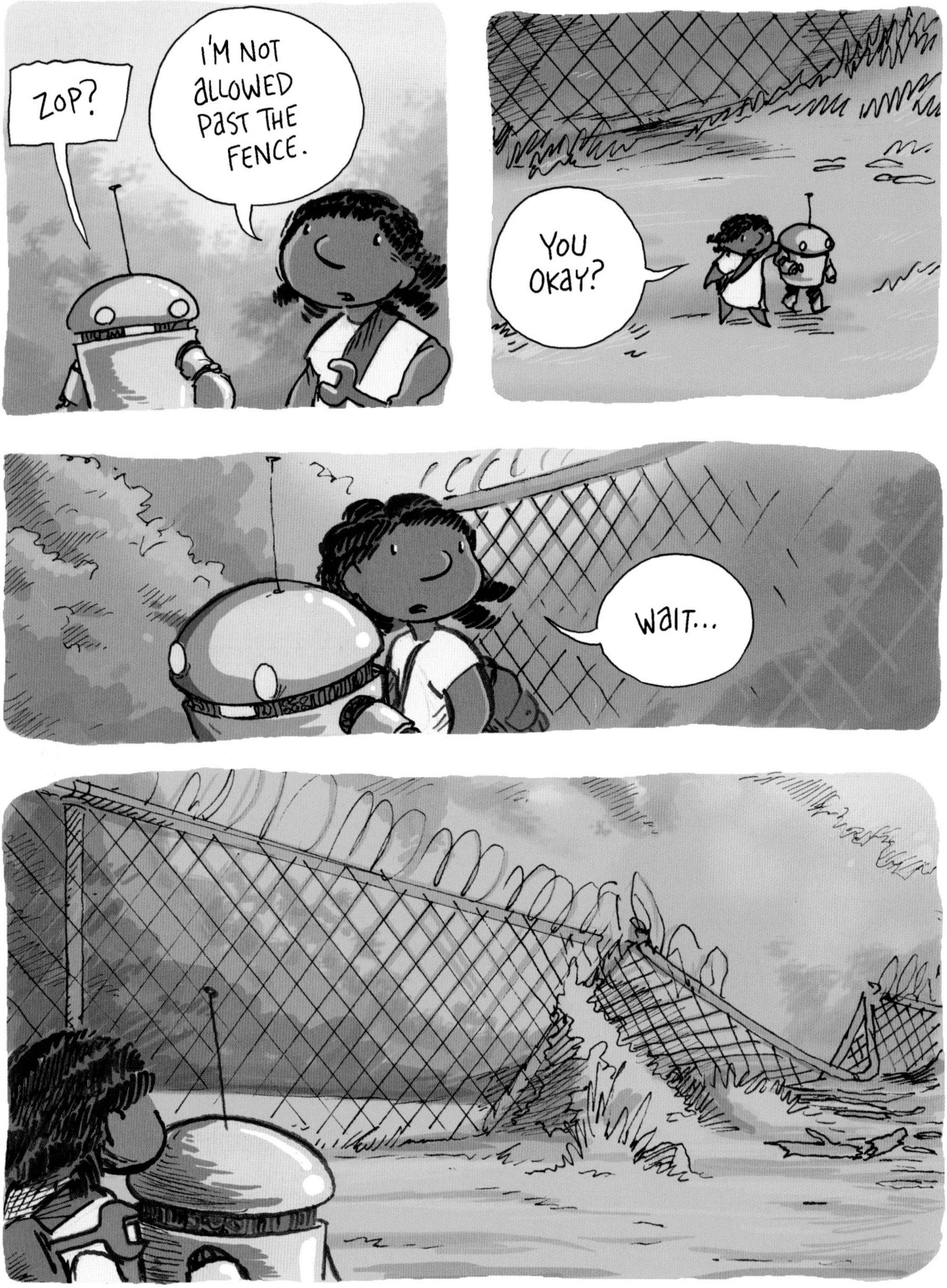
ZOP?
I'M NOT ALLOWED PAST THE FENCE.
YOU OKAY?
WAIT...

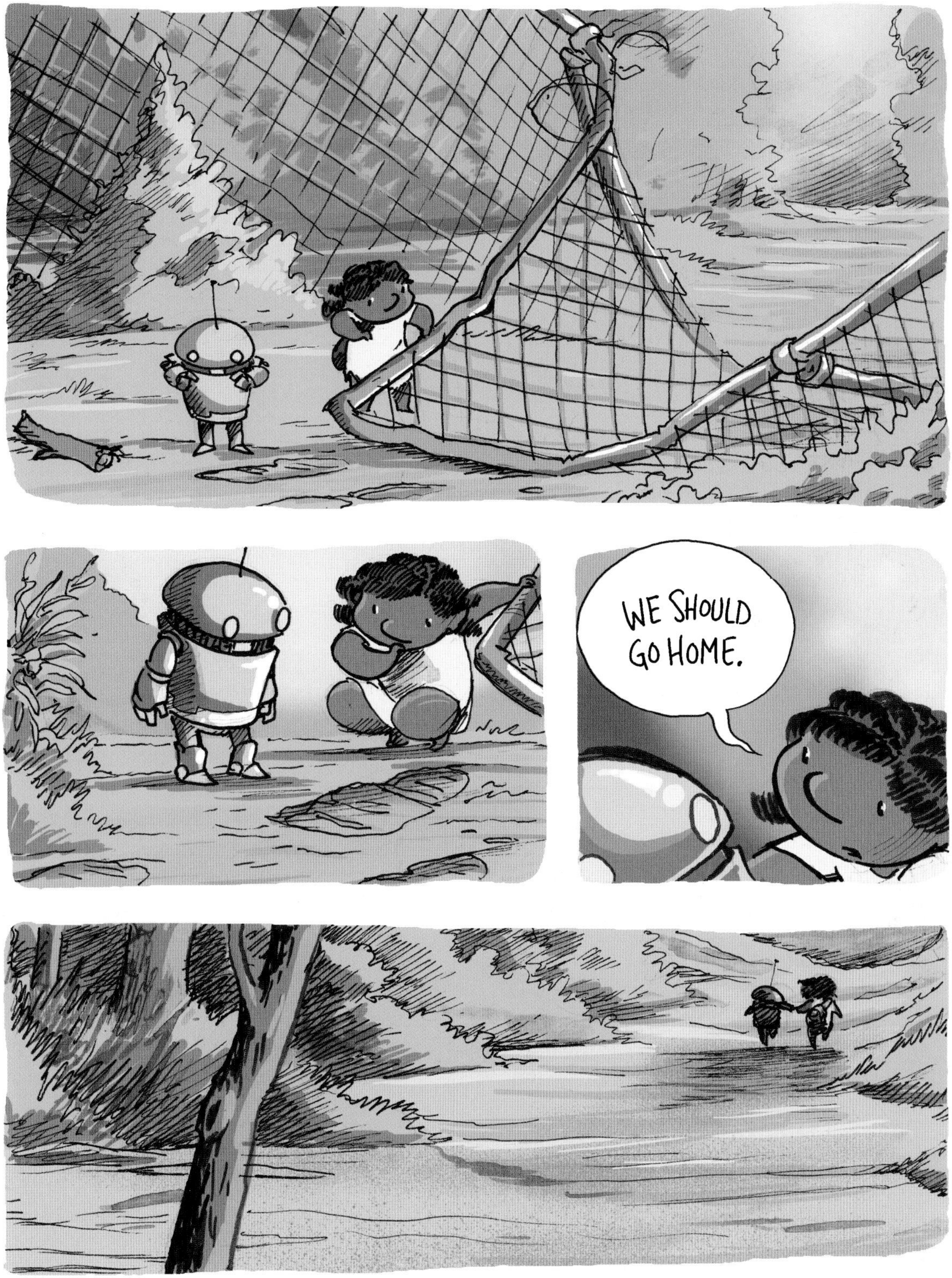
WE SHOULD GO HOME.

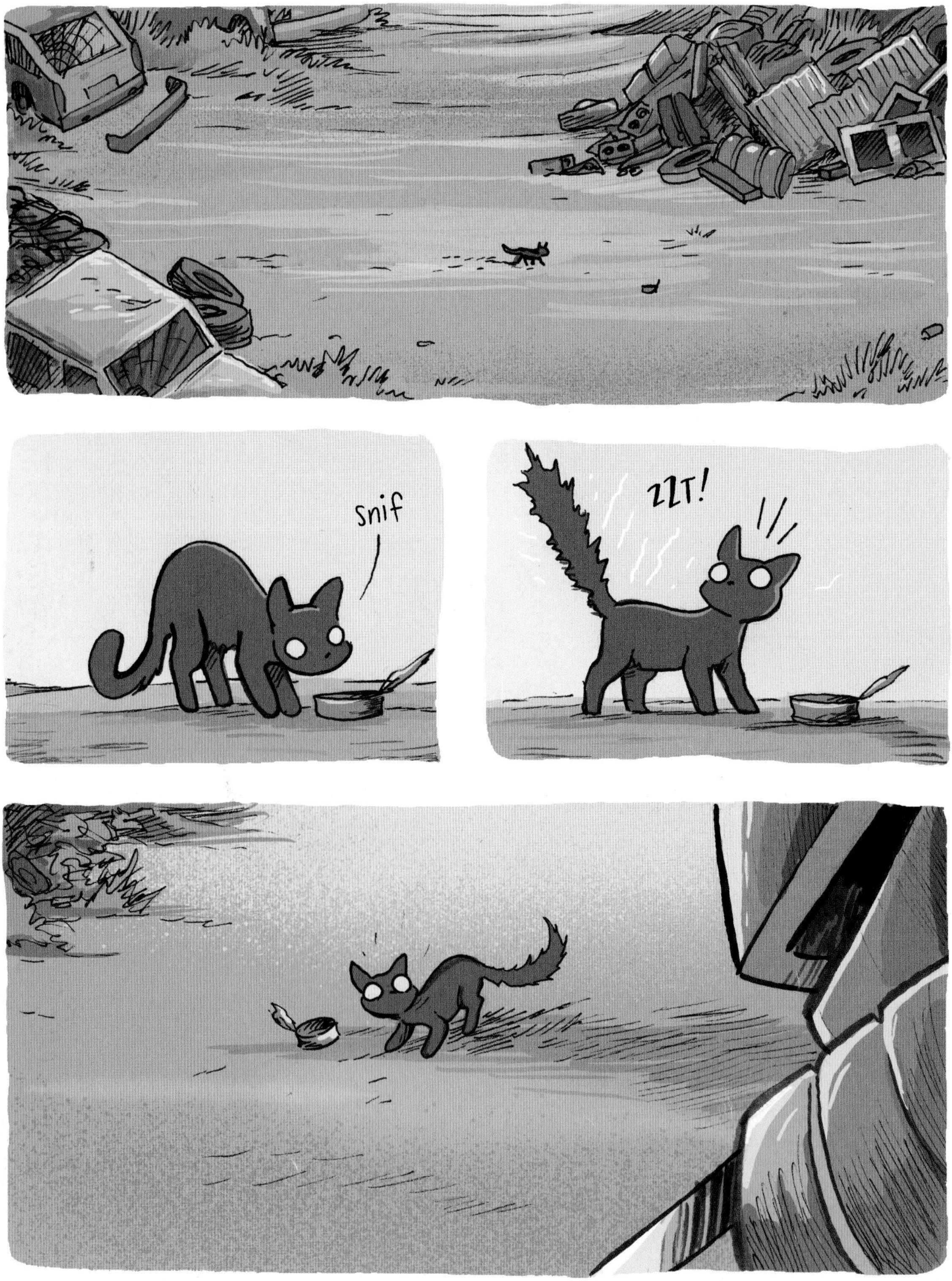
snif
ZZT!

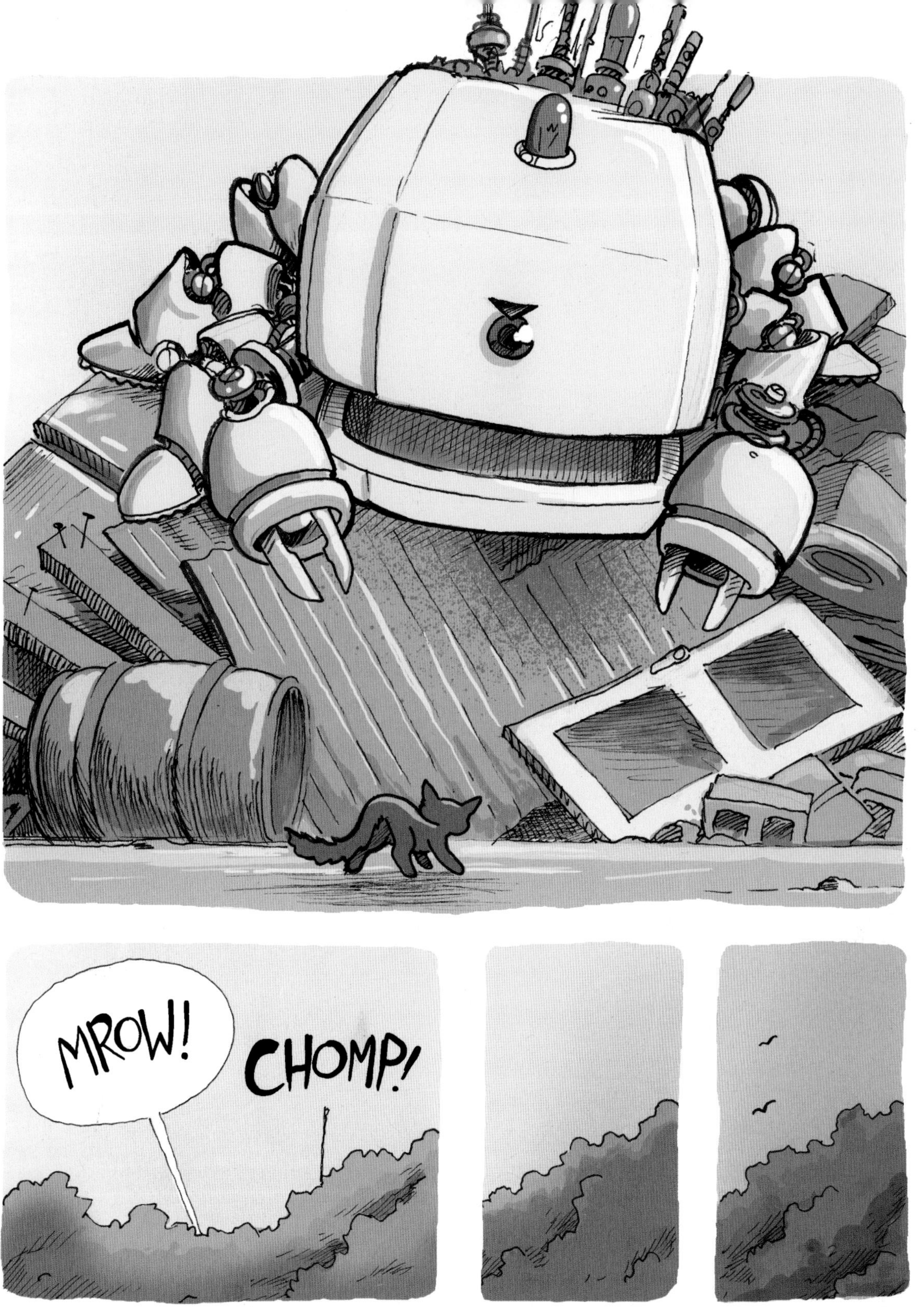
MROW!
CHOMP!

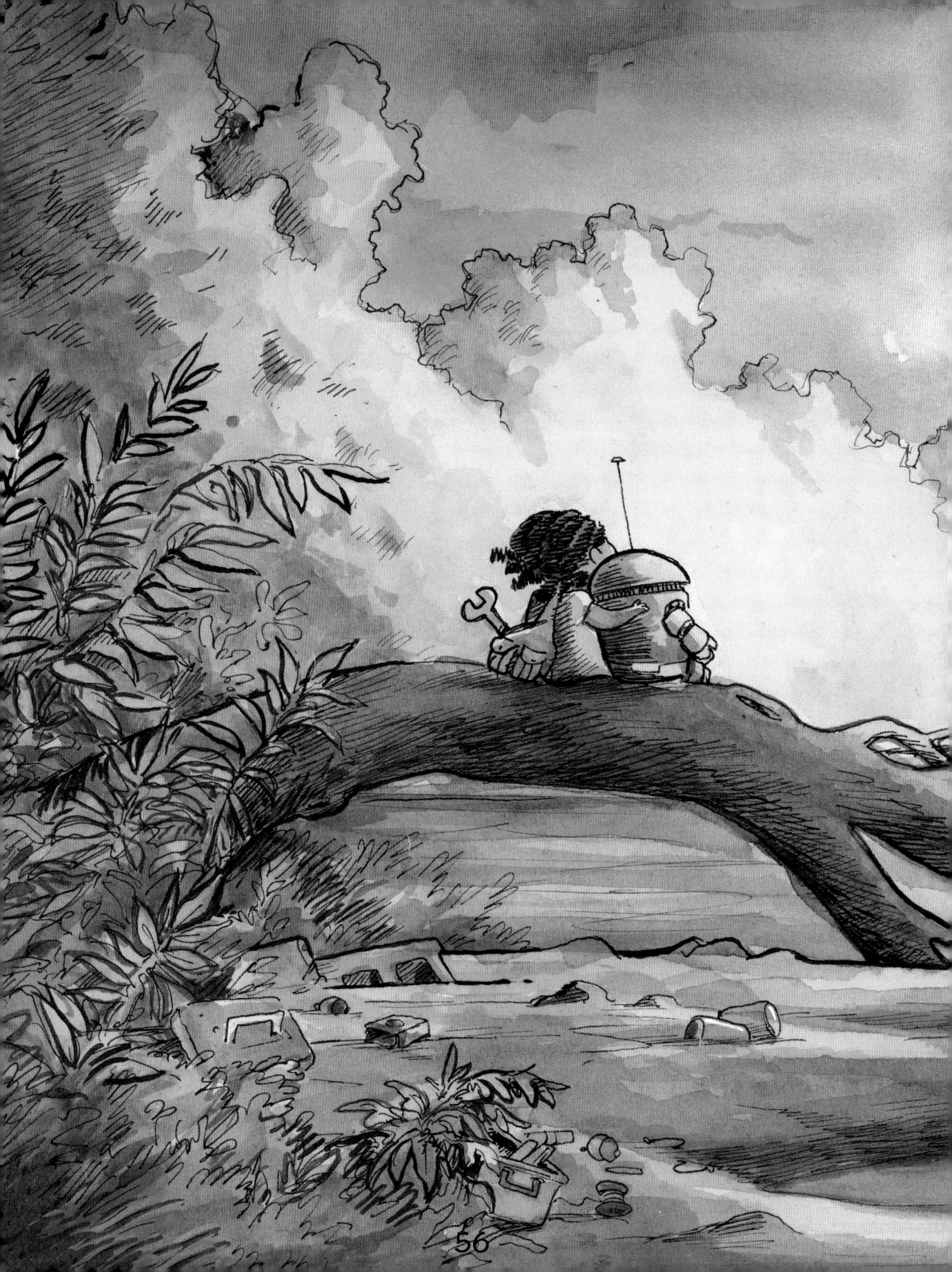

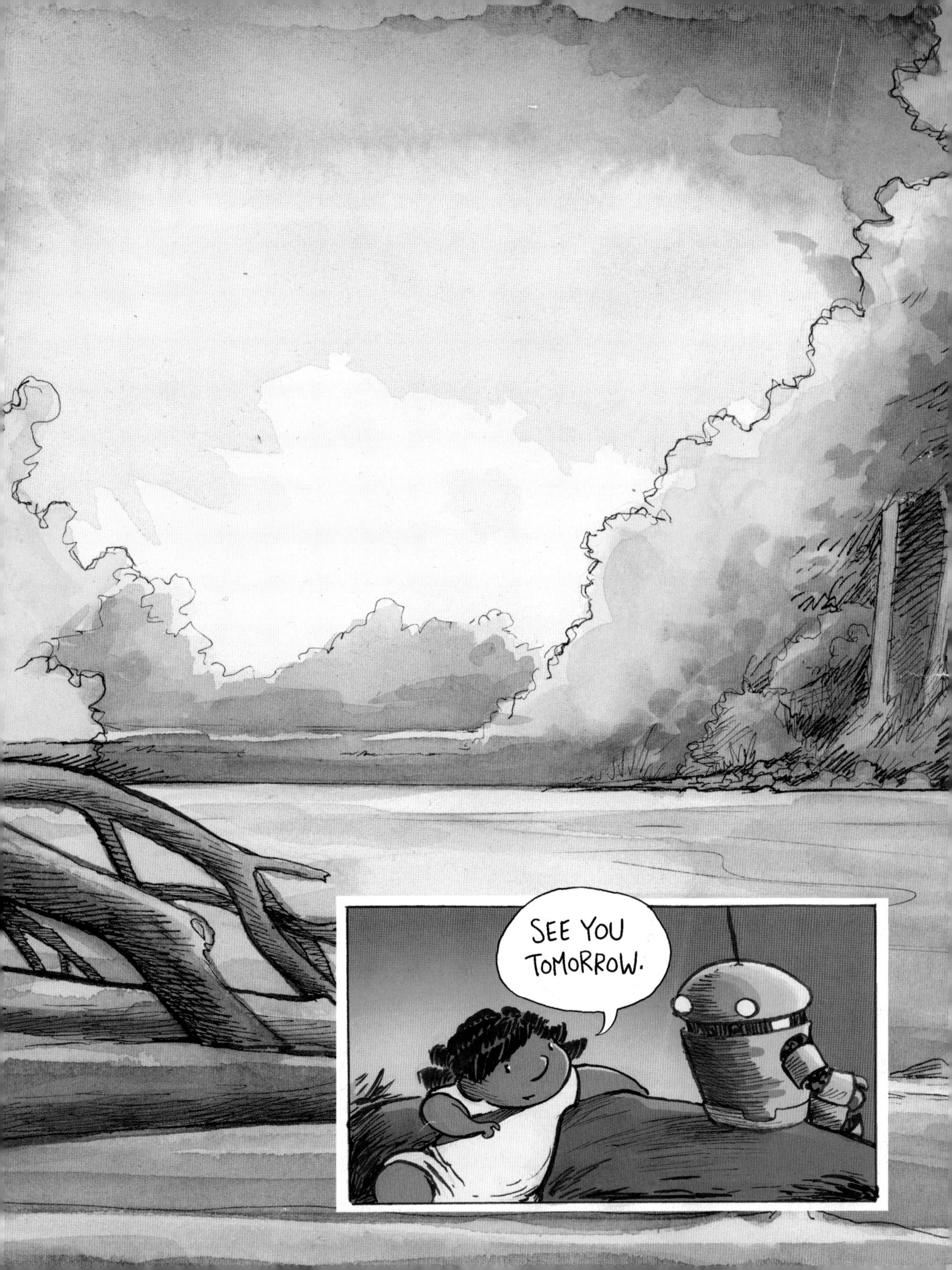
SEE YOU TOMORROW.

CHAPTER FOUR

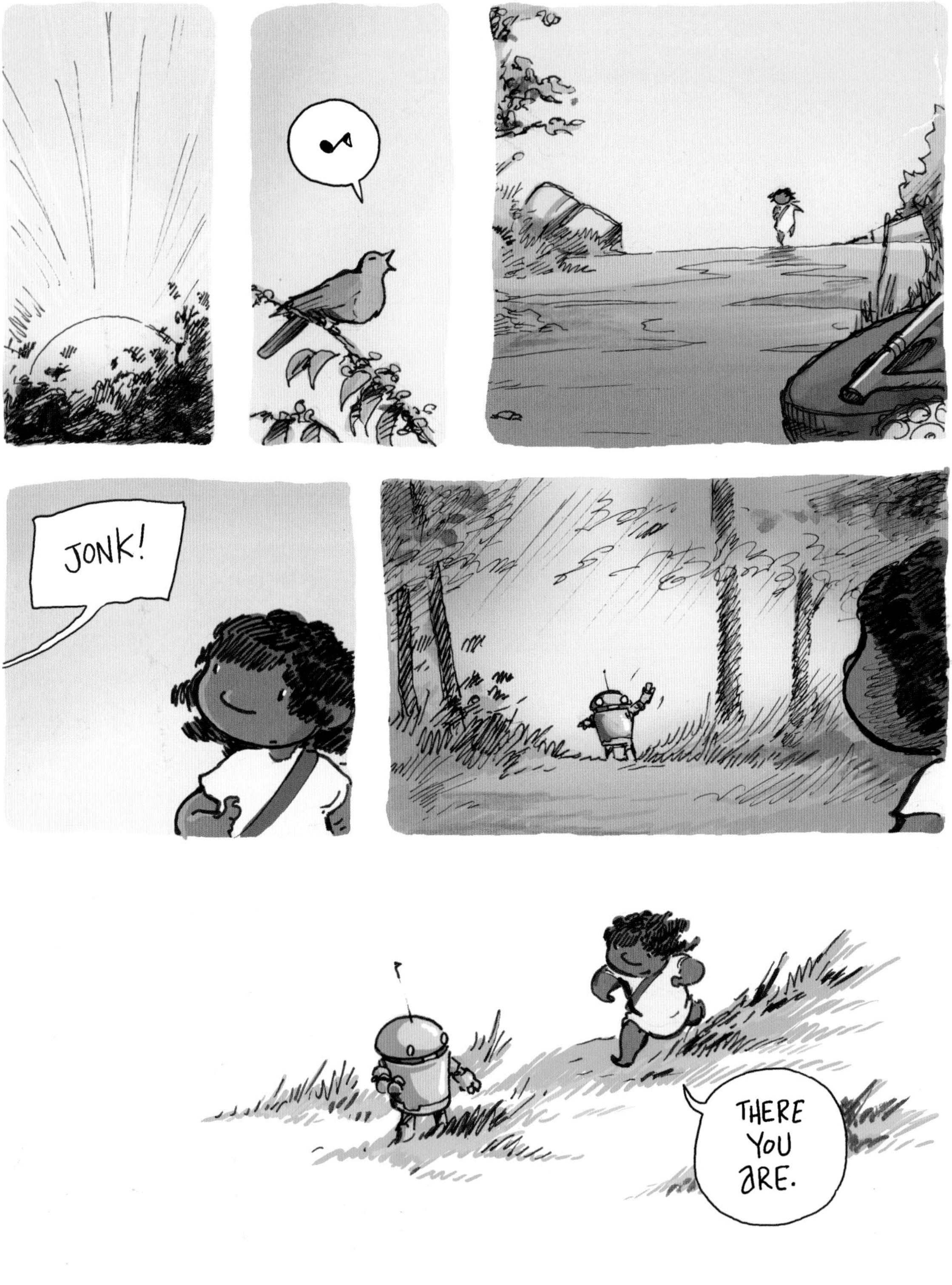
JONK!
THERE YOU ARE.

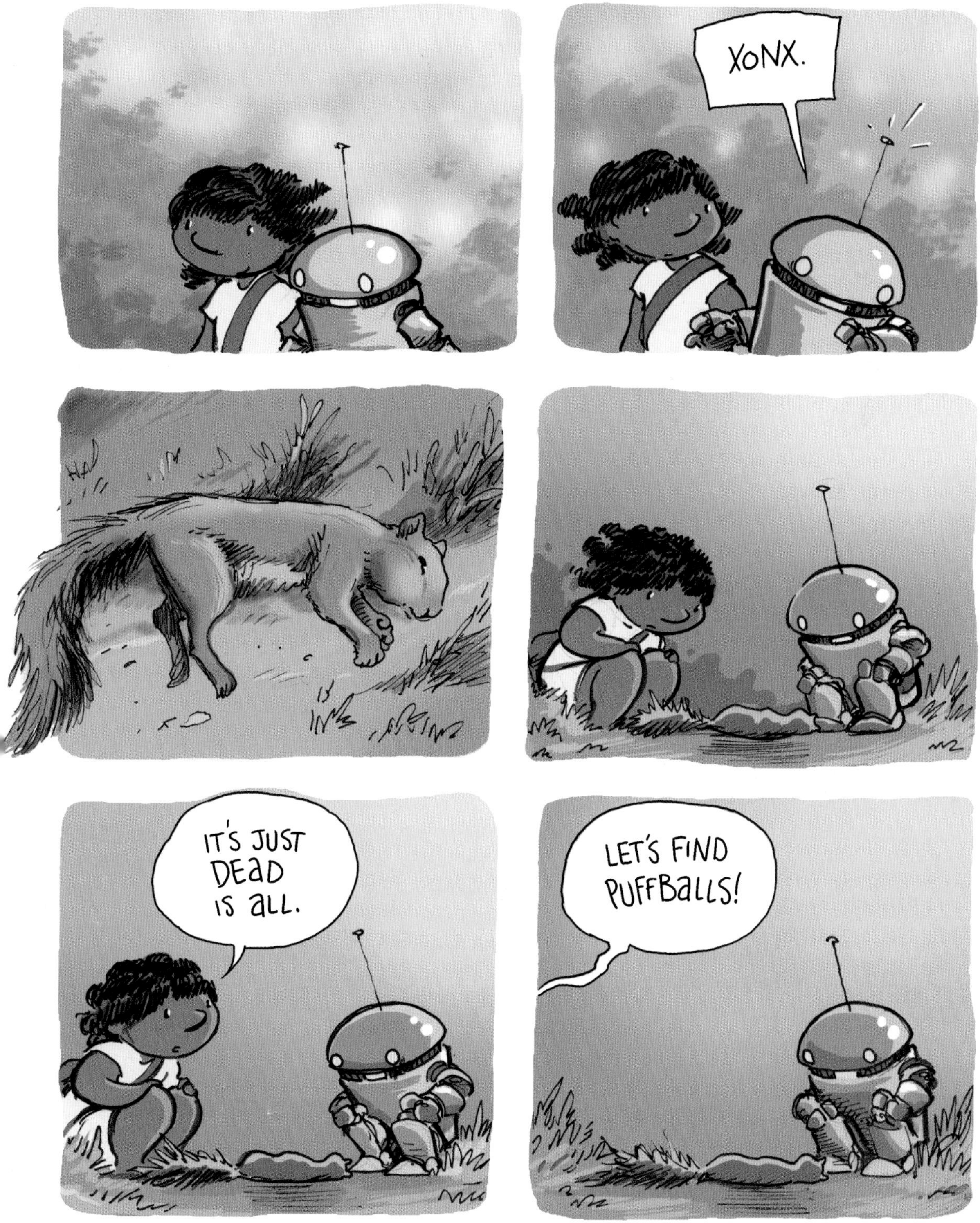
XONX.
IT'S JUST DEAD IS ALL.
LET'S FIND PUFFBALLS!

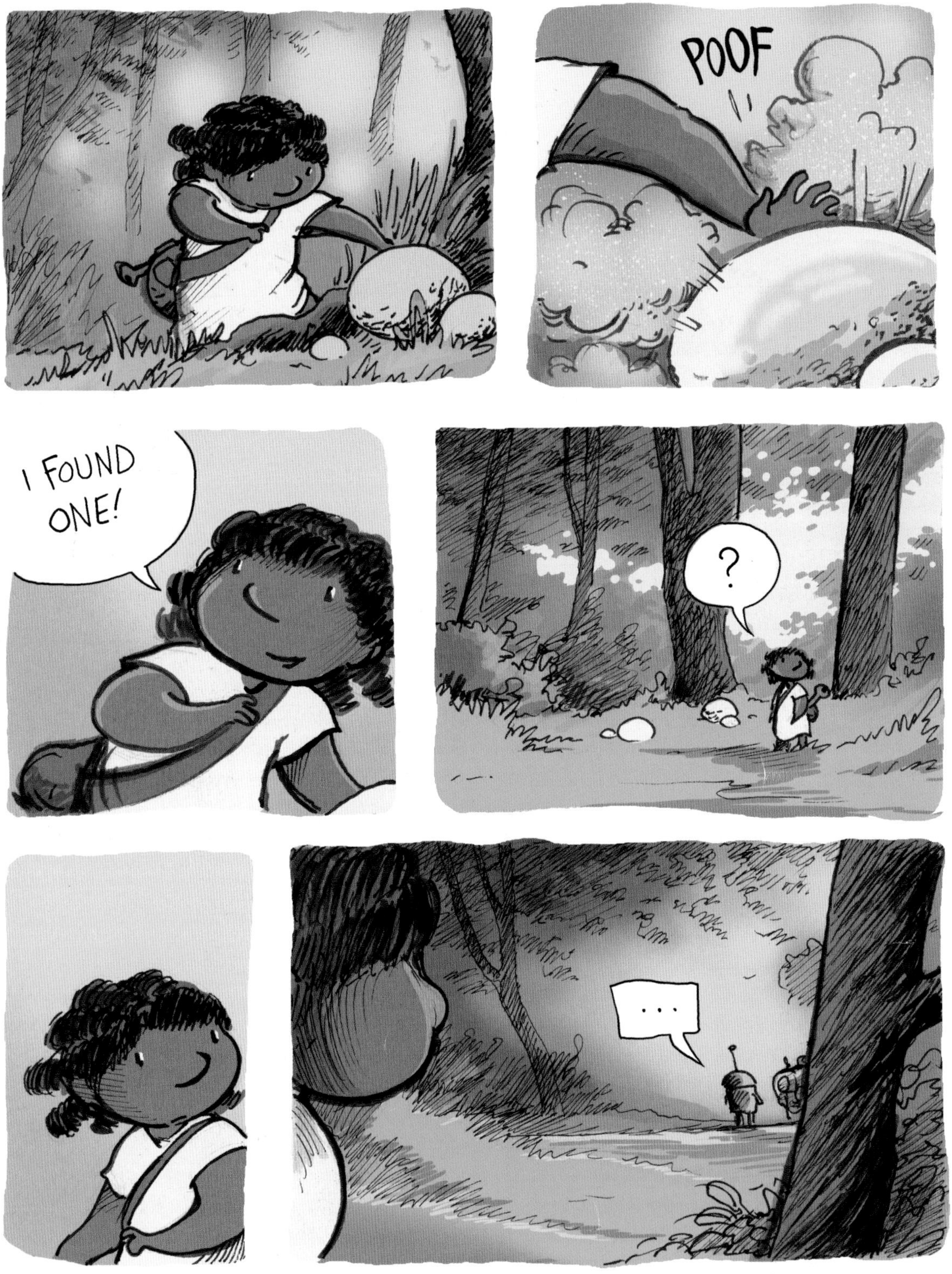
POOF
I FOUND ONE!
?
...

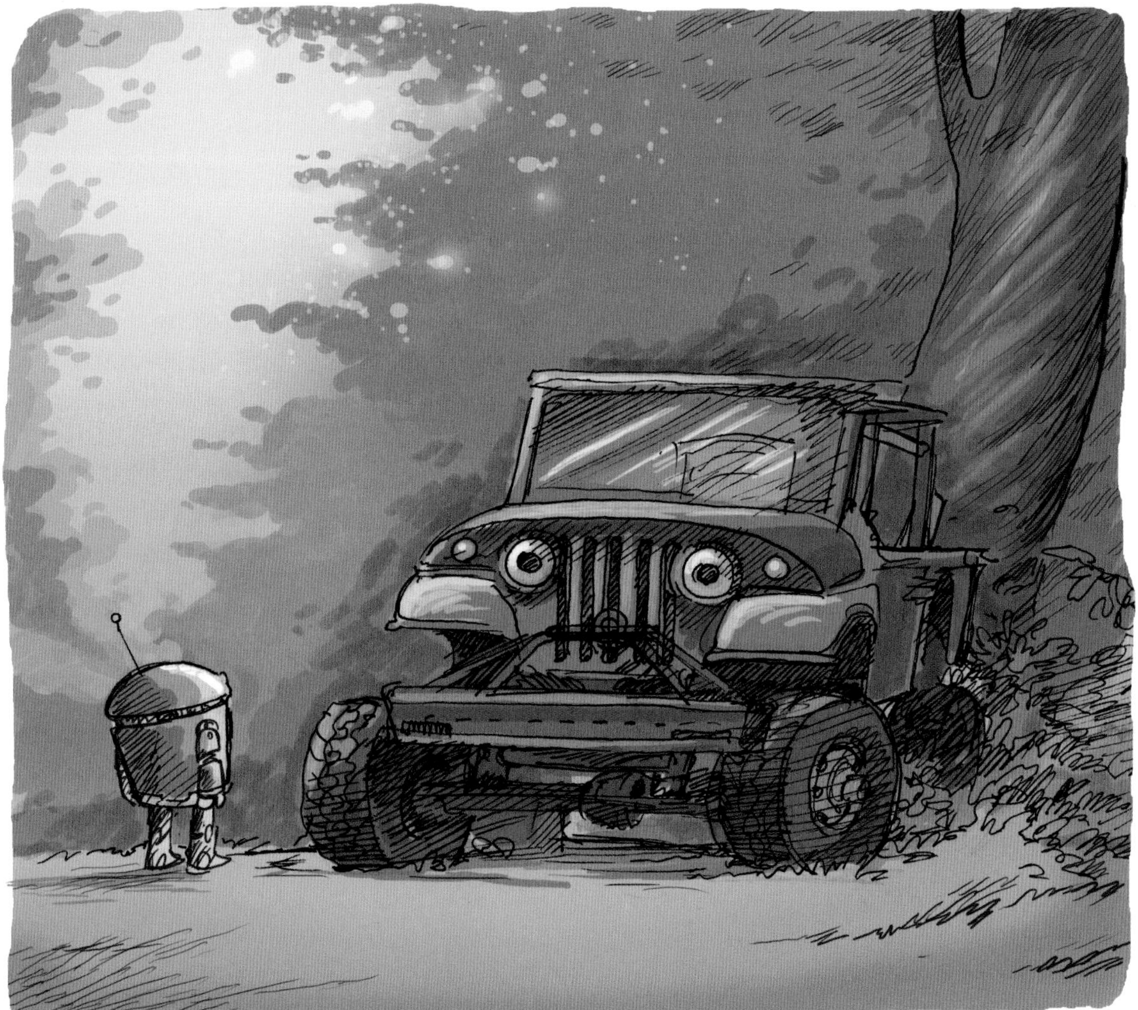

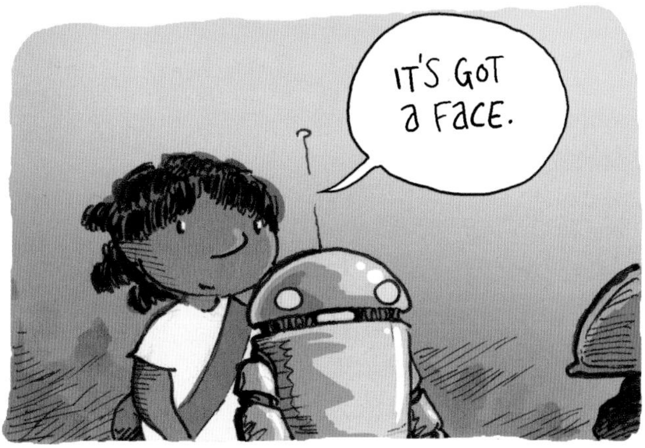
IT'S GOT a FACE.
?

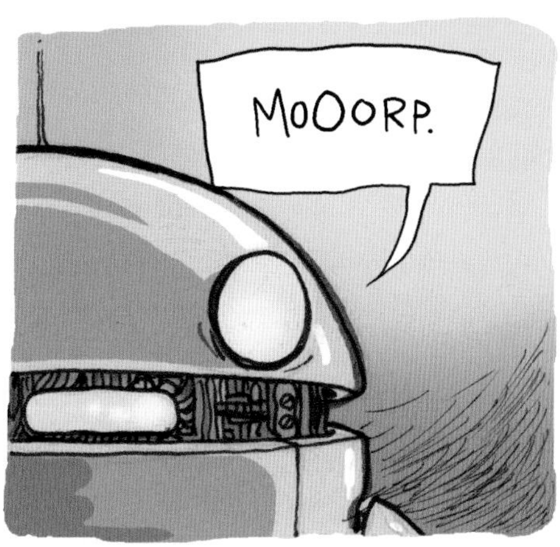
MoOORP.

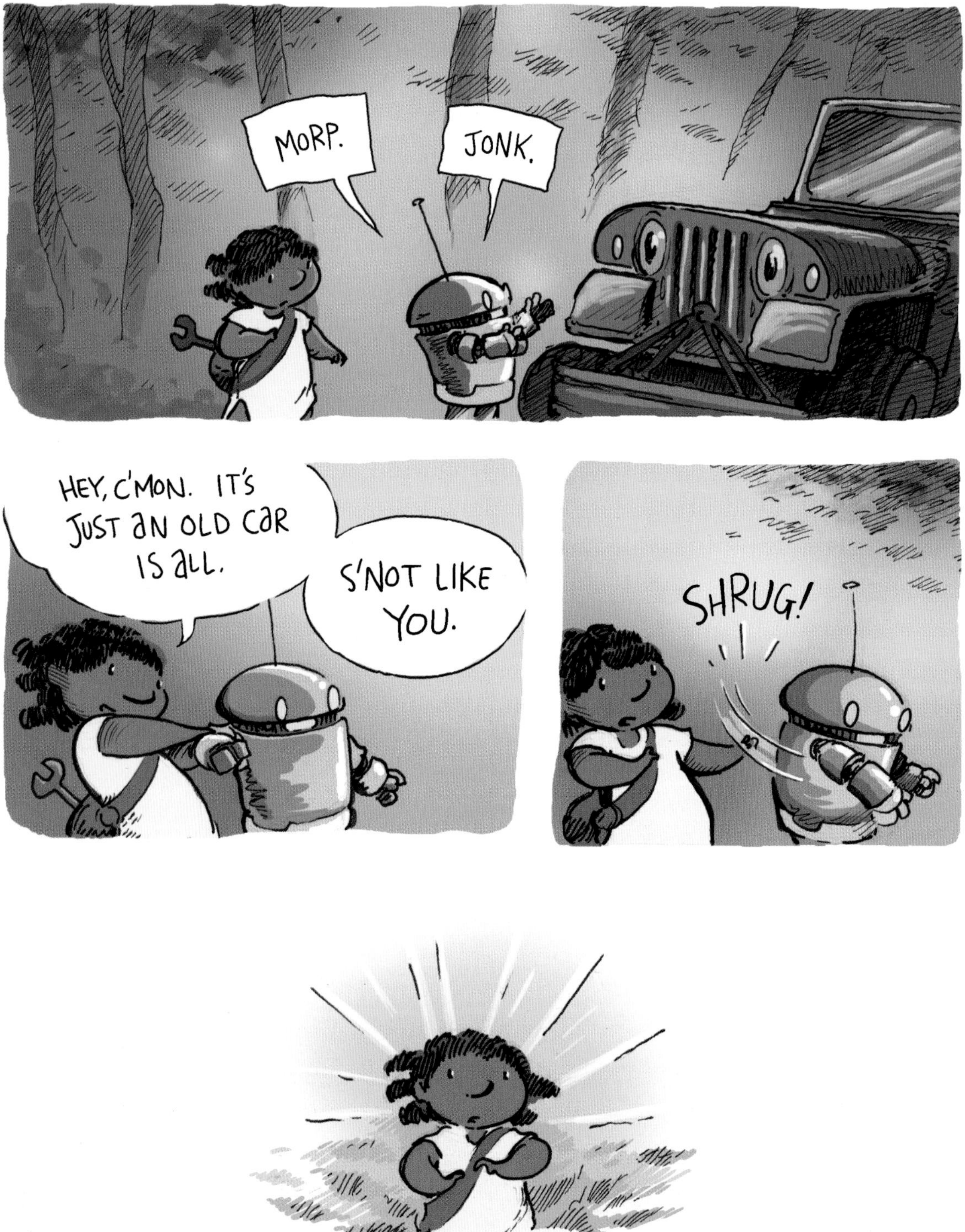
MORP.
JONK.
HEY, C'MON. IT'S JUST AN OLD CAR IS ALL.
S'NOT LIKE YOU.
SHRUG!

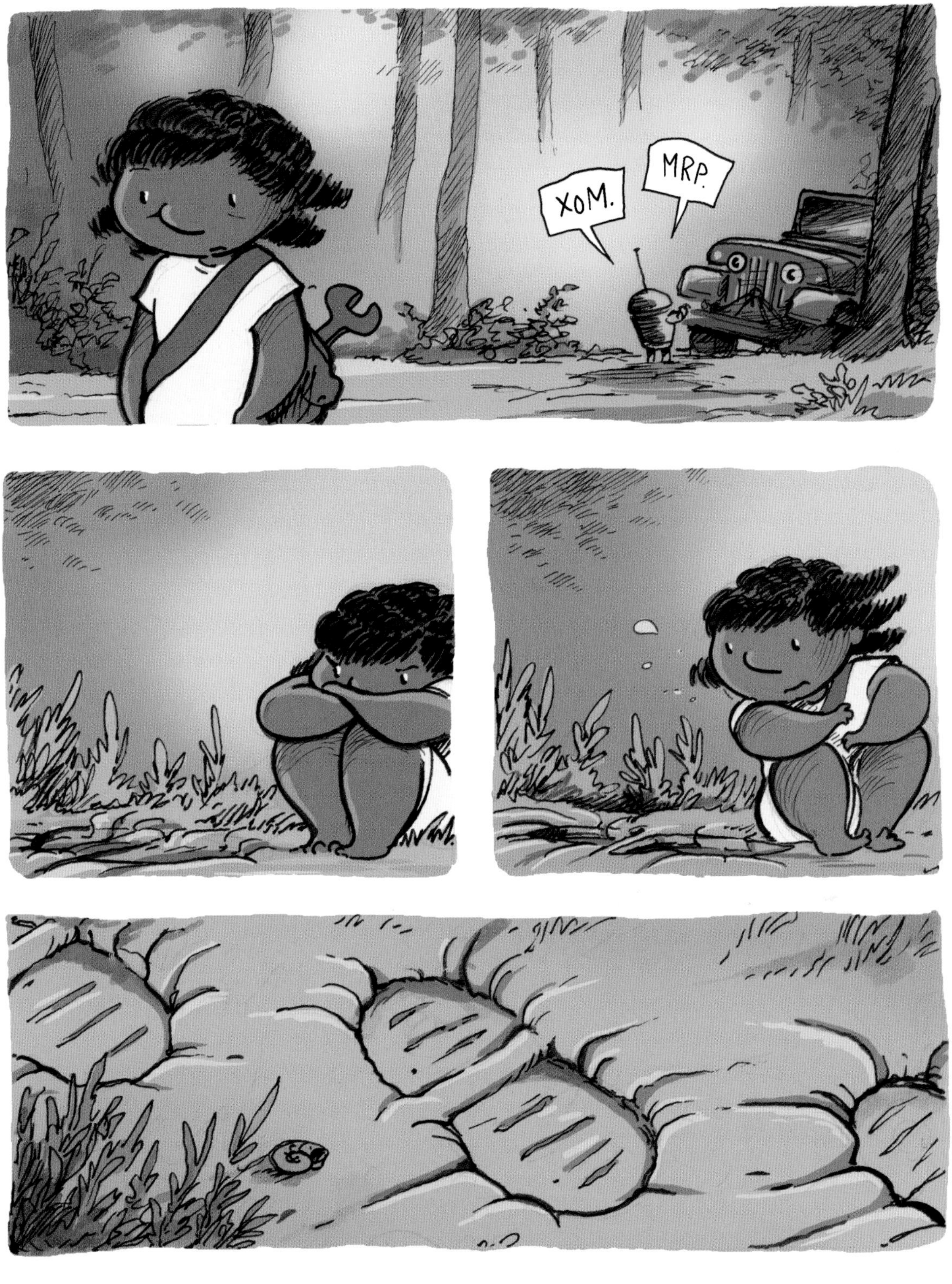
XOM.
MRP.

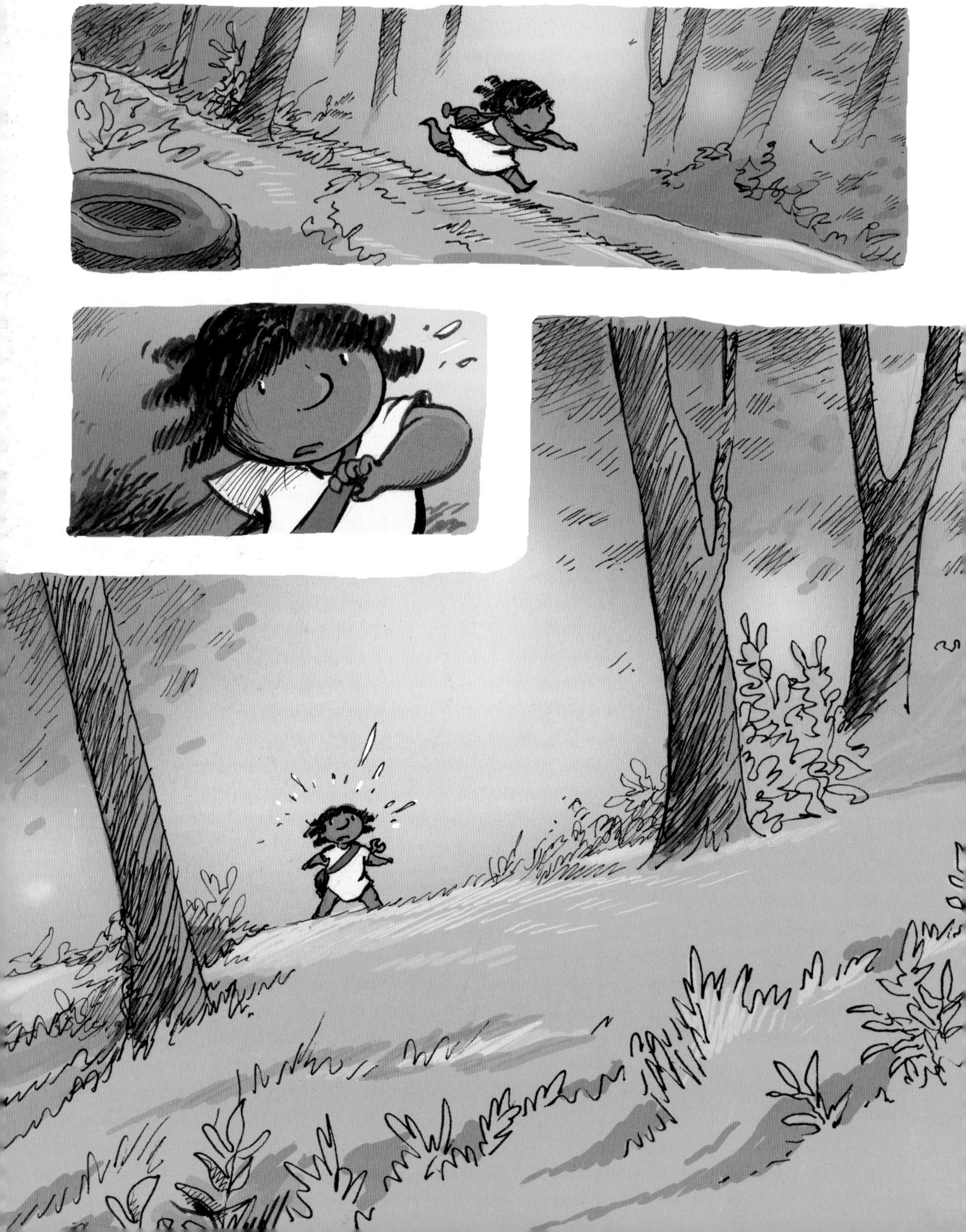

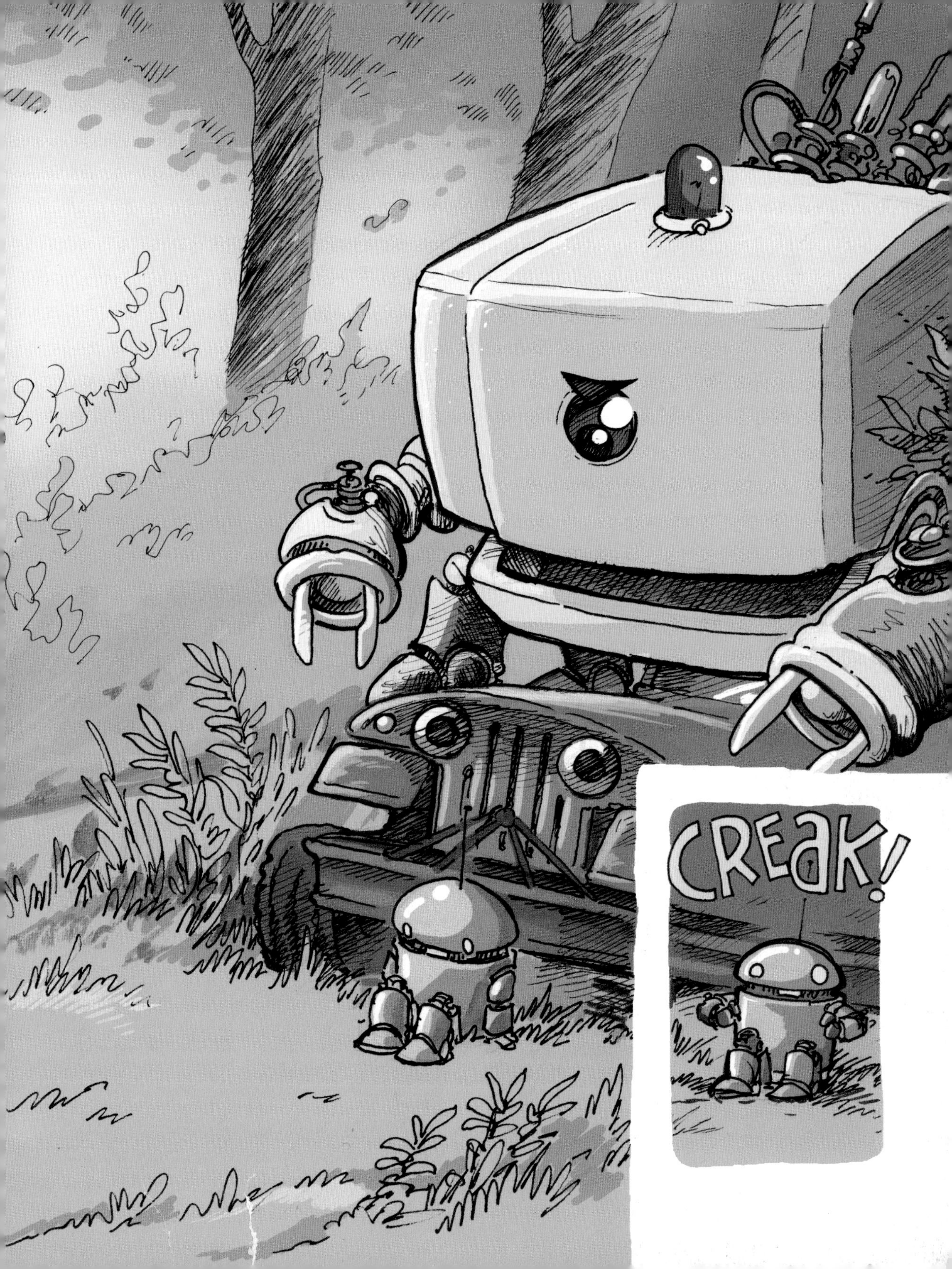
CREAK!

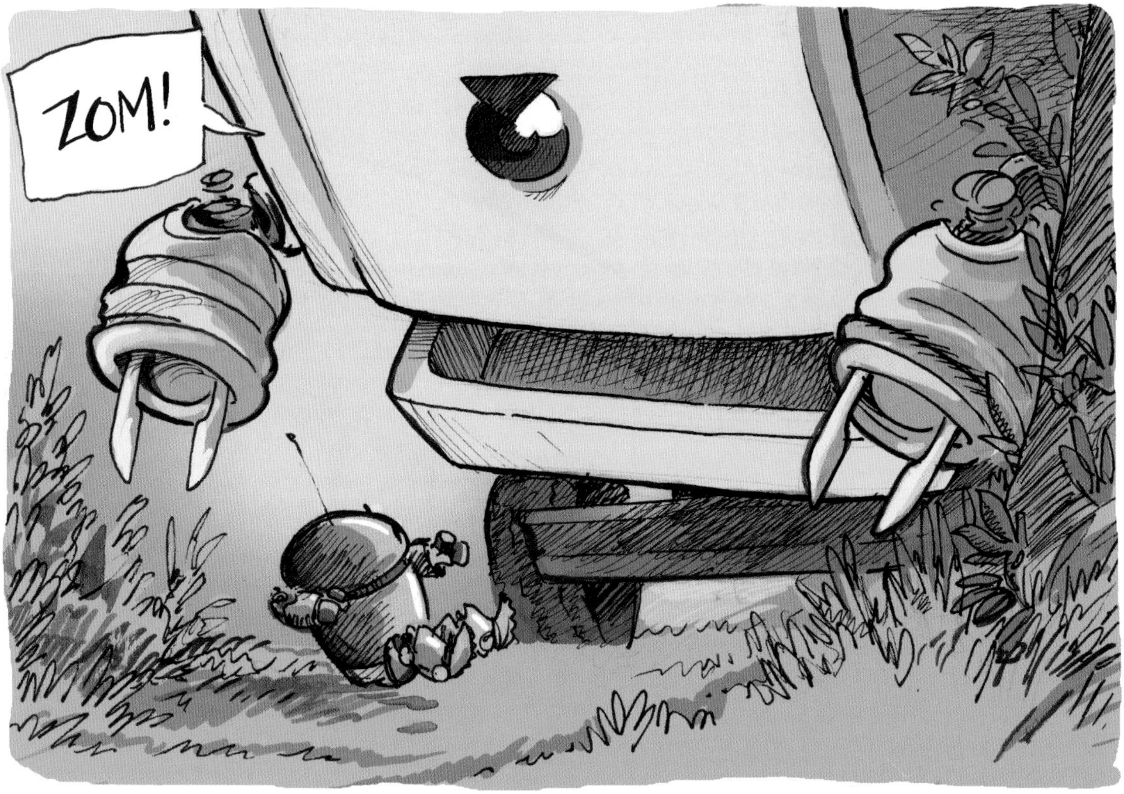
ZOM!

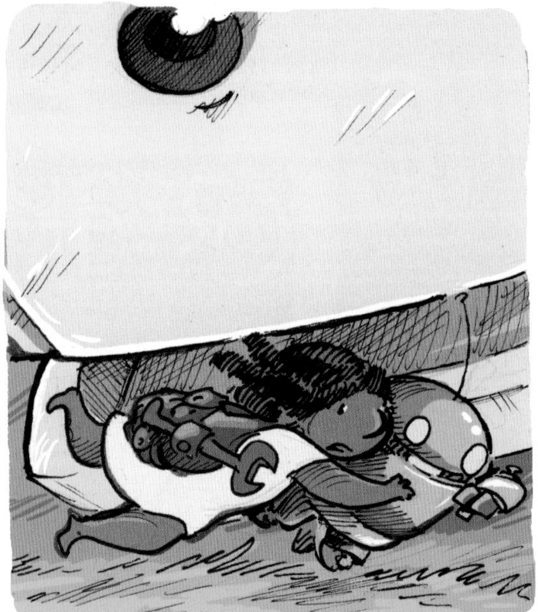

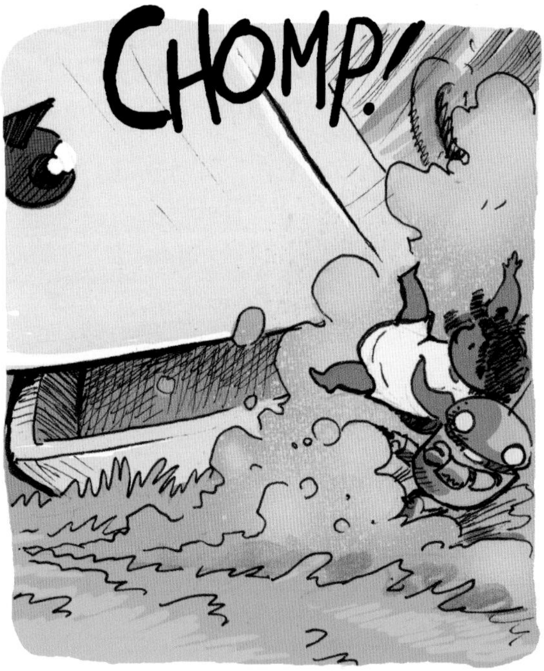
CHOMP!

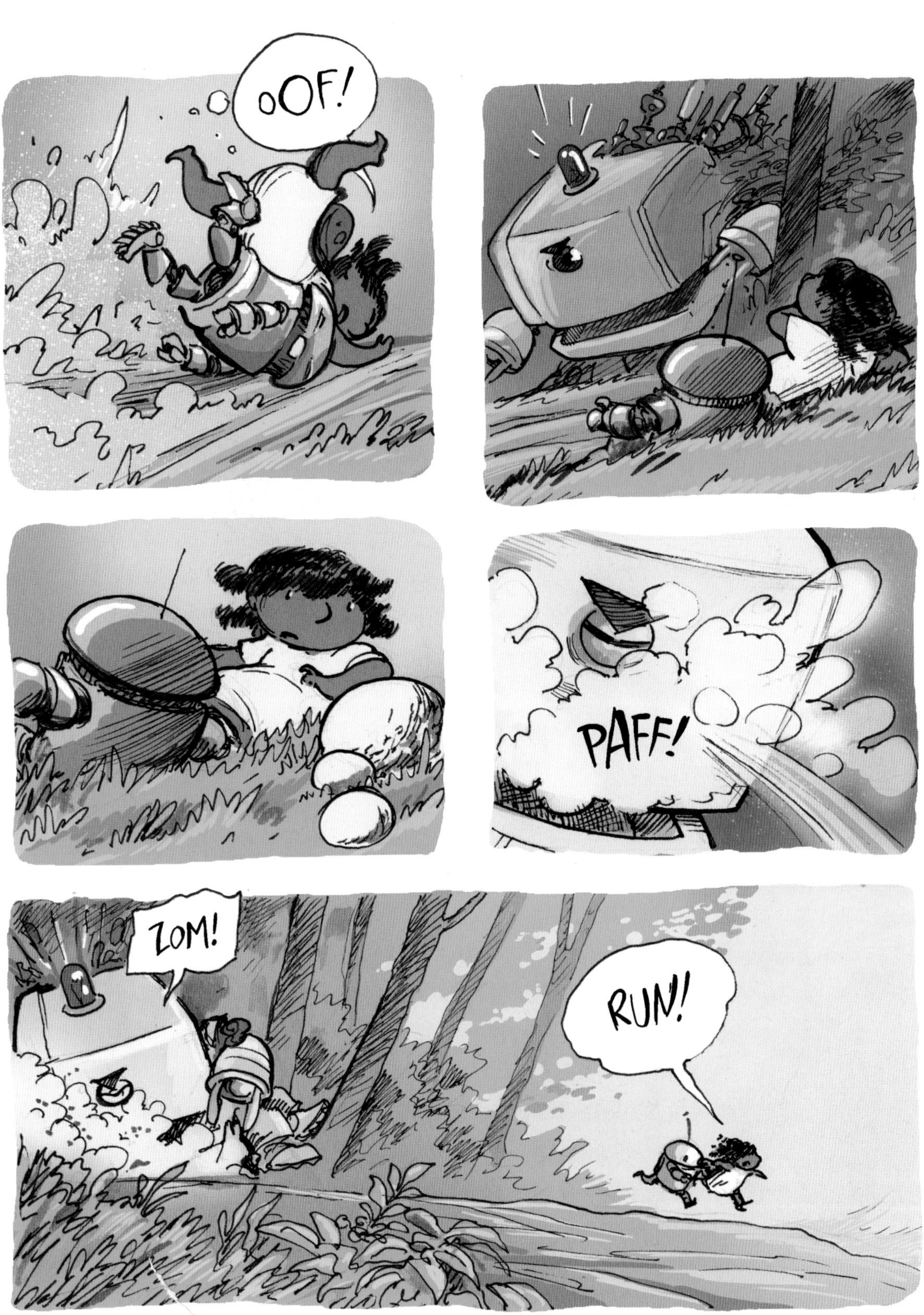
oOF!
PAFF!
ZOM!
RUN!

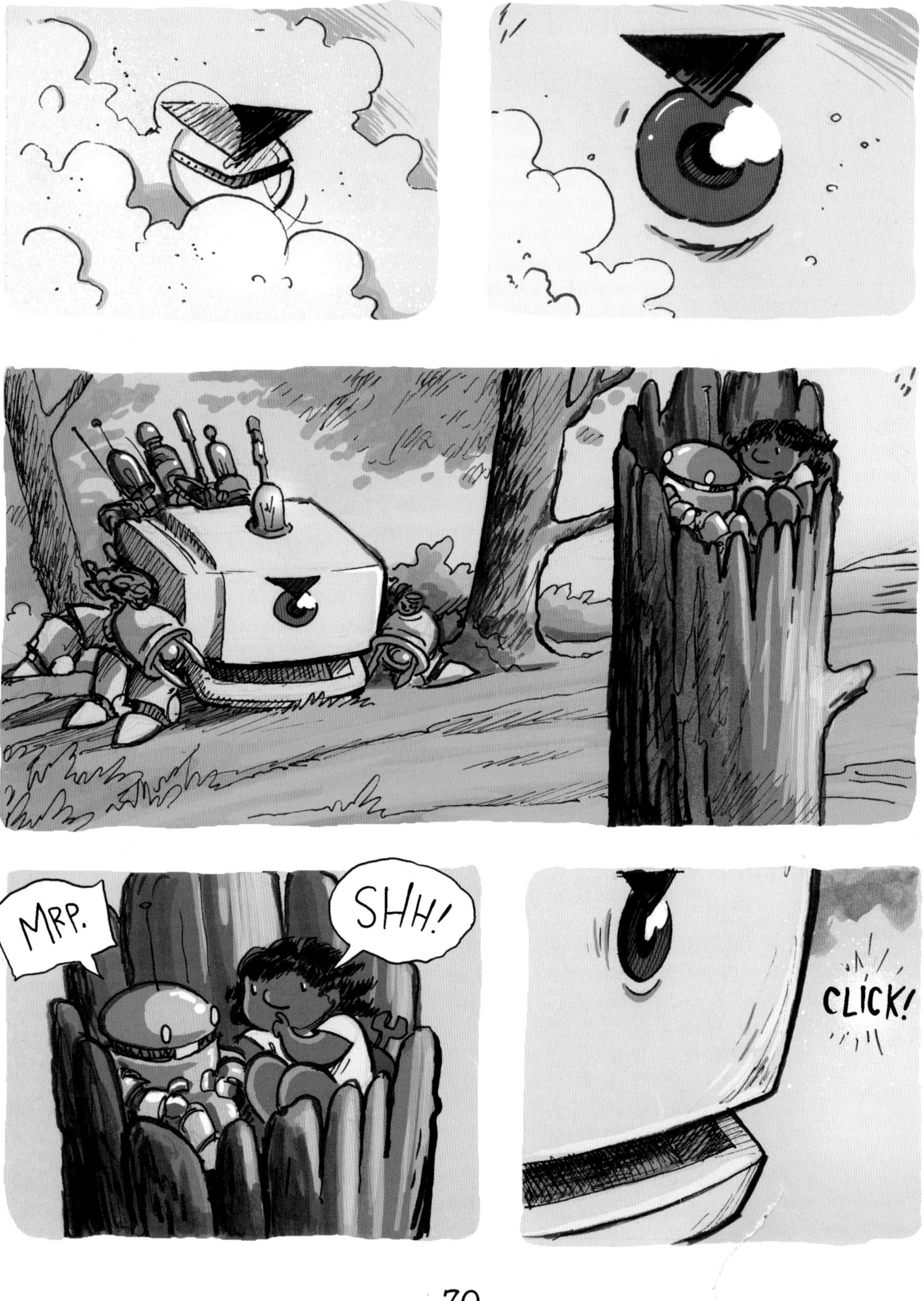
MRP.
SHH!
CLICK!

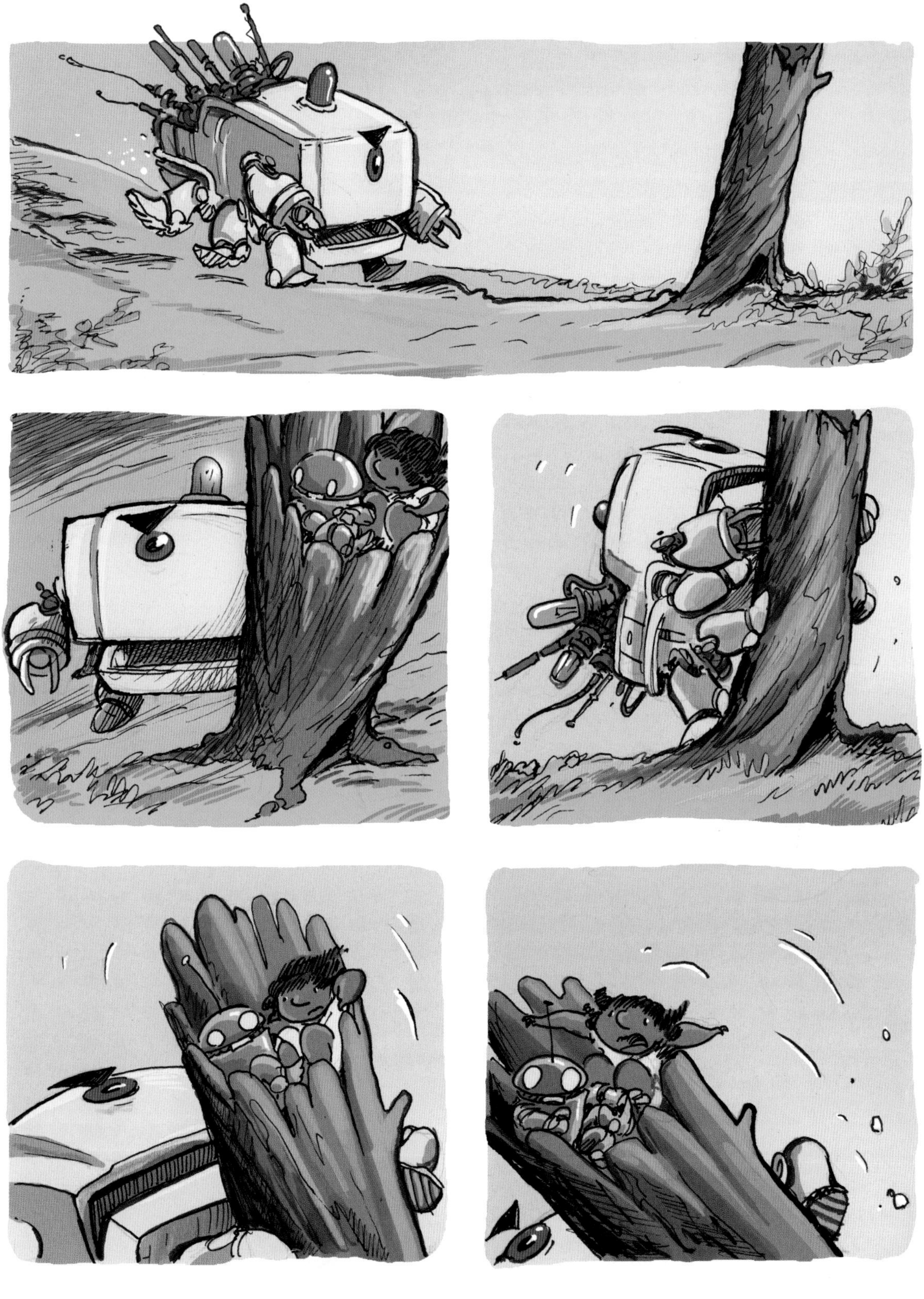

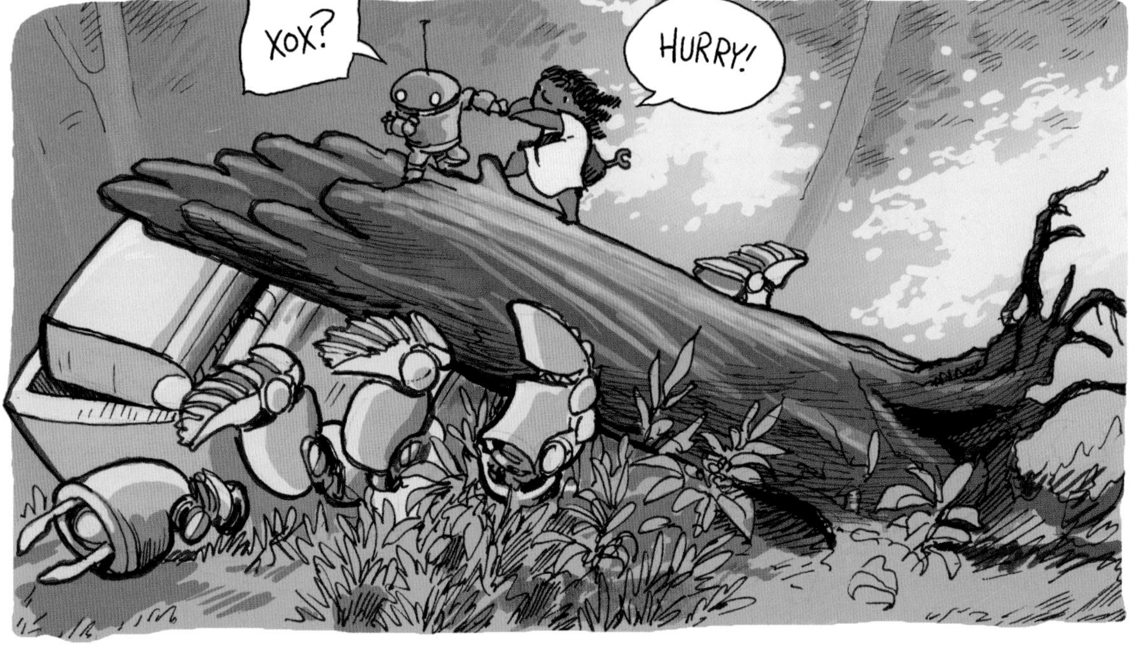
XOX?
HURRY!

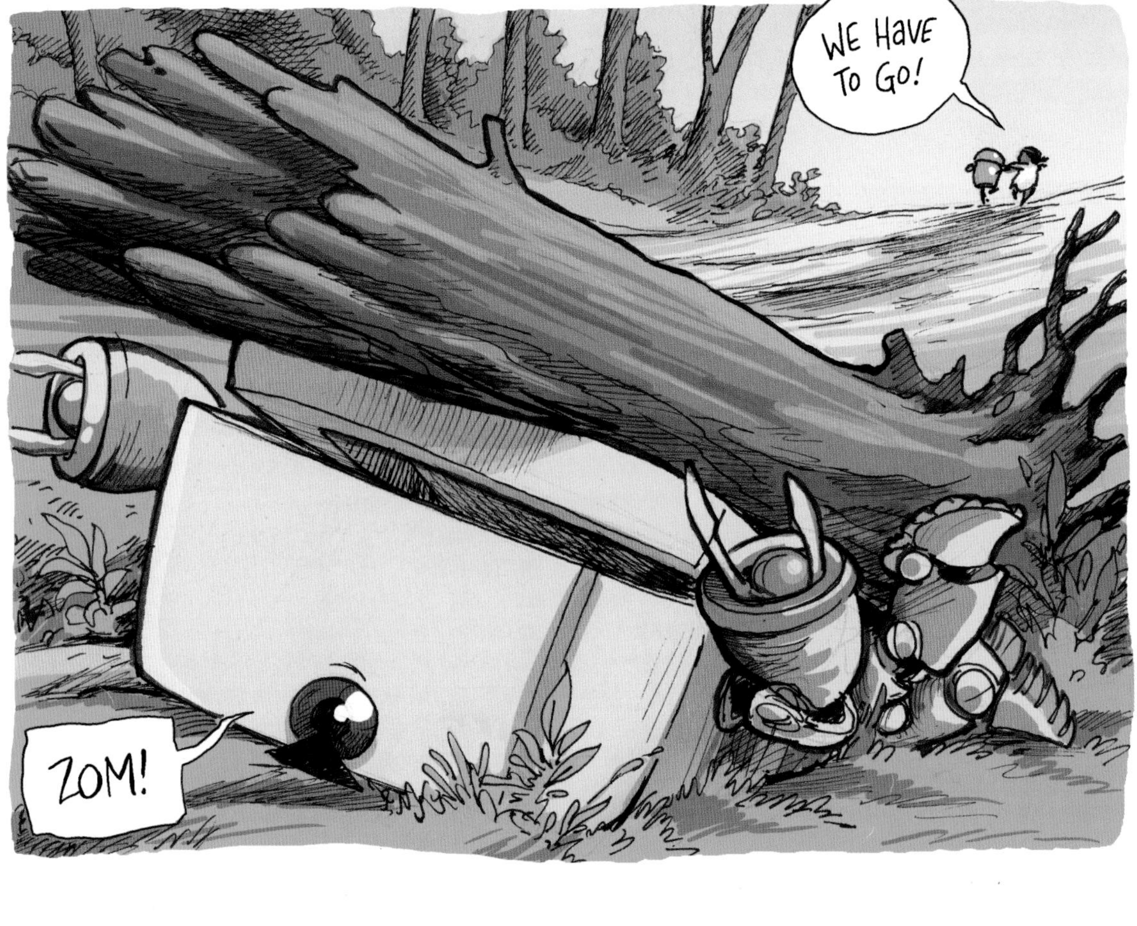
WE HAVE TO GO!
ZOM!

CHAPTER FIVE

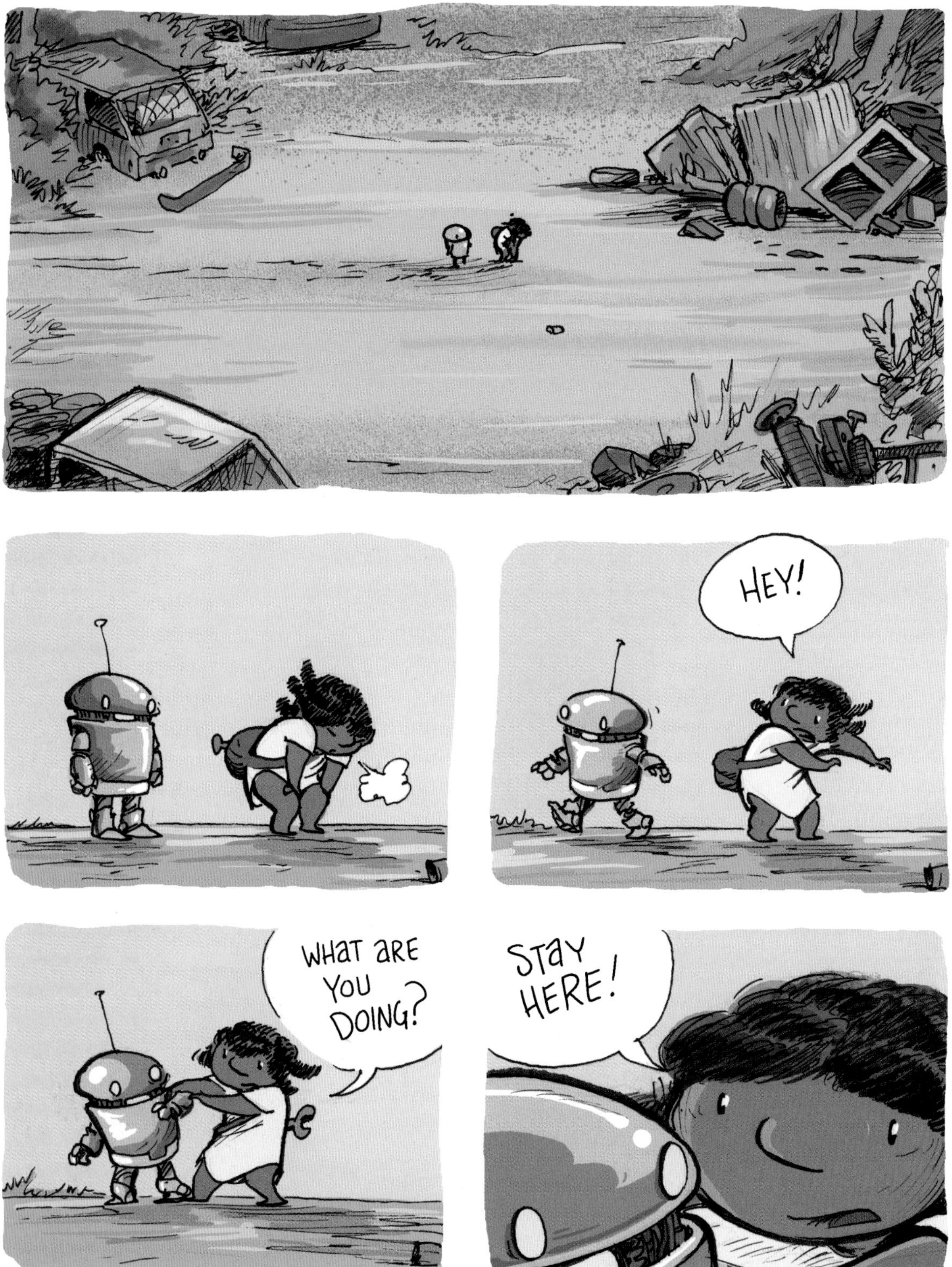
HEY!
WHAT ARE YOU DOING?
STAY HERE!

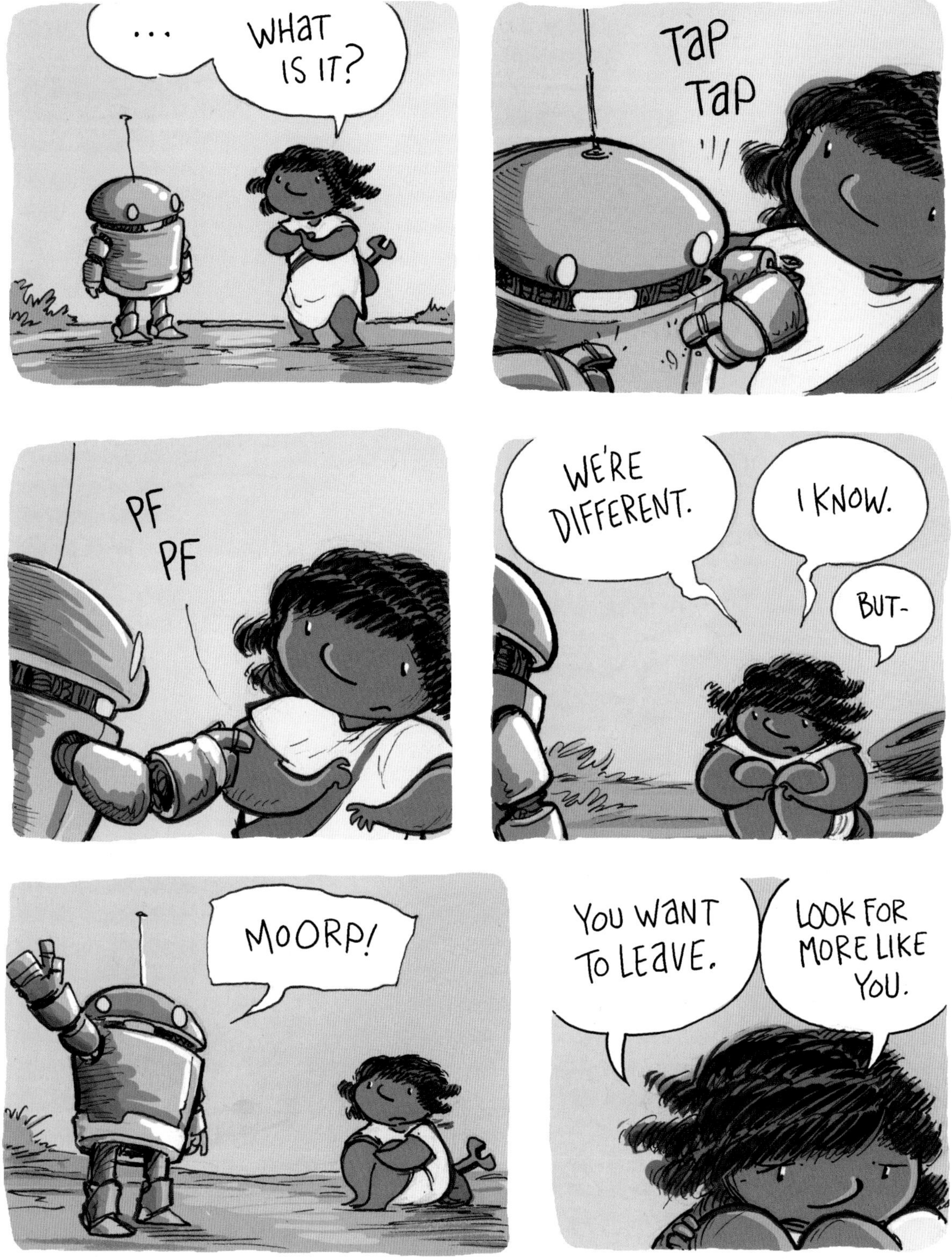
...
WHAT IS IT?
TAP TAP
PF PF
WE'RE DIFFERENT.
I KNOW.
BUT-
MOORP!
YOU WANT TO LEAVE.
LOOK FOR MORE LIKE YOU.

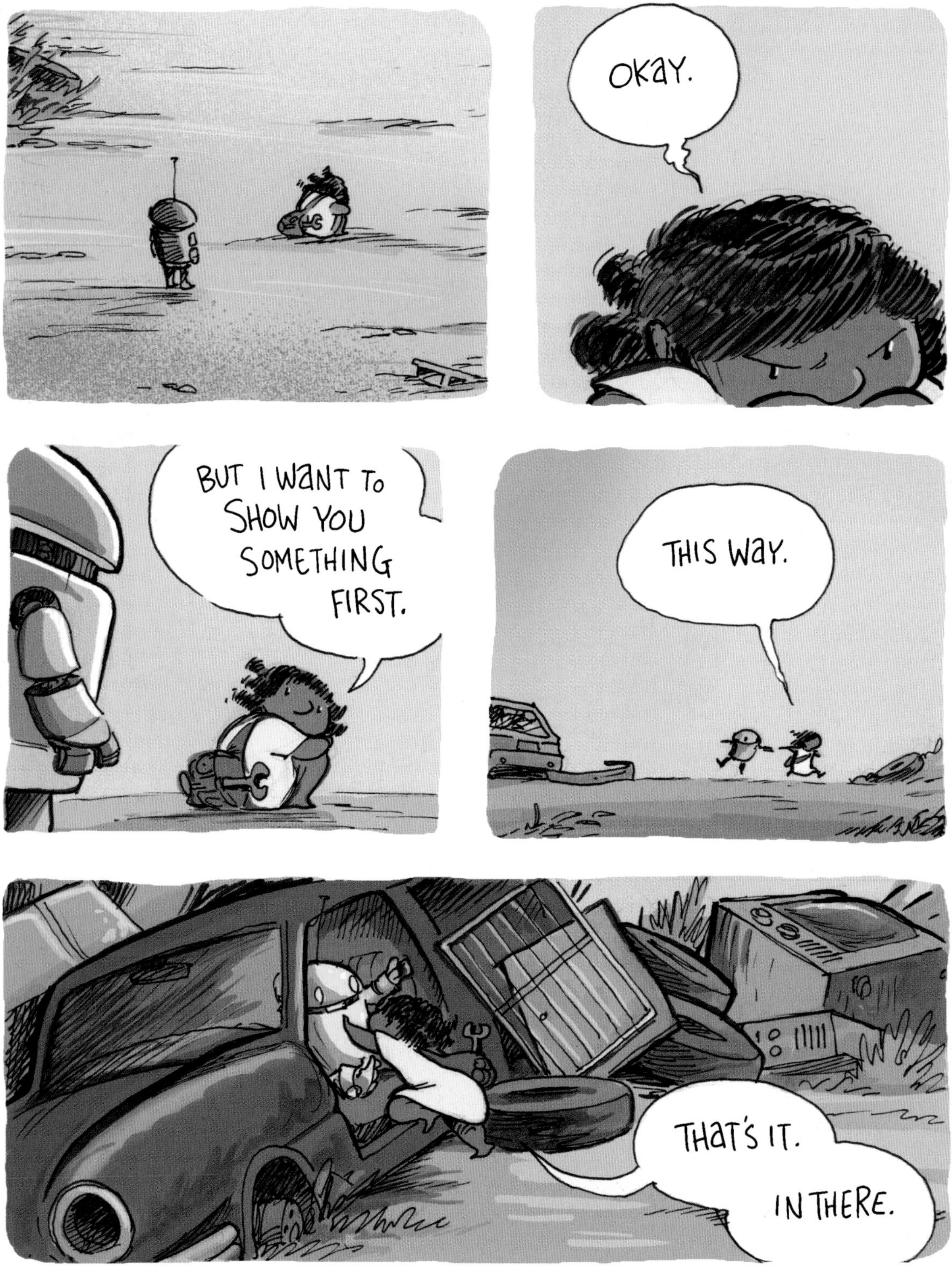
OKAY.
BUT I WANT TO SHOW YOU SOMETHING FIRST.
THIS WAY.
THAT'S IT.
IN THERE.

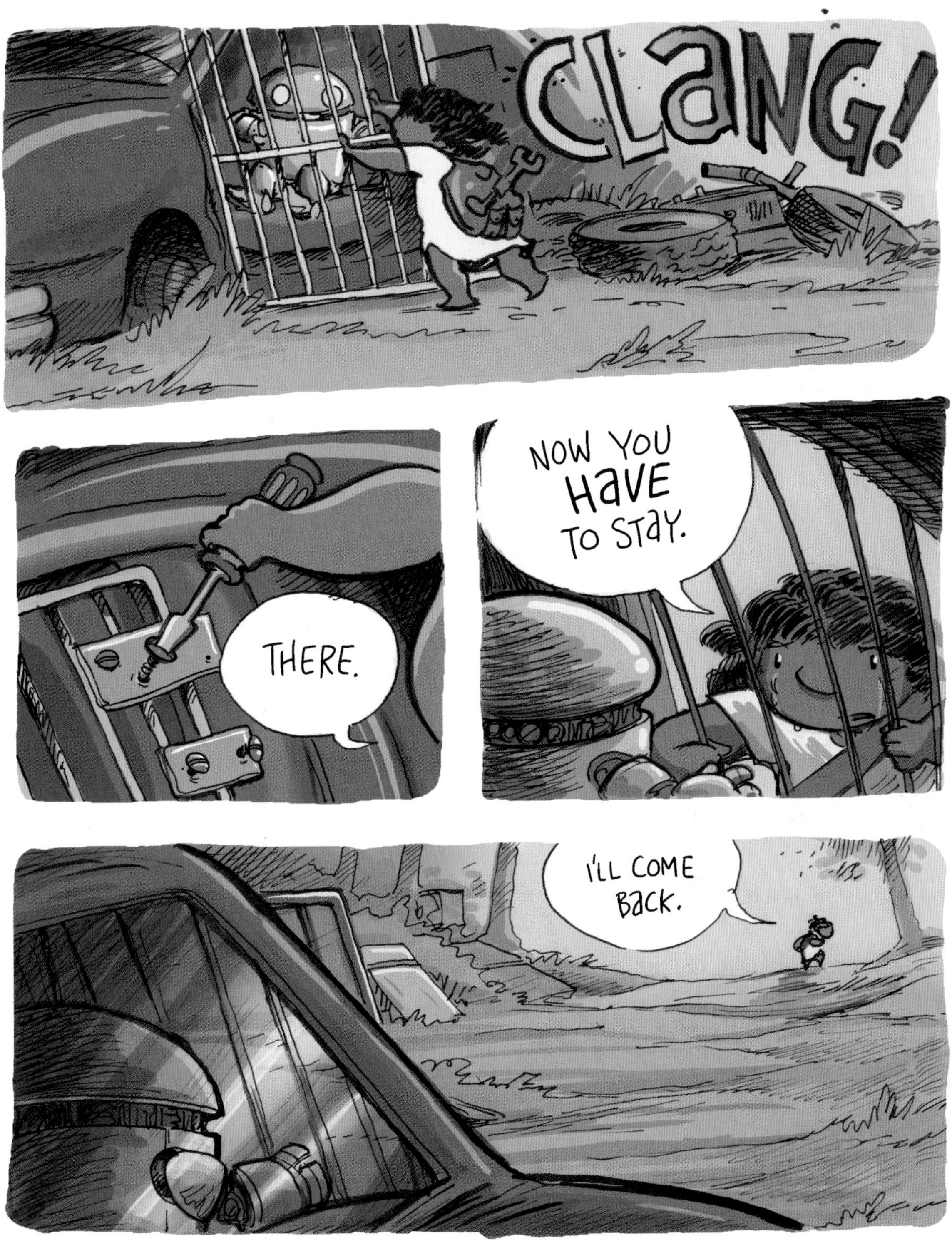
CLANG!
THERE.
NOW YOU HAVE TO STAY.
I'LL COME BACK.

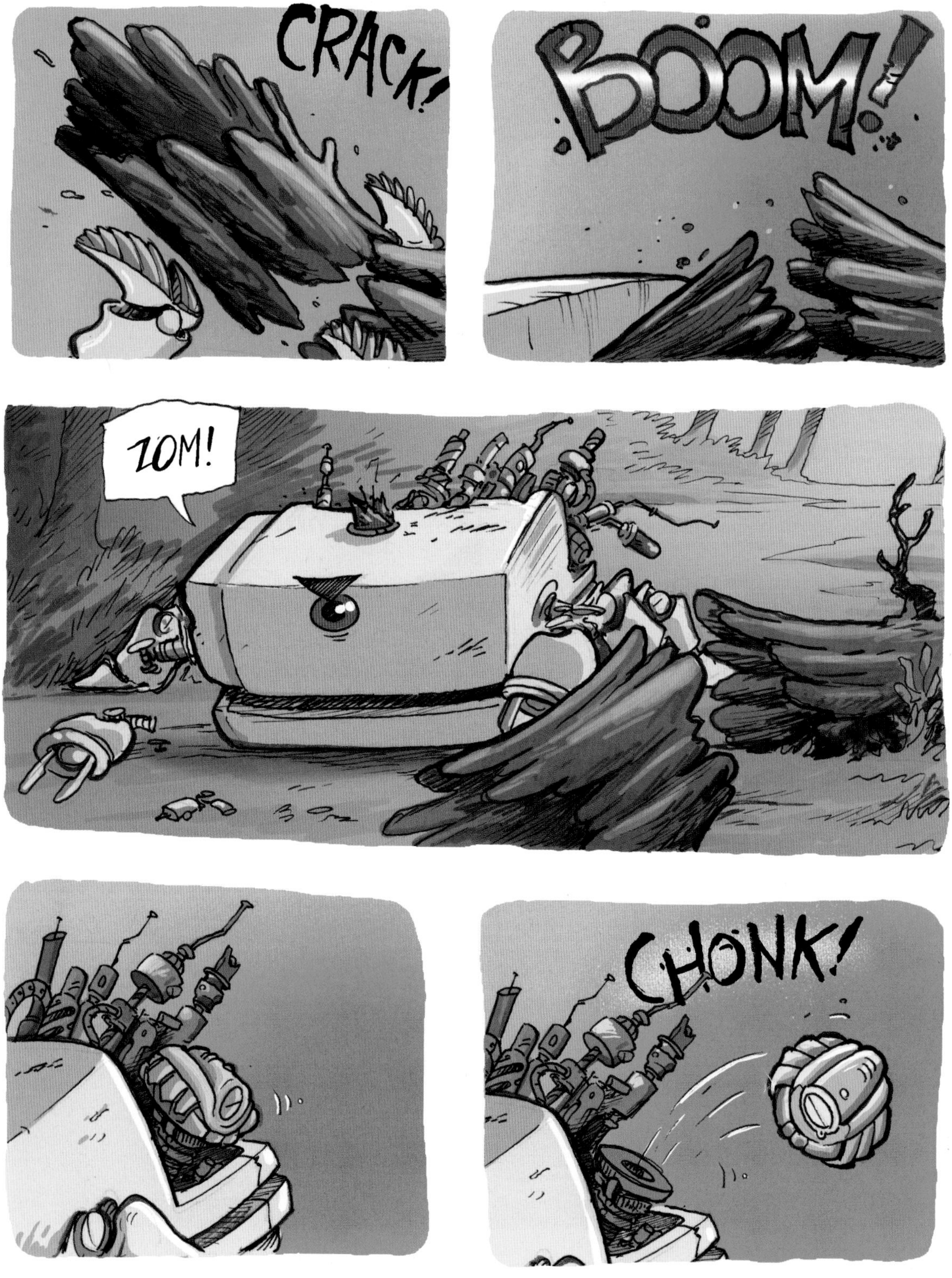
CRACK!
BOOM!
ZOM!
CHONK!

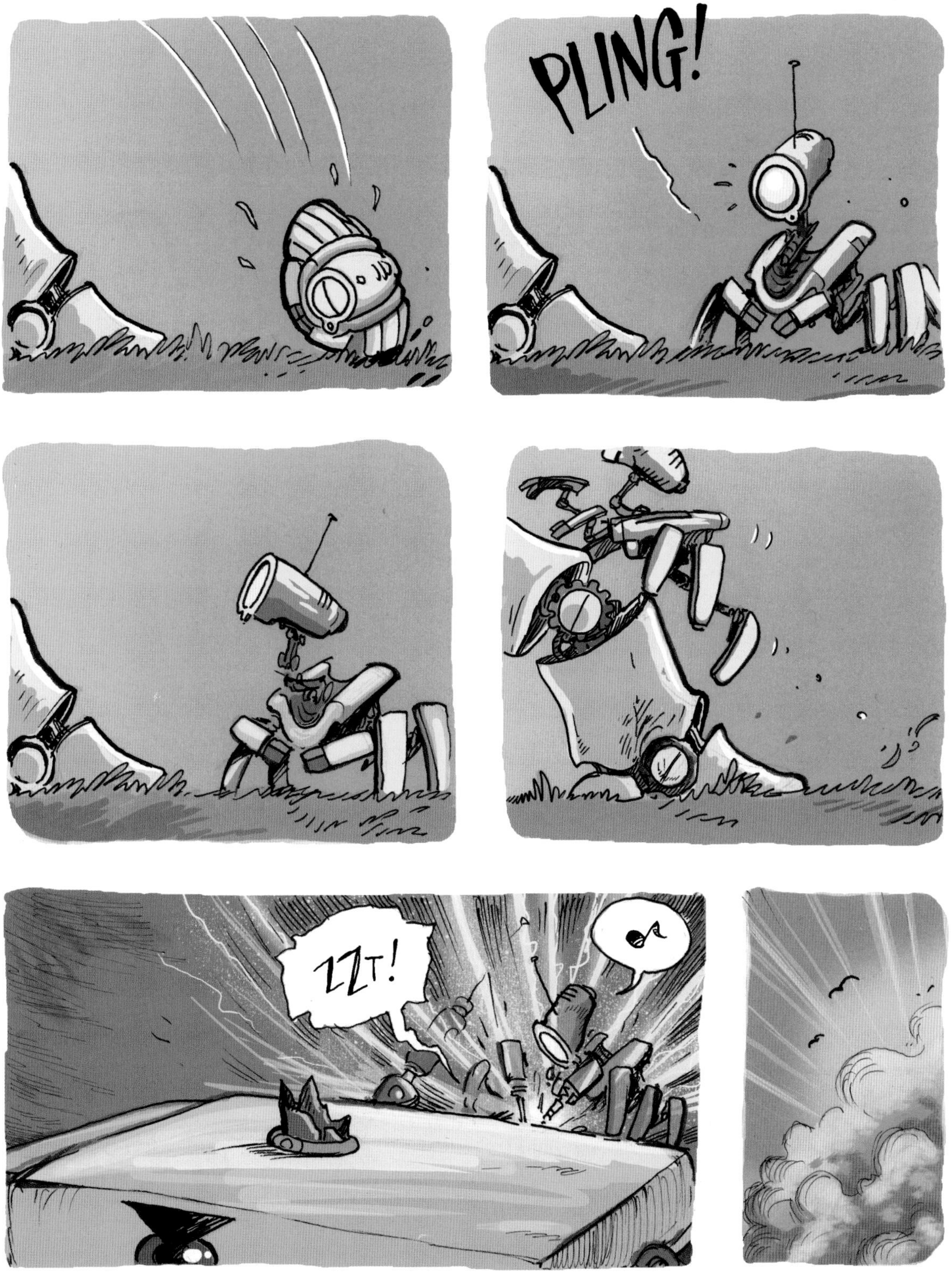
PLING!
ZZT!

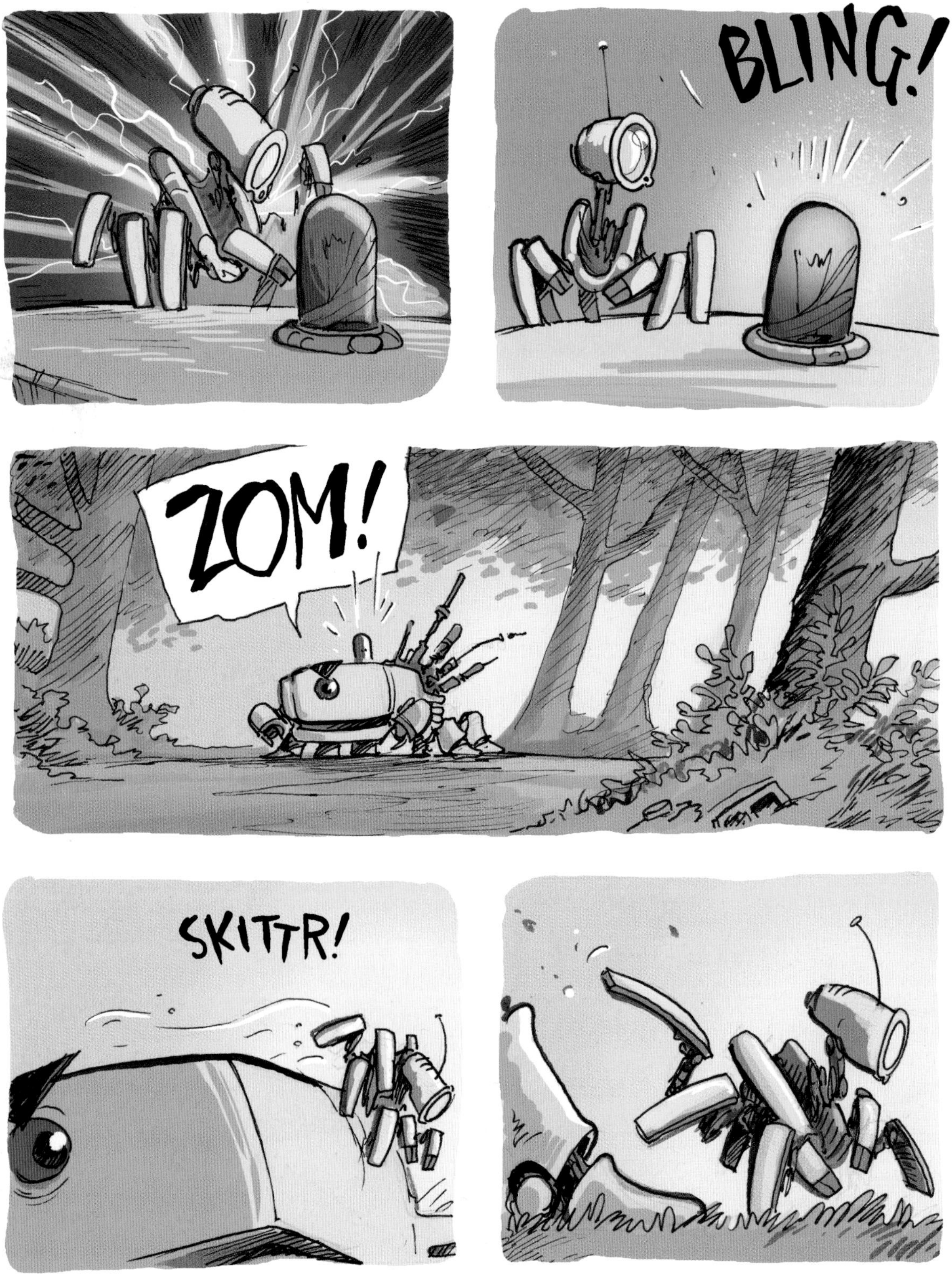
BLING!
ZOM!
SKITTR!

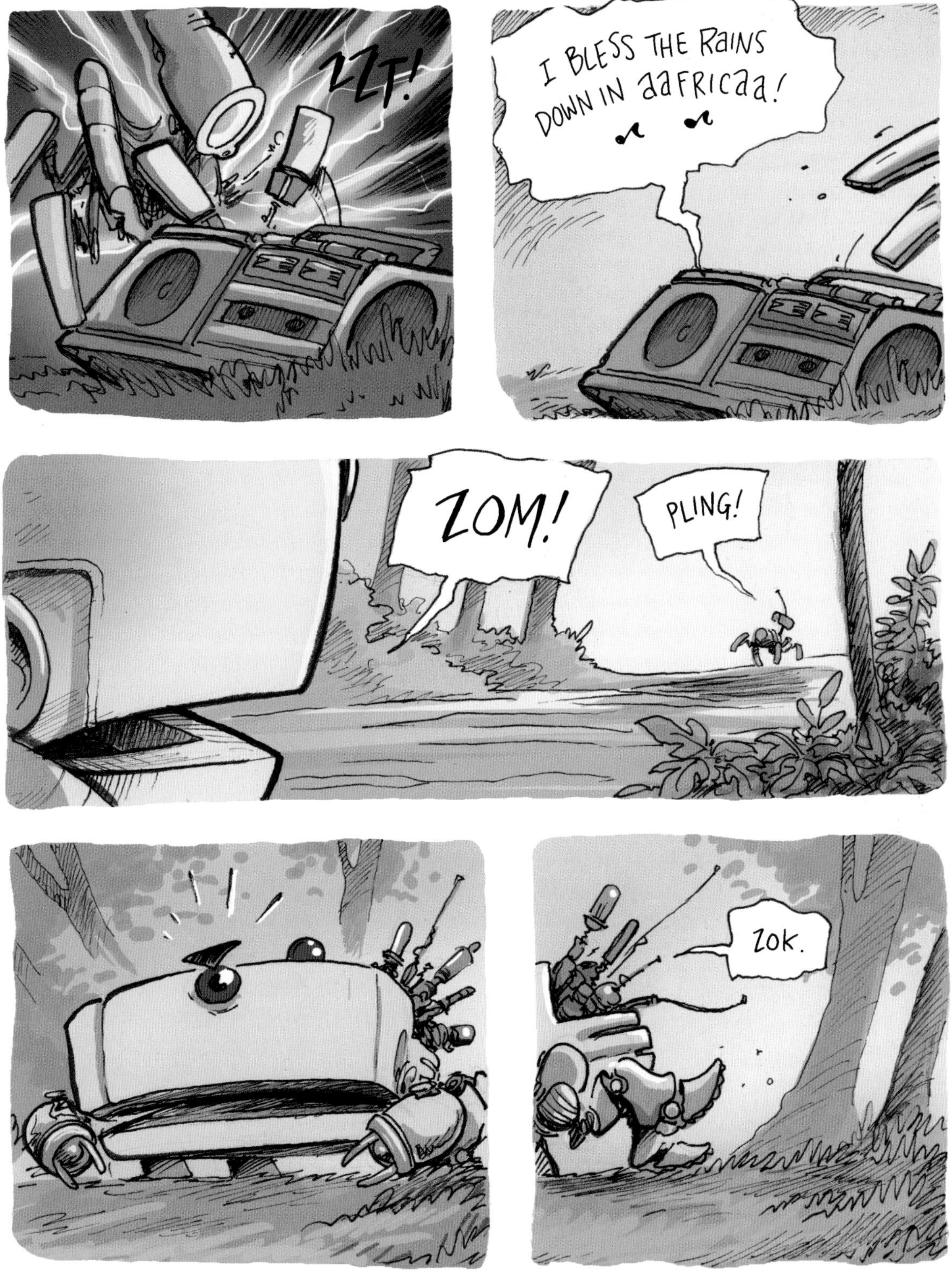
ZZT!
I BLESS THE RAINS DOWN IN AAFRICAA!
ZOM!
PLING!
ZOK.

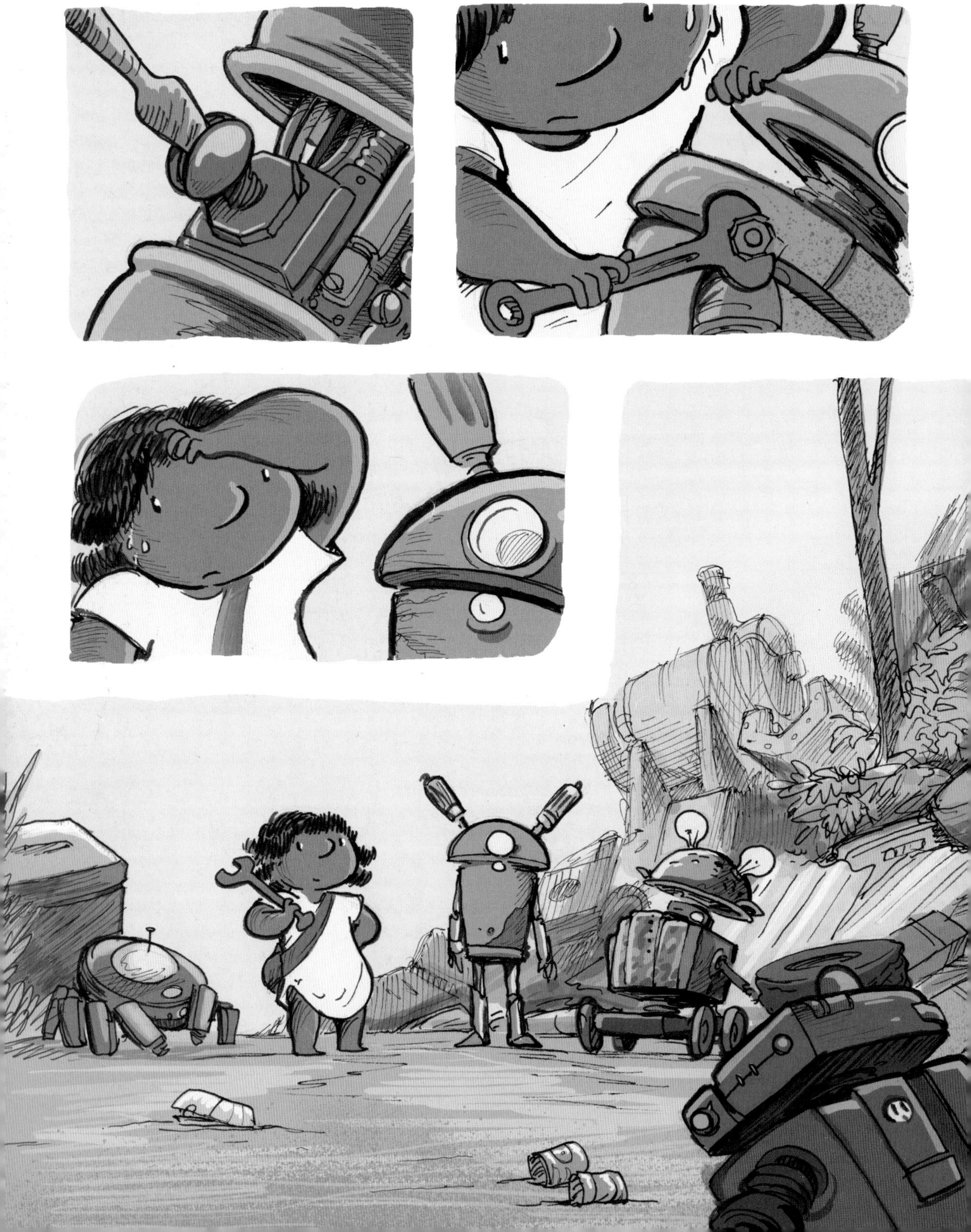

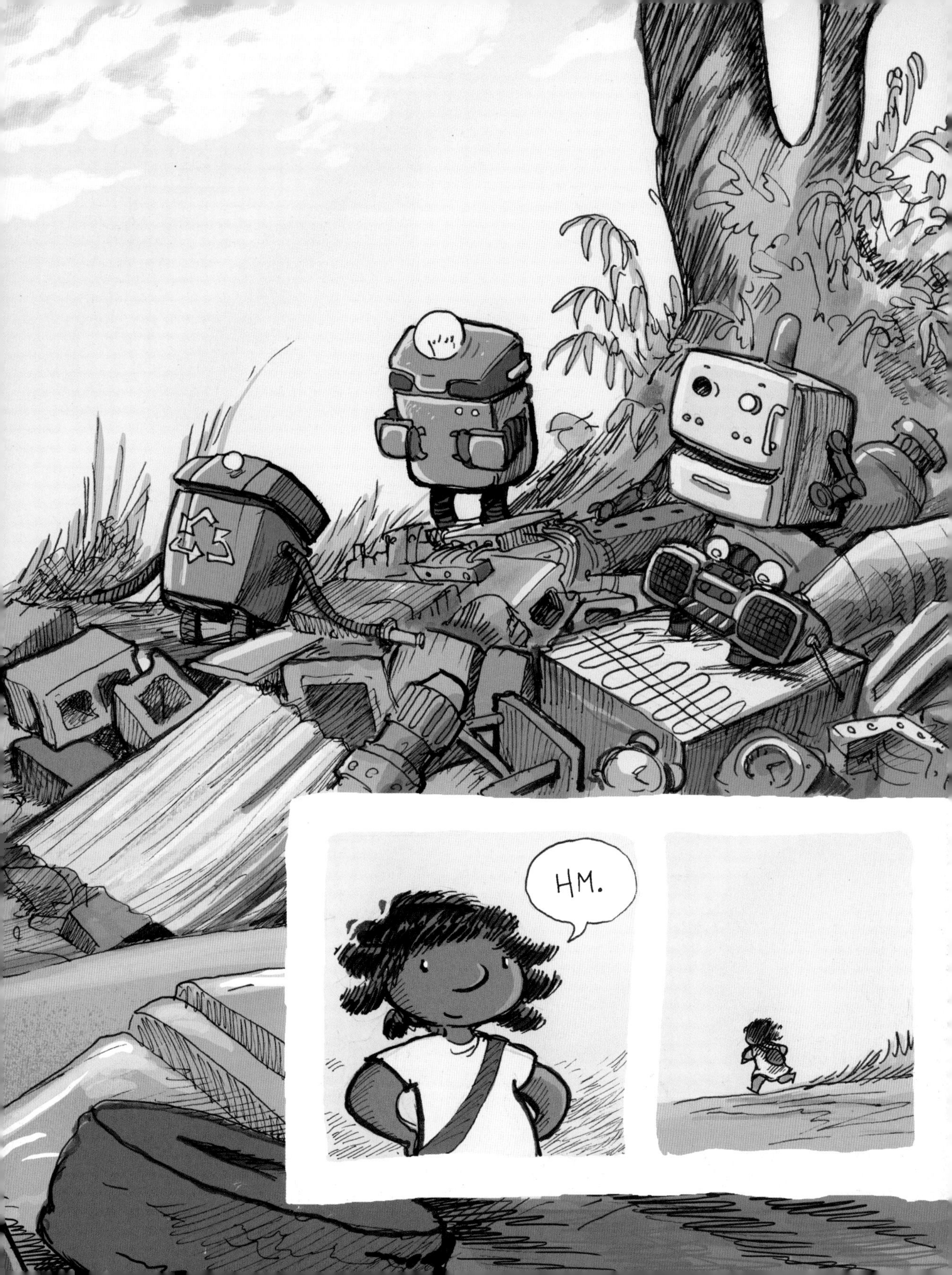
HM.

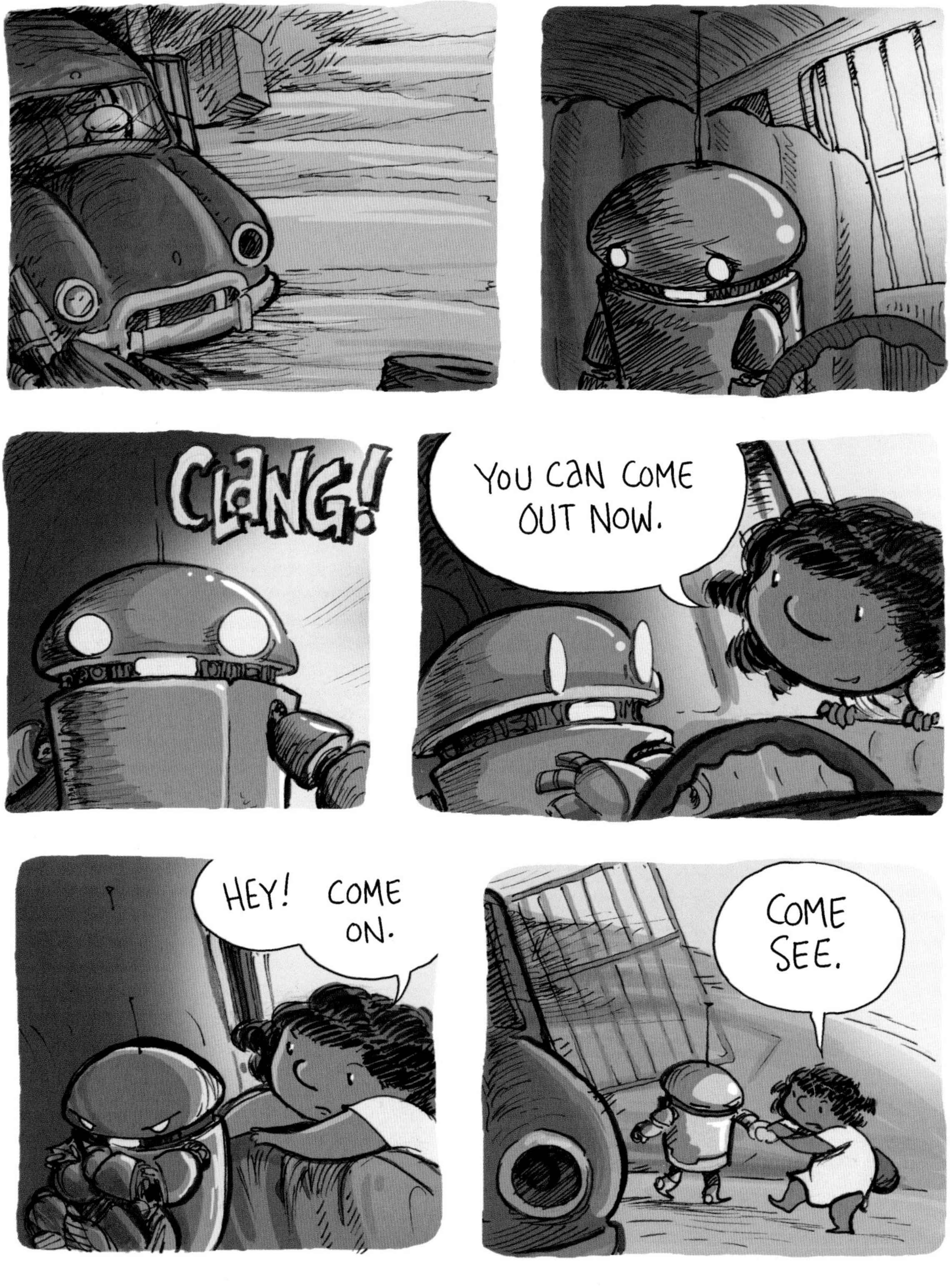
CLANG!
YOU CAN COME OUT NOW.
HEY! COME ON.
COME SEE.

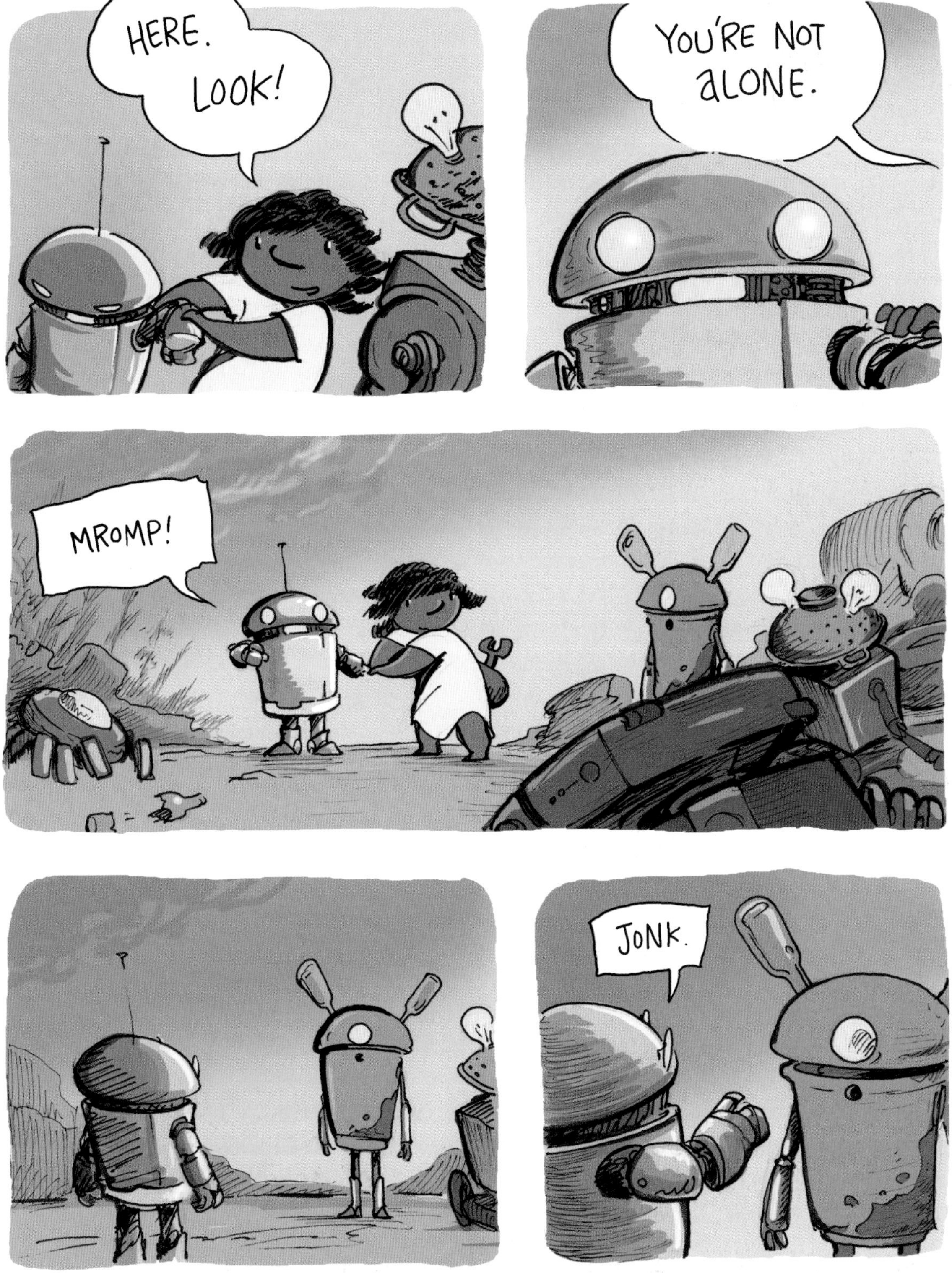
HERE. LOOK!
YOU'RE NOT ALONE.
MROMP!
JONK.

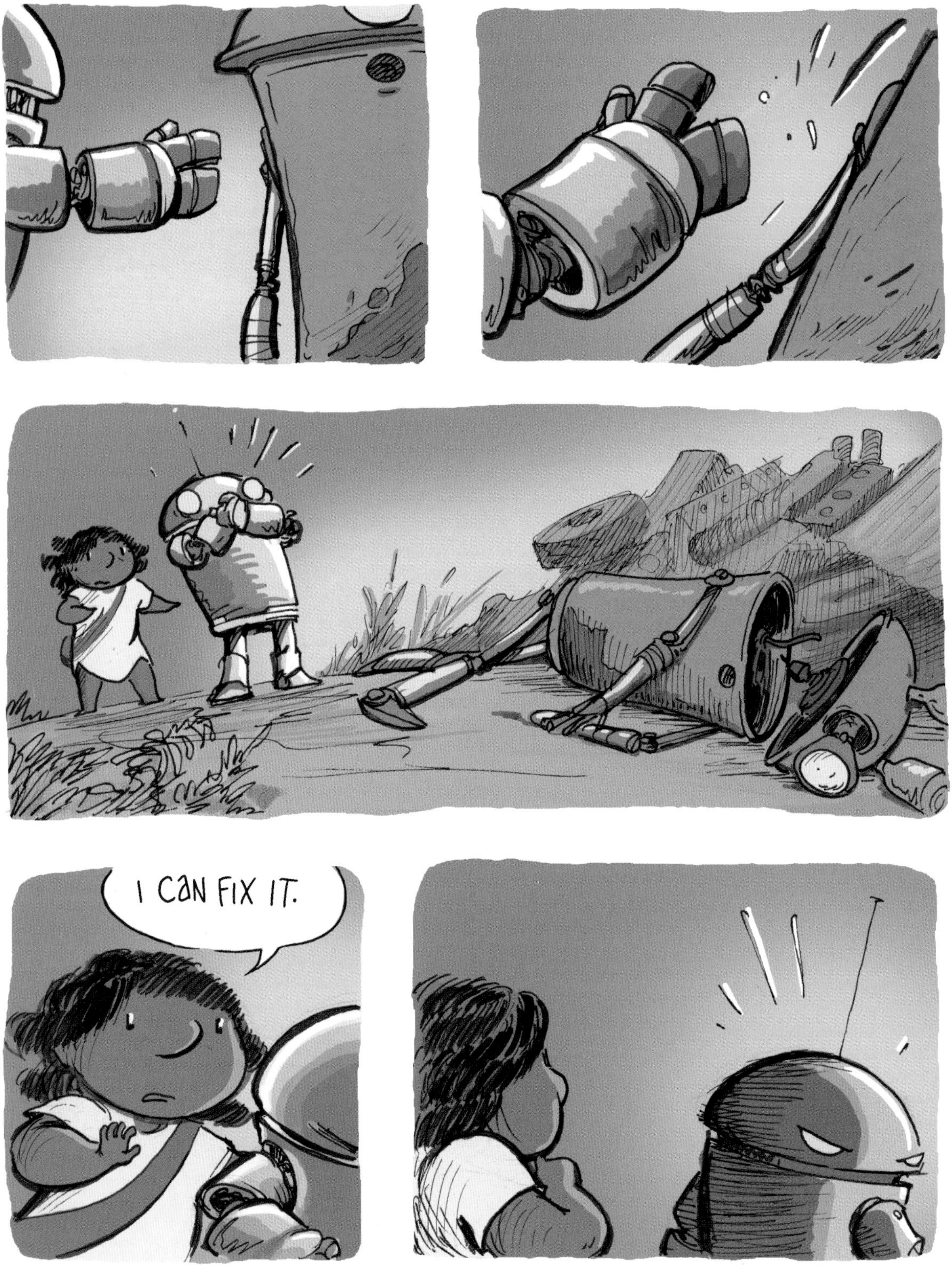
I CAN FIX IT.

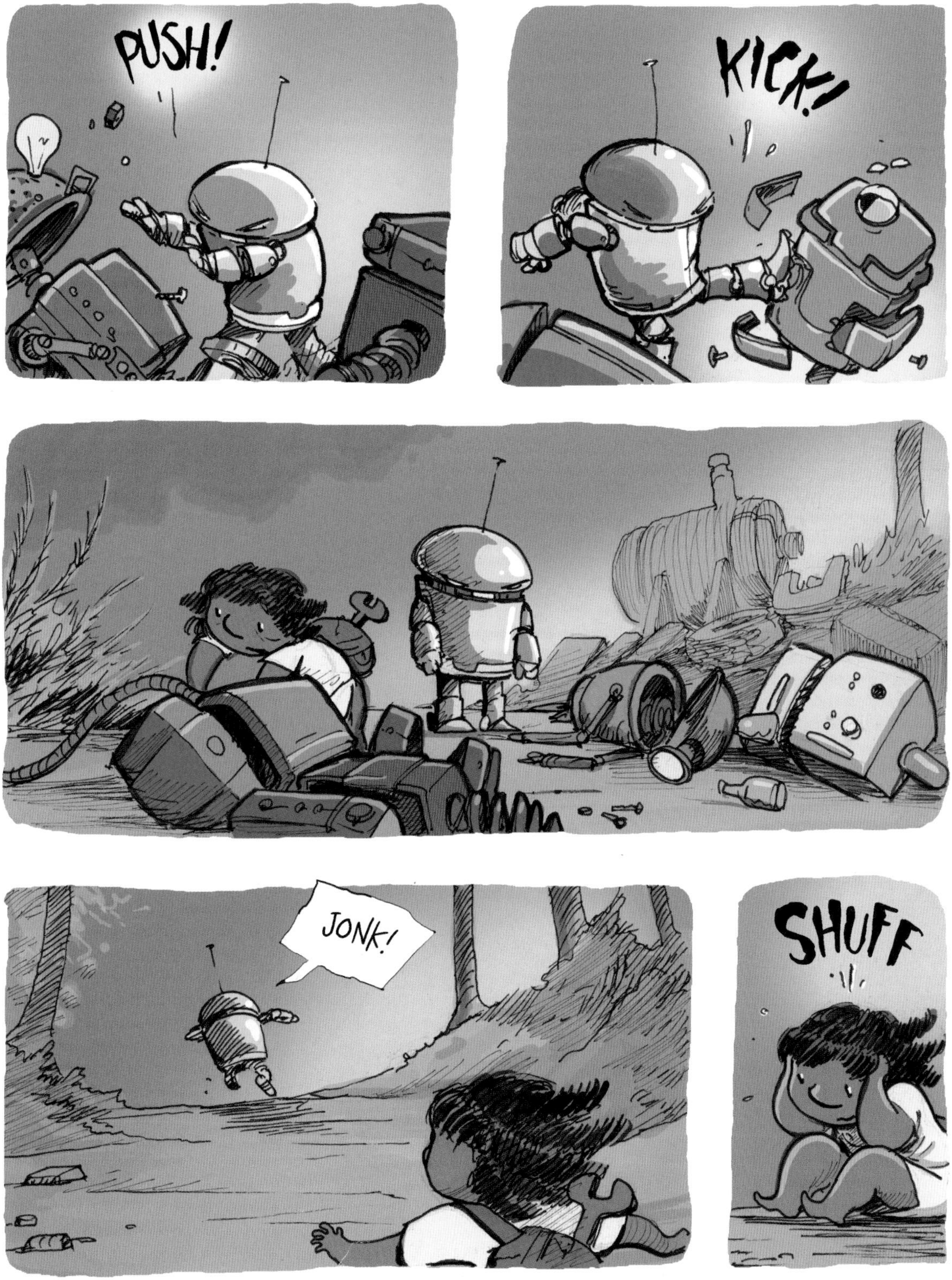
PUSH!
KICK!
JONK!
SHUFF

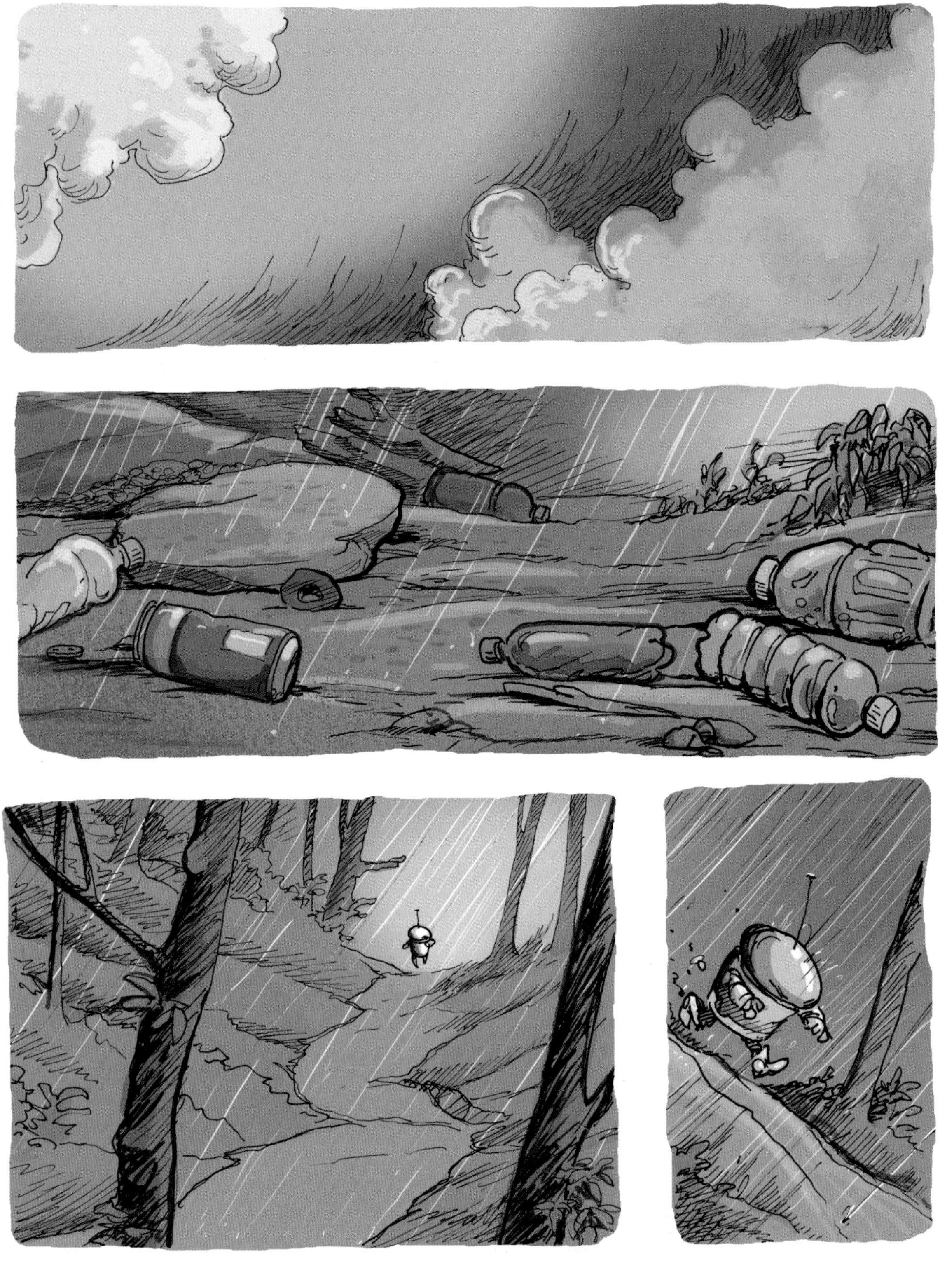

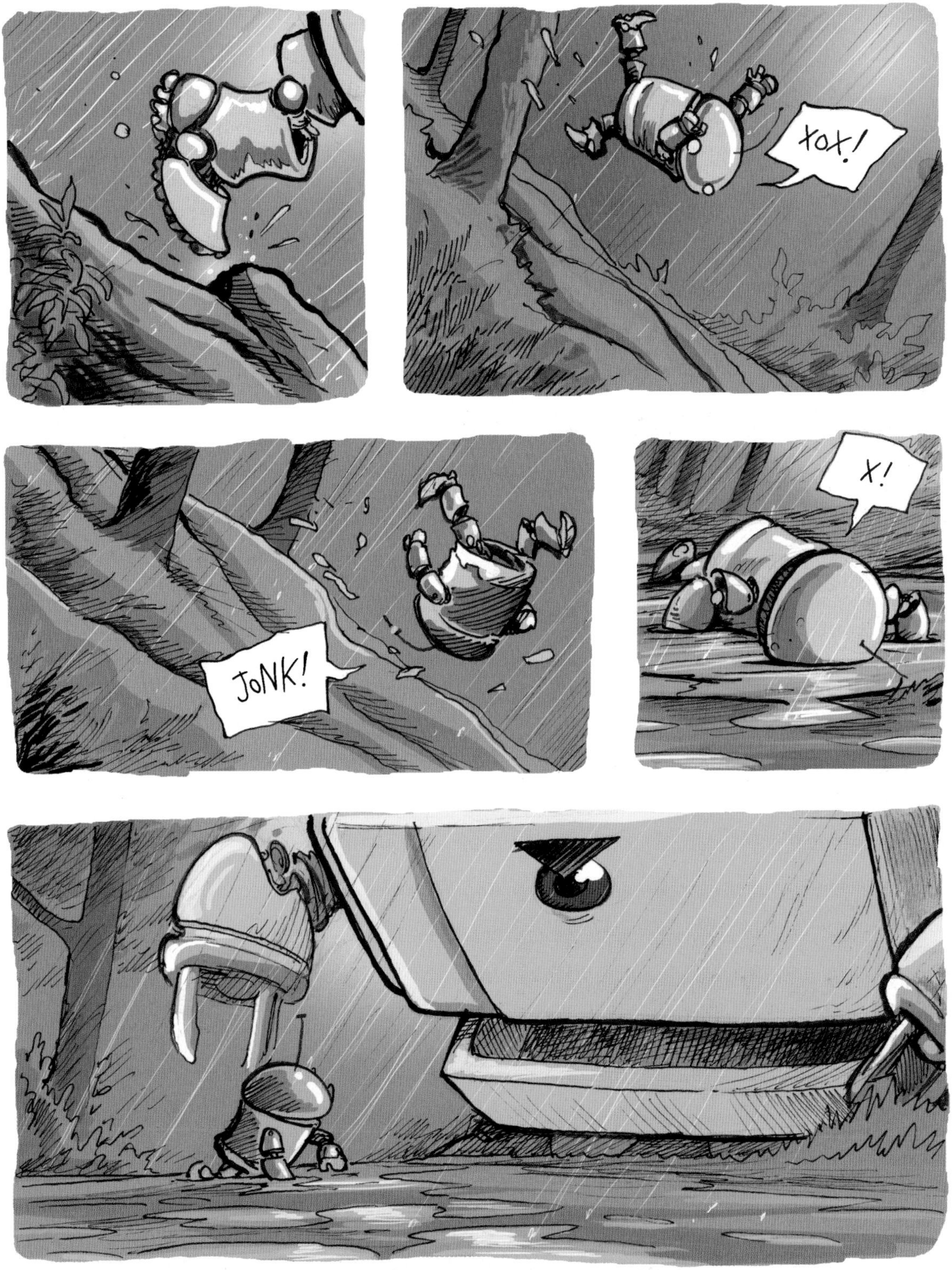

XOX!
JoNK!
X!

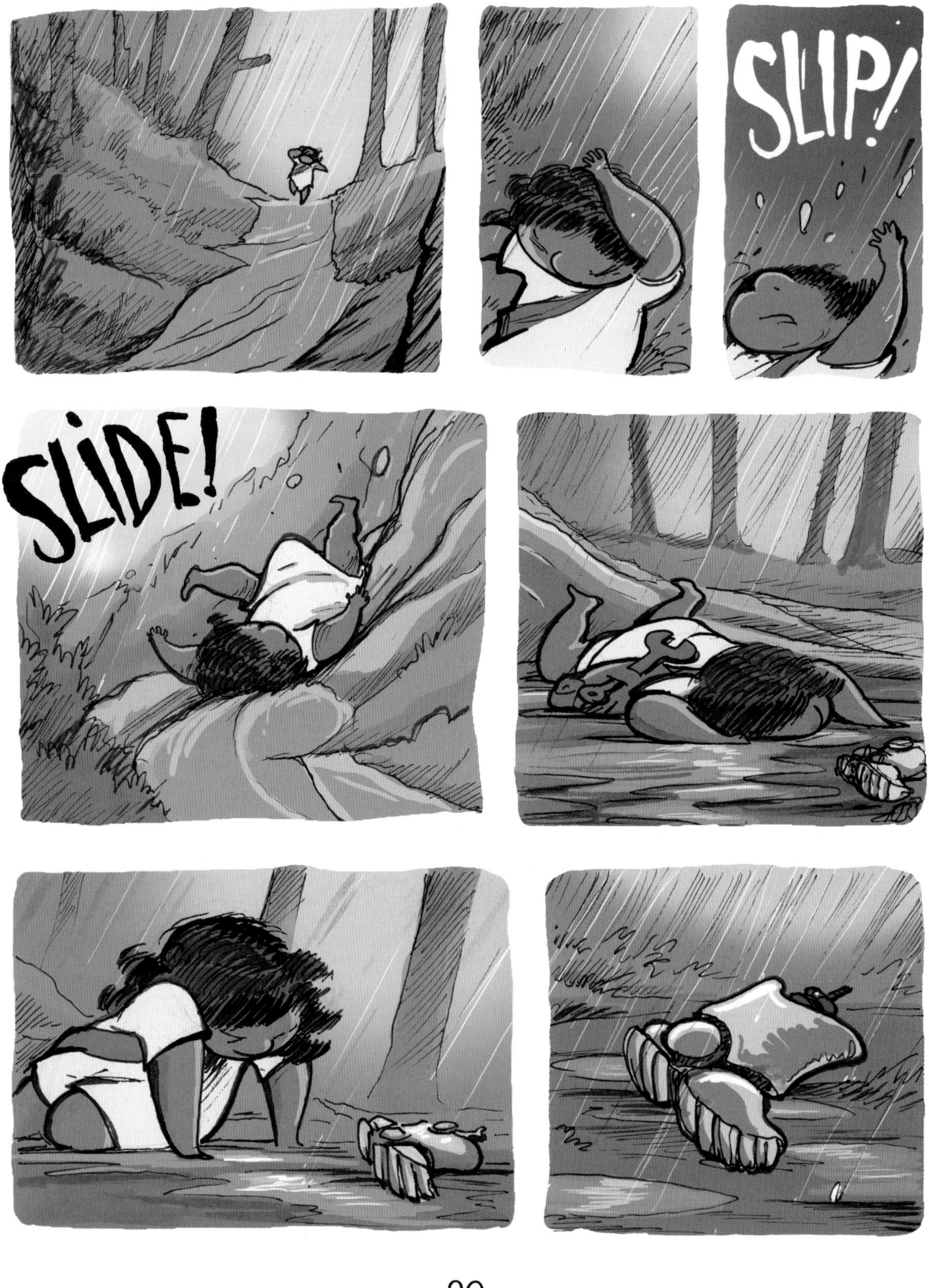
SLIP!
SLIDE!

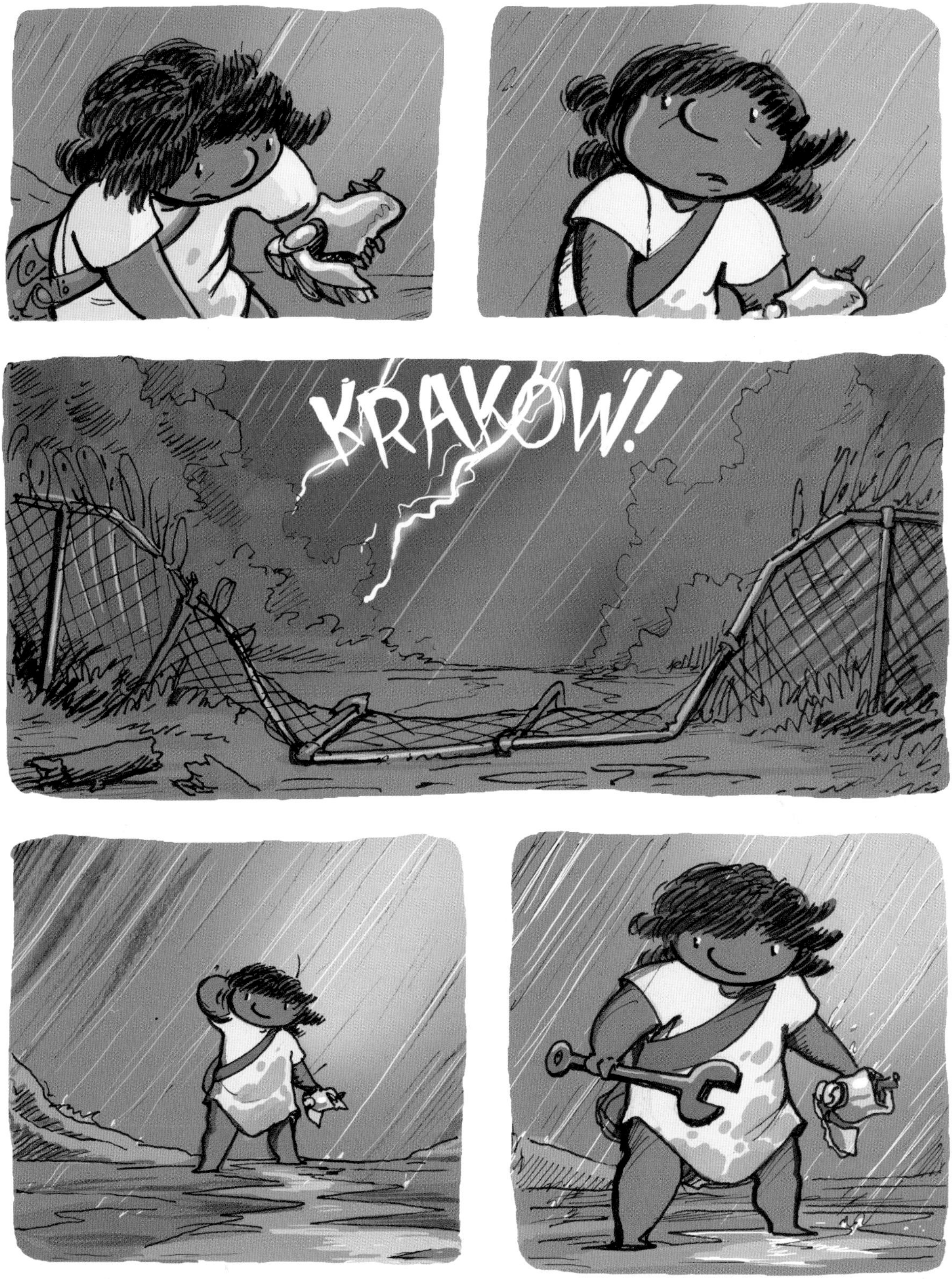
KRAKOW!

CHAPTER SIX

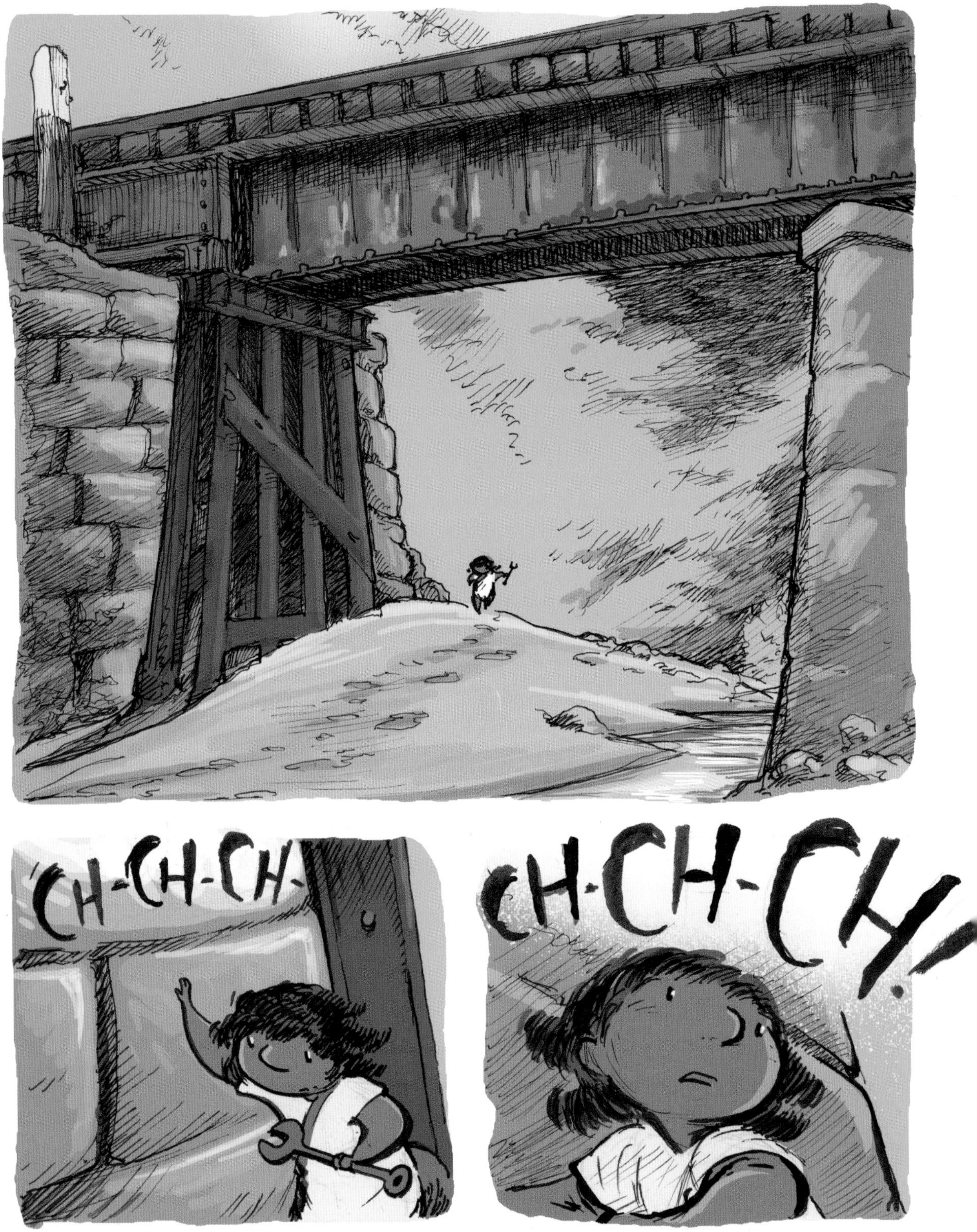
CH-CH-CH-
CH-CH-CH!

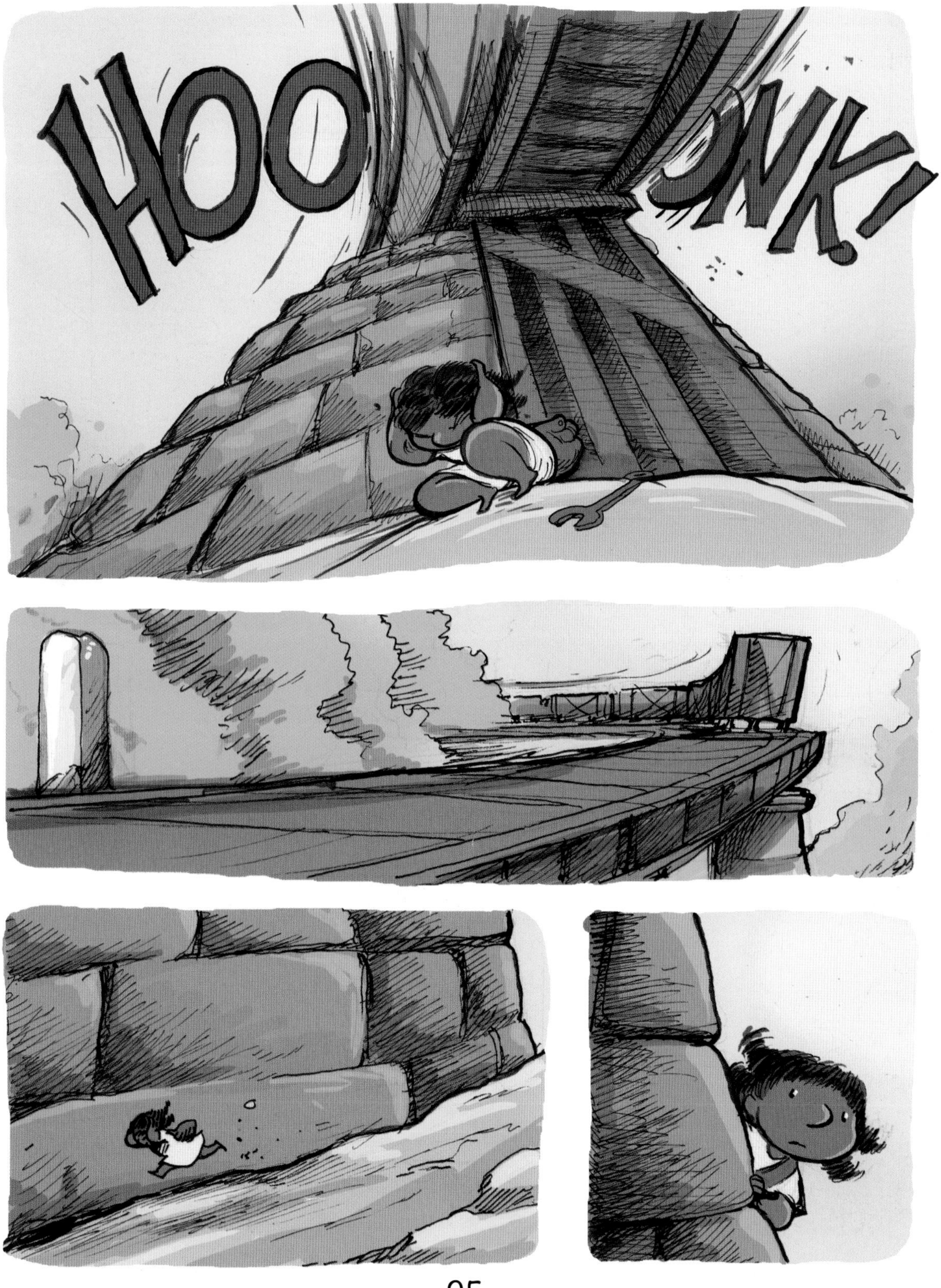
HOOONK!

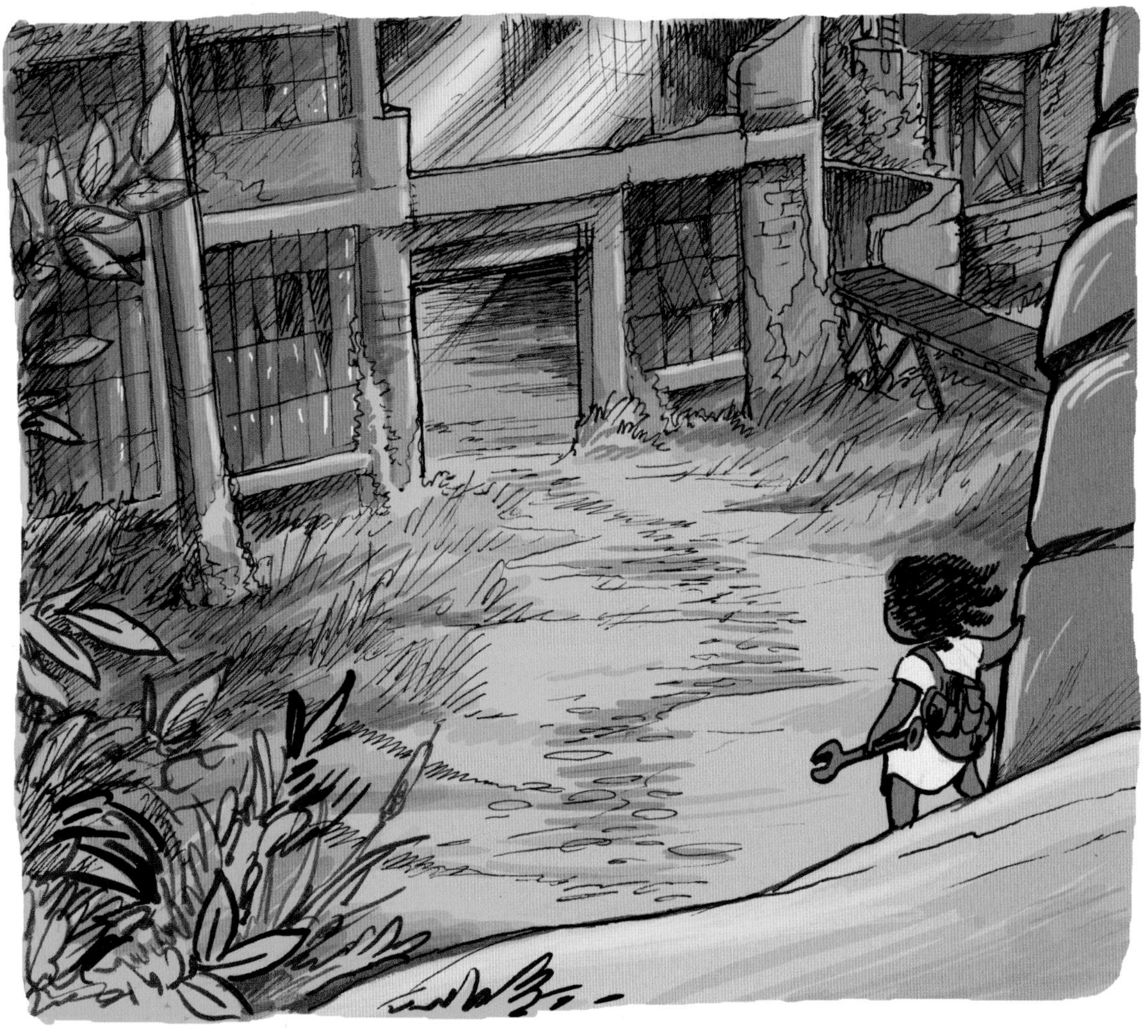

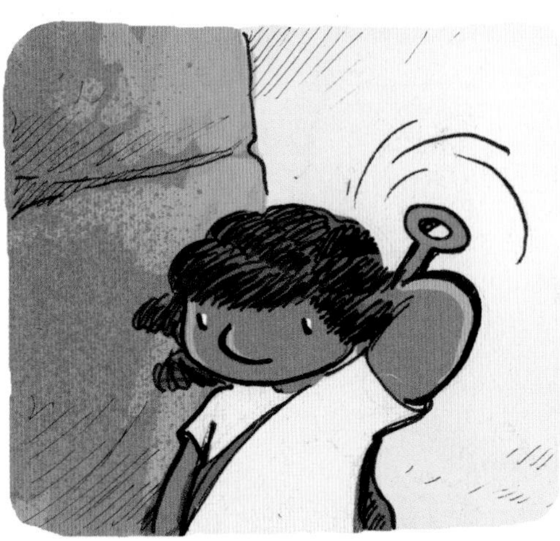

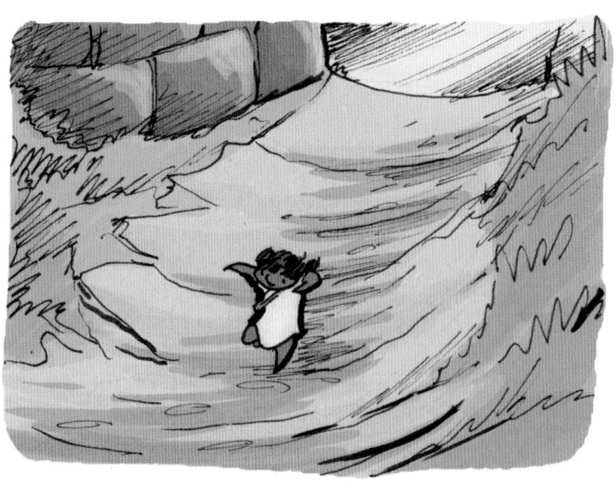

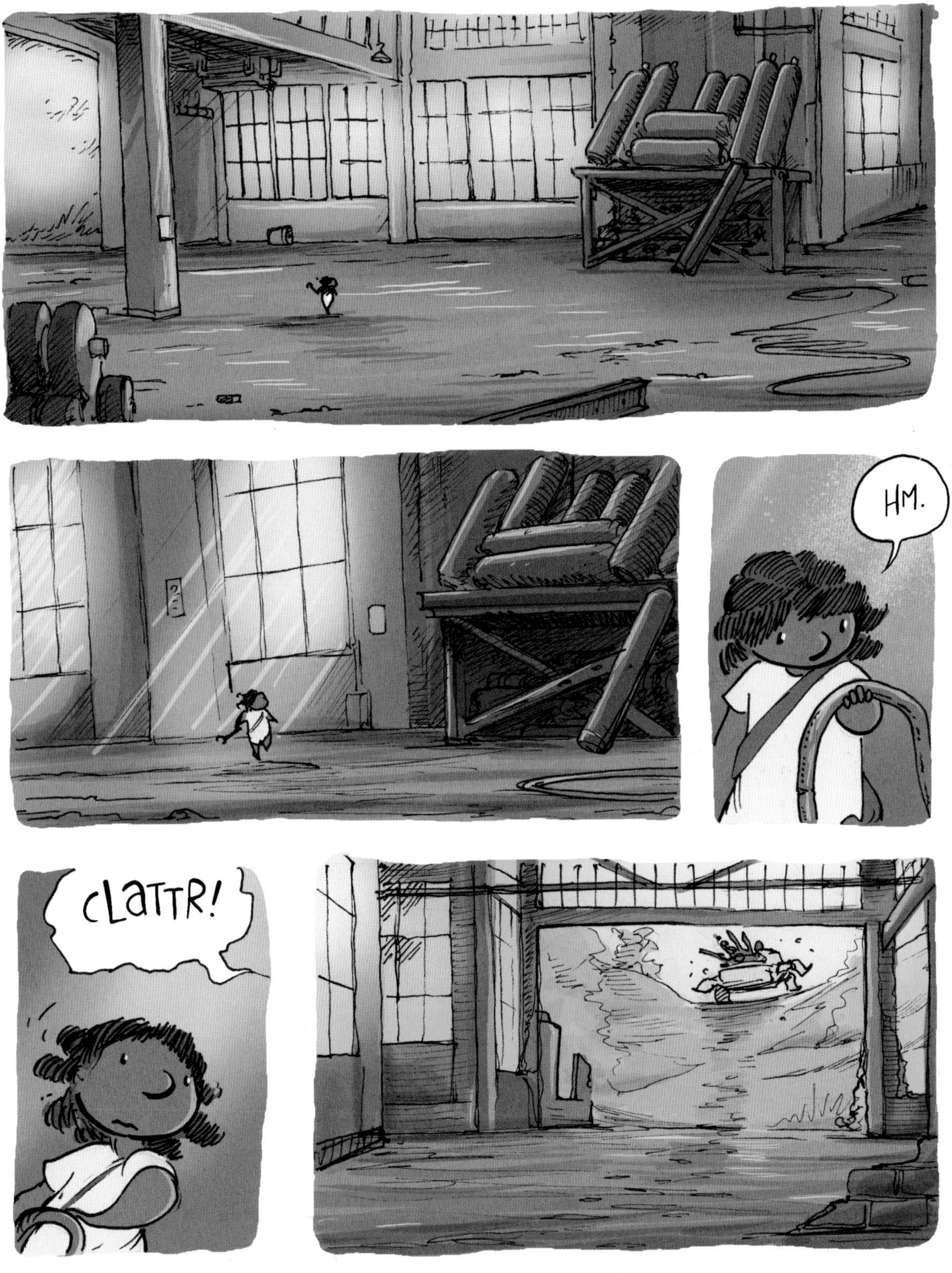
HM.
CLATTR!

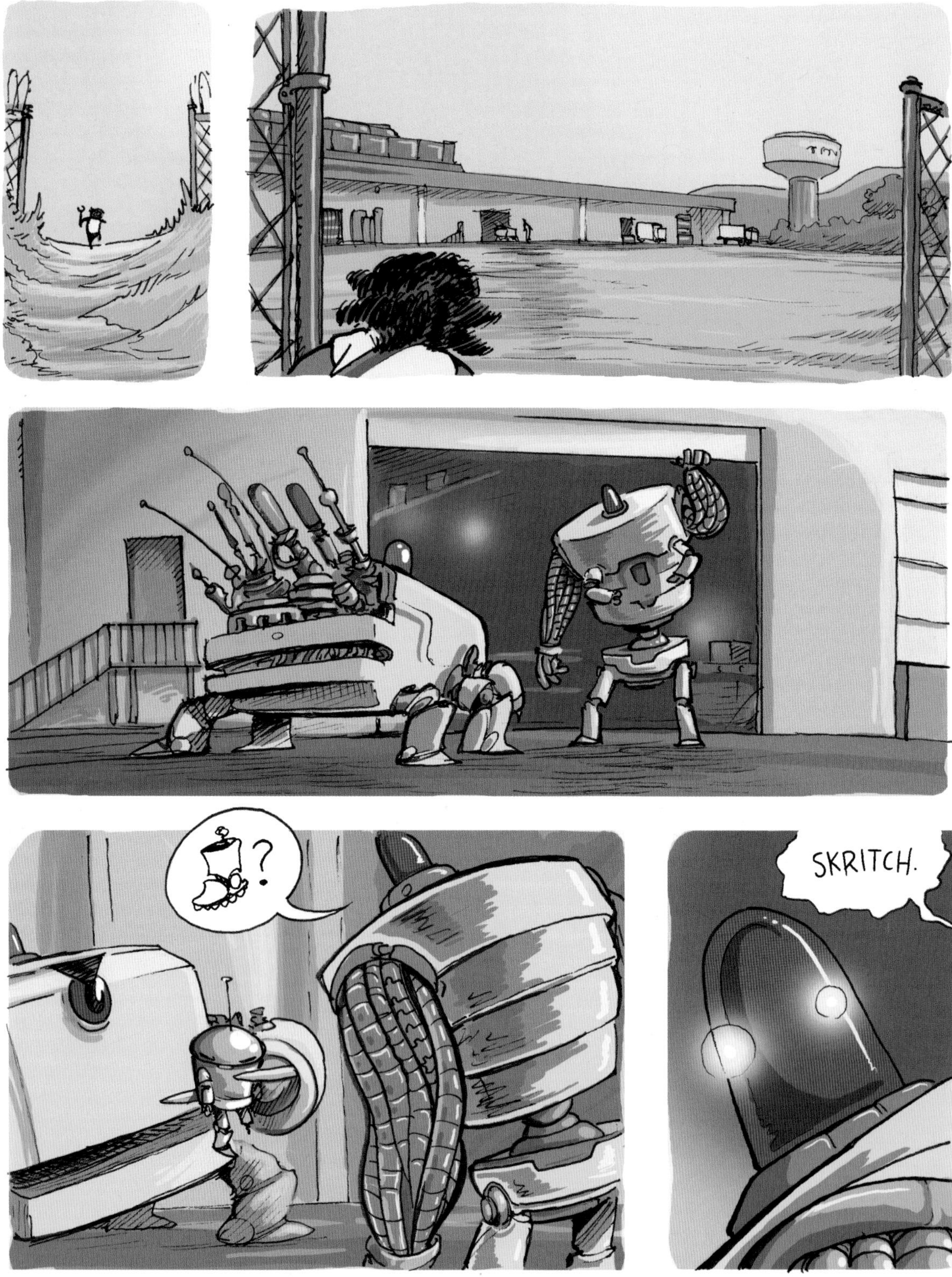
SKRITCH.

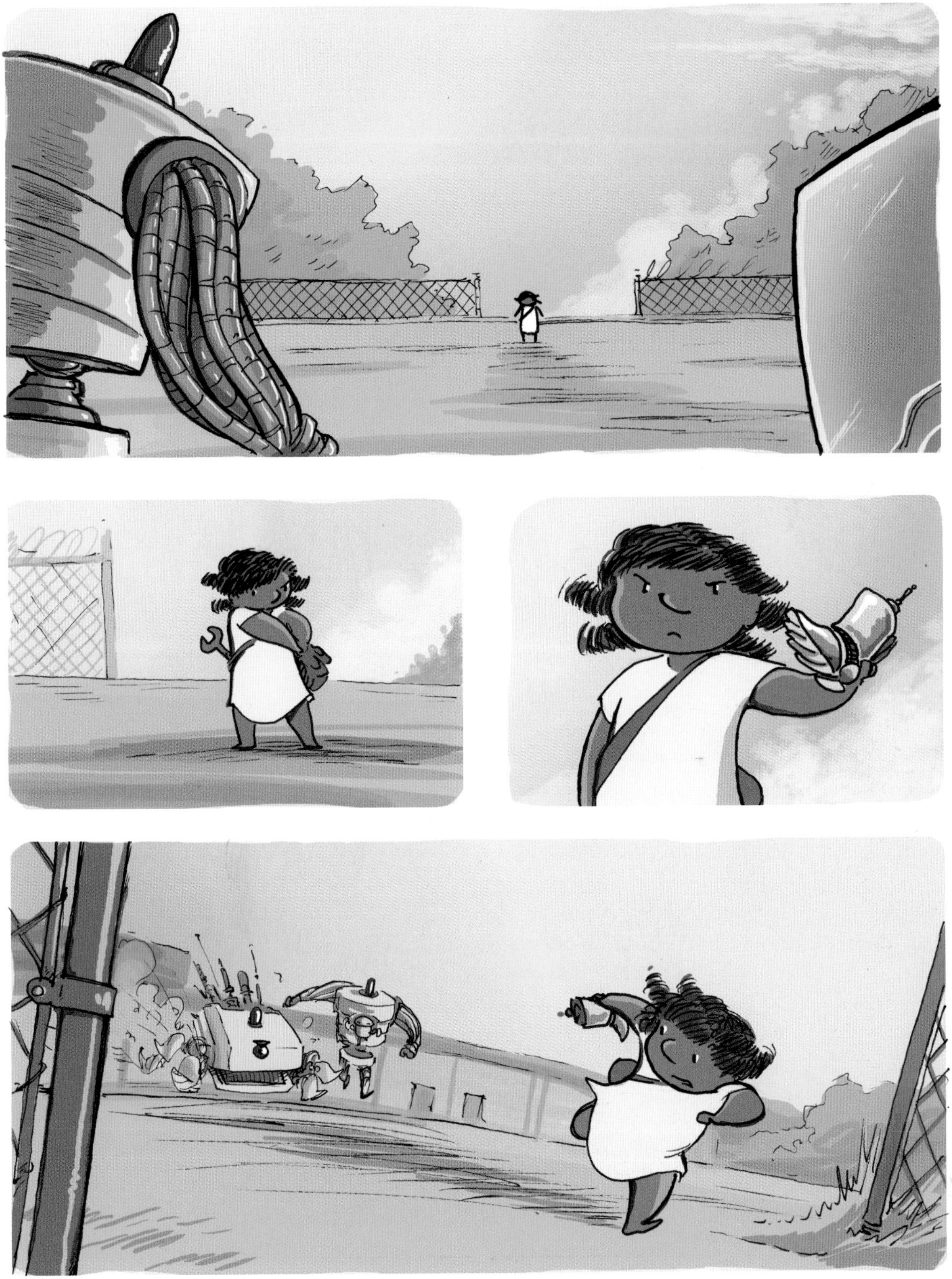

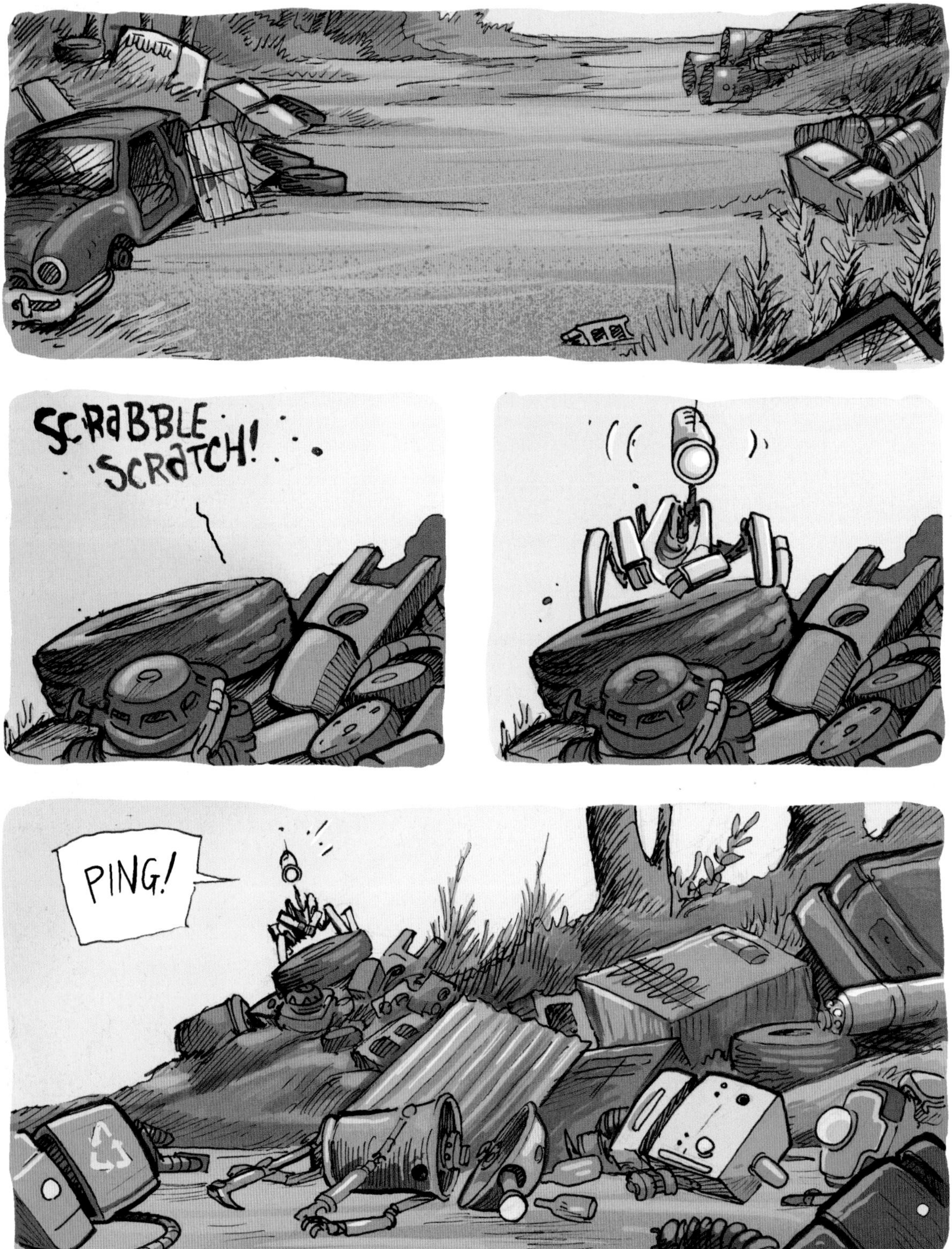

SCRABBLE
SCRATCH!
PING!

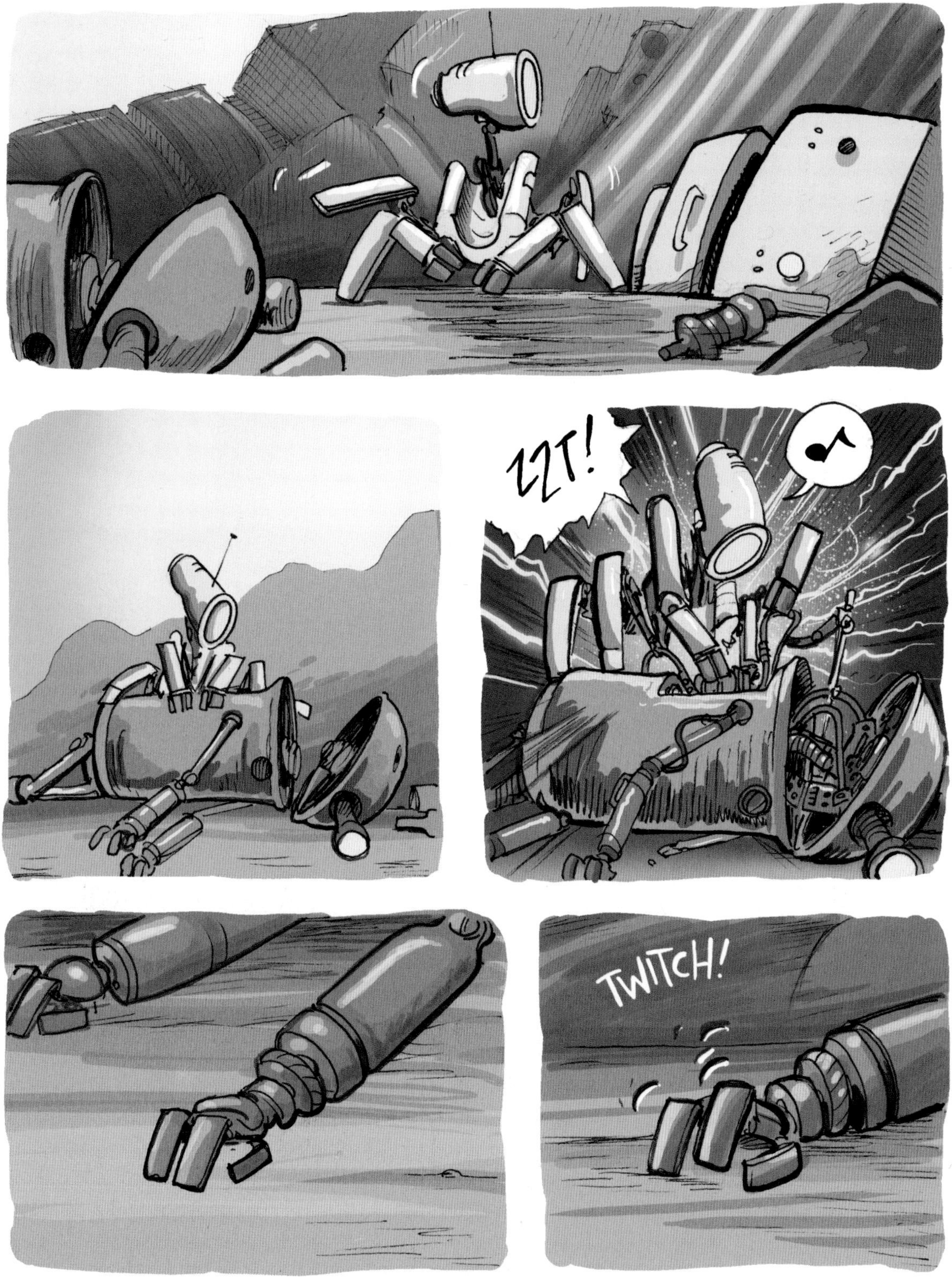
ZZT!
♪
TWITCH!

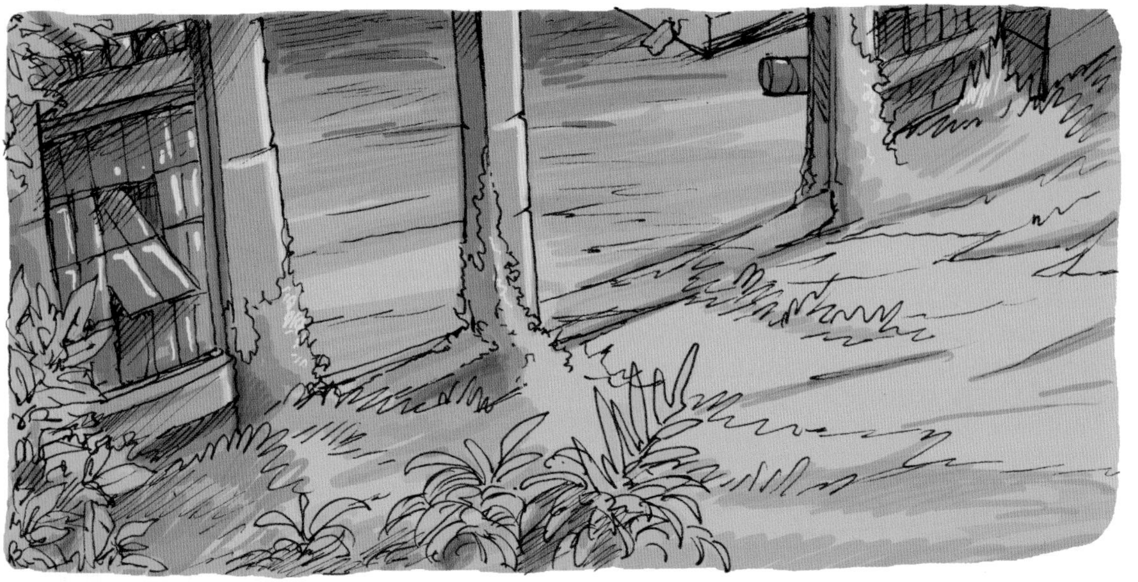

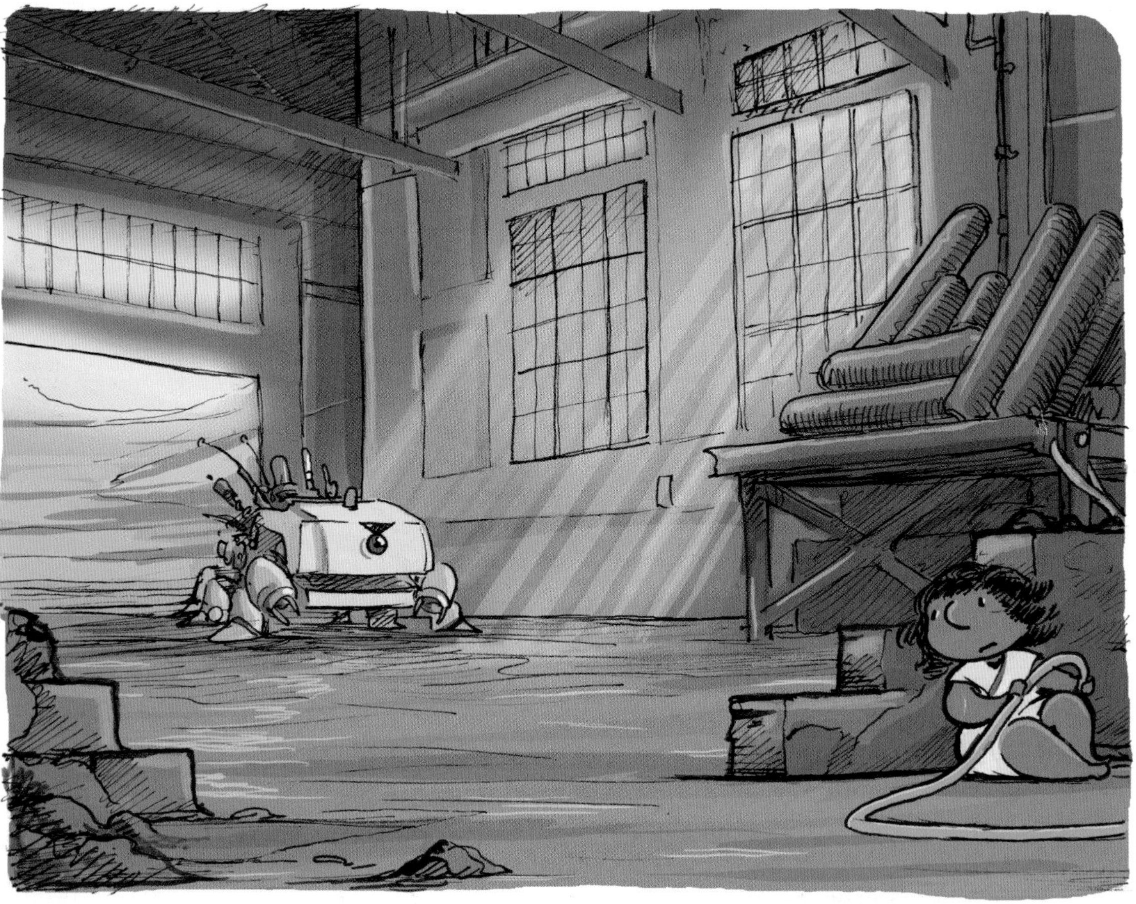

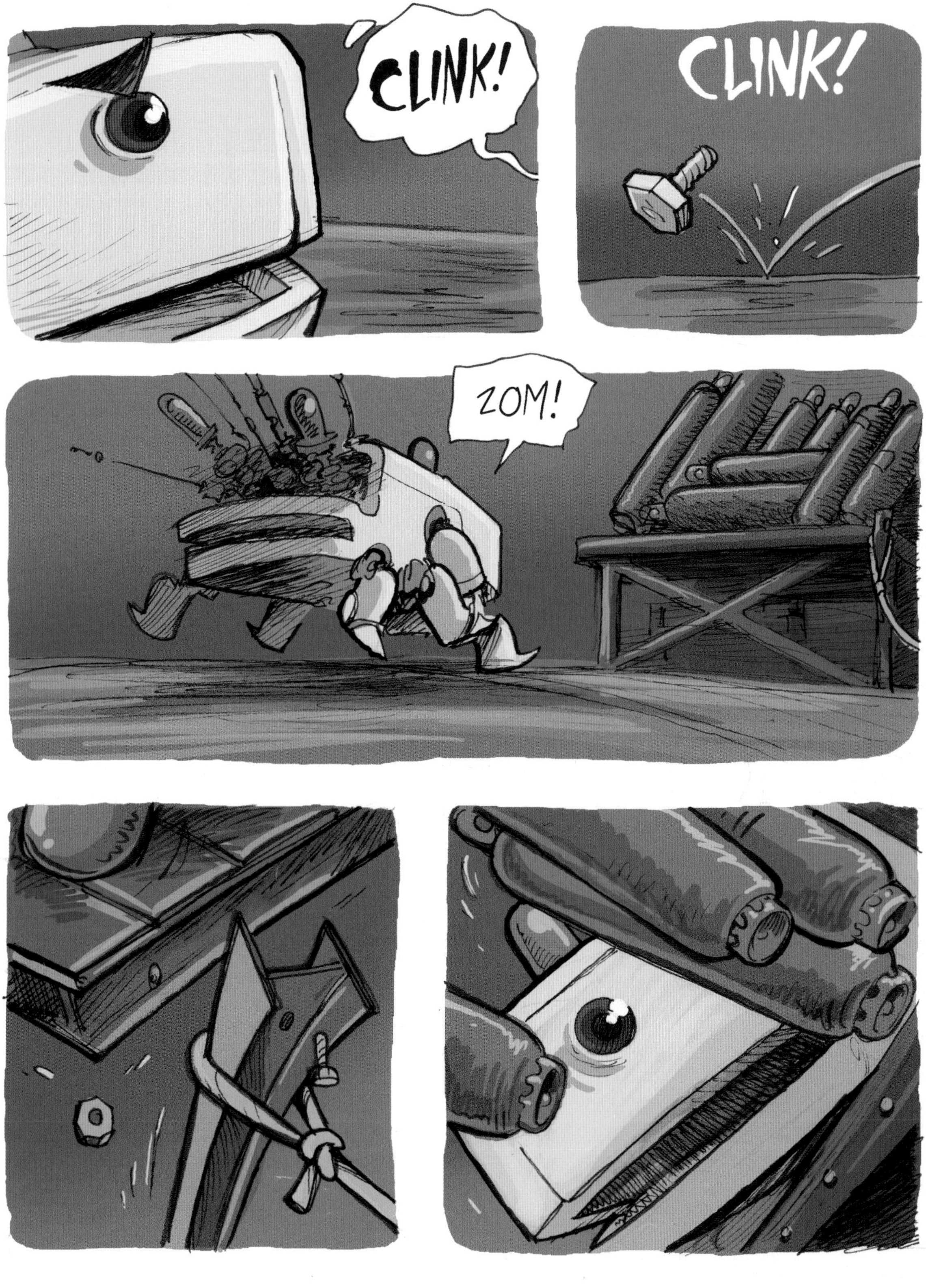
CLINK!
CLINK!
ZOM!

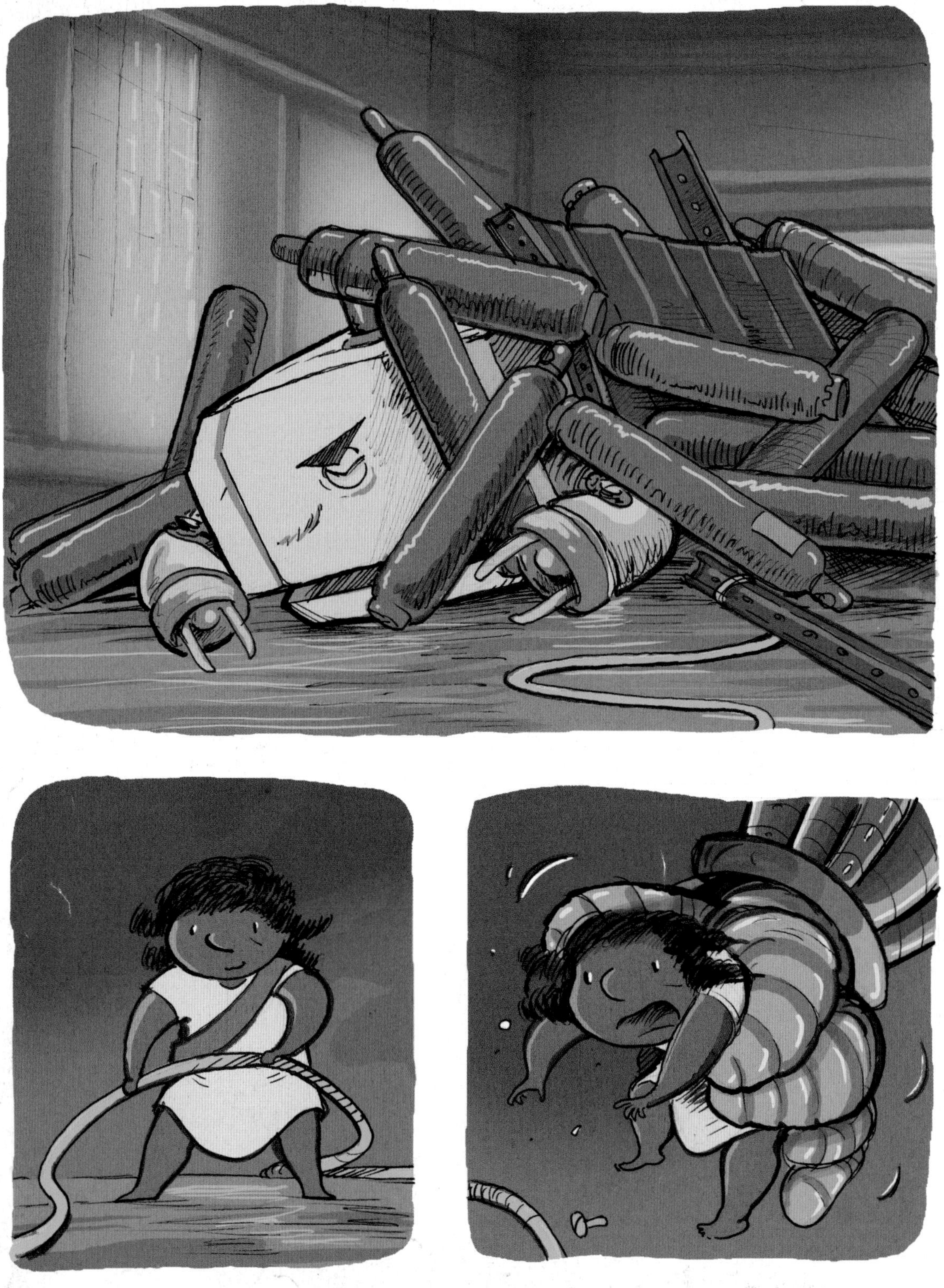

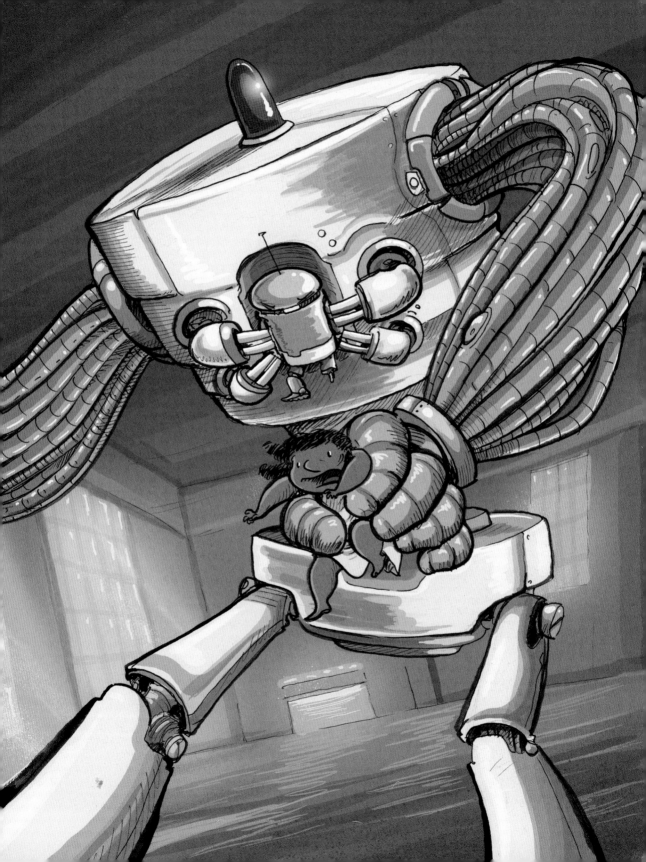

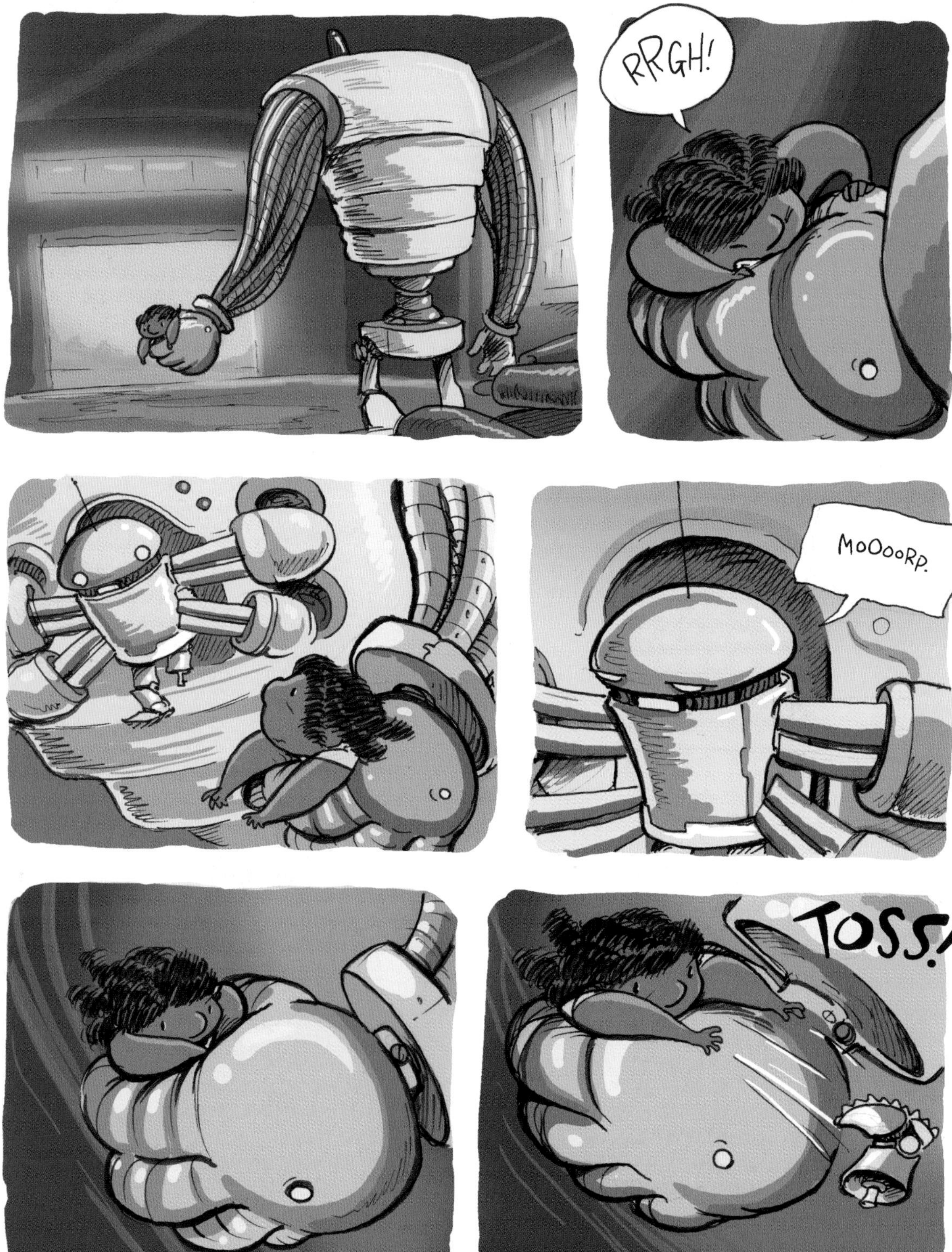
RRGH!
MoOooRP.
TOSS!

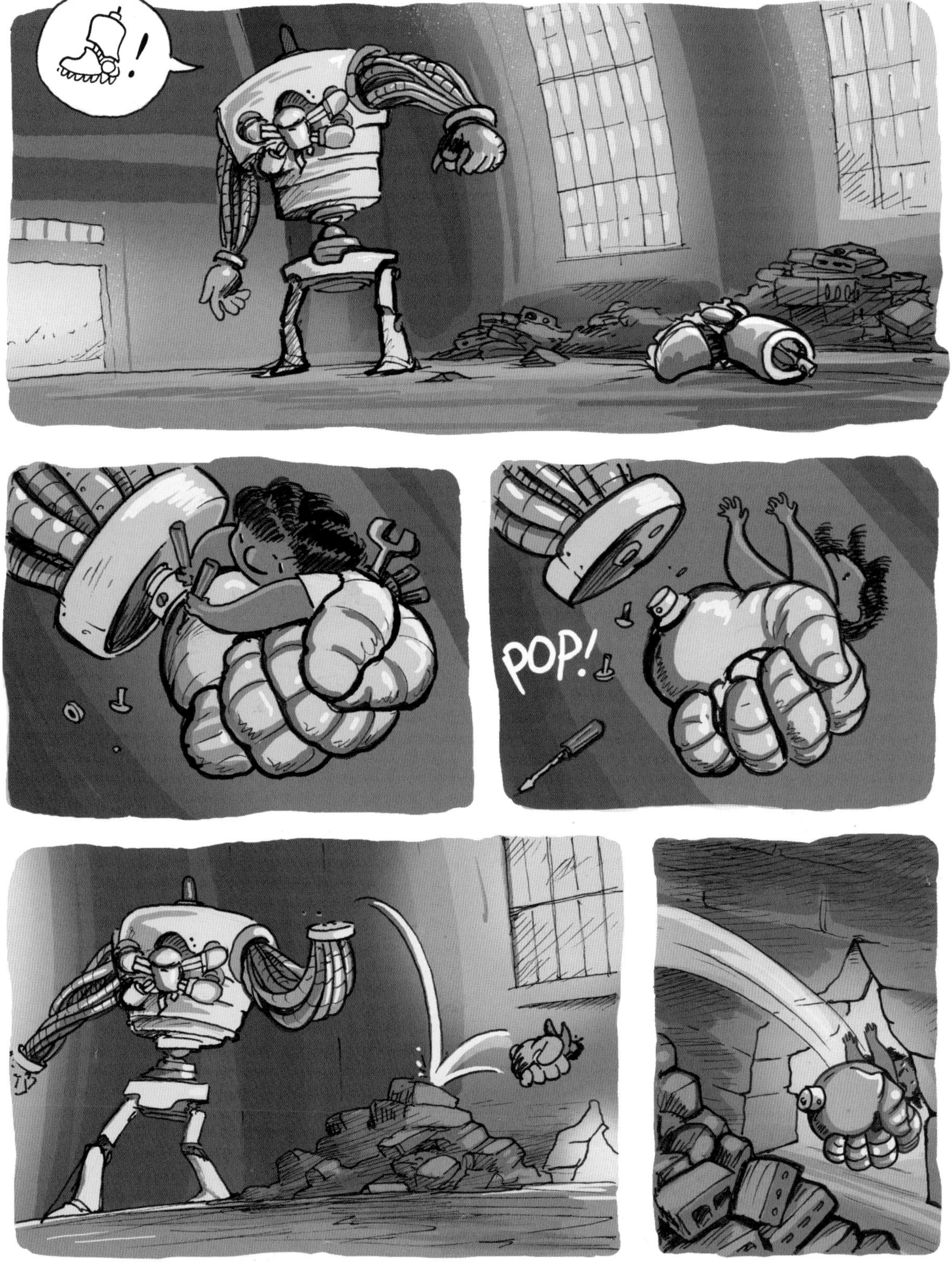
!
POP!

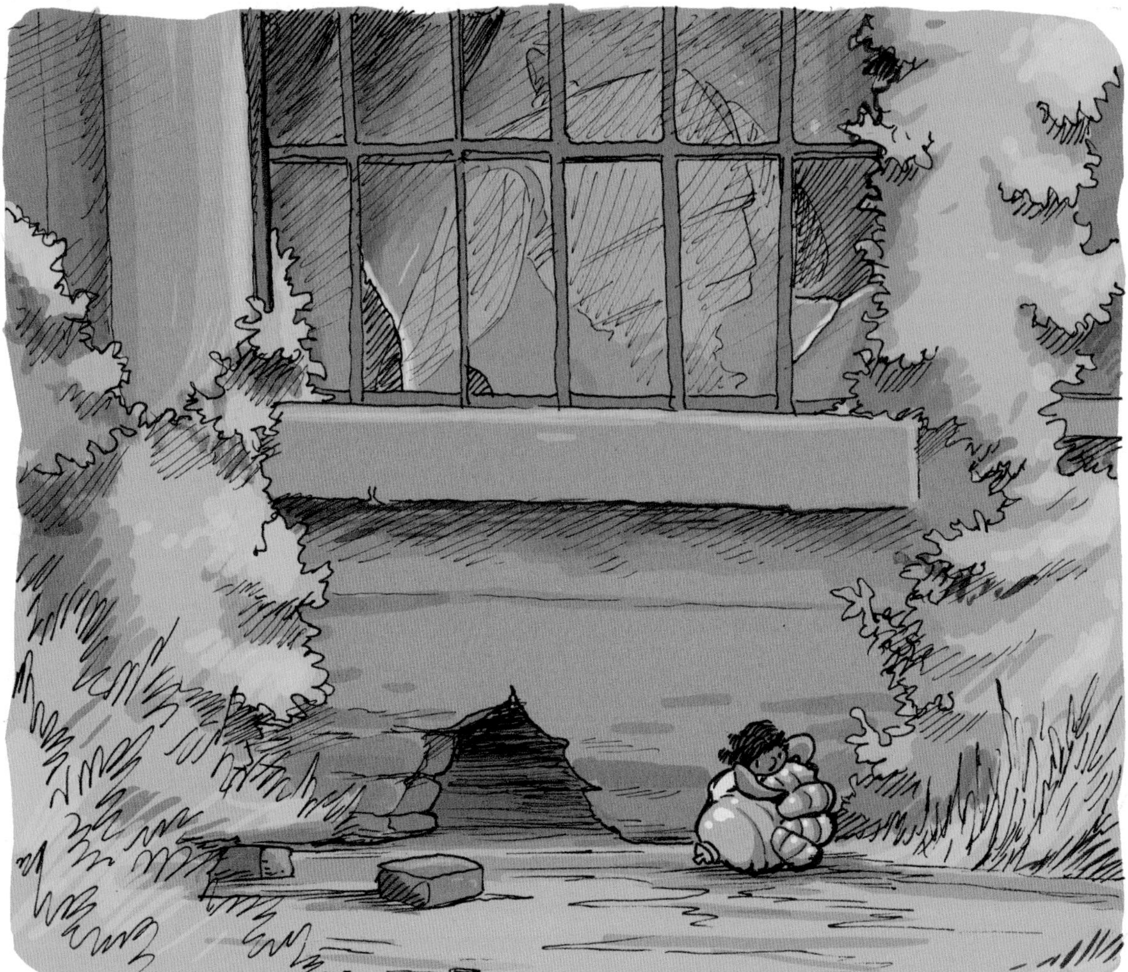

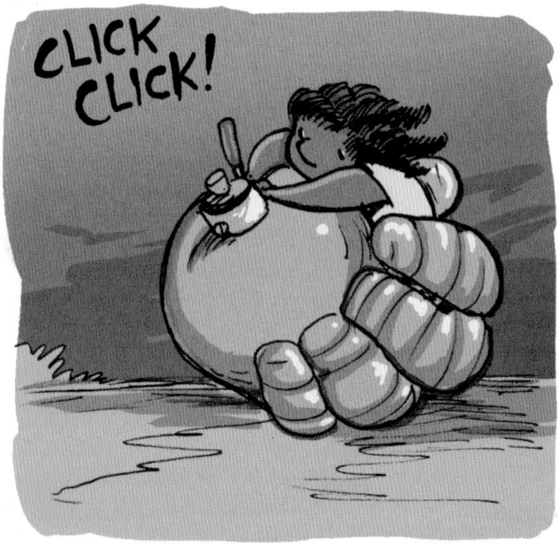
CLICK
CLICK!

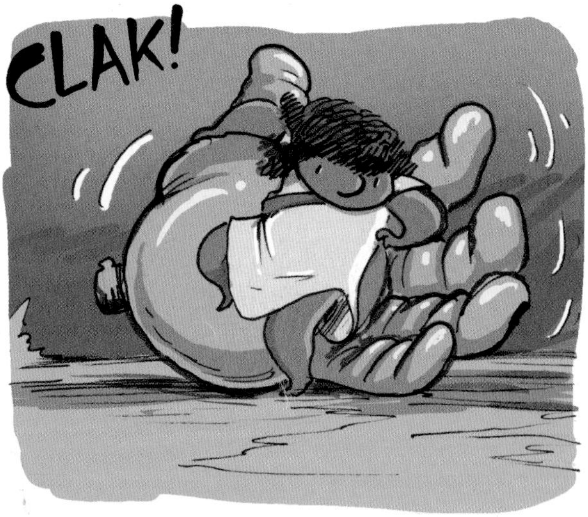
CLAK!

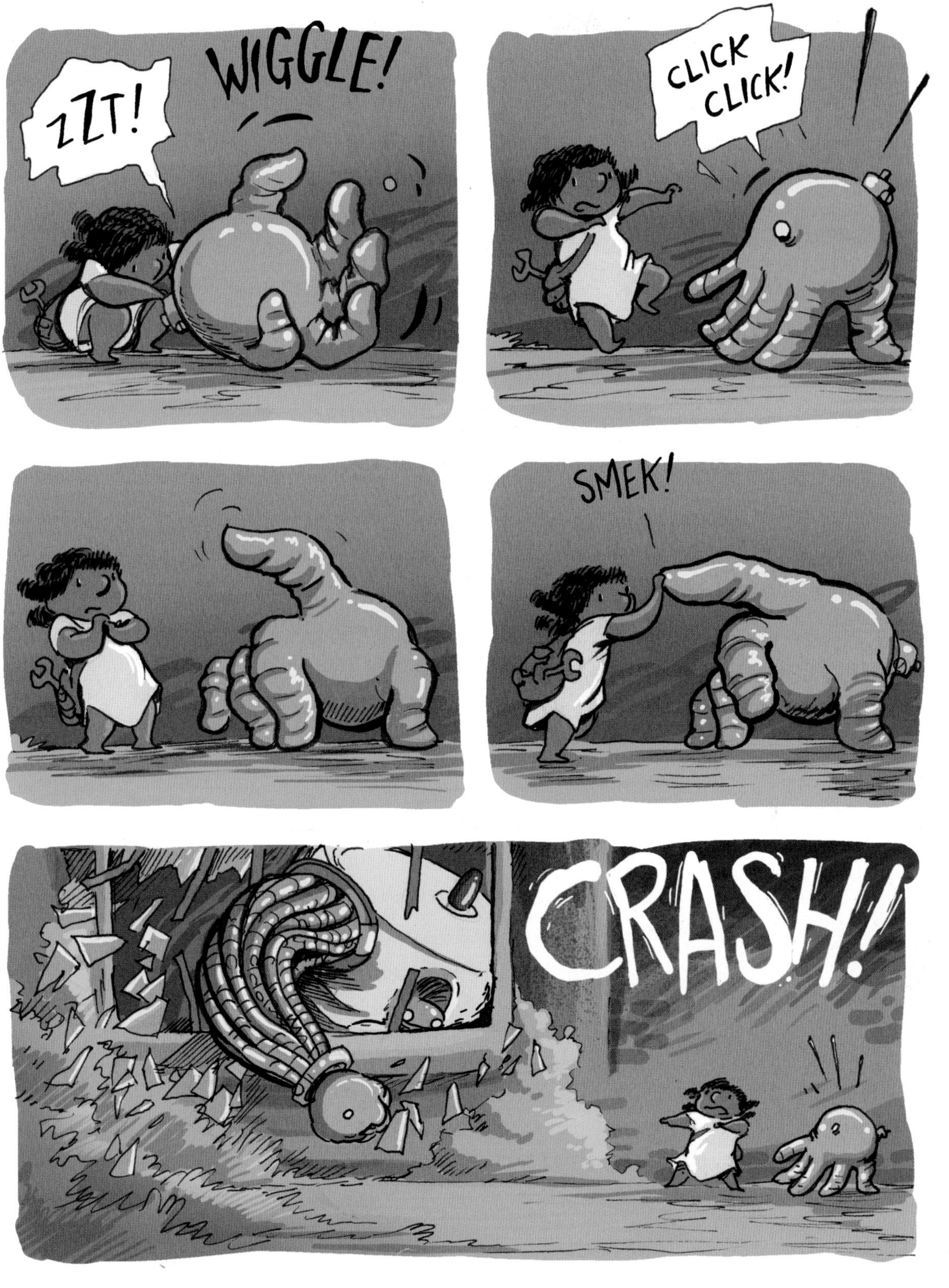
ZZT!
WIGGLE!
CLICK CLICK!
SMEK!
CRASH!

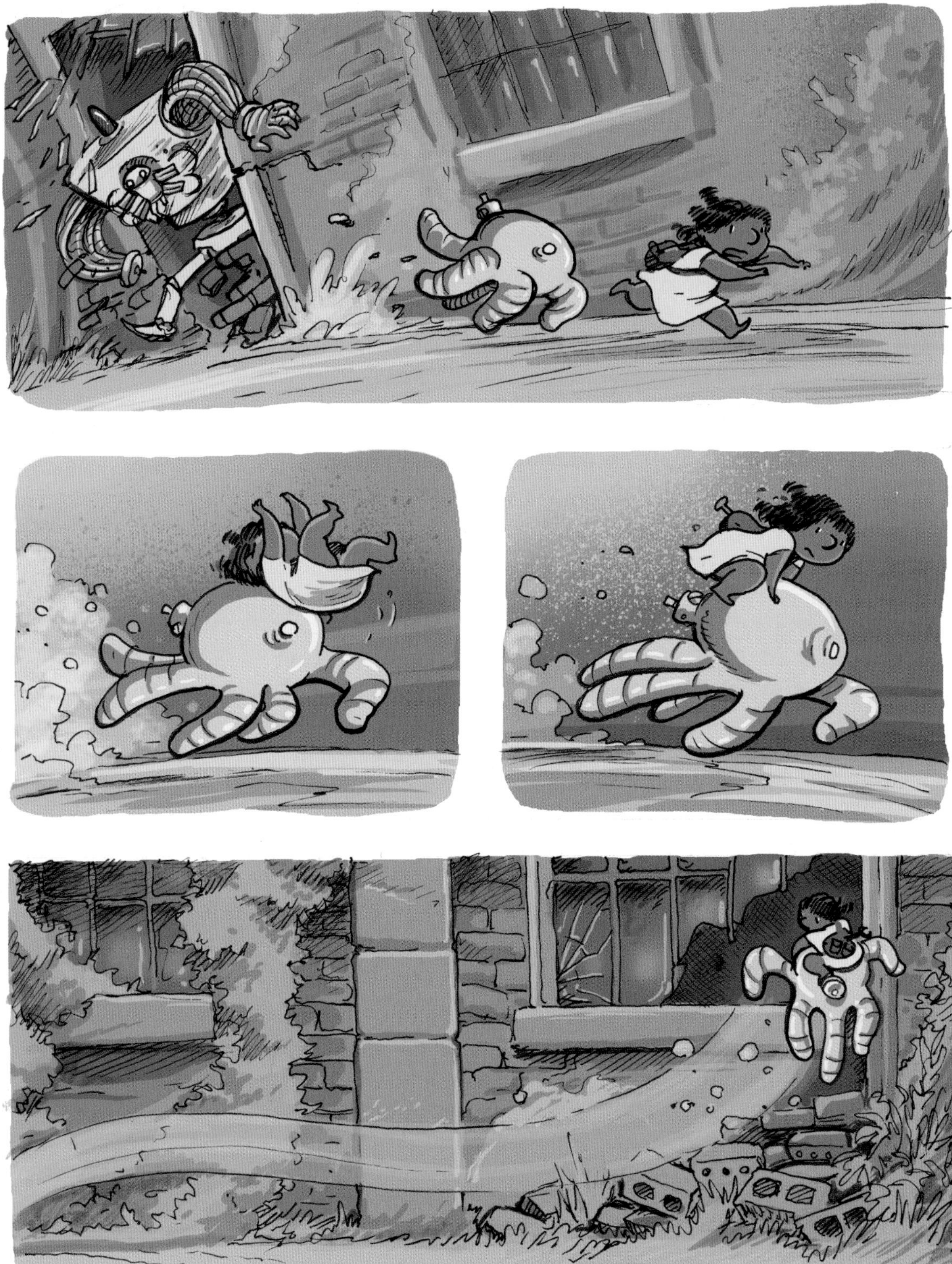

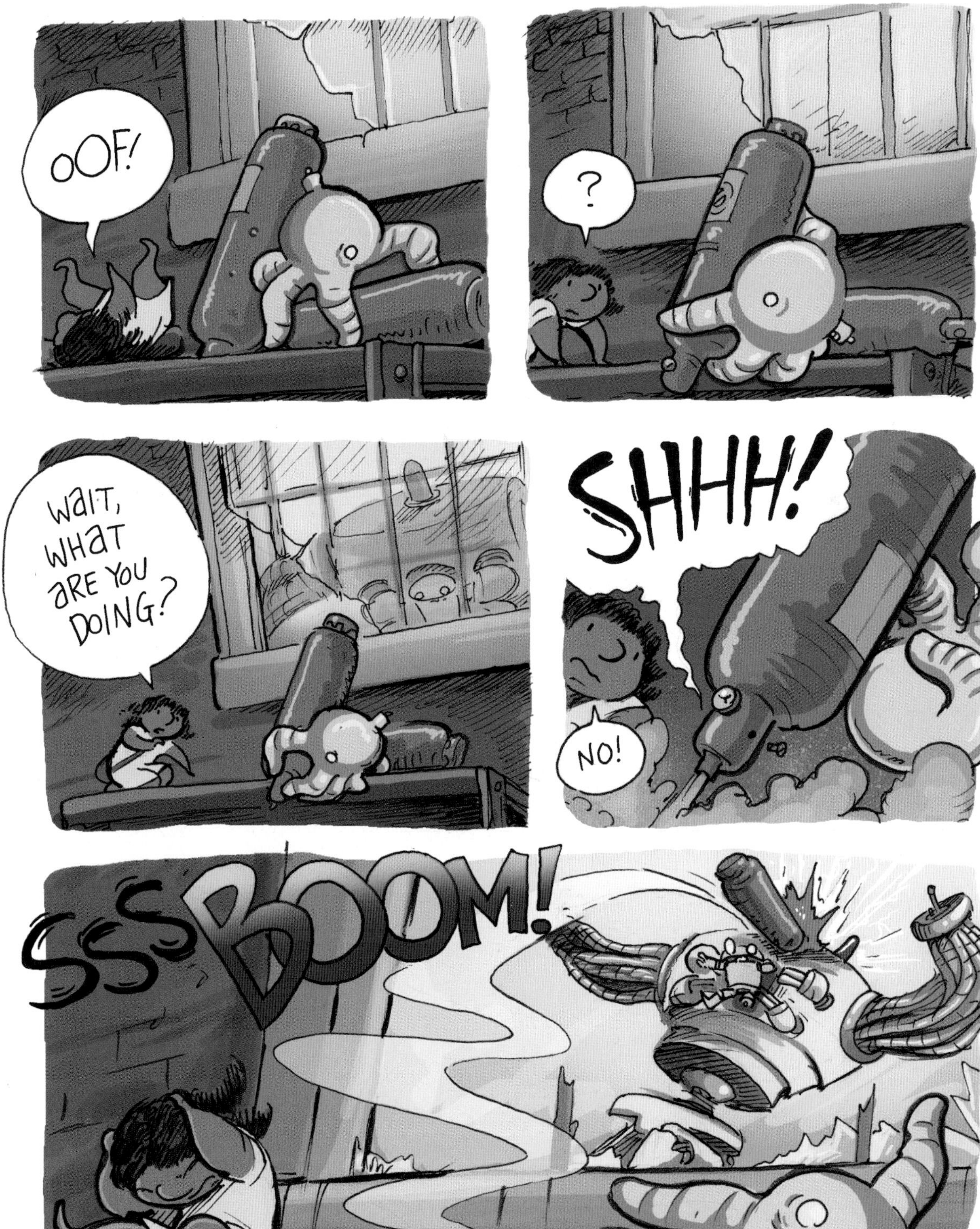
OOF!
?
WAIT, WHAT ARE YOU DOING?
SHHH!
NO!
SSSBOOM!

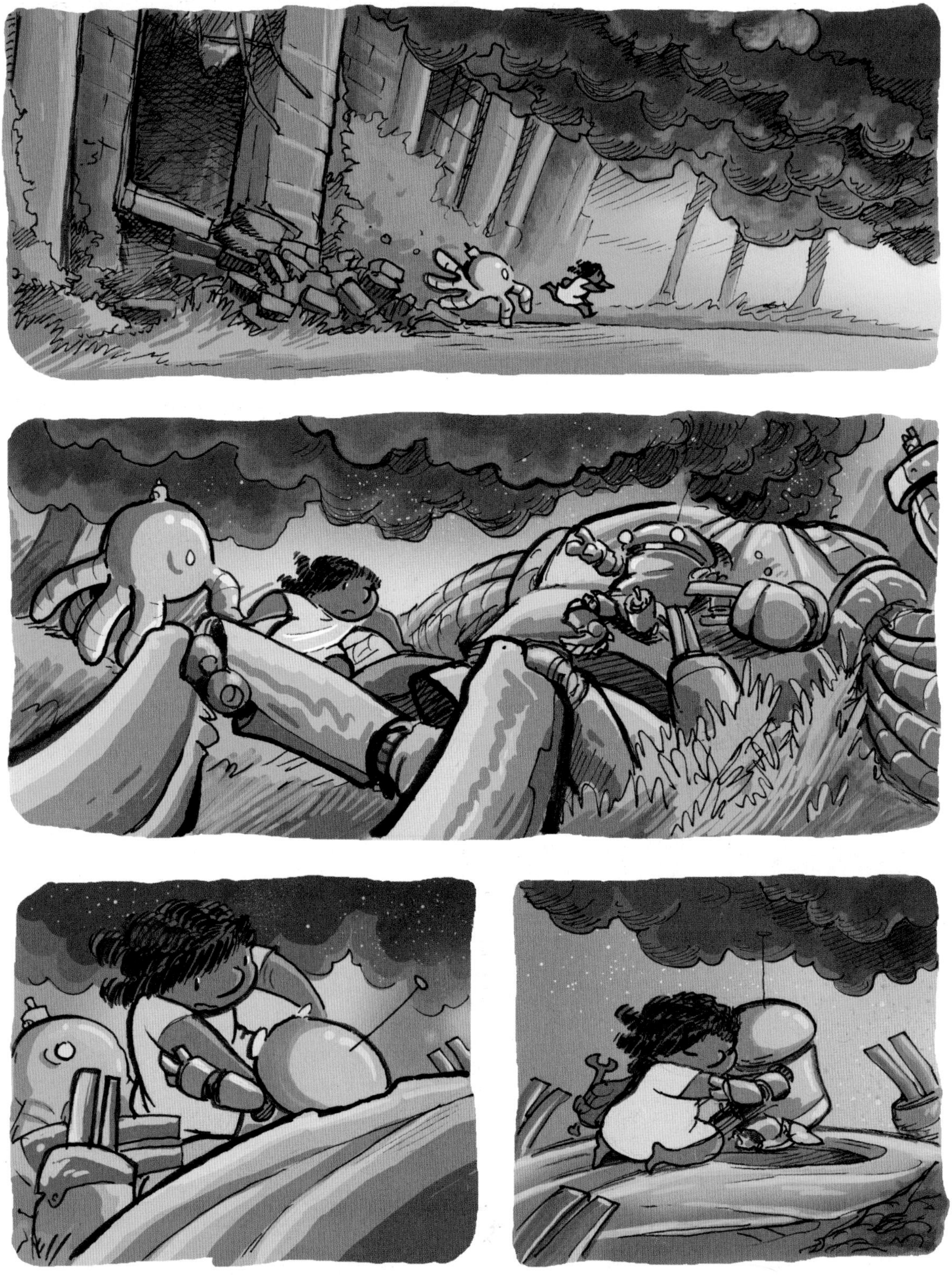

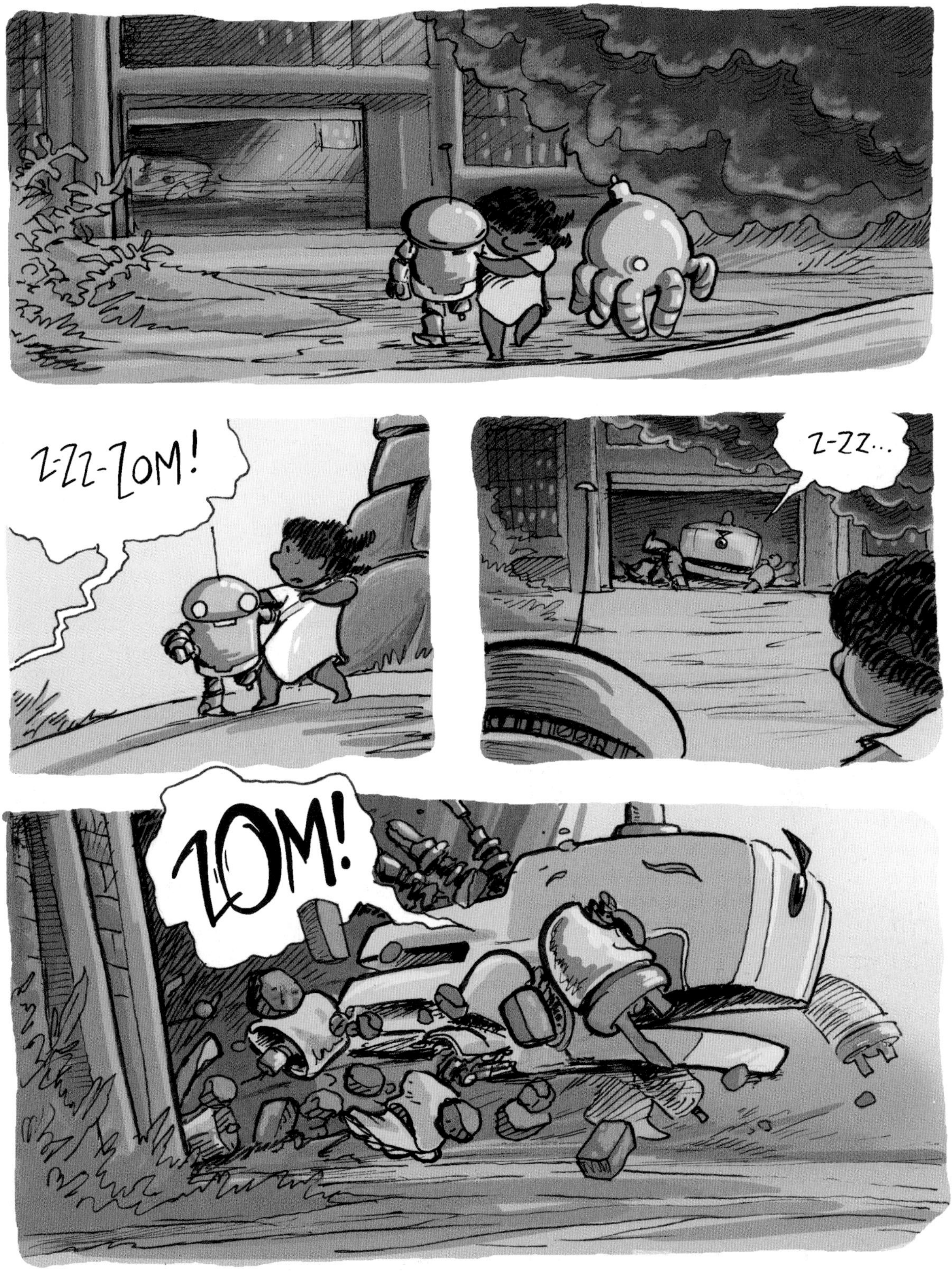
Z-ZZ-ZOM!
Z-ZZ...
ZOM!

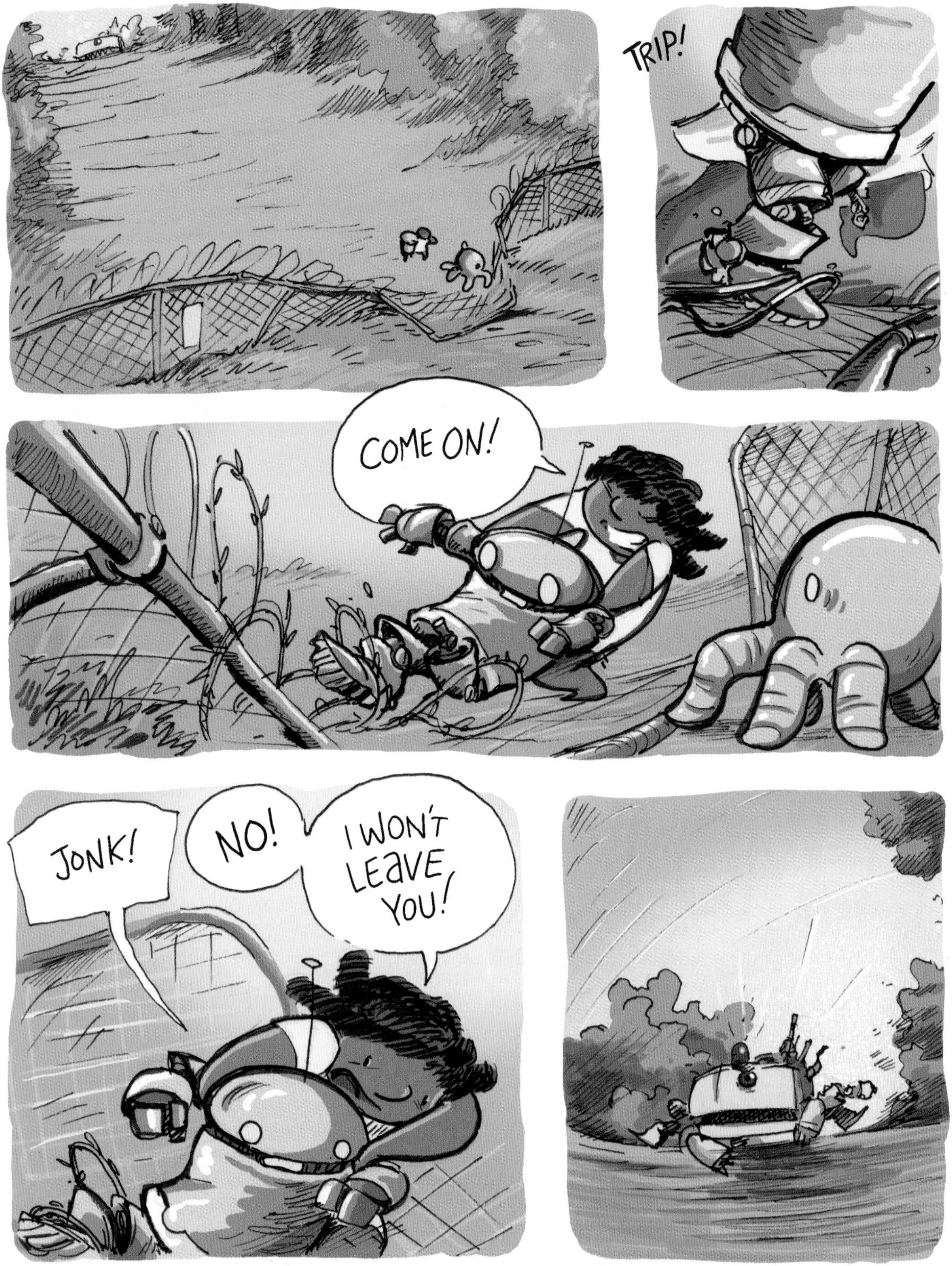
TRIP!
COME ON!
JONK!
NO!
I WON'T LEAVE YOU!

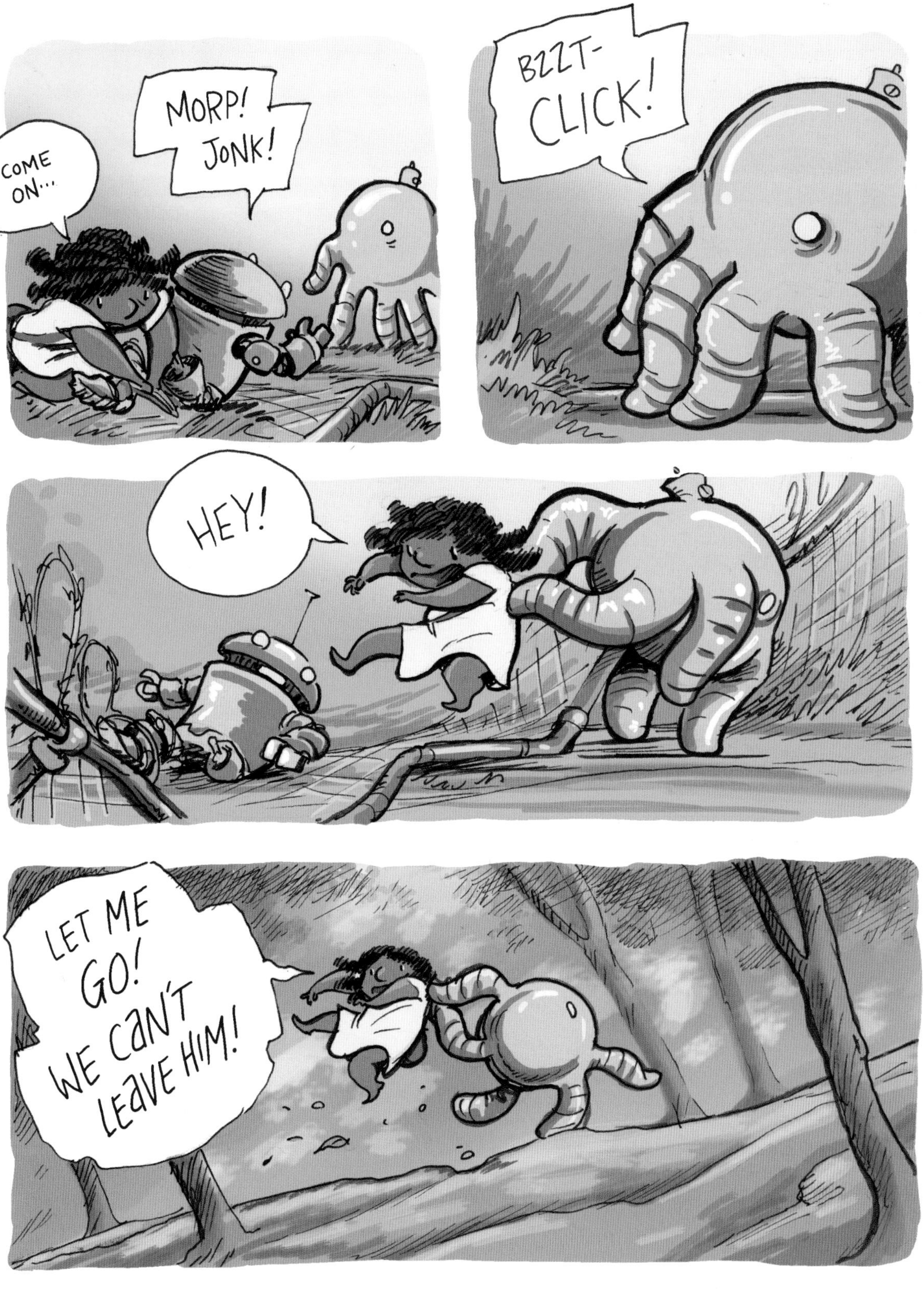
COME ON...
MORP! JONK!
BZZT-CLICK!
HEY!
LET ME GO! WE CAN'T LEAVE HIM!

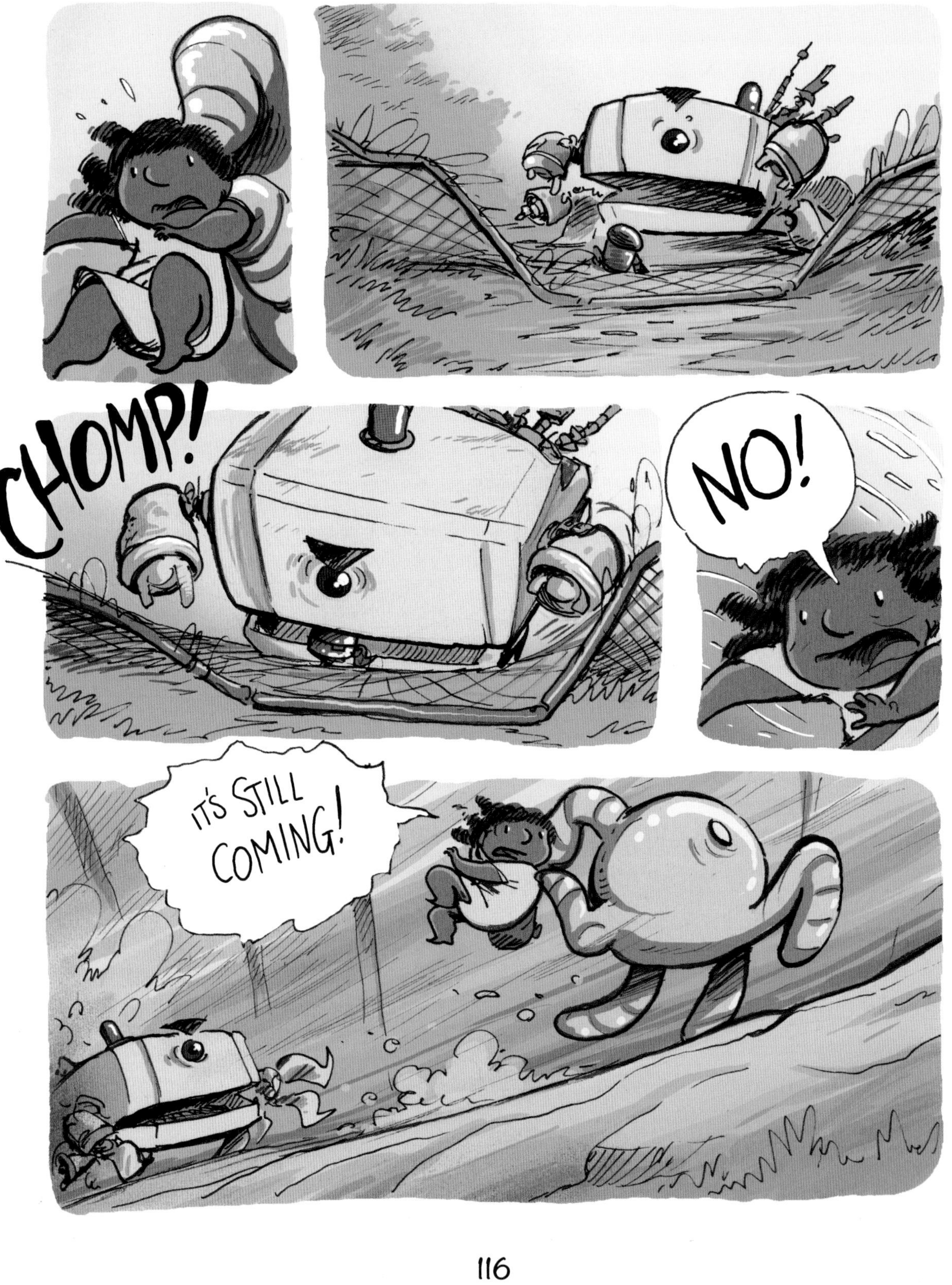
CHOMP!
NO!
IT'S STILL COMING!

CHAPTER SEVEN

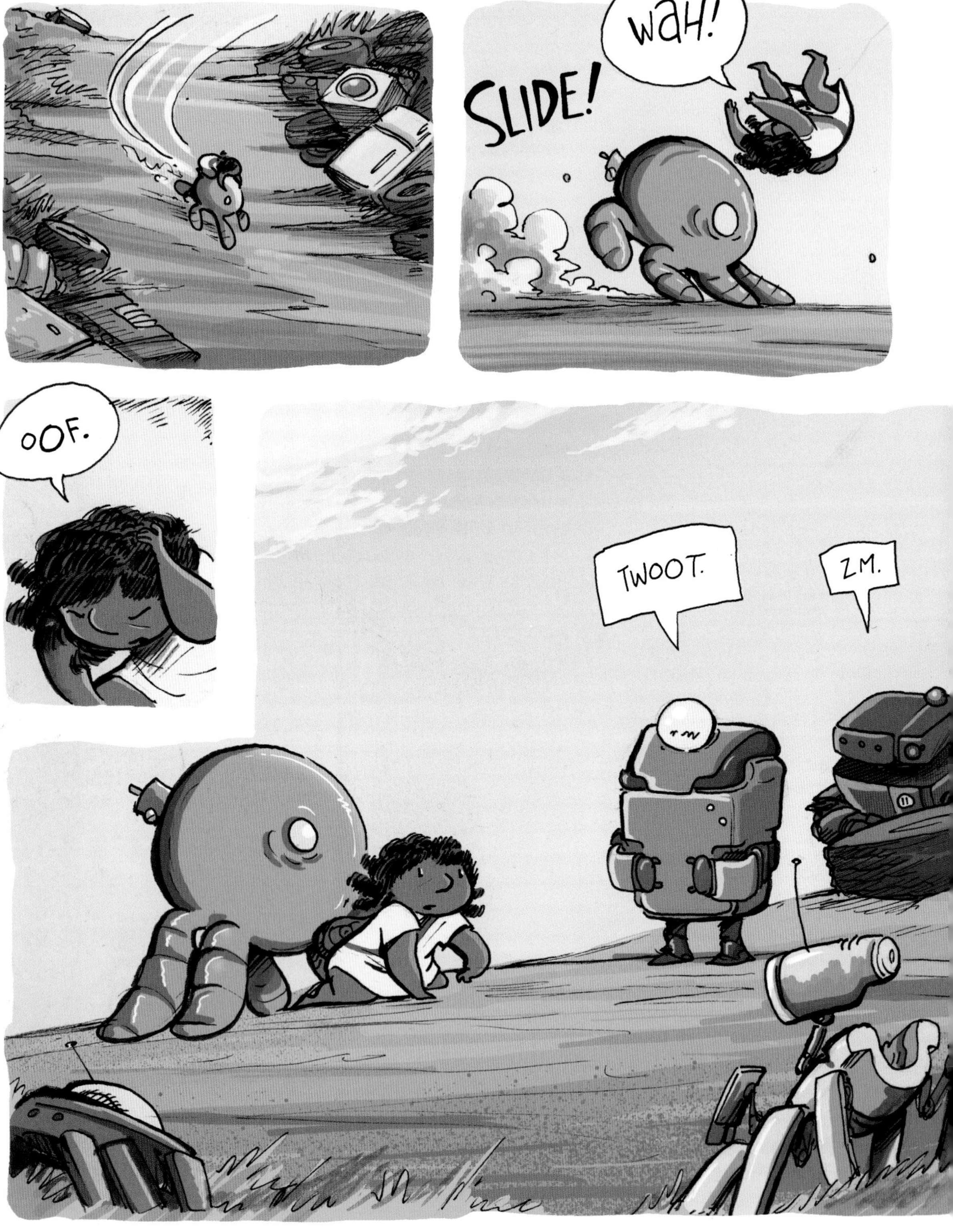
SLIDE!
WAH!
OOF.
TWOOT.
ZM.

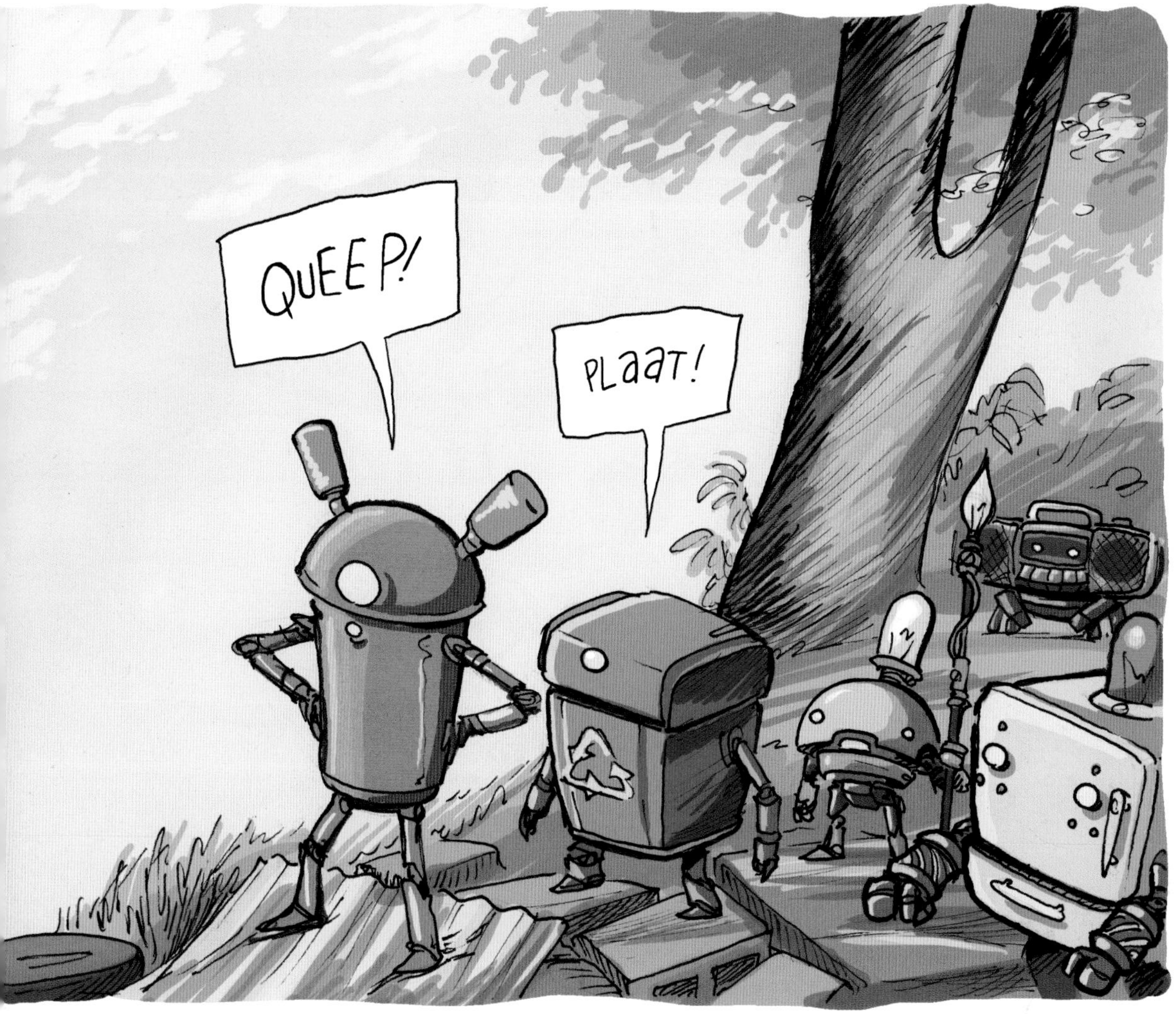
QUEEP!
PLAAT!

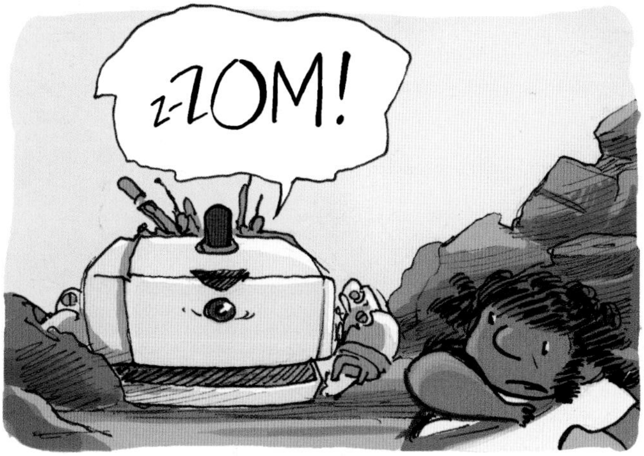
Z-ZOM!

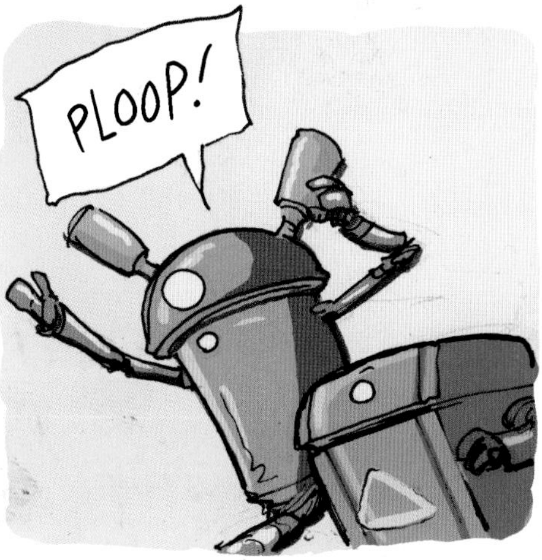
PLOOP!

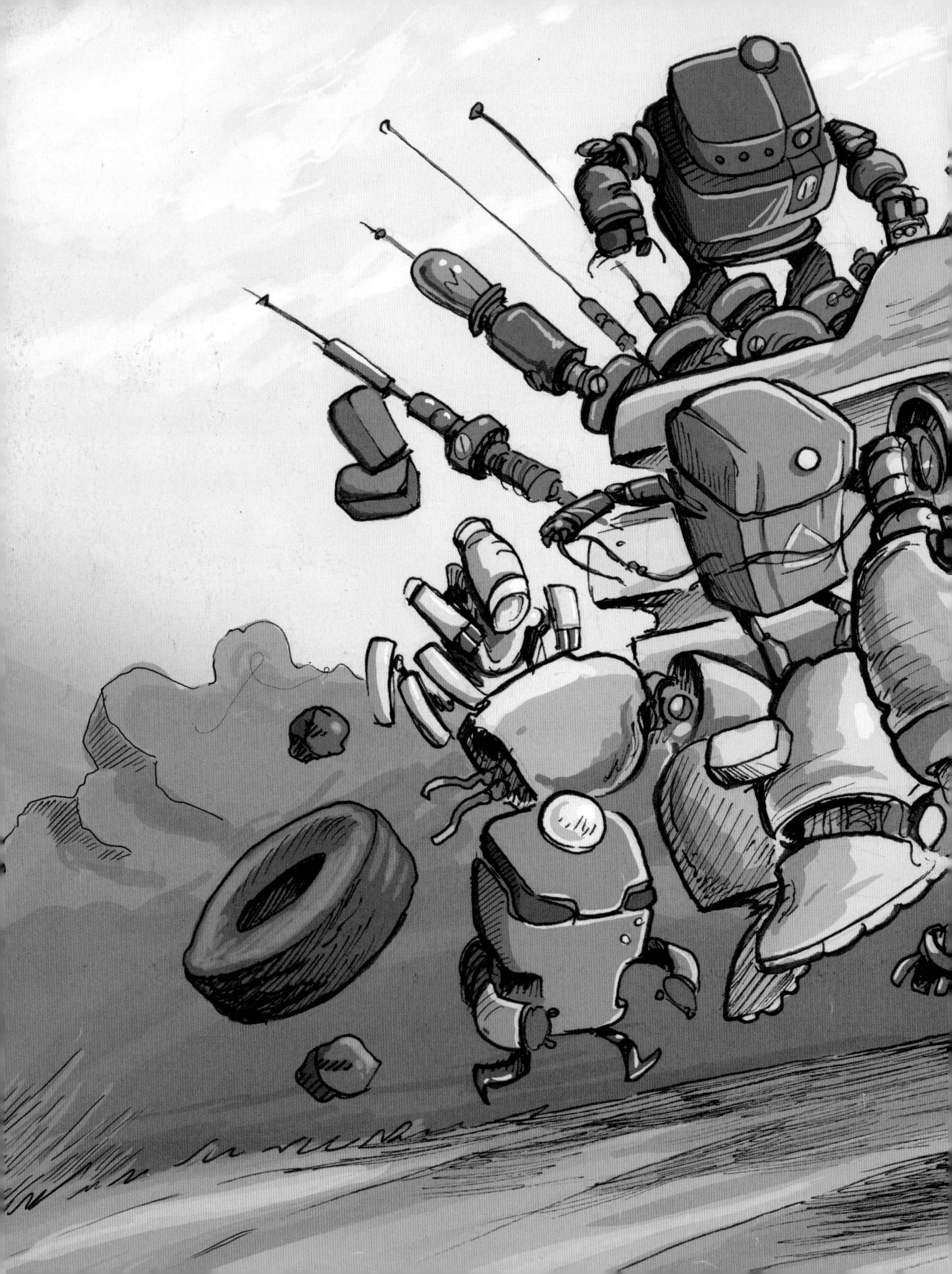

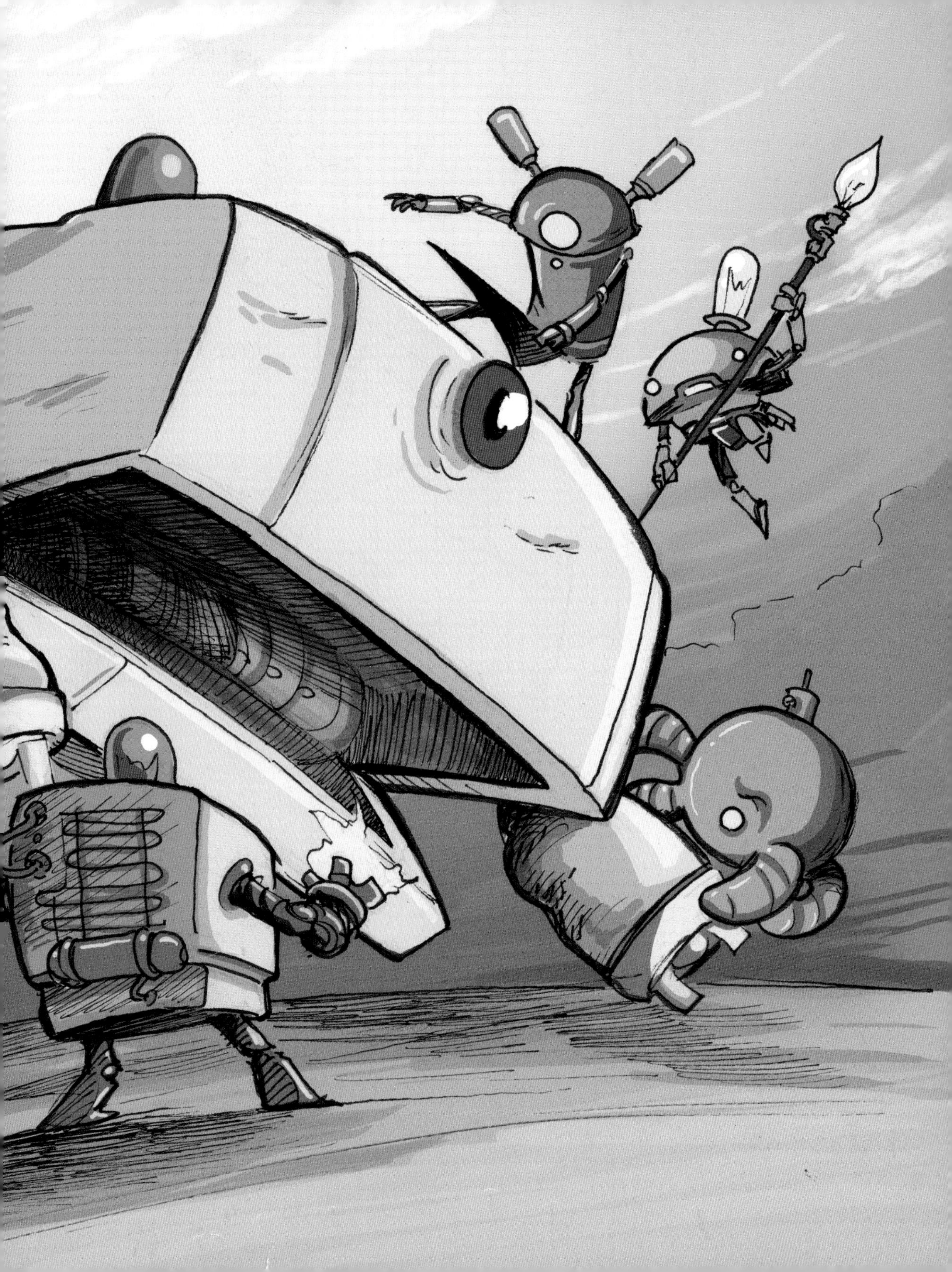

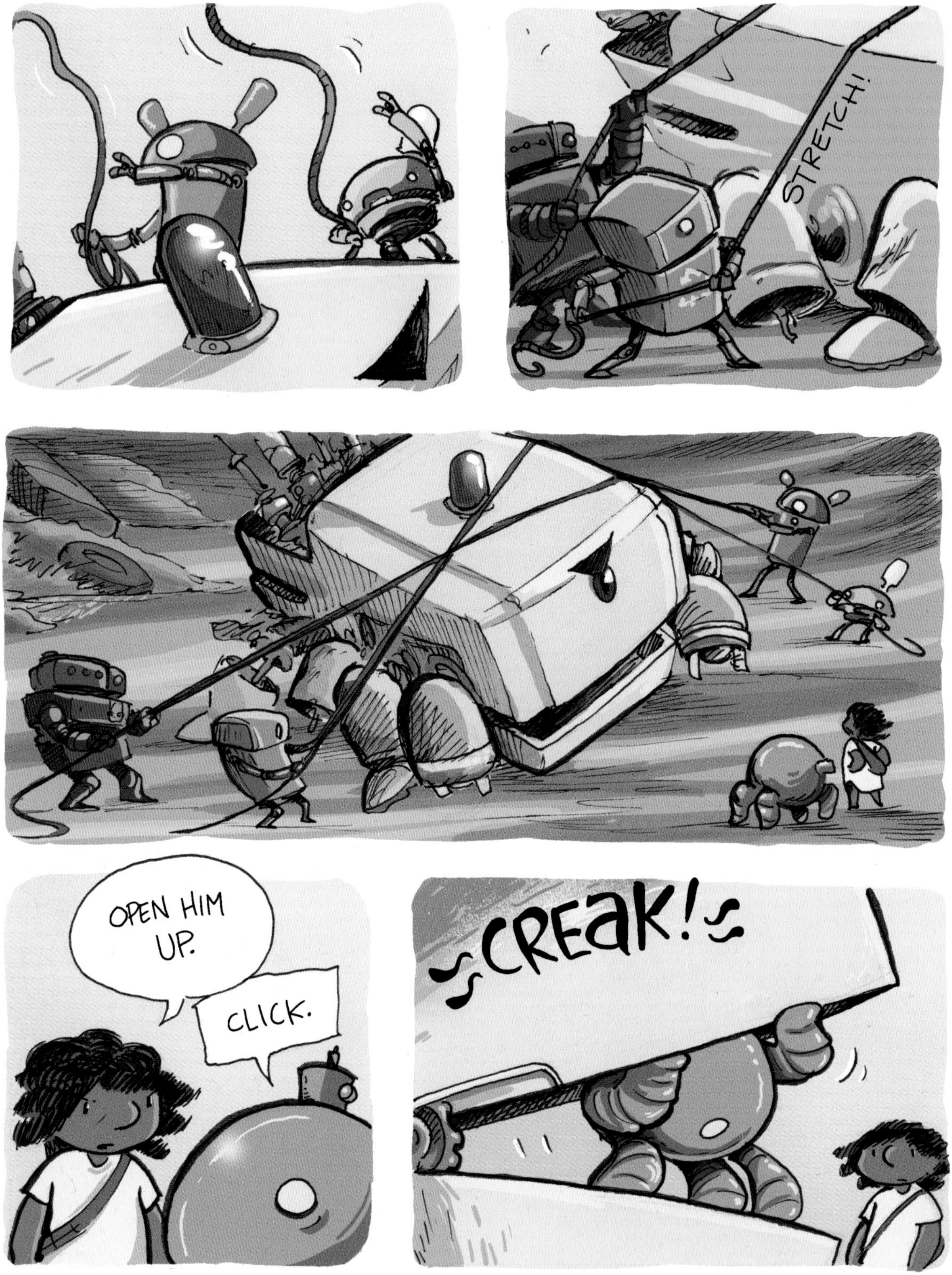
STRETCH!
OPEN HIM UP.
CLICK.
CREAK!

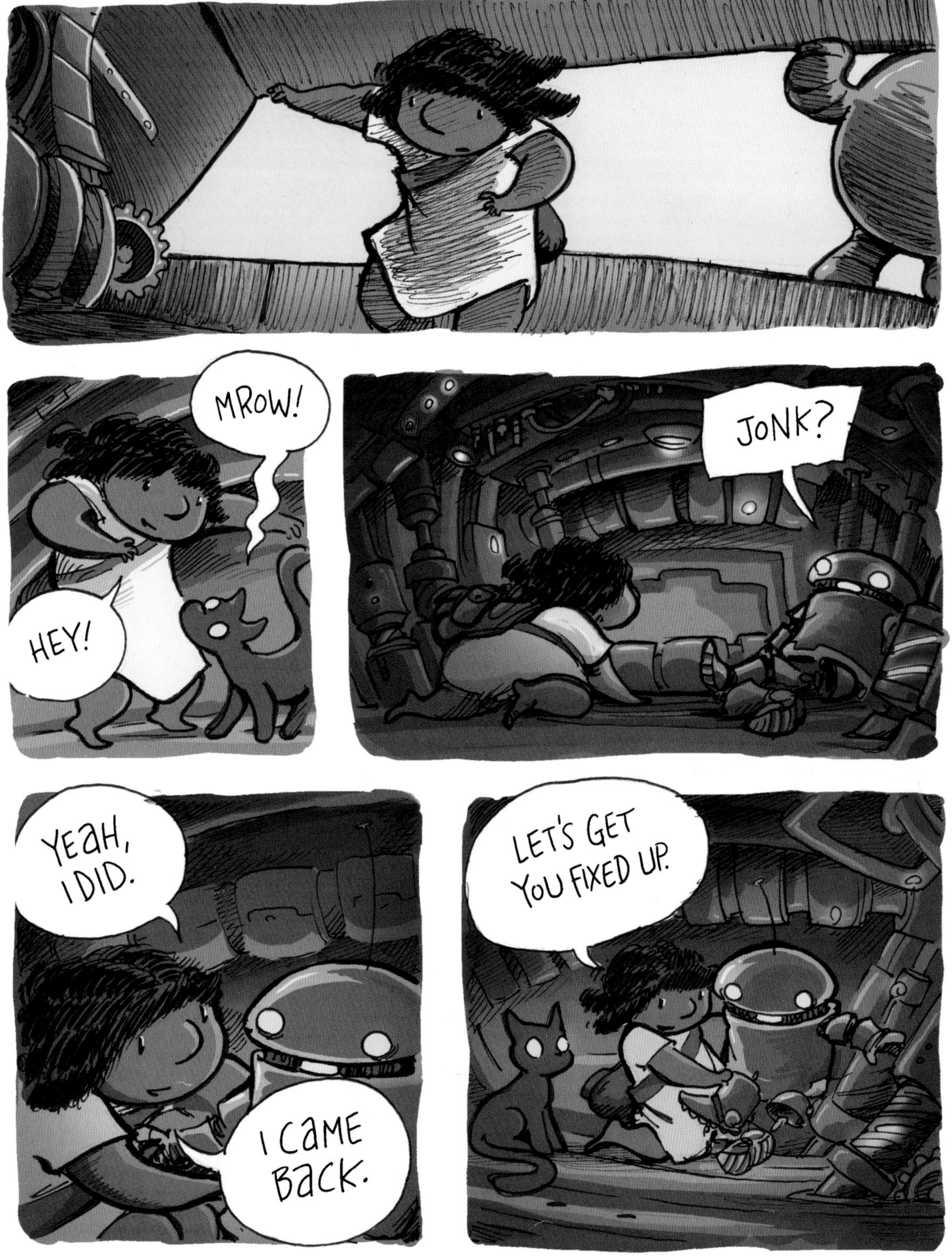
MROW!
HEY!
JONK?
YEAH, I DID.
I CAME BACK.
LET'S GET YOU FIXED UP.

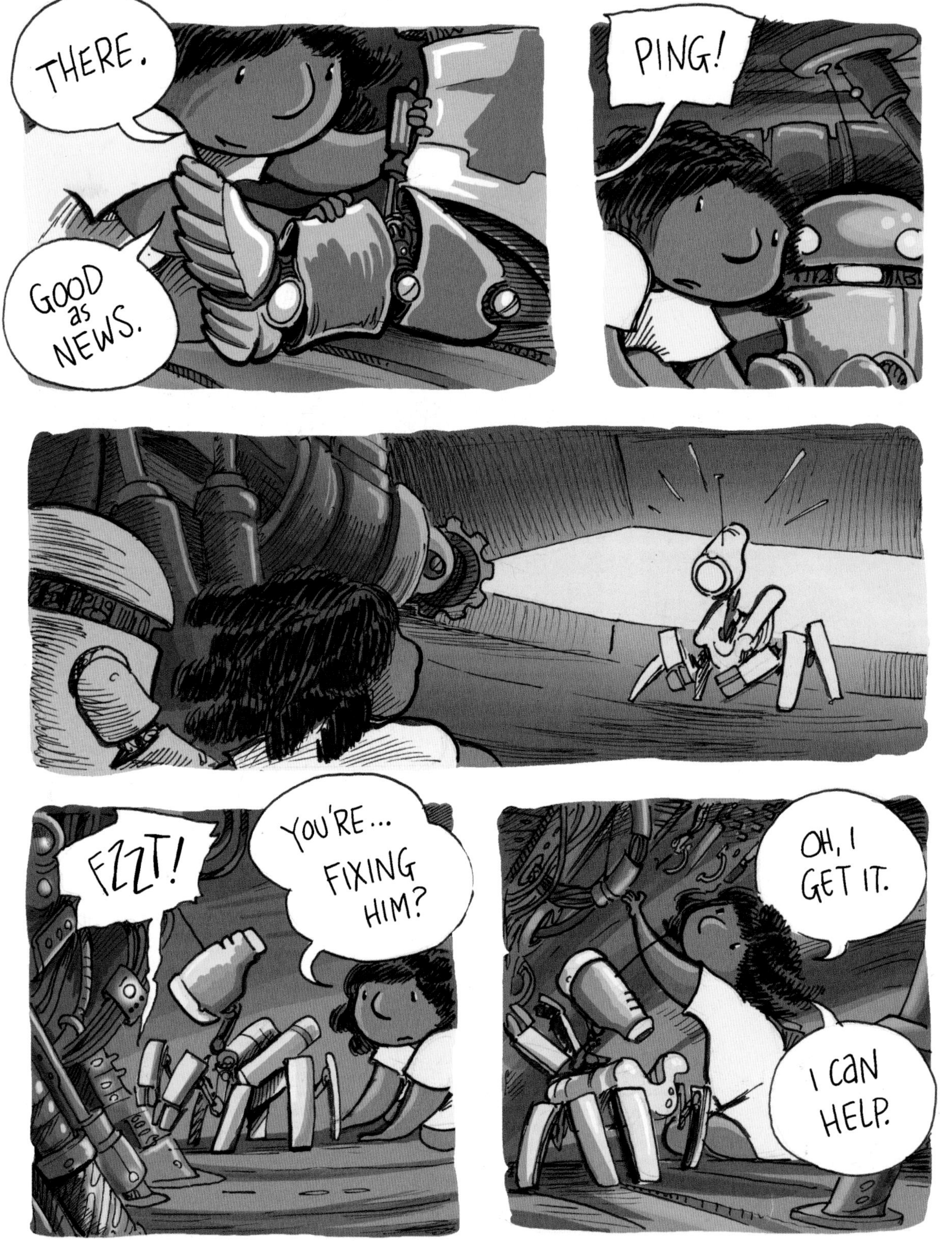
THERE.
GOOD as NEWS.
PING!
FZZT!
YOU'RE... FIXING HIM?
OH, I GET IT.
I CAN HELP.

FZZZ

BLING!

YOU CAN LET HIM GO NOW.

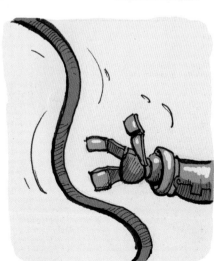

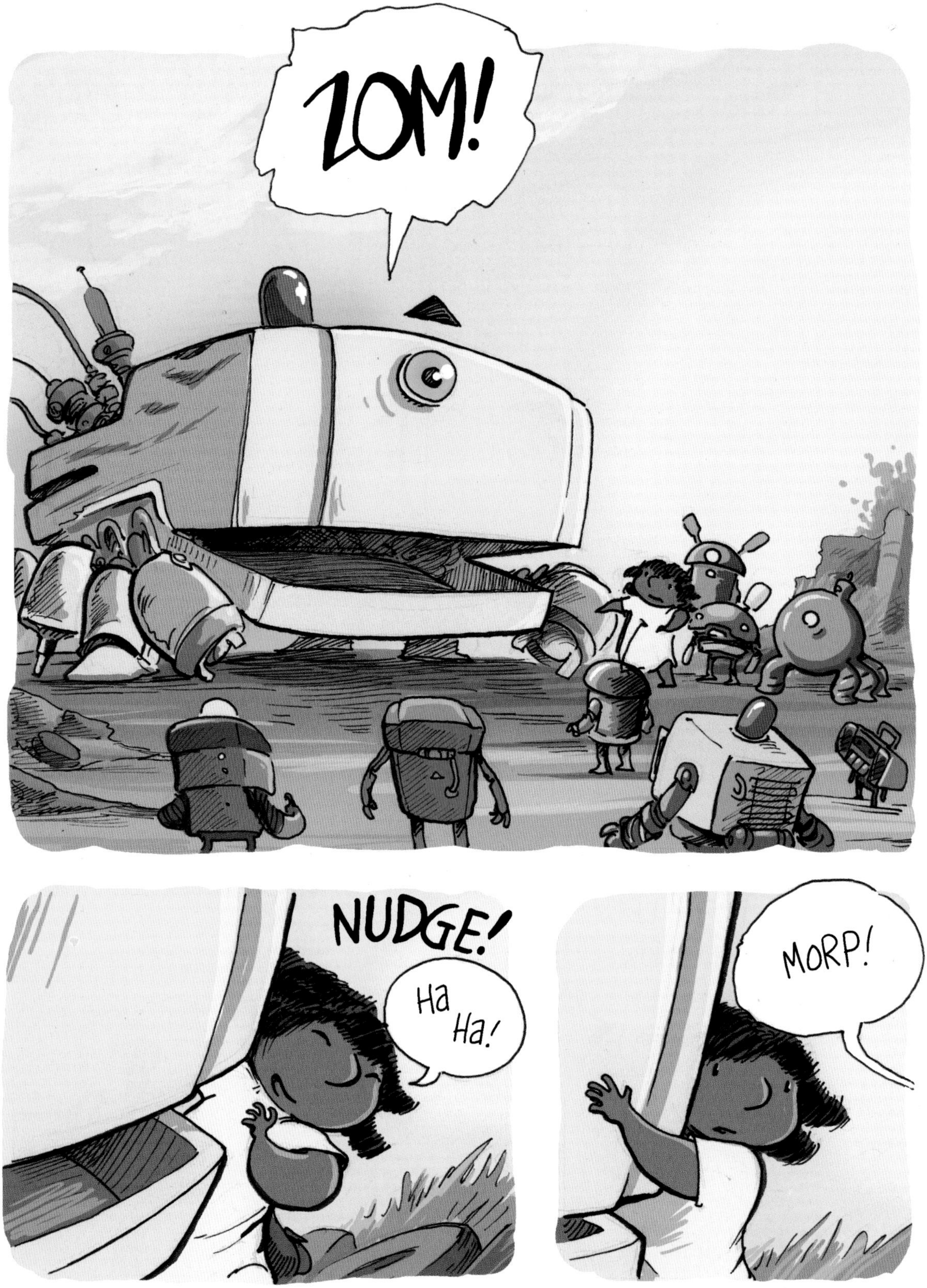
ZOM!
NUDGE!
Ha Ha!
MORP!

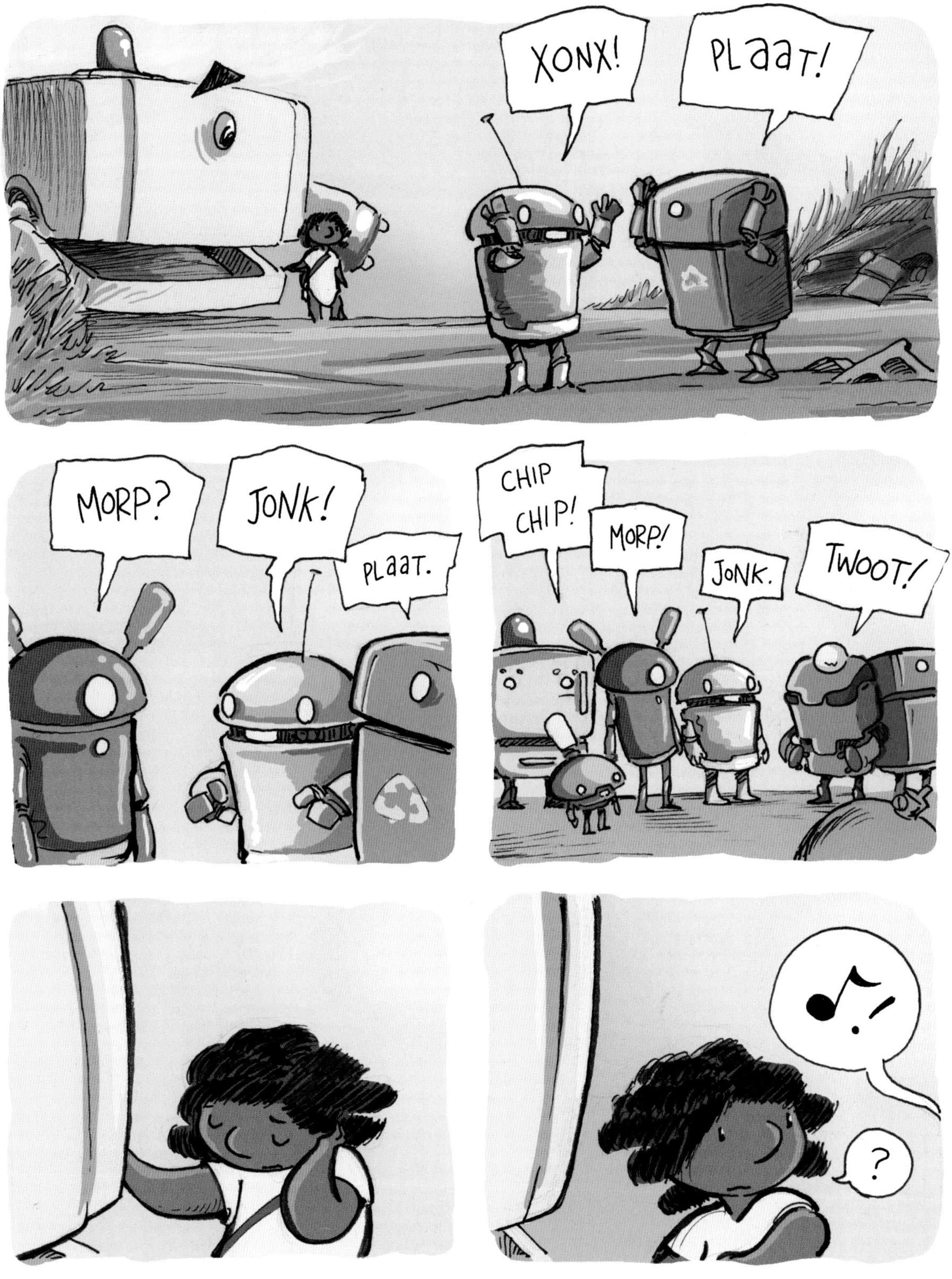
XONX!
PLAAT!
MORP?
JONK!
PLAAT.
CHIP CHIP!
MORP!
JONK.
TWOOT!
?

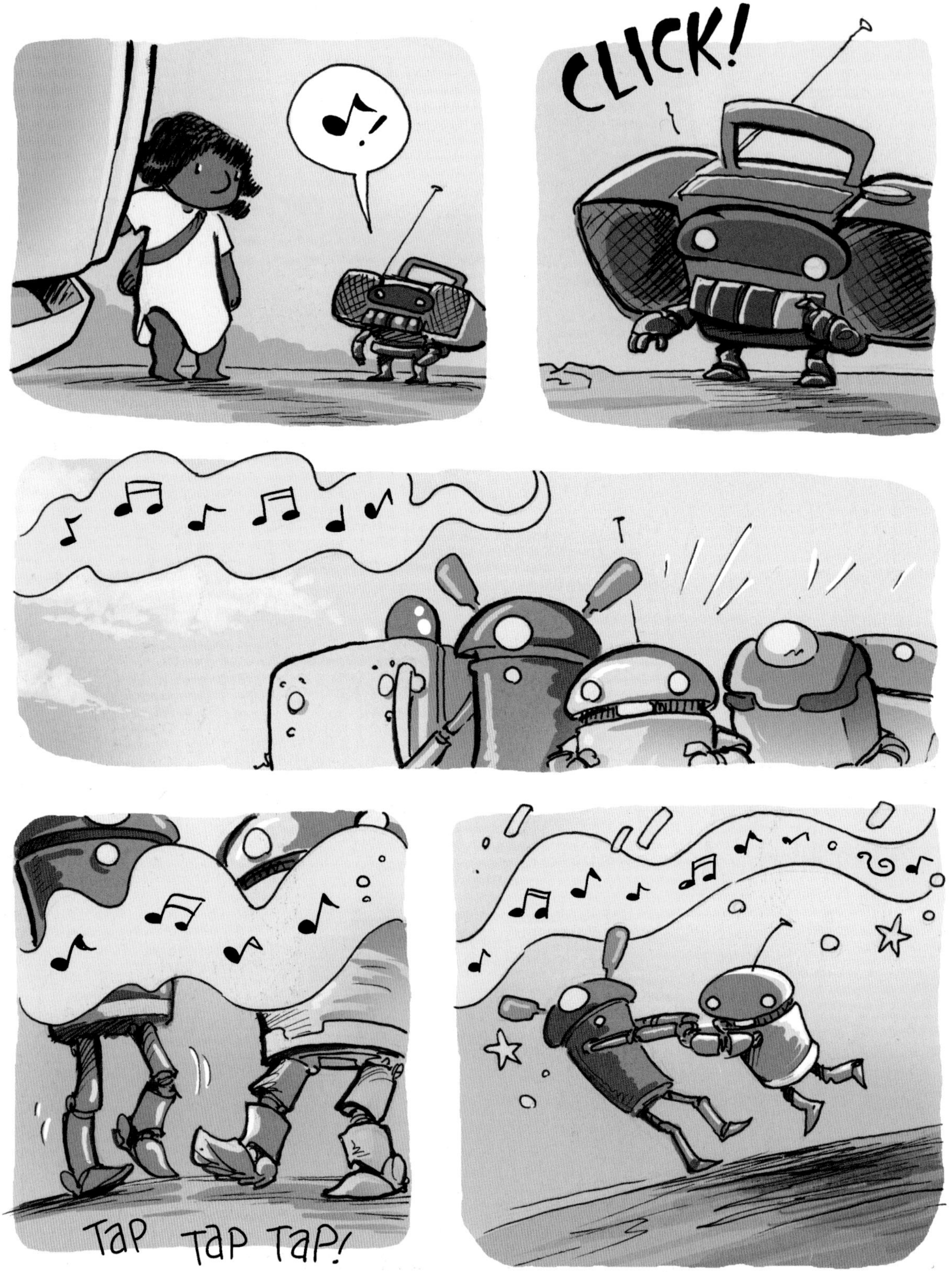
!
CLICK!
TAP TAP TAP!

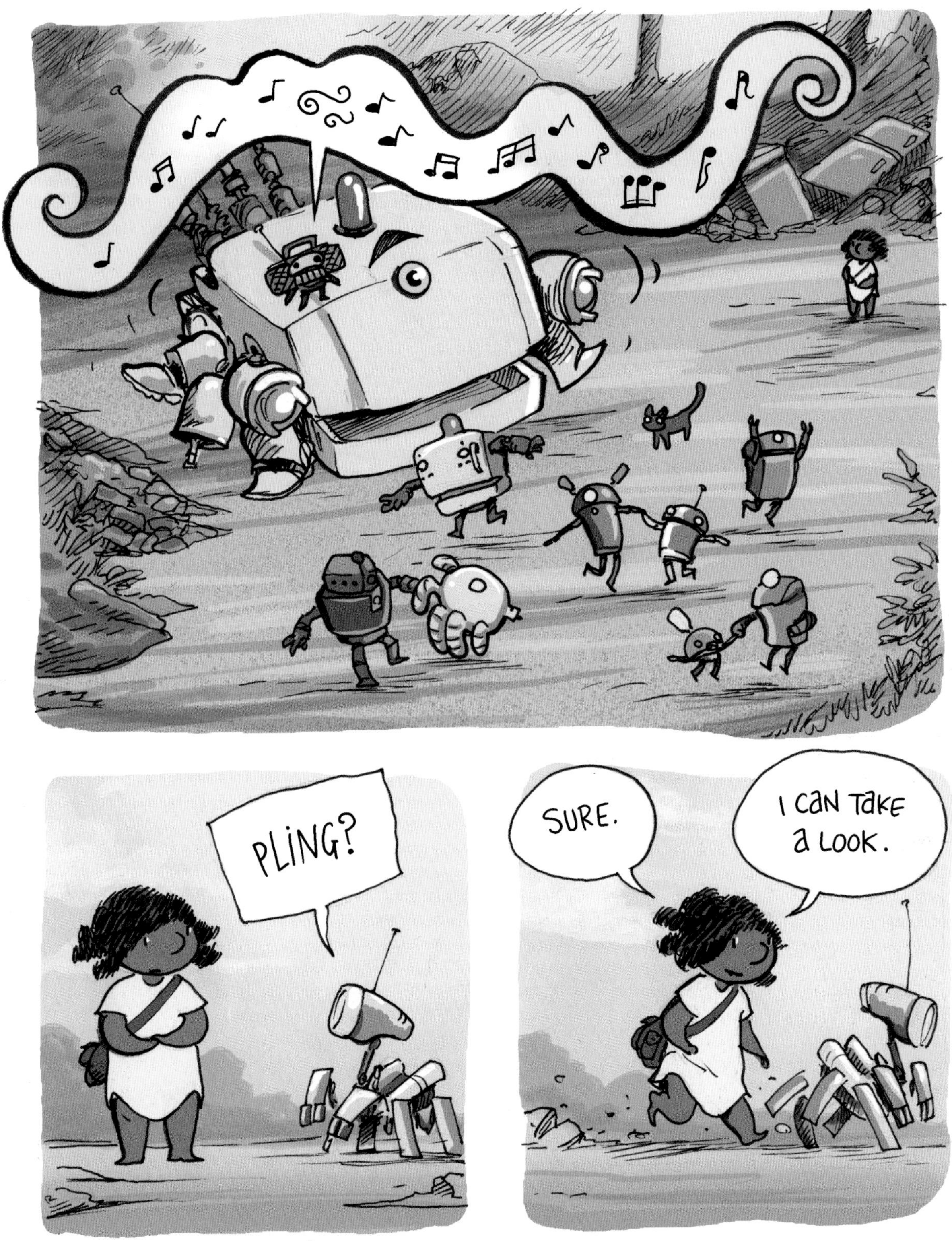
PLING?
SURE.
I CAN TAKE A LOOK.

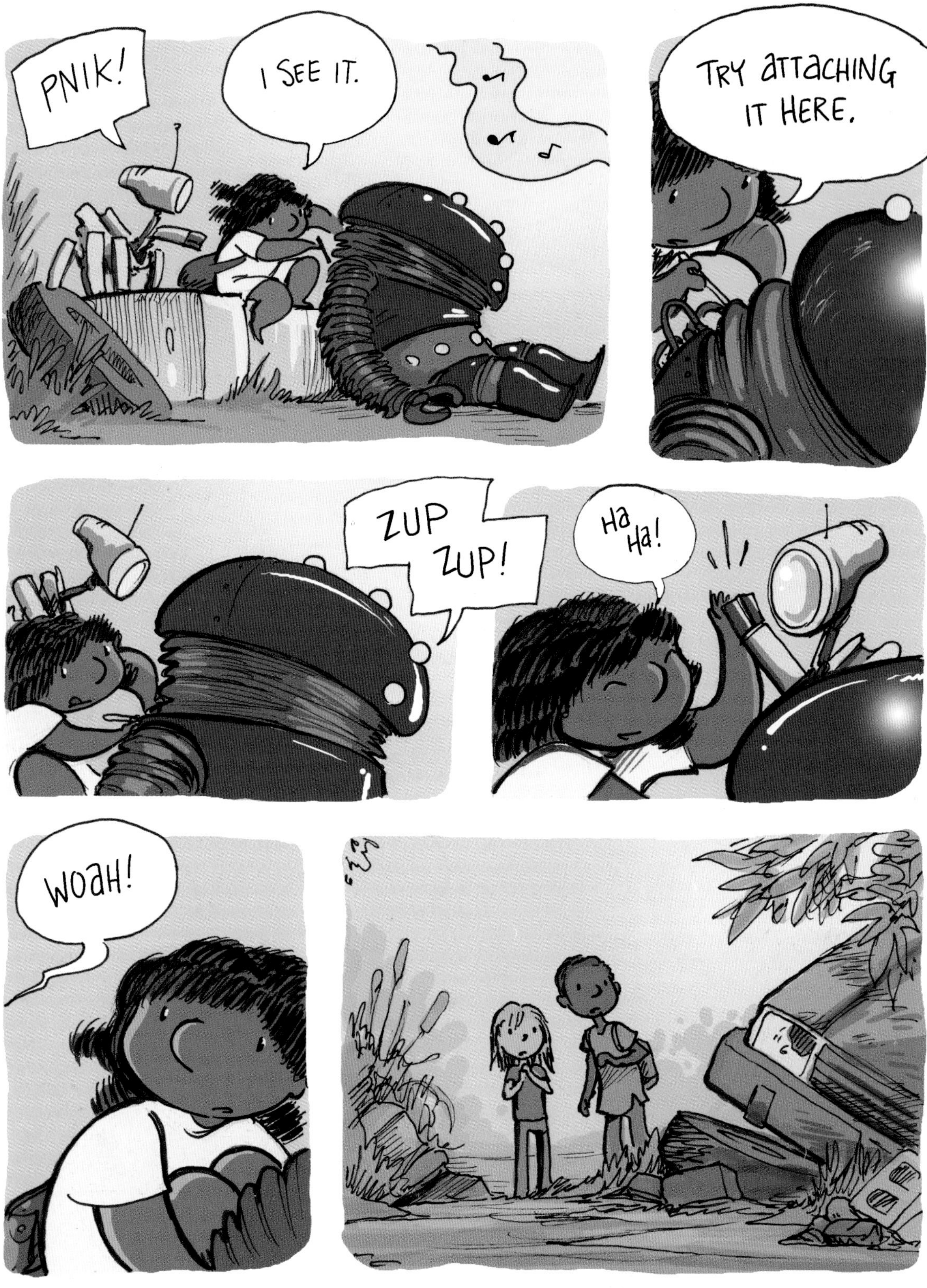
PNIK!
I SEE IT.
TRY ATTACHING IT HERE.
ZUP ZUP!
Ha Ha!
WOAH!

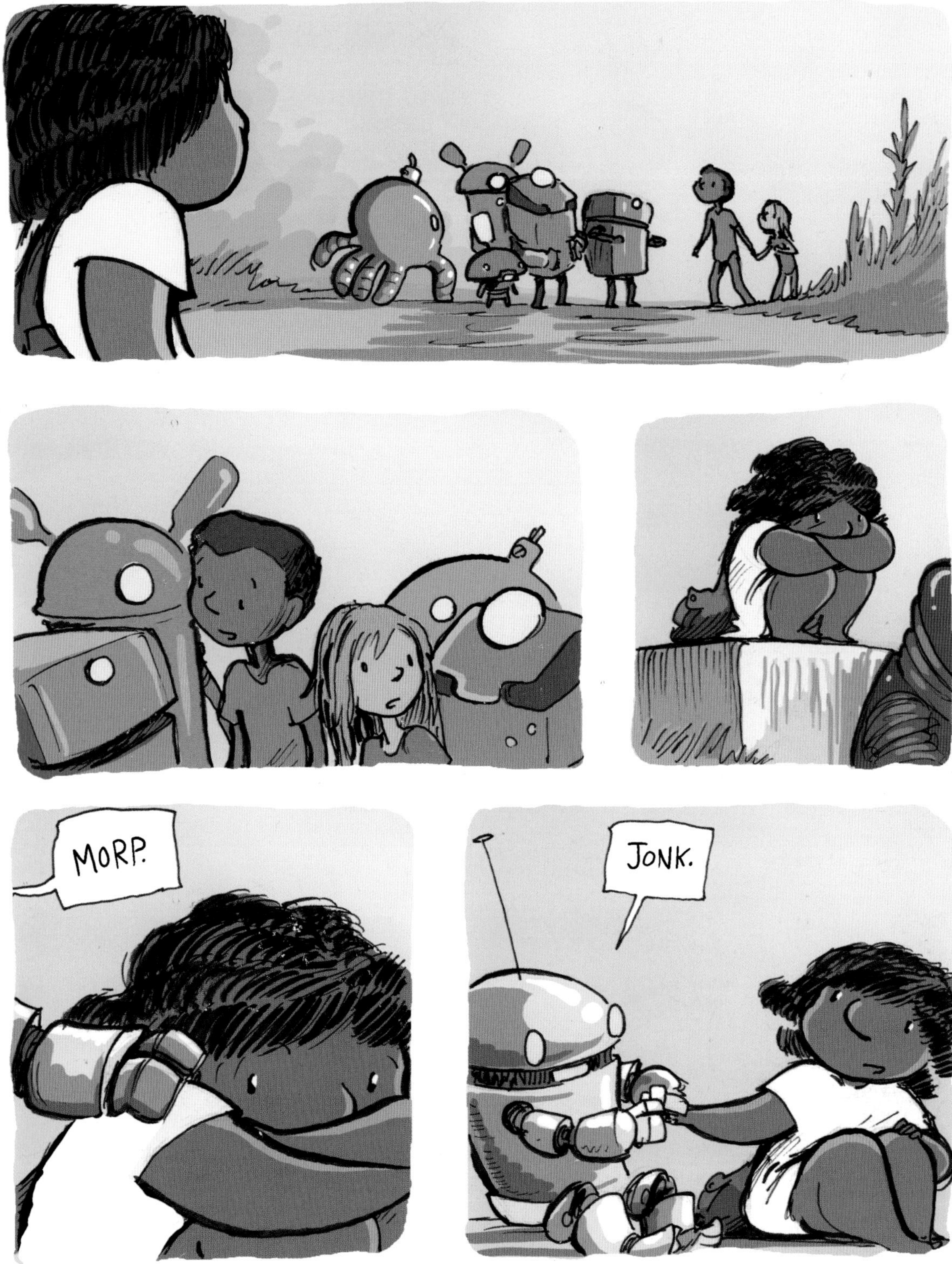
MORP.
JONK.

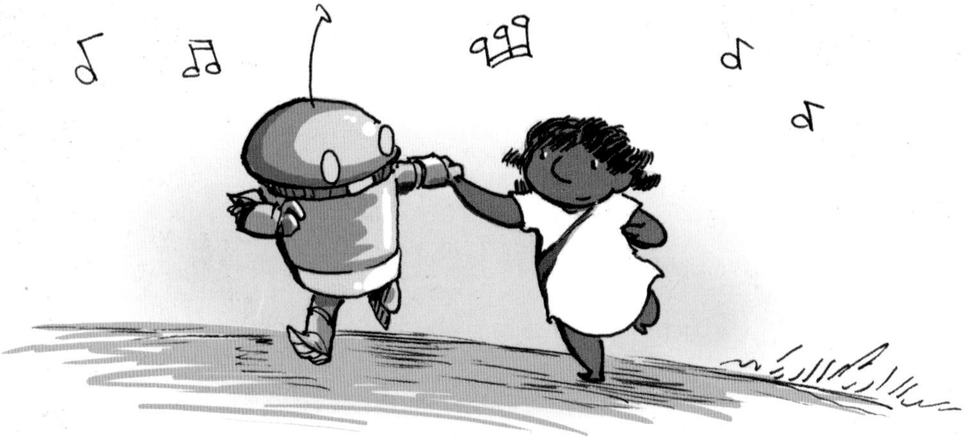

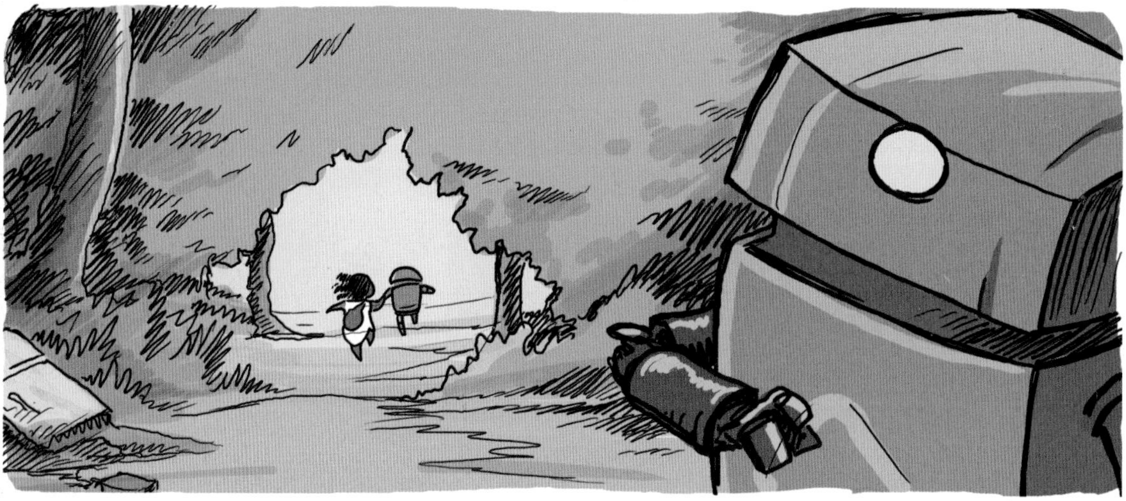

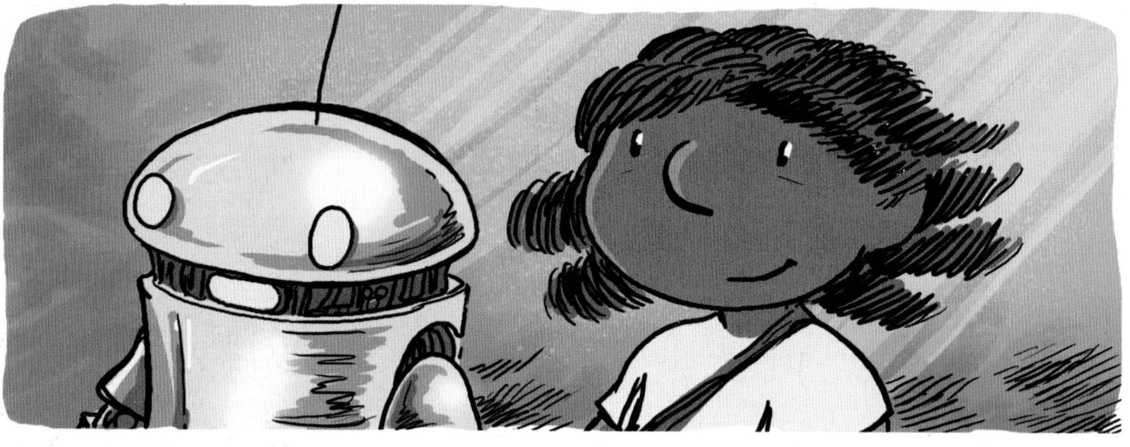

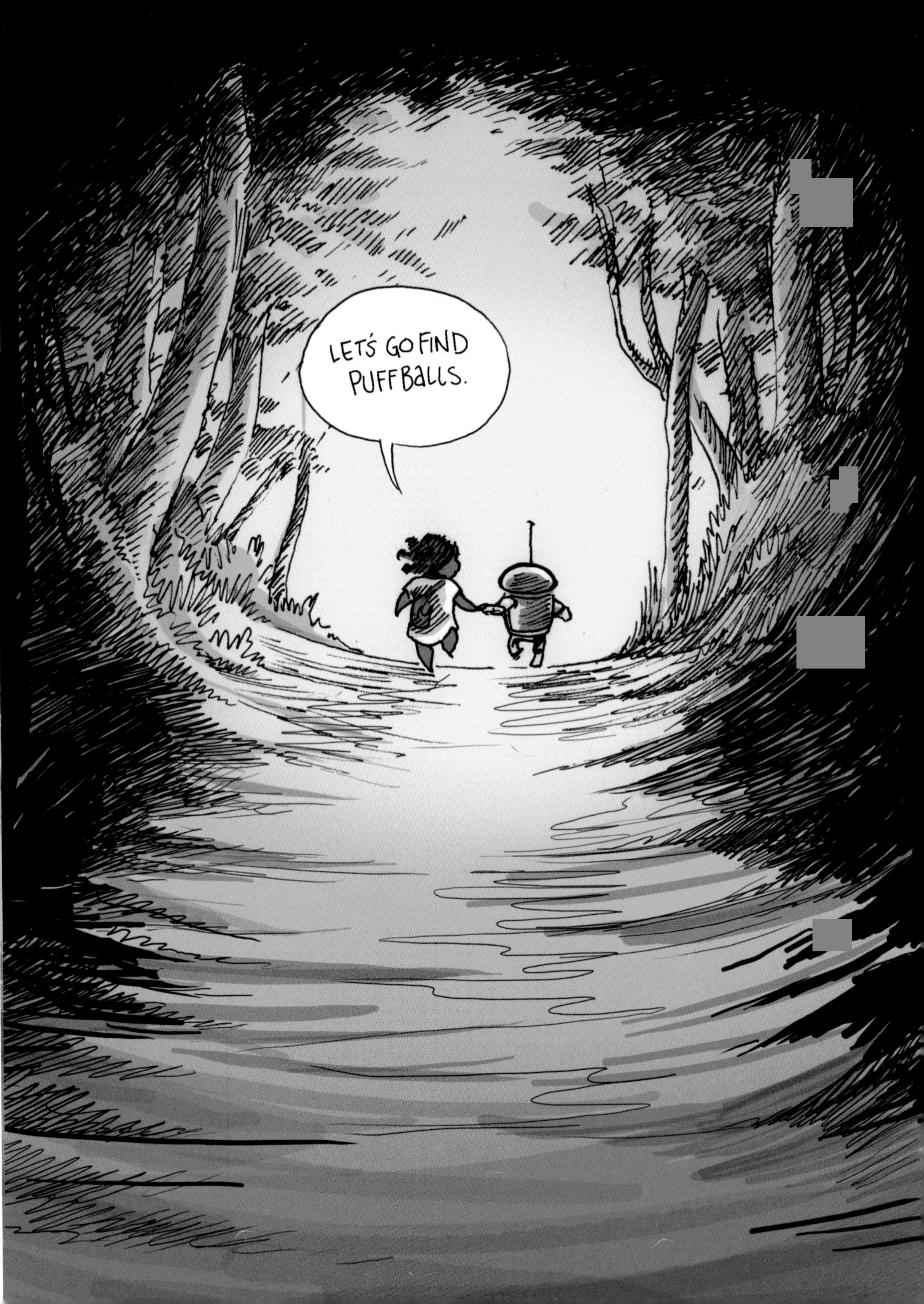
LET'S GO FIND PUFFBALLS.

THE END

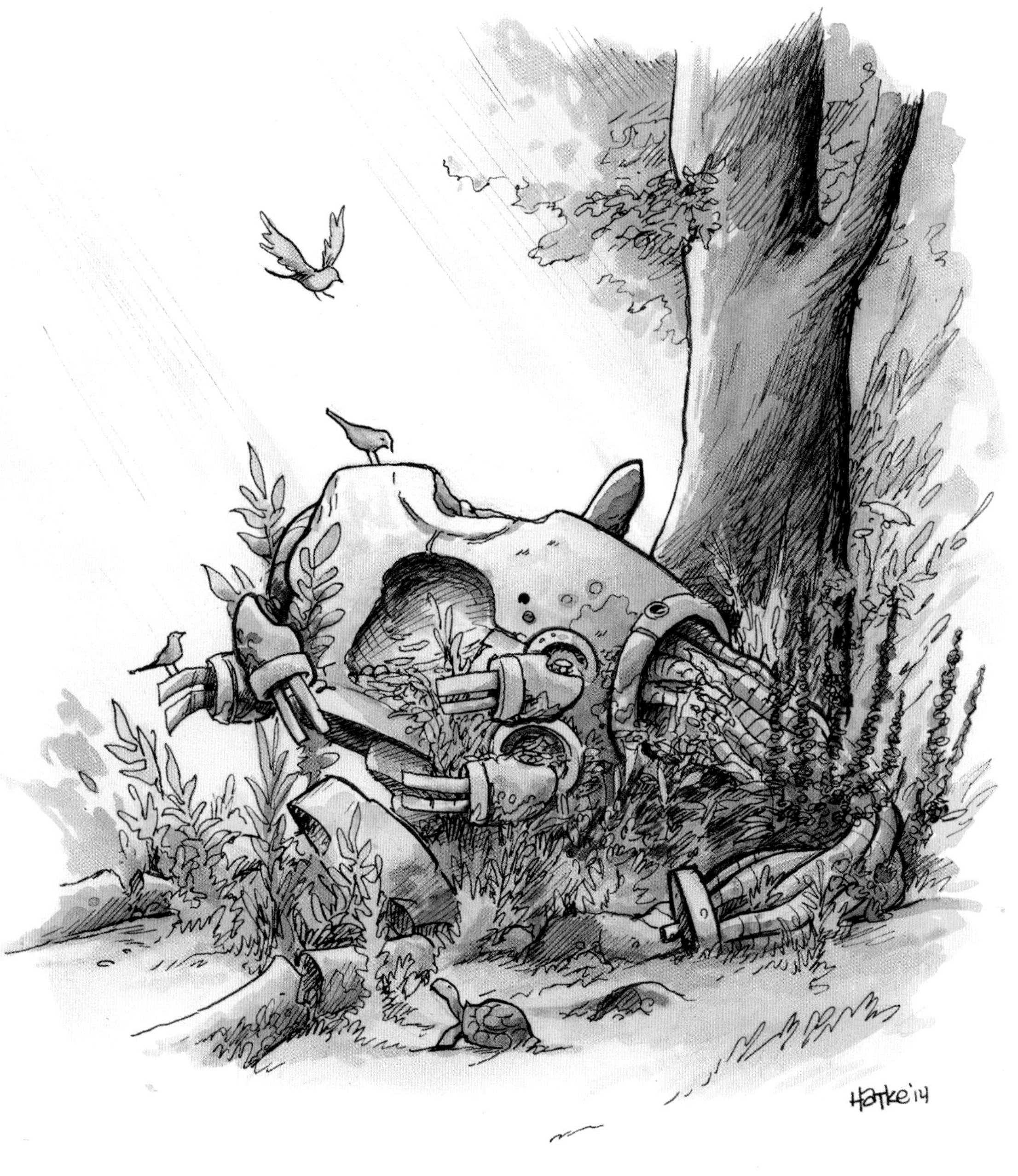
Hatke '14

ACKNOWLEDGMENTS

A big thank you to everyone who helped me make this book! Thanks to Calista, my editor on this project, and to the whole crew at First Second: Mark for sage advice; Danielle for a fantastic cover and layout; and Gina for being amazing. I'm lucky to work with you.

Thanks once again to my agent, Judy Hansen, for keeping me from getting lost in the woods.

Thanks, as always, to my wife, Anna, for making it possible for me to work at home, and for being patient when I made her pull the car over so I could take pictures of junked cars on the side of the road. And thanks to my daughters, Angelica, Zita, Julia, and Ronia, for checking on my progress every day. Particular thanks go to Julia for posing as a reference for some of the pictures of the Robot Girl.

Special thanks go to Louis Decrevel for help with coloring and for catching a few inconsistencies in the art. I probably would have turned this book in late without you, Louis.

And finally, thanks to my online friends who followed the very first Little Robot comics. Y'all are the best.

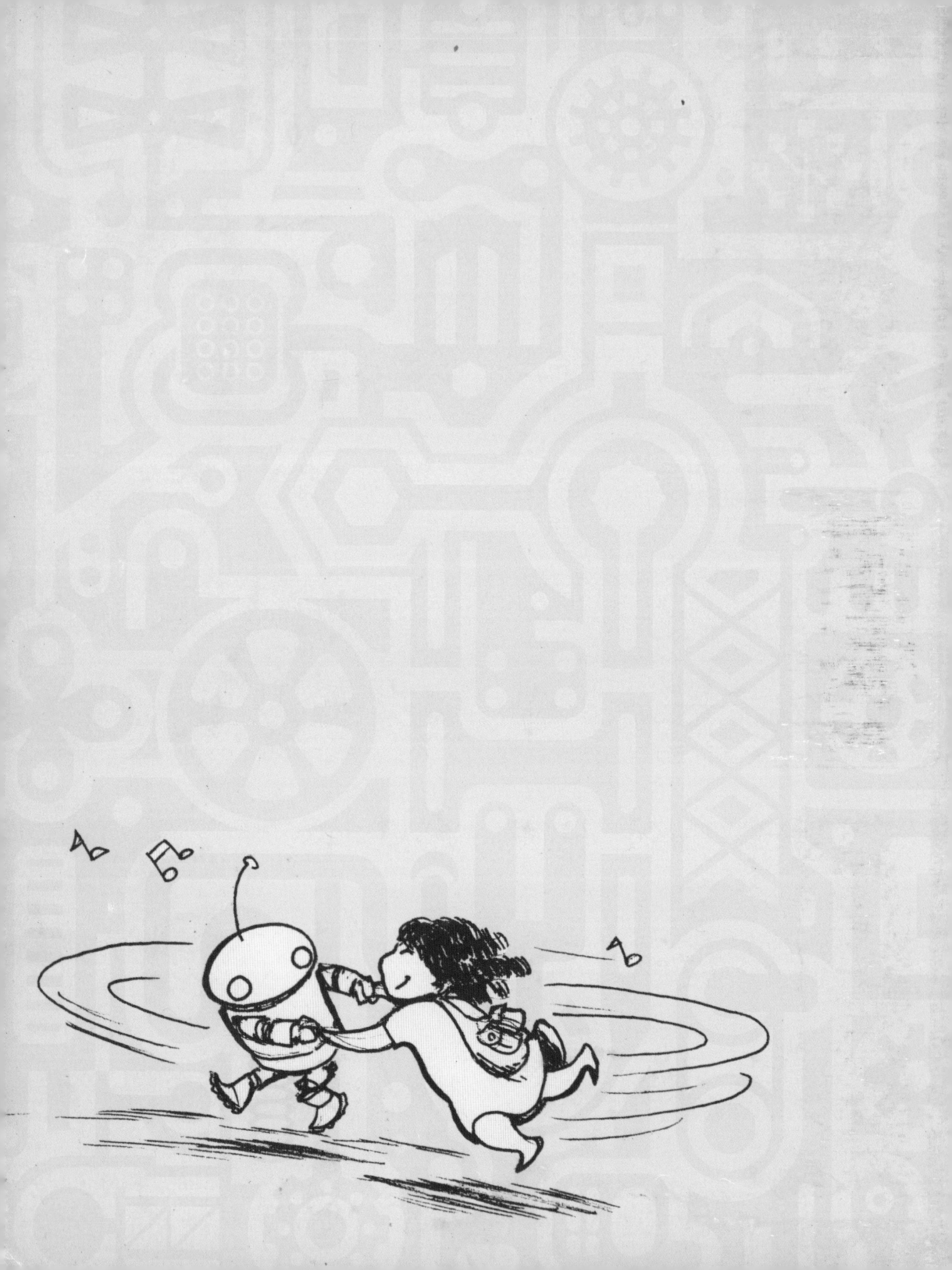